Prim
Wolves (

Lindsey Devin
© 2022
Disclaimer

All rights reserved. No part of this publication may be reproduced, distributed, or transmitted in any form or by any means, including photocopying, recording, or other electronic or mechanical methods, without the prior written permission of the publisher, except in the case of brief quotations embodied in critical reviews and certain other noncommercial uses permitted by copyright law.

This is a work of fiction. Names, places, characters, and events are all fictitious for the reader's pleasure. Any similarities to real people, places, events, living or dead are all coincidental.

This book contains sexually explicit content that is intended for ADULTS ONLY (+18).

Contents

Chapter 1 5
Chapter 2 21
Chapter 3 36
Chapter 4 52
Chapter 5 64
Chapter 6 72
Chapter 7 81
Chapter 8 102
Chapter 9 114
Chapter 10 122
Chapter 11 132
Chapter 12 152
Chapter 13 165
Chapter 14 173
Chapter 15 184
Chapter 16 200
Chapter 17 215
Chapter 18 228
Chapter 19 235
Chapter 20 242
Chapter 21 253
Chapter 22 264
Chapter 23 273
Chapter 24 292
Chapter 25 303
Chapter 26 316
Chapter 27 328

Chapter 28..335
Chapter 29..342
Chapter 30..354

Chapter 1

"Come on, Reyna," Fina said. She sat down at the small dining room table in my quarters. "Don't you think this has gone on long enough?"

It was mid-morning, and I had nothing on my schedule for the day. It'd been two months since my wedding to the Bloody King, Elias of Nightfall. No longer was I Lady Reyna of Daybreak-- I was now Lady Reyna of Nightfall, Queen of Frasia. I had beautiful lodgings, attentive handmaidens, and my two closest friends, Fina and Adora, as members of the court. I'd attended fine luncheons and dull meetings, familiarized myself with the way the Nightfall Court runs and the day-to-day business there.

I'd spent more time in the library, too, but I couldn't seem to muster the energy or the desire to delve further into my research. What was the point of trying to figure out why the Fae disappeared when I had no real leads, and no one wanted to talk about it?

I leaned my chin into the palm of my hand, at the seat across from Fina. "What do you mean?"

"The moping," Fina said.

"I'm not moping."

"You're definitely moping." Fina leaned back in her chair, raising her eyebrows pointedly.

My handmaiden Amity swept into the room, pushing a cart laden with breakfast. I'd taken to having the morning meal in my quarters, a slow start to the day before I had to begin my royal duties. I pulled my silk robe tight around my shoulders. Amity murmured her greetings, then set down a fine spread of breads, eggs, and fresh fruit, alongside steaming mugs of coffee.

Fina wrapped her hands around her cup and peered at me. "When's the last time you stayed with the king?"

"What?" I huffed. "That's none of your business."

"Come on," she said. "He's your husband."

"And we have separate rooms," I said. "So I sleep here."

Fina sighed. We'd had this discussion multiple times over the past two months. As much as I loved Fina and Adora both, they didn't understand the pain I was still carrying. I hadn't wanted to be queen—and I hadn't wanted to marry Elias. I'd lost so much to gain the throne: my future, my freedom, the family I'd thought I had, the man I'd thought I'd loved in Daybreak. The King's Choice—and Elias—had taken all of that from me.

How was I supposed to forgive him for that?

Fina peered over her shoulder to the door that connected my quarters to the king's. She sighed. "He's not in there, is he?"

"He starts his days early, as far as I know," I said. "Usually he goes for a run in the woods."

Sometimes I heard him in his quarters, in the gray light of dawn. Electricity sparked on my skin when he shifted, and when I closed my eyes, I saw his powerful wolf form behind my eyelids. My own beast howled with the desire to join him, to shift and take off through the woods together, but I kept her on a leash. No matter what animalistic desire I had for him, it didn't overpower the betrayal, and the grief.

After the wedding, he'd tried to break through my walls. He'd tried to talk to me, with gentle words and hands, touching my shoulders and lower back. Every time I'd pull away. He'd left me gifts, too, gowns and cloaks and fine foods and even fancy ceremonial weapons from different packs and different kingdoms. I merely ignored them.

Now, after two months, his efforts had slowly petered out. He'd stopped trying to speak with me in private. No more soft glances in the halls or in our shared sitting room. No more gifts, no more longing sighs. Our lives had melted into a dull routine, where we only saw each other at court functions, where we had a silent agreement to play the role of king and queen.

Sure, I was the one who had turned him away, but a small traitorous part of me was hurt he'd stopped trying. Two months wasn't that long—and he had a lot to make up for. He'd given up quite easily. I wasn't going to be the one to mend the rift between us. I was the one who'd lost everything. He'd basically forced me into this marriage, and if he wanted my love, he had to earn it.

I wanted him to be a partner—to treat me like an equal. I'd had more than enough of finery in Daybreak. What I lacked was trust. I wanted him to earn my *trust*. Sometimes it felt like more than a *want*. It felt like a *need*.

But how could I ask for something like that?

"And you don't go with him," Fina said. "Of course not."

"I don't need to run to keep my head on straight," I said. "I have better control of my wolf than that."

"Right," Fina said, sounding exceedingly unconvinced.

Rue knocked on the door and stepped inside. "Good morning, milady," Rue said brightly. It'd only taken a dozen corrections to get her to stop calling me 'Your Highness.' "I've been instructed to bring this to you immediately. Seems it's important."

She was carrying a delicate silver tray with a single letter on top of it.

I thanked her and, taking the letter, quickly opened the envelope. I expected the usual kind of communiques that came to my chamber: a notice about scheduling changes with the court, or information about a visiting diplomat, something important but fairly dull. My eyes widened when I read the paper's actual contents.

It wasn't court business at all. It was a simple handwritten note from the king.

You will join me for dinner at sundown, it said in his narrow hand. *I look forward to enjoying your company.*

I huffed as I threw the letter down on the table between Fina and me. She craned her neck to read it. "That's nice," she said. "Dinner plans like you're still courting. Romantic."

"It's not an invitation," I said. "It's a demand. He's always doing this—ordering me around left and right. This is supposed to be a partnership, but he still treats me like he owns me."

"You don't seem to be treating him like a partner, either," Fina said gently. "He wants to have dinner with you. He knows if it's a question, you'll say no."

"Well, that's my right," I said.

"Sure, it is," Fina sighed. Amity and Rue busied themselves cleaning up my quarters and ensuite, purposefully distancing themselves from our conversation. Fina scooted her chair closer to the table. "Reyna, can I speak to you as your friend? Not as a member of the court?"

"Of course," I said, even though I was sure that meant I wasn't going to particularly like what she had to say.

"Giving the king the cold shoulder isn't going to change the fact that you married him," Fina said.

"What am I supposed to do, then?" I asked. "Just forgive him for everything he did? Be his happy little trophy wife?"

"No," she said, "that's not what I'm saying at all. But I do think you're blaming *him* for things that aren't really his fault."

"Like what?" I shot back. He was the one had brought me here, he'd led the Choice, he'd killed Griffin, he'd chosen me. It was all him.

"Well," Fina said, "He's not the reason your ex showed up here to challenge him."

I pressed my lips together and said nothing.

"And it's also not his fault that the Duke of Daybreak was in on it. And I can't tell you not to grieve." She sipped her coffee and gathered her thoughts. "It's just—I don't see what you gain from pushing him away. You're stuck with him. And keeping the king at arm's length is just going to make everyone miserable, including me and Adora."

I glanced up as a new bolt of guilt cut through me. "What do you mean?"

"People are starting to wonder if everything is all right between you two," Fina said. "Adora and I have been smoothing it over, but there's only so much we can do. If you two seem weak, it could cause problems for his reign. Both internally and externally."

"...What do you mean?" I asked again.

"I mean if rumors start, someone might come knocking for another challenge," Fina said. "Nothing has happened yet, but I'm trying to be honest with you."

I picked at my breakfast, my appetite suddenly gone. Was that true? Was my disdain so obvious that it could threaten his rule of the kingdom at large? I was grieving, true—but I didn't want anyone else to suffer because of me.

"It's just so frustrating," I admitted. "Everything is decided for me in this life."

"You can change that," Fina said gently. "But not without the king."

I leaned back and dramatically flung my arm over my eyes, cutting the tension between us. "Ugh. I hate this."

Fina laughed at my theatrics. "Is it really that bad?" she teased. "Being queen? Having a super gorgeous, powerful husband who wants to have a nice dinner with you? A great breakfast brought to your quarters every morning?"

"You're right," I said. "I'm being childish, aren't I?"

"Just a little bit," Fina said with a smile. "It'd serve you well to look forward instead of backward."

"All right. I'll go to dinner. I'll be nice to him. But I'm not apologizing."

Fina laughed again, bright and surprised, then leaned forward conspiratorially. "You know, that's very Nightfall of you."

"What?" I balked.

"Nightfall wolves never apologize," she said. "At least not with their words. It's all action with them."

I sniffed and said nothing.

"Just saying," Fina said. "Maybe you fit in here a little more than you think."

The rest of the day, Elias was in meetings with his generals down at the barracks near the manor. I spent the day reading in the solarium, and on the grounds with Amity and Rue, gazing at the tree line to the forest as I turned over Fina's words in my mind. As much as it pained me to admit it, she was right. I couldn't undo what had been done—I was queen, regardless of what I wanted. And if I wanted to carve out a life of my own, I had to do it with the king. He'd extended the olive branch multiple times, only for me to knock it away.

I could be his queen, and his partner in leading Frasia. But I didn't know if I could be his wife, or—a shiver ran down my spine at the thought—his *mate*. What my wolf wanted and what I needed were two different things, and I was still figuring out how to negotiate them.

But we could start with dinner.

When the sun began to set, I made my way back to my chambers to prepare as the king had 'requested,' first with a hot bath.

"What will you wear tonight, milady?" Amity asked as she helped me, freshly scrubbed and soaped, out of the enormous tub. "Has the king asked for anything in particular?"

"Oh, I don't know," I said. "You and Rue choose for me, please?"

Amity lit up with glee, then composed herself. "Of course, milady. We'd be happy to."

I smiled at Amity in the mirror, then took the towel from her hands and gestured for her to leave the ensuite. I'd let the girls choose my outfit while I dried and styled my hair. I knew what I was doing at this point; their care was helpful but not a requirement. They both seemed to enjoy the fine gowns a lot more than I did, and admittedly I enjoyed seeing their delight when they were allowed to dress me like a doll. All the pieces in my wardrobe were provided by Nightfall, anyway—and plenty of them had been given to me by the king himself in the days after our wedding. The girls would gain more pleasure out of choosing one than I would.

I braided my hair in the mirror, so it fell in a long blonde plait over my shoulder, then sighed and peered at my own reflection.

I wore the exhaustion of the past two months on my face. Sometimes when I looked in the mirror, I hardly recognized myself at all. With a sigh, I pulled on my fine silk underclothes, then padded back into my quarters. The girls had chosen a simple black dress for me, slinky black fabric that hugged my frame but not too tightly, with delicate straps and dark lace detailing the neckline. It was formal, but simple and comfortable—they knew my taste. Amity sighed, pleased, and then dabbed a small amount of stain on my lower lip. No full makeup tonight. I had to look nice, of course, but this was just dinner with my husband.

I tried to focus on what Fina had said. It'd be easier for us both if we could be civil. This could at least be a starting point.

The girls shifted into their wolf forms, then escorted me through the manor to the formal dining room. I was getting more comfortable with the cool silence of the place, and the familiar click of wolf claws on the polished floors. Sometimes I missed Daybreak, with its warm salty breezes and the familiar distant roar of the ocean, but the freedom I had in Nightfall made up for it. In Daybreak, I was always looking over my shoulder, waiting for the next demand from the duke's staff or a reprimand from my tutors. Here in Nightfall, I could roam the halls without interruption.

I approached the ornate door. The leather-clad guard bowed and pushed the entrance open, welcoming me inside with a murmur.

I'd never seen the formal dining room so empty. Despite the lack of people, it was still welcoming, the table dotted with low candles and the curtains drawn to create a cozy atmosphere under the vaulted ceiling. In the corner, a string trio played quietly. I was grateful for the music—it was a lot better than whatever awkward silences I knew would characterize this dinner.

Elias was seated at the head of the table, in a plain shirt worn loose at the collar, his dark hair tied back with a leather strip. A shadow of a beard dusted his jaw, and there were faint circles under his eyes. It appeared that the meetings he'd been stuck in all day had worn on him. We were quite a pair. Despite his visible exhaustion, he still looked handsome. The broad-shouldered King of Frasia worn out after another day of leadership.

As I approached, he stood up and pulled my chair out at his right-hand side. His gaze traveled over me: not with a leer, but like he was making up for lost time. Recollecting once more what I looked like. I swallowed. His hand brushed over the bare skin of my back as I took my seat, and he took his.

His eyes burned as he watched me. They lingered on my lips for a long moment, and then he seemed to snap out of it. He cleared his throat and picked up the decanter of wine in between us, pouring a glass of the rich dark liquid for each of us. It should've felt ridiculous, being the only two people at this big table, but it felt cozy with the empty space of the table dotted with candles, and the two of us pushed close together like it was an intimate dinner.

Internally, my wolf whined, longing to burst forth and cuddle close to Elias, soothe his exhaustion with familiar licks and nuzzles. That wasn't going to happen, though. We could be civil, but not that close. Not yet—maybe not ever. I ignored her whines.

Two servants came out, and covered the table with fine dishes: roast chicken, vegetables, bread, and bright salad. It smelled delicious, but it wasn't extravagant. I would almost say it was homey. Elias sighed with relief as he carved the chicken and served my plate before his own.

"Thank you for joining me, Reyna," he said.

"Of course," I murmured in response. I swallowed. "How were the meetings today?"

"Oh, just fine," Elias said with a shake of his head. "I prefer seeing the generals rather than some of the other court members, at least. But the most important meetings are the most tedious." He sighed and took a sip of his wine.

"What do you mean?" I asked.

He shook his head. "You'll see in time, I'm sure."

"You don't need to be so condescending," I said.

"I'm not," he said with a quirk of his eyebrow. "I mean the more you settle into your role as queen, the more you'll have attend these meetings, with or without me."

I blinked. "Oh."

That seemed to amuse him as he cut into his chicken. "I do believe that should be a major benefit of having a partner in leadership," he said. "Splitting the duties."

"I suppose so." I was surprised to hear it, though, as I did still often feel like I was nothing more than a prize he'd won. "You would trust me to handle royal business alone?"

"Certainly," he said. "You're smarter than most of the people on the court already." His voice didn't indicate flattery, but simple fact.

I felt my cheeks flush regardless. "If you say so."

He laughed quietly. "Admittedly it's not a hard bar to clear. But that was one of the most important traits for me in choosing a queen. Someone who can play the games leadership requires but can also improvise when necessary."

"My improvisations don't always seem to go over well," I said.

"Well, you're currently Queen of Frasia, so you seem to have turned out all right," he said with a small smile.

"I suppose so." I took a sip of my own wine.

That was what I wanted from him. Trust. Acknowledgment of my individual capabilities. When he spoke to me like this, it was easy to feel like we could have a future together. Like maybe I didn't need to resist him.

The rest of dinner passed in quiet, if sometimes stilted, conversation. Elias complained about his more incompetent court members and brainstormed upcoming changes to the tax code. I chimed in with questions and thoughts, here and there, and we kept the conversation carefully on topics of Efra and Frasia at large. Not about us or our relationship—our *marriage*. It was like were business partners instead. I found it was easier to settle back into feelings of civility with this careful boundary drawn between us. Maybe Fina was right. If we could find common ground between us as leaders, the rest of our lives could be a lot easier.

And it was easier for me to see him as the king, and not just as Elias. It hurt less. It made more sense.

After we finished eating, the servants swept in to remove our plates and replace them with small flagons of rich, dark sipping chocolate. The steam itself tasted sweet, floating up to surround me as I stirred the mug with a tiny silver spoon. It looked almost comically diminutive in Elias' huge hand, but it didn't seem to bother him at all as he lifted it and took a meager but grateful sip of his drink.

"Listen." He set it down and fixed his eyes on me. "Thank you for joining me for this meal."

"You're welcome," I said, my attention focused on my own drink. I didn't want him to think that I had forgiven him for what he'd done to my life—only that I could potentially speak civilly to him when circumstances required.

"I invited you here because I have a proposition for you."

I glanced up. "A proposition?"

"I've been called on a diplomatic visit to Shianga," he said. "That was the reason for the meeting with the generals today. Typically for meetings like this, I'd send a member of the court in my stead, but this is a sensitive issue, and I don't trust a representative to play it correctly."

"Right," I said, unsure of where he was going with this.

"I know we have our differences," he said gruffly, "but I'd like you to join me on this trip."

I set my mug down so quickly the chocolate nearly sloshed over the edges. "What? Join you?"

"Yes," he said. "It'll be a lot of diplomatic bullshit—honestly, the Shiangan king can be a real pain in my ass—but it'll be good for you to start being involved in that kind of thing firsthand. Plus—" he flushed faintly "—I thought it might be good for us to spend some time away from the manor. Shianga's a lovely country with some of the finest cartographers in the world. I know that interests you. It'd be a nice place to spend some time."

I stared at him, slack-jawed. Shianga. The land of the dragon shifters. I'd read so much about Shianga, even learned how to use some of its famed, elegant weapons in my training, but never in my life did I think I'd get a chance to travel there.

He met my gaze steadily, but there was a glimmer of uncertainty there too. "Does that interest you?"

"Interest?" I was still shocked. "Elias, I—I'd love to go."

He sat back, a pleased smile playing on his lips. "I thought you might. Good. I'll begin the travel preparations and we'll plan to leave next week. There are a few things we'll need to cover." He stood up and smoothed his shirt down, then wrinkled his nose as he turned over the logistics in his mind. "Certainly, there are court members we'll need to bring with us as part of the party, and we'll need to go over the expectations that Shiangan royalty will have for—oof!"

I cut him off in the middle of his sentence by throwing my arms around his neck. I'd done it before I'd even realized what I was doing, so overwhelmed by the sheer excitement of going to Shianga. I'd always dreamed of traveling, and now it was really going to happen.

I was going to see Shianga with my own eyes.

Elias' hand drifted to my lower back as he returned the hug gently, like he was afraid of spooking me. I realized then that this was the most I'd touched him in nearly two months. My wolf was responding with delight, begging me to press closer and bury my face in his neck. I pressed my lips together and slowly stepped away. My fingertips dragged over the skin of his nape as I did so, and that bare amount of contact alone sent a zing down my spine. How was it possible he still had such an intense effect on me?

I cleared my throat and folded my hands awkwardly in front of my body. "Thanks, I mean," I said. "For inviting me to come."

"Well, you are the queen," he teased carefully.

"It'd make just as much sense for you to leave the queen here to manage the day-to-day affairs," I said. "So, thank you for not doing that."

"Eventually I'll just send you on all these boring diplomatic trips alone so I can manage the court at home," Elias said with a sigh.

He had no idea the sheer amount of delight that filled me with. I bounced barely perceptibly on the balls of my feet, resisting the urge to start clapping with glee. The world that had felt so closed off here in Efra was starting to open up in front of me again.

"What members of the court typically travel with the king and queen?" I asked.

"Whoever you'd like," Elias said. "I assumed you might want Fina and Adora with you as part of your convoy."

"I did hope I could invite them," I said. "If it wouldn't be too much trouble."

"Not at all," he said. "The Nightfall convoy is almost always the smallest to travel in, no matter how many wolves I bring along."

"I'm not sure if that's a good or bad thing," I admitted.

"Nor am I," he said with a smile.

For a moment we stood staring at each other just a few paces apart. Elias' gaze flickered to my mouth for a brief moment, but he didn't move. My wolf whined again, longing for closeness—he was right there. Right within reach. But this offer was still part of being partners in leadership—I was still learning to trust him. My wolf had never doubted Elias, though. Not for a moment. I'd denied her instincts for a long time, and sometimes I still questioned them.

But had she ever steered me wrong?

It was in Daybreak I'd learned to distrust her. It was a hard habit to shake. The ferocity of her desire still cowed me, made me nervous. I couldn't rely on my wolf to guide me completely. At least, not yet.

"Well," he said with a small smile, "Lady Reyna. Thank you for dining with me."

He swept into a formal bow. I couldn't help but smile in return, sweeping into a curtsy before I left the dining room and returned to our quarters alone.

Chapter 2

"Gods above," Fina said, squeezing my forearm as she watched the carriages pull up. We were waiting outside the manor in our heavy cloaks, our trunks packed and ready. "I can't believe this is really happening!"

"I know," Adora said. "Shianga! I had to get new dresses made to prepare for the heat!"

"It's hot," Fina agreed, "but it's a beautiful country. I haven't been in years, since I visited with my court for a diplomatic engagement, but I was so young I couldn't appreciate it. It's going to be amazing to be back!"

"I hope so," I said. I was getting a little nervous—as excited as I was to be going on such a big journey, I was still traveling as the queen. I was in plain slacks and a heavy cloak for travel, but I had plenty of freshly made fine gowns as well.

"Good morning, ladies," a warm, unfamiliar voice boomed. A woman strode toward us, in dark trousers and heavy boots, with a loose white shirt worn over her broad chest and shoulders, and a plain, heavy cloak fastened across her collarbones. She carried a short sword at her hip but it didn't have the decorative gilding that many ceremonial sheaths had. Everything about her was functional. Her dark red hair was pulled back into a high ponytail, with braids wound through it, a striking contrast to her tan complexion. Around her neck she wore a fine gold chain with pendants on it that looked suspiciously like teeth.

"Glad to see you've made it out to the carriages on time. We've got a long way to travel." She swept into a bow. "Your Highness."

"Um," I said.

The woman broke into a broad grin. Her teeth were sharp, wolfish even in her human form. "Right," she said. "We haven't had the pleasure. I've heard plenty about you, though. I'm Kodan, one of the king's generals."

I blinked in surprise. "Oh," I said. "Of course, Kodan—lovely to meet you."

She laughed. "Not expecting a general to look like me, huh?" she asked.

"Oh, no, it's just--" I stammered, my cheeks flushing.

"I get that sometimes," Kodan interjected. "It's fine. I've been quite busy the past few months but the king has requested I join the Shiangan envoy as head guard. Happy to be of service." She turned to Fina and Adora. "I'll be joining you in your carriage, if that won't disrupt your travels."

Adora was staring wide-eyed at Kodan like she'd never seen anyone like her before. Fina looked delighted and hopped forward to shake Kodan's hand.

"Of course, General," she said. "We'd be delighted for you to join us. I'm Fina of Duskmoon, and that's the Lady Adora of Starcrest. Here, I'll show you to the carriage. Where did you say you were off on assignment to?"

Fina tugged Kodan toward the carriage by her muscular bicep, and Kodan looked somewhere between impressed and amused. Adora trailed after them, looking just as confused.

The front doors of the manor swung open again and Elias appeared, with no fanfare at all. He was dressed casually for travel, too, and the only sign he was the king at all was the fine golden clasp keeping his cloak closed over his shoulders. His staff followed behind him with his trunk and bags, and immediately busied themselves packing the largest carriage in the center of the lineup.

He stood at my side, his hands folded behind his back. "I see you met General Kodan."

"She's quite a character," I said.

"That she is," Elias said with a low laugh.

"Is she close with the court?" I asked. "I'm surprised I haven't met her before now."

"She's been busy managing some of the military details while I was focused on the Choice," Elias said. "She's not too fond of the more ceremonial events so it wasn't too much of a loss for her."

I got the feeling there was more to that story he wasn't telling me, but I didn't push. "I see."

"She is a close friend of mine, as well," Elias said. "We grew up together as pups. I'm relieved she'll be taking on a role as a member of the royal guard."

"I see," I said again.

He glanced at me, and his lips formed a playful smile. "Do you find yourself jealous?"

"I could be," I shot back, "if you'll answer me one question."

"Of course."

"Did she ever kick your ass when you were younger?"

He barked a loud, surprised laugh. "As a matter of fact, she did."

"Then yes," I said, "I'm a little jealous."

Elias laughed again, shaking his head in disbelief. He set his hand gently at my upper back and guided me toward our coach.

"We're in this one," he said. "Kodan and your handmaidens will be behind us, and more of my staff will be in the front. Shall we?"

I nodded and pulled my cloak tighter around my shoulders. "No reason to linger, I don't suppose."

I stepped into the carriage. It was luxurious and comfortable inside, with plush bench seating and space to spread out. All five of us could've easily ridden in here together. I settled onto the bench and pulled off my cloak, spreading it over my lap instead against the slight chill. Elias sat across from me, leaning comfortably back against the bench and glancing over his shoulder to peer at the driver.

After a moment, the horses lurched into motion, and the vehicle began to rumble over the streets of Efra, heading toward the western gate. I peered out the window as we rode, taking in the now-familiar sights of the city: the taverns already bustling with activity, the street vendors selling their wares, the blacksmith spitting smoke into the crisp air, all while citizens moved around in both human and wolf form. Seeing wolves lope around the streets had initially made me uncomfortable, but now it was such a regular part of my day, I found it odder not seeing any at all.

I still kept a tight leash on my wolf, though—I needed to keep my faculties about me if I was to be a capable queen. I was still learning to lead like a wolf of Nightfall, to move between my animal instincts and my human logic fluidly. I wanted to do that, but sometimes it felt out of reach, like I'd never fully understand what it meant to live with the animal in me.

"I expect the journey to only take two days," Elias said. "They'll just be long ones."

"Right." I'd already been extensively briefed on the details of our travel by my handmaidens, but I could tell Elias wanted to fill the silence.

"We should cross into Shianga tomorrow. The climate won't change until we make it through the mountain pass along the border. I trust you had your dresses made?"

"Of course," I said. "Though my research says it won't be too warm—not like the humidity of Daybreak, at least."

"Ah, yes," Elias said. "I almost forgot."

I glanced at him, brow furrowing. "What do you mean?"

"Just that you fit so well in Nightfall," he said. "It's easy to forget you weren't one of us your entire life."

Internally, my wolf flicked her ears, unsure how to take that particular comment. It felt like a compliment—but at the same time, just another way I was losing myself to the roles I had to play. I pressed my lips together and turned my gaze back to the window.

The ornate city gates closed behind us. The road led through the fields on the western side of the city, where wolves tended their farms, and then into the tree line of the familiar forest. The sturdy trunks and canopy created a tunnel-like effect as we traveled, which didn't make for very interesting scenery outside the window. I settled back onto the bench seating and curled up on the seat, legs folded under the warmth of my cloak. I rifled through my rucksack and fished out one of the novels I'd packed for the journey.

Before I could open it, Elias cleared his throat.

I stuffed down my irritation and tried to remember what Fina had said. Everything would be easier if we could be civil to each other. He was my husband, after all. So I kept my book closed and met his dark eyes.

"How has your time in the manor been?" he asked. "Since we haven't seen too much of each other since the wedding."

There was no accusation in his voice, just resignation. And that was a mild way of describing my anger and avoidance of him. He could've mirrored my own rage right back at me, but instead he'd asked me to dinner, invited me to join him on this trip, and was now extending another olive branch. It didn't make up for what he'd done—but a bit of idle chatter was nicer than a slow-simmering rage.

"Just fine," I said. "I've been enjoying the library."

Elias frowned minutely—I wouldn't have noticed it at all if I hadn't spent so much time during the Choice cataloguing small changes of expression to try to get a handle on his moods. I knew he wanted more from me, more openness, but if I was honest with him now about how I felt, it would only start another fight. I didn't want to tell him how lonely I was, even with my two closest friends with me at the manor. I didn't want to explain how I still felt trapped in my role as queen, even with all the freedom he had given me so far, leaving me to my own devices.

He knew how much he had hurt me. We didn't need to rehash that again.

I wanted to forgive him. I was *trying* to forgive him.

"I've noticed that," he said, nodding toward the book in my hands.

I nodded back and offered him a small smile. The silence spread out awkwardly between us, broken by the rattle of the carriage on the rough road and the occasional bird call from above.

Elias sighed. "Right. Well. Enjoy the book." He turned to his own rucksack, then pulled out a stack of documents and turned his attention to those instead.

I almost asked what they were—information having to do with the purpose for this trip? But I was grateful for the quiet in the carriage. We'd have plenty of time to discuss details.

The hours rolled by as I lost myself in the novel, stopping only when the carriage paused so we could stretch our legs and share a quick meal at a clearing in the woods. At the afternoon break, Kodan and Elias were sharing a brief conversation, heads together over the documents the king had been reviewing in the carriage. Fina, Adora, and I were stretched out on a blanket on the grass, sharing a simple meal of bread and cheese.

"Kodan is so interesting," Fina said, her voice slightly awed. "She's been all over! She has stories from what seems like every corner of the globe."

I burned with envy—not from Kodan's extensive travel, but just from the chance Fina had to pick her brain in private. It made climbing back into the carriage with Elias even more frustrating. As we made our way back onto the road, Elias looked just as irritated as me as he reviewed the documents.

By sunset, we had made it out of the forest and back onto the bald streets of Frasia, then to the inn we were staying at for the night. It was a large timber and brick building with a thatched roof, and a lamp burning over the sign that declared its unfortunate name: the Bloody Nightingale. It was the largest structure for miles, with the others around it mostly small subsistence farms.

Elias climbed out of the coach first and stretched his arms luxuriously overhead. His spine popped, and he groaned with pleasure. "Gods, I hate those carriages," he grumbled. "I have half a mind to run the rest of the way."

"I don't know if that'd make a great first impression," I teased.

"Oh, gods," he said again. "Don't make me think about all the pomp and circumstance we'll have to go through. Let's at least get a good meal first."

"Good gods in the highest heavens, I need a drink," Kodan said as she clambered out of her carriage. Fina and Adora were on her tail, laughing. Kodan waved us all toward the inn. "This place has the finest braised lamb you'll ever taste. Let's go, I need a brandy."

My mood lifted over our boisterous, laughter-filled dinner, with the five of us crowded around a table in the corner of the busy inn. It was clearly doing double duty as the only good tavern around for miles. The braised lamb *was* delicious, and Kodan ordered a round of brandy for all of us as the rich soup and crackling fire soothed the aches I'd received from the long day of travel. She ran the table like a professional, sharing stories of bar fights and drunken mishaps. Here, briefly, I remembered the moments I'd had with Elias in private, during the Choice, before we were king and queen. When all of us had a moment to step out of our required roles, it was easy. Elias was generous and insightful and let Kodan tell jokes at his expense. I loved spending time with Elias the man, and Elias the wolf. It was the king that caused problems. But when his knee pressed against mine under the table, I didn't move away either.

After dinner, the elderly but quick-moving innkeeper led us upstairs and showed us to our rooms. Kodan, Fina, and Adora were in one room, with two single beds and some space on the floor, while Elias and I would share a bigger bed. Elias thanked the innkeeper with a hefty sack of coin—the inn was crowded, and it was a miracle we got rooms at all.

"I know this isn't ideal." He closed the door behind us, softening the noise of the tavern downstairs to a low murmur.

The space was small, occupied mostly by the bed and the tiled mosaic hearth with a low fire burning. There was a sheepskin rug on the hardwood floor in front of the hearth. Elias nodded at it. "I'll sleep there."

"On the floor?" I asked.

"It's quite comfortable in my wolf form," he said. "I wouldn't want to invade your privacy."

I swallowed. We hadn't shared a bed since the wedding—I always chose to stay in my own quarters. His deference surprised me.

"That's not necessary," I said. "I think we're capable of sharing a bed like adults."

"Or wolves," Elias said with a careful smile.

I nodded and busied myself pulling my toiletries from my rucksack, willing the flush to leave my cheeks. "Sharing is fine. I won't make the King of Frasia sleep on the floor."

"But you know I would do it," he said. "If you asked."

I looked up. Elias pulled off his cloak and hung it on the hook by the hearth, then rubbed the back of his neck, his dark eyes watching me carefully. His gaze was warm, like a physical touch, making my wolf whine with desire I felt in my chest. Being away from the manor was already making the icy barrier I'd built against him start to melt.

"I'm stiff from the travel," he said. "Go on a run with me?"

I balked, defenses snapping back up, even as my wolf leapt to attention. "A run?"

"Sure," he said. "Just a quick jaunt through the fields. It'll loosen me up, get some energy out. And the moonlight always helps with the aches."

"You can't be serious," I said. "Someone might see us."

"That's no problem." Elias undid the top few buttons of his plain shirt, then rolled the sleeves up to his forearms. It was a casually handsome motion, one that made my gut clench with the desire to step closer, and feel those hands on me again. I pushed that inclination deep down inside. "We're still in Frasia," he continued, "and most of the folks out here are wolves, or familiar with them. Seeing wolves on a run isn't anything strange."

He raised his eyebrows. "Why does it make you so nervous?"

I undid the plait in my hair, just for something to do with my hands. "It's just the way I was raised, I suppose. I'm still getting used to it."

"To what?" he asked.

"Shifting," I said. "In Nightfall, everyone shifts so... so carelessly."

"It's not careless," he said gently. "It's natural."

"It was different in Daybreak," I said. "From the moment I could walk, my father ingrained in me that I needed to control my wolf. That shifting too often was a sign of weakness."

"Our wolves are our strength," Elias said. "It doesn't serve us to keep them locked down—to pretend that they aren't part of us."

"I don't deny that," I said, even though a twinge in my chest suggested that might not be completely true. "It's just a different relationship than the ones the Nightfall wolves have."

Elias nodded slightly, brow furrowed like he was still trying to figure me out.

I sighed. "I suppose it's another thing I took as truth from my father, when he wasn't even my father at all." He'd done nothing but lie to me my whole life—it was like I had to now re-examine everything I knew about myself, my past, and my future, to untangle his deceptions from my reality.

"I have something for you," Elias said abruptly. He gestured for me to step closer.

I moved to stand in front of him, and the closeness of his strong body, the warmth of the fire, and the brandy in my veins all made me want to lean closer, to press against him. Bury my face in his neck and inhale his soothing, masculine scent. I didn't, even as my wolf complained internally.

"Here." He pulled a delicate brooch from his pocket made in the shape of a moth. The body was made of fine silver, and the wings were inlaid with moonstones. "This is for shifting. It allows you to keep your clothes intact, should you desire to shift, and protect your modesty."

That would make it easier, I had to admit—not having to stash clothes and sneak around nude. It felt a little more civilized. I'd seen Amity and Rue use something similar. Was this a tactic used more by the lower-class wolves? I wasn't sure, but I was still surprised by the surge of gratitude I felt at this small, attentive gesture.

"Thank you," I murmured.

Elias fastened the brooch onto my shirt. Then his touch drifted to my shoulder, then my cheek, slowly enough that I could pull away if I wanted to. I didn't.

"Will you trust me?" he asked.

"What do you mean?"

"Come run with me," he said. "We'll sleep better."

If I said no, he'd go running, and I'd have some coveted time alone in our tiny room, after spending so much time together in our tiny carriage.

But the air was crisp outside. The moon was full and high in the sky. My wolf whined, pacing and pawing eagerly.

"All right," I said. "Just a quick run."

Elias' face broke into a gorgeous, wolfish grin. How could I be expected to say no to that?

He led me back outside, out the backdoor of the Bloody Nightingale where a small garden had been planted. He stripped briskly—no moonstone for him—and left his clothes hanging on the garden fence. I hardly had a chance to admire the curve of his muscle in the pale moonlight before his wolf exploded forth in a crackle of power. His broad paws hit the soft earth with a thud. Elias shook out his dark pelt, then tipped his big head at me expectantly, ears perked forward and tail wagging like a puppy.

I took a deep breath, letting the cold air fill my lungs. I tipped my head back, closed my eyes, and let my wolf take control.

Choosing to shift felt different than my wolf forcing my way out. Power moved down my spine, then a cool energy surged from my core and danced down my nerves all the way to my fingertips and toes. The shift rippled over me as my wolf gleefully sprang forth.

My paws hit the ground. I took another long inhale through my newly elongated snout, and in this shape the air was rich: the legumes growing underground, the lamb cooking in the kitchen, the smoke from the hearths inside, the strong smell of dirt and moonlight. I shook out my bright white pelt, too.

Shall we? Elias' voice rumbled in my head. His eyes gleamed pure gold as he watched me, jaw barely parted enough to reveal a hint of teeth.

I perked my ears forward. I'd almost forgotten that—that he could communicate with me in this shape so easily. It felt good, though, to hear his voice so intimately. I lunged forward and nosed roughly at his neck, inhaling the warm, familiar scent. *Yes,* I said in response. I wasn't sure he could hear me, until he rumbled a low acknowledgment in his chest and knocked his head affectionately against mine.

Behind the Bloody Nightingale, the bald roads were vast and rocky, peppered with boulders and a few spare trees leading to the distant forest. It was vast and open, untended, uninhabited—freeing.

Elias turned around, then dug his back paws into the dirt and exploded off of them, bounding onto the bald. I yipped in delight and chased after him. We sprinted as fast as our wolf-shapes could run; the wind combed through my pelt as if to graze me, and my nose caught the many sweet scents. I chased after Elias, hopping over rocks and dodging trees as we ran and ran, chewing up the distance carelessly.

He was right. It did feel good. It felt incredible. I ran faster. My heart pounded hard, blood singing in my veins as my muscles worked, shaking off the stiffness of travel and the frustrations of the past few months. It all slid off me like rainwater. I barked happily; we approached a large boulder jutting from the bald like a turtle's shell and I charged it, ran up its sloped face to the top and then leaped off, gleefully careening into Elias' bulk and knocking him onto his side. He yipped back playfully and snapped his jaws at me. We tussled like that in the bald for a few minutes, playfighting, until I had him pinned.

His gold eyes gleamed as he bared his throat in submission. I nosed at his exposed neck affectionately, then leaped off him and back up, head lowered in an invitation to play, tail wagging.

He looked up and released a low, sonorous howl. The sound made my whole body shiver with pleasure, and I thumped my tail against the ground as I sat back on my haunches and instinctively echoed him. Our twin voices filled the cold night air.

It was so easy to be together like this. I only wished our royal lives were as simple.

Chapter 3

The next morning, I climbed into the carriage feeling shockingly well-rested. Elias had been right about the run—I'd slept like the dead on the slightly too soft mattress. I slept even better with the heat of Elias' body next to mine. He'd been perfectly respectful all night too, keeping his distance from me. If I'd woken up first with my nose pressed to his nape, well, he didn't need to know that.

The mischievous glimmer in his dark eyes, however, suggested he might. "That run seemed to serve you well," he said as he set our rucksacks inside the carriage. "Should make for a more pleasant ride today. Are you sore at all?"

"No, should I be?" I asked, rubbing my neck.

"Not particularly," he said. "Just from the roughhousing last night. You were quite spry for someone who rarely shifts." He set his hand at my neck where I was rubbing it and pressed his thumb into the muscle. It *was* slightly sore—that was why the contact sent delicious warmth spiraling through me.

I swallowed and stepped out of his reach and into the carriage. "Just because I don't shift constantly doesn't mean I'm a weak wolf," I said.

"I never said that."

I bit my tongue before I started another fight. Why was it so much harder to communicate with him as a human than as a wolf? I took my seat in the carriage and pulled out my novel.

"Good morning, Your Highnesses," Kodan said cheerfully as she strode up to our carriage. She carried a wax-wrapped package in one hand and a large flask in her other. "Some snacks for our journey today. And coffee." She handed them to me, and I took them gratefully. "Innkeeper said the augur indicated some bad-looking clouds in the distance. We should do our best to outrun them."

"Is that a metaphor?" Elias asked.

"No, she meant the actual weather," Kodan said. "So we'll be moving at a slightly brisker pace if the horses can take it."

Elias nodded. "Then let's get moving."

"Pray the gods give us speed," Kodan said, and threw up a sloppy salute.

As it turned out, the augur was right. We had passed six hours of the journey through the balds when the sky darkened with dense clouds overhead. The mountain pass separating Frasia from Shianga loomed in the distance, as the closer we got, the rockier things became, and the horses slowed their pace over the rough, hilly terrain.

Elias cursed under his breath as he peered out the small window of the carriage. Fat flakes of snow began to fall—just a few carried by the howling wind rattling the coach. And then more flakes. Then ice. Then the wind began to slam into us hard enough to rock the wagon on its wheels. I gasped and braced my arms against the sides, wrapping myself tight in my cloak as the blizzard worsened.

"I had expected a storm," Elias growled, "but not anything like this."

The carriage ground to a halt, trapped in the middle of the balds by the howling wind. I couldn't see anything outside of the small window, just a flurry of white.

There was a brisk knock at the door. Elias slid it open and cold wind raced into the carriage like it had been waiting to come inside. I grimaced and pulled the cloak even tighter around my body.

"The horses are blinded, Your Highness," Kodan shouted over the wailing tempest. Her red hair and black cloak whipped wildly around her, though she seemed indifferent to the cold. "We can't progress further."

"We can't stay here, either," Elias said. "Only the gods know when the storm will break. We need a camp."

"I thought the same. Shall I scout for a nearby site?"

"I'll come with you," Elias said. "Reyna, wait with the other ladies in Kodan's carriage, please."

I nodded. Typically, I didn't like being bossed around, but being squished between Fina and Adora for warmth sounded like exactly the right place to be.

The king wrapped his arm tightly around my shoulder, using his bulk and the cloak to shield me from the worst of the blizzard as he guided me toward the other coach.

"Be safe out there," I said.

He grinned. The cold didn't seem to trouble him, either, even as the wind caught his dark hair and sent it whipping around his face. "I'll find us a nice place to stay," he promised. "Nicer even than the Bloody Nightingale."

"Bar's low, then," Kodan said. She closed the door with a wink.

I leaned close to the window. Elias and Kodan both shifted, and through the blizzard I could barely make out their immense shapes. Kodan was nearly as big as Elias was, but leaner, and her pelt was dark brown, but shot through with the same shade of red as her hair. The two wolves lowered their heads and loped off into the blizzard, quickly swallowed by the storm.

"Sit," Fina said after a moment, gesturing to the space between herself and Adora. They were seated on the same bench, both curled up in big Starcrest cloaks against the cold.

Adora smiled and brandished a fine silver flask. Her cheeks were ruddy from the cold. "I have a little brandy, too."

"It's barely mid-afternoon!" I said with a laugh. I sat between them and curled my feet up under my body, immediately grateful for the warmth. I leaned back against the seat with a sigh.

"And we might be here a while," Fina said. She took the flask from Adora's hand and took a swig.

"I don't know what they think they'll find," Adora said. "It'd do better just to let the snow build up around the carriage. Let it act as insulation."

"Even a blizzard this strong wouldn't be enough to cover the carriage," Fina said. "Those poor horses."

"The staff's already got blankets on them," Adora said. "They'll be just fine."

"You Starcrest wolves are so tough," Fina said. Then she passed me the flask. "How are things in the private royal carriage? I heard some howls last night—did you go for a run?"

I turned red with embarrassment. "Ah, I hope it didn't disturb you."

"Disturb?" Adora asked. "I love the sound of a howl in the evening. Makes me feel safe."

"Me, too," Fina said. "I was glad to hear it. Are things okay between you two?"

I took a tiny sip from the flask. The brandy did warm me, and I sank a little deeper into the bench seating. With my cloak wrapped around me like a blanket, I could lower my nose into the fur collar and savor the warmth.

"They're better," I admitted. "Getting better."

Fina smiled, and kindly didn't press for more. "Good. Here, Kodan has been teaching us this crazy card game from Askon. Want to play?"

We hunkered down with the cards, prepared to wait a long time for Kodan and the king to return—but it was only about an hour before there was a knock on the carriage door. Elias was at the other side, flushed and grinning, with Kodan next to him, still in her intimidating wolf-shape.

"We've found a place to stay nearby," Elias said. "We can fit the party and the horses inside, and we'll leave the carriages until the storm passes. Kodan will take you ahead to the site, and I'll help the staff get the horses through the snow."

The three of us climbed out of the carriage and shifted into our wolf shapes. The cold was far less bracing in my wolf form—honestly, it almost felt *good* sluicing through my thick fur. I stuck my nose into the white flakes, savoring the shock of cold, then buried my face deeper in a snowbank and shook it over my head and down to my hackles. It was a crisp, refreshing sensation.

I flicked my ears, feeling someone's gaze. When I looked up, Elias' eyes were glowing gold as he watched me with a small, affectionate smile.

In this shape, it was harder to hide my feelings. My tail wagged against the snowbank.

Fina nudged my flank with her nose and yipped. Her pelt wasn't as thick as mine, and she was obviously still cold. I snapped to attention and followed Kodan's tall, lean wolf through the snow.

Fina's head was low in her animal shape, her tail between her legs, and even Adora with her pelt of similar thickness to mine looked a little more than displeased, her ears lying flat against her skull. I understood why—it was cold and windy, and we had no idea how far we were traveling to this unknown campsite. And yet I couldn't help but have a bit of a spring in my step.

What was a journey without a few troubles? I'd been so stuck in the rhythm of life in the manor. It was all the same: sleep in my huge bed, have a lavish breakfast, attend meetings, walk the grounds, read in the library. Just the same few activities over and over. I hadn't realized how *bored* I was until this journey had given a much-needed jolt of novelty.

Even the edge of danger felt good. I'd much rather travel like this—in my wolf shape, through the storm, alert and aware of the threats around me—than be packed away, bored by a novel in the carriage.

I flicked my ears as I loped along. Part of me knew that was a big realization. The first instance in which I would ever *prefer* to be in my wolf's shape, instead of my human form. But in circumstances like this, it just made sense.

Kodan led us to a formation of boulders near a steep hill. The boulders leaned against each other in such a way that they created a fairly large cave, big enough to fit the whole party, and the horses, too. The four of us hurried into the entrance. The darkness fell over me like a shroud, as did the sudden quiet, as we were shielded from the raging wind. I shook out my pelt. Fina whined, her ears lying back.

Even in her wolf shape, I could see Kodan rolling her eyes. She yelped at Fina, then flopped onto her belly. Fina trotted over and pressed against her side, burying her nose in Kodan's dense, coarse fur for warmth.

Adora lifted her nose slightly, then tipped her head at me slightly, as if to say, *we're tougher than that.*

Only then did I realize I couldn't speak to them the same way I could speak to Elias.

Before I could think too hard about what that meant, a loud whinny caught my ear. I peered out of the mouth of the cave. Elias had two horses in hand, and his three attendants managed the other four. Kodan nudged Fina, then stood up and shifted back into her human form. Adora flopped down where Kodan had been, and Fina rumbled gratefully.

It was crowded in the cave with the horses and the whole party, but it was cozy, too, especially with the storm raging outside. I shifted back into my human form and helped Elias brush the horses and cover them with cleaner blankets.

"I know it's not ideal," he said again, as he had in the Bloody Nightingale. "This will extend our travel time a bit, and—"

I laughed and patted his forearm. "I know you can do a lot, Your Highness, but I don't expect you to control the weather."

His expression softened, and he nodded in acknowledgment—or maybe gratitude.

Kodan and one of the attendants built a firepit in the center of the cave, just under a small opening in the top to filter out the smoke. The attendants had brought provisions, too, and once the fire was roaring and the cured meats were unpacked, it was warm enough for even Fina to shift back.

By the time we were set up in the cave, the sky was almost completely dark, though the storm still raged outside. I sat next to Elias on a blanket, with the rest of the party making a circle around the cheerful flames. Elias had uncorked a flagon of wine, warmed it on the fire, and poured a small glass for each of us.

"I haven't camped like this in a long time," he hummed.

"When's the last time?" Kodan asked. "Back when you were a pup?"

"I think so," Elias said. "It had to be when we were still in the old Nightfall."

Kodan whistled low. "Yeah, so about a hundred years ago."

Elias clicked his tongue and flicked a twig of firewood at Kodan's face as she laughed. I found myself laughing, too. I was so used to seeing Elias as the serious, unflappable King—but Kodan brought out a younger-seeming, more playful side of him.

"You're older than me, remember?"

Kodan cringed. "I try not to."

I pressed my shoulder against Elias', and he adjusted slightly so he could wind his arm around me. I told myself it was the chill and the tiredness that led me to do this—but the contact felt good. Grounding. I took a sip of the warm wine.

"What was it like?" I asked. "Old Nightfall?"

"Old Nightfall?" Fina asked.

"Our former pack lands," Kodan explained. "We lived on that territory until I was ten."

"And I was six," Elias said. "Even as a boy, I knew that land was going to be the death of us." He tugged me a little closer, his arm around my waist, but his gaze was fixed on the flickering blaze. "The old territory isn't far from here, actually. Cold and dry and impossible to farm. We were always struggling. Struggling to eat, to hunt, to build, to survive. I remember that it had a particularly harsh winter. The snow never seemed to stop and had driven the elk across the mountain pass to Shianga. Nothing to eat but salted pork and crusts of bread. The pack elders were dying—even the toughest wolves couldn't survive that cold."

Even Kodan's jovial demeanor flattened at the memory.

"So," Elias continued, "my father, the pack alpha, traveled with a small party to Efra, to ask the crown for aid. More than anything we needed food, but my father also hoped the crown would take in some of the pack and lodge them for the winter while we rebuilt in the spring, so we could avoid more unnecessary deaths. At that time the King of Frasia was an old man. My father was confident he would see the value in protecting the lives of innocent wolves."

The King of Frasia. At that time, the king was my grandfather, Constantine. My heart sank.

"He went, he pleaded his case to the king, and then the king turned him away."

"What?" I pulled away just enough to stare at the side of his face, though he was still looking into the flames. "He said *no?*"

Elias laughed a small, sardonic laugh. "He hardly waited for my father to finish talking before he turned him away. He wouldn't even give them lodging in Efra for the evening. He turned them right back out into the wilds to return to Nightfall."

"What was the reason?" I asked. My father had never mentioned this in my entire life. All the stories I'd heard of Nightfall as a young wolf were narratives of their ferocity and their bloodthirst—and how they showed up at the gates of Efra hungry for wolf-flesh and tore my innocent grandfather limb from limb.

"He suggested that Nightfall's woes were the gods' desires," Elias said without inflection. "And that if we did not survive, perhaps it was better for the wolves of Frasia to weed out the weak."

I was stunned to silence. The Duke of Daybreak had always spoken of Constantine as if he were a benevolent god himself, ruling over Frasia with kindness and fairness. But a kind king would never have turned away a pack in need. There was no reason for it—no reason other than cruelty and hatred.

"When my father returned to Nightfall and told his counselors what had happened, obviously there was outrage," Elias said. "It was briskly decided that if the King of Frasia believed the gods wanted to cull the wolves for weakness, then Nightfall would speed up that process."

Kodan smiled faintly.

"It wasn't an easy decision," Elias said, "but my father was trapped between a rock and a hard place. The pack would either succumb to death by the elements or death in battle fighting for a better life. He chose to fight. He never wanted glory—he simply wanted our pack to survive, and to be able to uplift all the packs in Frasia, not just our own."

"Gods rest his soul," Kodan murmured. The story hung in the air for a moment, over the crackling fire, and then Kodan asked, "Does anyone want to hear about the time Elias chased a squirrel into a tree and then got stuck?"

The rest of the evening passed with lighthearted stories from our childhood, but I had trouble focusing on the jokes and the laughter. I was still trying to wrap my head around the story Elias had told. The terrifying wolves of Nightfall were just a scraggly bunch of starved peasants? Fighting for their lives instead of fighting for glory?

As the fire lowered to embers, we all shifted into our wolves to sleep. It was easier to share warmth after shifting, piled against each other around the fire as protection from the cold. I nuzzled close to Elias, willing his familiar scent to calm the thoughts that were racing through my head, even in my wolf form.

You okay? his voice rumbled in my mind.

Yes, I responded. *I just didn't know Constantine had turned away Nightfall when they needed help most.*

Elias' ears flickered. *I imagine that's not the story they told you.*

It's not, I responded. *I think there might be a lot I don't know.*

Elias nuzzled closer then licked my snout, just once, a gentle soothing motion. Somehow, in the quiet of the cave, I was able to fall asleep.

I awoke at dawn, before everyone else, and the world was still. I padded out of the cave and stretched luxuriously, from the tip of my snout to the tip of my tail, then took a deep inhale of the cold morning air. The balds were covered in a layer of pristine snow, untouched save for a few animal footprints here and there. The sky was clear and the sun was shining high overhead, already beginning to loosen the hold the snow had. It wouldn't be too hard to get the carriages moving in this weather.

I was considering going on a run—a thought I never would've considered before this journey—when Kodan stepped quietly out of the cave. She was in her human form and was already leading one of the horses outside.

I shifted quickly back into my human form. "Good morning," I said.

"Morning," Kodan said. "Just going to start to hitch up the horses, since I'm awake. We should get moving soon."

"I'll help you," I said.

"That's not necessary—"

"I'm awake, too," I said with a grin. "We can let the others get a bit more sleep."

Kodan nodded. We led two horses each away from the cave and back to where we'd left the carriages in the middle of the road.

"You know," Kodan said as we hitched the horses back to the carriages, "I've known the king his whole life."

I glanced up at her, fighting down a spike of nerves. I wondered if she might threaten me a little. I'd already gotten the sense that she was quite protective of Elias, like an older sister.

"When his father… When he became king, something in him changed," she said. "He closed off. He had a lot of responsibility on his shoulders, and he was young, and the way he ascended to the throne was…less than ideal."

Less than ideal? What did that mean? All I'd known was the previous king had died, but the circumstances were unknown.

Kodan smoothed her hand down the horse's neck. "I advised him against holding the Choice, you know."

"You did?" I asked, furrowing my brow.

"Yes," she said. "It's part of the reason the council sent me on assignment during the event. They knew I'd cause trouble if I was on site."

"Why?" I asked. "Were you two ever…?" I flushed. That was none of my business.

"Together?" Kodan asked with a toothy grin that looked a lot like Elias'. "No, he's not my type. I was against the Choice because I didn't want to see him give up another piece of his life for the throne. He's sacrificed a lot, and I wanted his personal life to be *his*, not another role he had to play for Frasia."

I laughed, low. "Honestly, I can relate to that."

"I can tell," Kodan said. "I'm saying all of this because when he's with you, I see some of that old Elias."

My heart beat hard in my chest.

Kodan busied herself checking the fastenings on the horses' yokes. "You're good for him," she said. "It's not what I would've expected from the Choice. But it's nice to see."

"Thanks," I said quietly. A strange warm feeling grew in my chest. I'd spent so much time feeling like a pawn and prize that I hadn't considered how I might be having an impact on Elias, too. Kodan seemed to think I was bringing him back to who he was *before* he was king. But I only knew him *as* the king. I felt like I'd just found a confusing tome in the back of the library, like there was another layer of information I had to uncover.

Maybe there was more to Elias than I'd given him credit for.

By the time we made it back to the cave, the rest of the party was awake and preparing to head out. As the attendants finished taking the horses to the carriages and put out the fire, Elias wrapped his arm around my shoulder and tugged me close to his side.

"I was wondering where you went this morning," he murmured.

"Just thought I would get some fresh air," I said, "before we spend another day in the carriage."

"You could always go on foot if you want," he said. "As your wolf."

Briefly, I considered it—but a whole night and day spent in my wolf shape seemed like a little too much. "If I do that, I'll be too exhausted to play Queen of Frasia for the Shiangan King."

Elias laughed, low and warm. "Well, we can't risk that."

The rest of the travel day passed without incident, and by the time the sun set, we'd already found a clearing to make camp for our last evening on the road. The Shiangan castle was just a half-day's travel away.

That night, instead of sleeping in a warm pile of wolves, Elias and I had a cozy tent of our own. It was a big, canvas tent—large enough for royals—with thick fabric and a small platform for a bedroll to keep us off the cold earth. I was smoothing out the blankets over the bedroll, wrapped tightly in my cloak when the king stepped into the tent. He'd spent some of the evening playing cards with us, and some in quiet discussion with his attendants. With a small amount of surprise, I realized I was happy to have him to myself.

His eyes flashed gold as he watched me carefully. "Are you cold?" he asked.

"I'm okay," I said. "Not too cold."

"You've got goosebumps." He stepped closer and brushed my blonde hair off my shoulder. His fingers trailed over my neck and nape, and my skin did prickle, though not from the cold. "Would you like me to sleep as my wolf again? I run hotter in that shape. It's like sleeping next to a furnace."

"No, that's okay," I said. "At the Bloody Nightingale... I slept better with you at my side."

"Even as a man?" he asked gently.

"Especially as a man," I admitted. Sleeping close as wolves was different—it was more instinctive, animal, functional. As humans, it meant something different. Something more.

"Well," he said with a small, almost hopeful smile, "I run fairly hot as a man, too, so you're in luck."

I curled up in our shared bedroll first, under the heavy blankets in just my underclothes. Elias pulled off his shirt, revealing all that broad, tan muscle, and then crawled in next to me.

"This all right?" he murmured as he set his arm at my waist.

"Yes," I murmured. "Much warmer."

It took hardly any time at all for Elias to sink into a deep slumber. I matched my breathing to his, slow and heavy, and snuggled a little closer to him. As I drifted toward sleep as well, I realized that even in the wilderness of Frasia, with an unknown kingdom on the horizon, I'd never before felt as safe as I did now with Elias holding me.

Chapter 4

"Good morning, lovebirds," Kodan said as she stuck her head into our tent. "Sun's up, and it's time for us to get moving."

Elias hauled me closer to his chest. He bared his teeth in Kodan's general direction and growled, but his eyes were still closed, and he was clearly still half-asleep. I laughed and let myself be cuddled, as Kodan rolled her eyes. Something warm in my chest glowed at his instinctively protective reaction—no one had ever cared for me like this. Maybe Kodan had been right when she'd said that *this* was the real Elias.

"Up!" Kodan said. "Five minutes before I come in and join this spooning session."

"Try it," Elias growled.

Kodan just laughed and left us alone in our tent. Elias blinked into wakefulness, then suddenly released his hold on me, like he'd only just realized how he'd been clinging. He sat up, propped on one elbow, and rubbed the sleep from his eyes. Then he looked at me, eyes warm. "You sleep okay?"

I pulled the sheepskin blanket around my shoulders. "I did."

"Good," he said. His eyes traveled over me, slow and luxurious, like he'd much rather spend a little more than five minutes in bed. "Unfortunately, Kodan is right. We should get back on the road. Should be able to make it to Shianga before it gets dark."

I nodded in agreement. The travel had been stressful, and I knew there was a lot on Elias' mind regarding the details of this diplomatic convoy. Once we were settled in Shianga, and had some real privacy, I'd talk to him. Not just about our relationship—whatever it currently was—but about my role as queen.

Kodan had said that I brought out the man he really was. I wanted to be his advisor. His partner in leadership. Not just a pretty face in the room, or the prize he'd won in the Choice. I was more than that, and I was beginning to think that together, we could do a lot more for Frasia than we could do separately.

I'd thought I'd moved from my father's iron cage to Elias' gilded one. Maybe, initially, it had been a cage—but maybe, just maybe, Elias had left the door wide open for me. I wasn't going to be stifled the way I had been in Daybreak. This trip was going to be a new start. The real beginning of my life as queen.

"You've got that dangerous look in your eye," Elias said as he tugged on a clean shirt.

"What look?" I said, snapping out of my reverie.

"Hard to explain," he said with a smile. "It's similar to the one I saw when you fought me in the arena, though. Determined? Maybe a little barmy?"

I chucked a sock at him. "Barmy?! You would speak to your queen like that?" I bit my lip to try to keep my smile from breaking into a laugh.

He dodged the sock, then chucked it back. "What? It's one of your finer qualities, in my opinion."

I stood up and started to get dressed as well. "Don't worry," I said. "It's nothing urgent. We can talk in Shianga."

He smiled. "I look forward to it."

The attendants packed up the campsite, as the rest of the party had just risen by the time we were ready to head out again. Kodan sent two of the attendants ahead as a scout, and they ran ahead briskly in their wolf forms. The last leg of the trip to Shianga was through the mountain pass. After about an hour of travel, we reached the narrow dirt path that led out of the crossing. The rocky side of the mountain was to our left, and to the right the terrain melted into grassy knolls, still dusted in snow from the storm last night. We climbed out of the carriages so the horses could better navigate things.

The remaining attendant walked in the front, leading the vehicles forward, while Elias and I walked behind them. Kodan, Fina, and Adora were bringing up the rear with a bit of distance between us. The pass was stunningly beautiful, with the snowy knolls climbing into another mountain, and the crisp blue sky was hardly broken by any cloud cover at all. Despite the cold weather, Elias was barefoot, moving silent and graceful over the hard-packed dirt.

"Gorgeous, isn't it?" he murmured, nodding toward the horizon. "I always love seeing the mountains after so much time spent in the forest."

"I've never seen them this close," I admitted. I'd known they were large from my maps, and from the paintings I'd seen, but viewing the rock up close was something different. I couldn't seem to get enough, my eyes drinking in every detail of the horizon and the featured face of the mountain.

"Never?" he asked.

I shook my head, trying to ignore the flush of embarrassment in my cheeks. "Never. The Choice was the first time I'd left Daybreak at all."

"What?" he balked. "*Ever*?"

I wrapped my arms around myself. "It wasn't by choice," I huffed.

"No, I'm not passing judgment," he said with a wave of his hand. "I'm just—I'm surprised, that's all."

"Why?" I asked. "Because I like maps?"

"No," he said, "because you're worldly."

I blinked at him. "What?"

"I do recall you chose a Shiangan sword to fight me with," he said, "not to keep bringing up the arena. But I was struck by that. No other competitor wanted it. They were challenging to wield."

"It's just a reflection of my training," I murmured, even as pride bloomed in my chest. "And my interests."

"Well," he said, "I'm glad you're coming with me on this trip, then. Maybe I'll have you show off some of those sword skills."

"Before I was sent for the Choice," I said as I gazed out toward the horizon, "my dream was to travel as far and wide as I could. I dreamed of seeing the entire world if I could."

"Do you no longer dream of that?" he asked.

"Well," I said, "now that I'm queen, it's not like I can take off for a trip whenever I'd like."

"Maybe not whenever," he said, "but your role as queen doesn't mean you can't leave Efra."

I looked over at him. He was watching me closely as we walked, his head tilted to the side slightly. The mid-morning sunlight brought out the flecks of gold in his warm brown eyes. The days of travel had turned the faint shadow along his jaw into a fuller beard, which made him look even more rugged and handsome than he usually did. The outdoors and travel suited him.

"But we have duties," I said. "We both do."

"Certainly," he agreed, "and often our duties will involve things like this. And, of course, the Nightfall Court is established enough that we can take trips for ourselves, too."

"Like a vacation?" I asked.

"Yes," he said. "Like a vacation."

I sighed and gazed back out over the horizon. The weather was beginning to improve, and the breeze was cool and refreshing as it rustled my hair.

"I don't understand," I admitted. "That shouldn't be a priority."

Elias hummed. We walked in silence for a few moments, and I could almost hear him gathering his thoughts. "Of course, our personal travels and engagements will come second to the duties that leading this country requires," he said. "But I didn't choose you to be queen as a way to punish you."

I pressed my lips together. It had felt, especially in the days leading up to the wedding, like he'd chosen me to be his bride simply because I was the one who had the audacity to not want it. In a way, part of me had assumed he wouldn't want me to be happy—or worse, he wouldn't care either way. Hearing him say aloud that wasn't what he wanted made my throat tighten unexpectedly.

"I want you to be happy," he said. "I want us to be happy together."

His candor shocked me. I looked back over and saw nothing but honesty in his eyes: honesty and perhaps a bit of nervousness. "You don't want to keep me locked up in Efra?" I asked, half-teasing and half-serious.

"I think if I tried to do that, you'd break out within the hour."

I laughed, surprised, and nodded in agreement. "I've done a bit of lockpicking in my time, it's true."

It was still dizzying to think Elias might not only let me travel as a diplomatic convoy, but travel *for myself.* Not as the Queen of Frasia—just as me. Reyna of Daybreak—no, of Nightfall. Maybe I could even begin to learn to draw maps myself from the court cartographers. The fantasy was just beginning to spin out in my mind when a sharp, loud bark broke through the quiet morning air.

One of the two king's attendants raced down the path, moving swiftly in his wolf form toward the convoy. Kodan swore loudly and rushed to our side. The attendant wormed past the caravans, nearly spooking the horses, then shifted back into his human form mid-run. He tumbled over the dirt before clambering to his feet, and Kodan caught his upper arm so he didn't slip off the pass and roll down the hill.

"General," he gasped. "Ambush."

"Ambush?" Kodan asked. "Where? By whom?"

"Waiting for the king," the attendant said through his heaving breaths. "Five men. We killed three. One escaped. Selwy captured the fifth. We don't know who sent them. He won't talk."

"Good work," Elias said in a low, furious growl. "I'd like to speak with the prisoner myself."

His voice sent a shiver down my spine. A memory flashed in my mind: Elias in the center of the ballroom, snapping the neck of a traitorous court member. Whoever had ambushed the scouts would face a fate much worse than that. He was still the Bloody King.

"Kodan," Elias said, "stay with the convoy and defend the women."

"Sir," Kodan said in acknowledgment.

"Thaddeus, show me to the prisoner," Elias said.

"I'm coming with you," I said.

"No, you're not," Elias said immediately. "There may be more men waiting. It's too dangerous."

"Then give me a weapon," I said.

"Reyna."

"I can defend myself," I said. "You've seen me do it." I crossed my arms over my chest and leveled him with my gaze. If Kodan was staying here, the king needed someone else to watch his back. And, as his queen, I wanted to be a part of this interrogation.

Elias rubbed his forehead. "Fine. But only because I don't have time to argue about this."

Kodan snorted. "Come on, Fina, Adora, we're taking a short break," she said.

"What's going on?" Fina asked as Kodan corralled them toward the carriages.

"We'll be on our way shortly," Elias said, his voice still a low, enraged growl. "Just sit tight."

Thaddeus, the attendant, shifted back into his wolf form. Elias and I shifted as well, then began to follow him at a brisk run, down the pass until we were on the other side of the mountain. Thaddeus led us into the tree line, then into a small clearing. In the center, the other attendant—Selwy, I assumed—sat on a stump, bandaging a thin gash on his shin. A blond man in peasant's clothing was hogtied and leaning up against a tree, blood dripping from his mouth as his chin tipped forward. The coppery smell made my nostrils flare.

There was something else under the scent though. Something vaguely familiar—a salty, almost resinous odor.

"Your Highness," Selwy said, and moved to scramble to his feet. He grimaced in pain.

The king rapidly shifted back to his human form. "Don't stand," he said immediately. "Tend to your wound."

Selwy slumped down with relief. I shifted into my human form, too, but Thaddeus remained in his wolf shape, hackles up and teeth bared at the prisoner.

"Who sent you?" the king growled. He kicked the prisoner's thigh roughly. "Speak!"

The prisoner just laughed, a drunken, gurgling sound, and spit blood into his lap.

"He hasn't said a word," Selwy said. "I tried."

"Then I suppose we'll have to take him with us," the King growled. "I can make this interrogation last as long as he wants."

The prisoner shifted slightly where he sat. Even covered in dust and blood, his shoes were clearly finely made, lightweight soft leather and a familiar style of buckle at the ankle meant for easy removal.

"Selwy," I asked, "did you see this man in wolf form?"

"No," he said. "Showed me a hint of it while we were tussling, but I kept him from shifting."

"What color were his eyes?" I asked. "Did you see?"

"Uh," Selwy said. "Brownish, I suppose? Reddish-brown, like mud?"

The recognition washed over me like a bucket of ice water over my head. Elias watched me, his own anger tempered by curiosity as I stalked forward to the prisoner. I knelt on the ground next to him, hooked my fingers in the neckline of his shirt, and tugged it down.

"I knew it," I hissed.

There was a small scar carved just under his collarbone: an X bisected vertically. To a casual viewer, it didn't look like anything special, like a strange brand or a knife fight gone wrong. But I knew what it was. Barion had explained it to me at the beginning of my training. *It's how you know who to trust,* Barion had said, pulling his own collar down to reveal the marking. *It's the sign of a servant of Daybreak.*

Once upon a time, I had trusted him. I'd trusted my family in Daybreak. But now there was nothing left but betrayal, and I was a wolf of Nightfall.

"He's a spy," I said. "He's from Daybreak."

Elias' eyes burned gold with his anger. "Step aside, please, Reyna."

This time I didn't fight back. I moved out of his way, standing at the edge of the clearing.

Elias loomed over the spy. "I've had it with you insufferable bastards," he growled. "First you try to take my throne. Now you try to ambush me in broad daylight? Have I not killed enough of you?"

The spy said nothing, just laughed, low and humorless as more blood dripped from his mouth.

Elias growled with rage. He gripped him by the hair and hauled the man to his feet, holding him at arm's length to keep the blood off of his clothes. Elias' shoulders tensed, then he grasped the spy's head in both hands and snapped his neck with one sharp twist of the arms.

I grimaced and closed my eyes. The dull crack echoed through the quiet forest, then the dull *whump* of the lifeless body hitting the forest floor.

"Good riddance," Selwy muttered. "Fucking asshole." He glanced at me. "Pardon my language."

"Mm, I agree," I said. "Fucking asshole."

Selwy snorted and carefully stood up. "Your Highness," he said to the king, "I suggest we leave the bodies for the runner to find. Should he return."

"Agreed," Elias said. He turned back to face me, and his eyes were still blazing gold with rage. Part of me wondered if it would've been wiser to bring the prisoner to Shianga with us, where we could potentially learn of his motivations. But perhaps that would've been crueler, to potentially subject this spy to the kind of interrogations the king might be capable of doing. I knew he could kill easily. I didn't think he had a sadistic streak. Yet…there was so much about the king I still didn't know.

We made our way back to the carriages, walking on two legs so we could help Selwy navigate with his bad one. Thaddeus hurried to brief Kodan. I turned to walk back toward the back of the carriages, and Elias caught me by the forearm.

"We're almost out of the pass," he said. "You'll ride in the carriage."

"I can walk," I said. "It's still rocky terrain."

"I know." Then he heaved a sigh. "Please. Just—for me?"

His voice wavered minutely, and that was enough for the argument on the tip of my tongue to melt away.

"What is it?" I asked. "What's wrong?"

"If we hadn't sent the scouts," he murmured, "they could've attacked us like sitting ducks. And we were just walking out in the open. One well-aimed arrow…" He shook his head like he was physically dispelling the thought. "I can't let anything happen to you."

I wanted to fight back and ensure him I could take care of myself. Perhaps I would have, if it hadn't been wolves of Daybreak who had ambushed us. Guilt gnawed at me. Had they been looking for me? Or was this just another misguided attempt to try to take the throne?

"Okay," I said. "We'll ride the rest of the way. Don't worry."

Elias' shoulders slumped minutely with relief. He smoothed his hand up to my shoulder, and then carefully set his hand at my jaw. "Thank you."

I leaned into the touch, turning slightly so the corner of my mouth brushed the warm skin of his palm. These hands had just killed a man without a second thought. And yet I felt so safe when he touched me like this—like we were the only two wolves in the world.

"All right!" Kodan hollered from the front of the caravan. "Ready to move!"

Elias dropped his hand. His golden eyes burned into mine for a moment, but this time, I saw no trace of anger. It was something else. Desire—and something more.

"Change into a gown, if you can," he said. "When we arrive in Shianga, we'll be meeting the king."

Chapter 5

By mid-afternoon, we reached the ivory gates of the Shiangan palace. The rest of our journey had been without incident, with Elias either on foot or in his wolf shape, keeping a careful eye on the horizon for any further threats. He was focused on ensuring no other spies showed their faces—it was almost overkill. I got the sense that something about the Daybreak spies had deeply unsettled him, but when I asked, he just shook his head, distracted. There was something he wasn't telling me. I'd done what he asked, though, trading out my dirtied, comfortable travel clothes for a simple tan silk gown under the usual cloak.

I'd have to question him about it all later, because as the gates rolled open, pushed by two immense guards in golden armor, my worried curiosity was overridden by sheer awe.

I pulled the door to the carriage open enough so I could lean out. The weather was warm; I shucked off my cloak and let the breeze tousle my hair. The carriage rolled smoothly down a well-paved narrow road, cutting through an immense, well-tended garden, carefully arranged with topiaries, flower beds, and immense sparkling fountains. At the far end of the garden, the palace loomed. It was a simple structure, a large, gilded rectangle with huge glass windows and skylights thrown open on the roof. It appeared to be mostly windows and ivory, reflecting the sun so the building glittered like a jewel.

And overhead, soaring in swooping choreographed arcs, were dragons.

Dragons, with elegant reptilian faces and immense, semi-opaque wings, their scales shining in shades of red, orange, blue, and rich green. They moved so elegantly, so sleekly winding around each other, that they looked more like fish darting around a pond. I gasped in awe, watching them turn and spin in the air as they followed our path toward the front of the palace.

The carriages stopped outside the huge doors, which were immense gold and ivory vines, wound over thick glass panels. The dragons overhead landed gracefully, two on either side of the door, then they folded large wings behind them and shifted back into their human forms. Their very tall, very muscular, very *naked* human forms. I squeaked and jerked back into the carriage and hoped I could blame the flush in my cheeks to the changing climate.

Elias stepped up to the carriage. He was still dressed in the clothes he'd traveled in—thankfully free of blood despite the encounter in the woods—but was now dressed in the delicate gold band around his head he typically wore in lieu of a dramatic crown. He offered his hand.

I gathered the silk of my dress in one hand and took his in my other, stepping carefully down the steps of the carriage and onto the road. Only up close did I see it wasn't paved at all, but done in mosaic, so carefully tiled it was smooth under the carriage wheels. Elias' grip was tight on mine, almost uncomfortably so, but I attributed that to his nerves. I'd never seen the king nervous, but being surrounded by dragons was as good a reason as any.

Elias stood in front of the doors with Kodan at his other side, and Fina and Adora were flanked by the attendants behind us. Adora was doing her best to stare anywhere but the guards, whereas Fina was grinning in delight as she took in the sights. She caught my eye and threw me a wink.

Then, the great glass doors slowly opened.

"Welcome!" the King of Shianga boomed. "My royal friends, I hope your journey was unremarkable."

He grinned at us, revealing all of his gleaming white teeth—and his canines, elongated and made of gold. He was taller even than the guards who flanked his doors, beating Elias in height by a whole head. Yet he moved with reptilian grace, accentuated by a golden robe so lightweight it seemed to shift like water over his broad, muscular frame. He spread his arms wide in greeting and the rings on his fingers glittered as they caught the natural light. On his neck hung a fine pendant of a dragon's head with rubies for eyes, matching the rubies encrusted onto his ornate crown. I'd never seen a man so tall and so striking. He commanded attention, not only with his gleaming clothes, but his overpowering charisma.

"King Draunar," Elias said. Despite Elias' lack of ornamentation, he matched the king in regality. "Apologies for our lateness. A blizzard blew through Frasia along the way."

"Ah, the weather—the one thing we kings cannot yet control." He took Elias' hand in both of his, in a firm shake. "Thank the gods you made it safely." Then his glittering green eyes turned to me. "And this must be the victor of the King's Choice."

"My wife," Elias said, "and Queen of Frasia, Reyna of Nightfall."

"I don't claim to know much of the intricacies of the demographics of Frasia," King Draunar said, "but I must say, Reyna, you don't look like a Nightfall wolf I've ever seen." He bared those golden canines again in a slow smile as his eyes slowly looked over my body.

"Um," I stammered under his burning gaze.

"There's no certain way for a Nightfall wolf to look," Elias said curtly. He tugged me closer to his side and wrapped his arm possessively around my waist.

"Of course," King Draunar said easily. He extended his hand toward mine. I accepted the handshake, and his touch lingered, fingers barely circling on the inside of my wrist.

Elias' grip dug into my waist. He growled, barely audible, seemingly on instinct. King Draunar laughed brightly, like Elias had delighted him.

"Come inside, please," King Draunar said, waving his hand grandly toward the palace. "I'll show you to your quarters."

He led us inside to the immense front room, with soaring, high walls and ceilings made entirely of skylights. The walls were pale and gilded, covered in ornate paintings of landscapes and battle scenes, and the floor was a vivid tile mosaic. Everything in the Shiangan palace evoked color and light; this room alone was so bright it nearly gave me a headache just walking in. King Draunar guided us into the southeast wing, through a pair of immense wooden doors.

"Here's where you and your party will stay," he said grandly. "I trust you'll find there's plenty of space. I'll have my staff unpack your carriage and tend to the horses, and leave you to get settled until dinner this evening—though I would appreciate a brief private meeting with you, King Elias."

Having an entire wing to ourselves—that was excellent. Perks of being royalty, I assumed.

Elias nodded. "Certainly. I look forward to it."

King Draunar's gaze lingered on me for another long moment, before he turned on his heel and sauntered back toward the foyer.

Elias sighed, shoulders slumping, and opened the door to the main quarters in the wing. The contrast to the main palace and the gardens was striking. The room had two big windows, but the plush, dark curtains were drawn, and the room was lit instead of warm, with glowing sconces on the red walls. The carpet was plush and dark under my feet, and the centerpiece of the interior was the immense gold four-poster bed, the black comforter itself embroidered with dragons. Elias closed the door behind us and rolled his eyes.

"Draunar's taste is so gaudy," he said. "I'd almost prefer to sleep outside."

"You know him?" I asked. I sat on the edge of the mattress, testing it. It was extremely soft—we might end up sleeping on the floor instead of sinking into this marshmallow. There was a fine sheepskin in front of the unlit obsidian hearth.

"Just his reputation," Elias said. "He certainly lives up to it." He leaned against the wall with a heavy sigh.

There was a light knock on the door, and Elias stifled a growl before he opened it. A pretty, young dragon in a maid's uniform nodded in deference, her hands full with a fine golden tray. Elias waved her in, and she set the tray down on the table, then left with a brisk curtsy.

"Lunch," Elias said. "That's nice, at least."

I joined him at the table for a meal of cold noodle soup in a clear broth, which tasted surprisingly refreshing in the cozy room. We ate in silence for a few moments. Elias' mind was obviously elsewhere.

I cleared my throat. "So," I asked, "you're meeting with the king after lunch?"

"Appears so," he said. "Straight to business."

"What exactly will you be discussing?"

"Likely updates on the skirmishes at the border," Elias said.

I resisted the urge to lean forward. I hadn't heard anything about the details of this diplomatic meeting, and I wanted to know everything, but I resisted the urge to pepper him with questions.

"East of here, where the three borders intersect," he said, "there've been some minor tussles between rogue wolves and the eagles of Cruora. The eagles can be a bit aggressive—I'm trying to stay ahead of any escalating conflict."

"Right," I said. "What do the dragons have to do with that?"

"I'd like to ensure a peace between Frasia and Shianga as a preventative measure," he said. "The eagles will be less likely to escalate any skirmishes if they're aware we have a relationship with the dragons. Hopefully, we can manage this with some adjustments to our trade policies, but we may have to cede some land at the border to Shianga as a show of good faith." He grimaced. "Though I hope it won't come to that."

"Well," I said, "from my time in Daybreak, I'm quite good at trade tax policy, should you need my eyes on it."

Elias hummed in acknowledgment but said nothing. His attention had already drifted. I pressed my lips together and returned to my soup. He had said he wanted me to be involved as a leader—but did he only mean being aware of his decisions? Instead of helping him make them in the first place?

He finished his noodles and stood up. "All right," he said, "I should go get this over with. The servants should be here momentarily with our things; you could start unpacking."

I blinked at him. Start unpacking? *That* was what he thought I should do right now while he initiated the meetings with the King of Shianga?

"And listen." Elias smoothed out the front of his shirt and adjusted his crown. "Keep your distance from the dragons. I don't..." He grimaced. "Things really need to go smoothly. So just keep your distance."

"What?" I asked. "What do you mean?"

He waved me off and hurried out the door, in a rush to get to the meeting. I slumped down in my chair and picked at the remainder of my noodles, my appetite gone. Disappointment sent my heart sinking toward my feet. What did he mean, keep my distance? Implying that my existence would cause trouble? After all that talk about wanting me to be able to travel, and wanting us to be happy together, and wanting me to be a part of the leadership—he was back to treating me like a possession. A prize, a pretty thing to look at, a bedwarmer.

I was naive to think he wanted anything else. I *was* a prize. Wasn't that the whole point of choosing a wife through the King's Choice?

With a huff, I stood up and threw open the curtains in the window. Our quarters overlooked the front gardens, which were dotted with staff tending the topiaries and planting fresh flowers in the beds. Dragons stalked around the landscape, too, in both human and reptilian form, the sun glinting off their fine scales.

It was a gorgeous day, and I had nothing to do until dinner. I wasn't going to be stuck locked up in here. Even if the king was worried about me—I could defend myself. He knew that.

It'd been too long since I'd had a proper, private conversation with Fina and Adora, too. I'd go find them—the king could unpack his own damn trunk.

Chapter 6

"Oh, Gods above," Fina said, grinning widely as she took a sip of a bubbly, sweet drink. "I swear Adora and I nearly knocked the carriage over when the guards shifted back to their human forms. I do *not* remember seeing that when I came here as a girl."

"I know!" I said. "I was shocked! And they just stood there!"

"I've never seen a royal guard act like that," Adora said. Her cheeks were flushed pink just talking about it. "It's so interesting."

"Interesting, huh?" Fina teased. She kicked at Adora's ankle under the table. "Maybe we need to find you a nice duke here to marry. Do Shiangans have those?"

I laughed and stole a sip of Fina's drink. It was crisp on my tongue and slightly fruity. Just sitting with them had lifted my spirits substantially. Even though Elias was getting on my nerves with his hot and cold behavior, my friends always made me feel better.

"Come on," I said. "I need to stretch my legs after that carriage ride. Shall we poke around the grounds a bit?"

Fina sprung to her feet. "Absolutely!" she nearly squealed. "I'm dying to get a better look around. And I'm fed up with the cold, the weather here is so much nicer already."

Adora looked a little less certain, but after some playful urging from both of us, she relented and came along. I led the way down a narrow hall in the wing, toward the far east side of the palace. A small door, made mostly of glass, led into a private courtyard. The three of us stepped outside, and two royal guards followed. They were tall and dressed not in ornate golden armor, but a more functional brown leather, not too different from Nightfall's uniform. They stood flanking the door, eyes forward, but decidedly not looking directly at us.

I wondered what their purpose was. Were the guards here to ensure our safety, or to ensure the kingdom's safety from *us?* The lack of privacy irked me. I had to be sure to watch what I said to the girls, lest they listen in and pass our conversation along.

"Oh, wow," Adora said. Her eyes widened as she gazed around the courtyard. "I thought the front gardens were impressive, but this is amazing."

Indeed, the area was lush. It was as if we'd stepped into the heart of the jungle. The plants here weren't carefully arranged and tended like they were in the solarium at Nightfall—here it was an explosion of color and life, as if the trellises and fence couldn't contain everything. Overhead, vines snaked around an ivory trellis and dropped heavy purple blossoms in full bloom; the tall grass was nearly up to our knees and soft to the touch. Immense ferns reached upward and outward, there were flowers of differing colors and sizes, as well as some big-mouthed flycatchers that moved lazily in the breeze.

I reached up and smoothed my thumb over the velvety petals of one of the flowers. "I'd love to have some of these growing in the solarium," I murmured. "Do you think we could sustain it?"

"I don't see why not," Adora said. "It'd be a fun project, regardless."

"What should we do while we're here?" Fina asked. "I know you'll have to do some diplomacy things—"

"Queenly things," Adora said.

"—Yes, queenly things," Fina said with a laugh. "But we should have some time to ourselves, too."

"Obviously, we need to see the tailor in town," Adora said. "I must know what that fabric was the king was wearing. It really looked like liquid gold."

"He seems like a character," Fina said quietly. "Those teeth! And the way he looked at you, Reyna…"

I swallowed. "He was perfectly polite," I said. That was true—he had been, but something about the gleam in his eyes had made me nervous. It wasn't anything I couldn't handle on my own though, and the last thing I needed was to make Fina and Adora worry about me.

"Still," Fina said. "He seems intense. But the grounds are beautiful. I wonder if I could get a hunting party arranged. I'd love to get a sense of the game in this part of the world."

I was grateful neither of them seemed keen to press on my brief interaction with King Draunar. Instead, we wandered the courtyard admiring the gorgeous plant life as we sketched out our plans for the next few days.

"I hope the palace has a library," I said, and Fina and Adora both groaned good-naturedly.

As we made our way back into the wing of the building, idly discussing plans to have tea before dinner, the door to the wing swung open. In marched a Shiangan guard I hadn't seen before: taller than the others, and in the same leather armor, but with gold gauntlets on his tan, muscular forearms. The men who had flanked the door to the courtyard saw him enter, and disappeared back into the courtyard like dismissed children. It jangled my nerves again.

"Queen Reyna," the man said sternly. "The king has requested your presence this afternoon."

I blinked. "What do you mean, requested my presence? Is he with my husband?"

"The king would like a private word with you before dinner," he said.

I balked. Alone? The image of his golden-toothed smile flashed in my memory. I folded my hands together in front of me and then glanced over at Fina and Adora. Adora pressed her lips together, and Fina offered me a small shrug. I knew we were all thinking the same thing: I couldn't exactly refuse the king. If I wanted these negotiations to go well, and to build up my reputation as a diplomat in my own right, I couldn't just blow him off because he'd smiled at me oddly when we'd first met.

But at the same time, my wolf had her hackles raised in my chest. Something felt off about this meeting, yet I couldn't put my finger exactly on what it was. It was the same feeling that had led me to slip a knife into my waistband just hours before Rona had attacked me in her wolf form. I'd learned it was best not to ignore it.

"Of course," I said politely. "I'm with my attendants, though, so I'd like them to join me."

The guard narrowed his eyes. "The king specifically requested a private meeting."

I wasn't just a guest in King Draugar's palace, though. I was the Queen of Frasia. I could make a few demands of my own. "I understand," I said. "But I must have my attendants with me. I'm happy to meet with the king as long as my attendants are welcome."

The guard kept his tight gaze fixed on me. I matched it with a kind smile, eyes wide and expression pleasant. He couldn't force me to attend, and he knew it.

"Fine," he said. "If they must." He sneered at Fina and Adora, clearly expecting them to excuse themselves, but they only smiled just as pleasantly. I suppressed a real smile of my own. I could always count on those two to back me up.

Defeated, the guard finally nodded and muttered, "Follow me."

He led us out of the guest annex and through the main foyer, past the ornate golden throne room doors - I realized I still hadn't seen the inside - and toward the western wing. The guard stopped in front of a plain wooden door just off the throne room, which was so unremarkable against the stone wall that I would've walked right by if he hadn't pointed it out. He knocked briskly once, then opened it.

This was evidently a study, small but intimate, with a deep desk and built-in shelves lining the walls, bursting with books of all shades and sizes. The hardwood floor was covered with colored woven rugs layered over each other. They were soft, even luxurious under my feet. There were no windows, but instead of a ceiling there was an immense skylight, and the sun's rays made the room feel warm.

King Draunar was leaning over his desk, reviewing some documents, and then turned with a smile when he heard the door open. He'd replaced his ceremonial golden robe with an elegant but slightly less intense outfit: an ivory-colored shirt and pants, which made his tan skin look like it glowed. The effect was only heightened by the jewelry still dripping off him. His green eyes flickered to Fina and Adora, and a scowl briefly crossed his face before it melted back into his welcoming smile. But I saw it happen. The fact that he was furious upon seeing the two only assured me that I'd made the right decision by inviting them.

"Good afternoon, Your Highness," I said politely. "You requested a meeting?"

"Queen Reyna," King Draunar said. "It's so kind of you to meet me on such short notice."

He stepped closer and took my hand delicately in his own, then lifted my knuckles to his lips and brushed them with a kiss. The contact made my wolf raise her hackles again, and I fought back the urge to bare my teeth when his eyes met mine. He beamed, revealing his golden fangs.

I tugged myself out of his grasp and folded both hands neatly behind my back. Then I took a delicate step back, putting some distance between us. "Certainly," I said. "How can I help you?"

"Oh, Queen Reyna, it's not your help I'm after." He turned back to his desk and opened one of the lower drawers, then pulled out a faded tube. With a smile, he held it out toward me. "Consider it a wedding gift."

The leather felt supple against my fingers. I pulled the top of it off and peered inside.

"Be careful removing it," King Draunar said. "It's quite delicate."

I could smell the age of the paper, strong and dusty from being packed away. The smell thrilled me—it was a library smell, a beloved one for me: the promise of mysteries and knowledge right at my fingertips.

"What is this?" I asked.

"Take a look," he said. He looked pleased at my reaction, his smile even wider as he gestured toward his desk.

Behind me, Fina sighed with the knowledge that we all might be here a little longer than I had initially expected. She and Adora took a seat on the small settee by the door. My curiosity about whatever was inside the leather tube quickly won out over my nerves about being here in Draunar's study. I carefully tapped the document out of the tube and unfurled it gently onto the desk. The sensory feeling was stronger now, as if an entire library was in one document, the familiar scent of dust and ink surrounding me.

"Gods above," I murmured as I drank it in.

It was a map of Frasia—ancient Frasia. Perhaps even from before it was officially a state. Pack territories were noted on the map, but without any of our hard borders, and the cities were recorded as villages and townships. The forests were larger, the dammed rivers still winding, and the coastlines slightly differently shaped. South of Efra, the territory marked was almost entirely Fae. And the Fae controlled the entire northeast peninsula, too. I hadn't even realized the Fae had history at all in the northeast.

"Where did you get this?" I asked.

"Oh, it's from my private archives." King Draunar's voice was so close to my ear, it was nearly a whisper. I started; I'd been so absorbed in the map I hadn't notice him creep up behind me, close as a shadow. I jumped and knocked myself back into his chest. But he steadied me with a hand on the upper arm.

From the settee, Adora coughed delicately.

I shifted to the side, putting more distance between us, but we were still close at the desk, enough that I could smell the amber-leather scent of his cologne under my beloved old-paper smell. I cleared my throat. "Do you know when it was drawn? I'm quite curious about the changing territories."

"I know quite a lot about it." King Draunar said. "I'm happy to share my knowledge with you, Queen Reyna."

"When did the Fae territories begin to shrink in the south?" I asked as I tapped my finger delicately against their realm on the map. "And for that matter, how long were they in the northeast? I have no record of that."

"There's quite a lot to discuss," King Draunar said. "Have lunch with me tomorrow and I'll be happy to share the historical knowledge I have."

I looked up at him. He was leaning against the desk with his arms crossed casually over his chest, one eyebrow arched curiously.

I rolled up the map and tucked it back into the leather tube. While I was still internally delighted to have such a rare artifact in my possession, I wasn't going to let King Draunar know that. He was using this gift to manipulate me—to what end, I wasn't sure. I couldn't understand his motivations, and that scared me more than his behavior. I could handle a creep. But a creep who was the King of Shianga, of that I wasn't so sure.

"Your Highness," I said, "I'm not sure what my husband would think of a private lunch between us."

King Draunar laughed, loud and booming, like I'd just told the funniest joke in the world. He shook his head. "Queen Reyna, it's just lunch. I wouldn't ask you to do anything your husband wouldn't approve of."

I frowned. He spoke of Elias like the two were old friends—when I knew that wasn't the case.

Or at least, I thought I knew.

"King Elias isn't the only one with decision-making power, I assume," King Draunar said. "I'd like to know you better as well—as your own woman, not just as the king's wife. It'll aid in our kingdom's peace talks. Don't you agree?"

I exhaled through my nose, suppressing a more dramatic deep breath. I glanced over my shoulder at the settee. Fina scowled, her focus on King Draunar, looking like she could leap to my defense at any moment. Adora had her hands folded demurely in her lap and her expression was carefully impassive.

There was no good answer here. Either I turned him down, potentially causing problems in Elias' negotiations, or I accepted a private lunch date without knowing what he wanted from me. If I had two bad choices in front of me, I was always going to pick the one that would give me more answers.

"Well," I said, "I do hope you'll pardon me, but I'd like to see what the day brings and send word in the morning. Would that be acceptable?"

The green in his eyes seemed to suddenly glow brighter, but only for a moment. I didn't need to see that to know my answer hadn't pleased him. He cleared his throat and stood up straight.

"Fine," he said curtly. "I'll expect word from your handmaidens in the morning."

Chapter 7

The rest of the afternoon was a whirlwind. By the time I made it back to my quarters, the Shiangan staff were nearly in a tizzy because I was apparently behind schedule to get ready. They dressed me in the finest gown I'd brought, black silk with a high collar and lace sleeves, letting my hair fall in pale waves over my shoulders before fastening the delicate gold crown across my forehead.

Elias met me just outside the quarters, already dressed himself in a fine black silk shirt and trousers, under a ceremonial cloak fixed with a gold wolf's head brooch. He still looked distant—like his mind was elsewhere, even as he offered my arm to guide me.

"Just try to get through this," he murmured as we walked towards the throne room. "Draunar is a bit of a showman. Smile and nod."

"What do you mean?" I asked.

He sighed. "You'll see."

The great ornate doors loomed ahead of us, made of ivory, and gilded with scenes of dragons swooping through a mountain range. Music was already playing behind them: pounding drums and bright horns, a high energy sound that was similar in tempo to the jigs of Nightfall, but the drums made it even more thrilling. My heartbeat synced itself up to the beat, and my nerves melted in anticipation. My time in Shianga had been odd so far—but the excitement of experiencing a new culture overwhelmed all of that.

The doors were swept open.

I gasped.

The throne room was immense, long and narrow with the entire back wall made of glass that revealed the large, gorgeously maintained courtyard behind it, exploding with plant life similar to the small one just off the guest quarters. The floors were mosaic tile, dizzying in their extensive color. In front of the glass was a dais and a polished ivory throne painted with gold, though King Draunar was not seated on it. At one end of the hall, the band indeed played on immense drums and golden horns, filling the room with melodies. The table in the center of the room was full of guests, who clapped at our arrival, though the noise was almost inaudible over the music. It was so *loud*.

"Where's the king?" I asked into Elias' ear.

"He likes to make an entrance," Elias said.

He led us to our seats at the table, seated across from each other on either side of the head of the table, where King Draunar's polished wooden seat sat empty. Across the table, I couldn't even speak to Elias over the din. The woman seated next to me, a beautiful, tall guest in a silvery gown whose dark hair was done in braids, directed my gaze up to the skylights above.

The skylights were all thrown open, so the evening sun and sweet air from the gardens permeated the room. Against the golden, cloud-filled sky, dragons were flying above us.

I gasped. There were so many of them, too; at least a dozen swooped and coiled around each other like they had when we'd first rolled through the palace gates. There was one that was larger than the others. His wings were immense, pale green against the yellow sky, but his scales were a rich emerald color, shot through with the occasional golden scale.

The dragon plunged through the air a few more times, spinning and turning expertly, then dove head-first toward the throne room. The music picked up as he moved through the open skylights. The power of his wingbeat was enough to make the empty wine glasses tilt precariously where they stood. His long, serpentine tail flicked once, and he bared his teeth in greeting. Even in dragon form, his fangs were golden. The guests hooted and clapped their delight, thrilled. I clapped along. It was an impressive display, but I certainly understood what Elias meant when he said King Draunar was a showman.

The dragon turned away from us, folded the wings into his body, then shifted back into human form, indifferent to his own nudity. Two attendants hurried forward and helped him into his golden robes and his jewelry, moving with practiced quickness and ease.

"Welcome, my dragons," he called. The music didn't even drop a decibel. "Please join me in welcoming our honored guests, King Elias and Queen Reyna of Nightfall. King and Queen of Frasia, enjoy the finest hospitality Shianga has to offer."

Then came an endless stream of dishes, and wine, and I turned on all the charm I had as I tried to make myself heard over the noise.

After a few hours, the room was finally shrouded in dim light and the music had lowered to something softer and slower. I'd finished my spiced drinking chocolate and final aperitif—and Elias had been pulled into a conversation with King Draunar and what appeared to be a Shiangan general. Fina and Adora had already excused themselves, and at my request had sent a servant to escort me back, too.

I caught Elias' eye again from across the room and raised my eyebrows in question. He nodded.

That was one of the nice things about marriage, I supposed. The unspoken communication.

I slunk out the throne room doors. One of the Shiangan handmaidens hopped to her feet. "Milady!" she chirped. "How can I assist you?"

"I'm sorry," I murmured. My voice was a little scratchy from speaking over the noise. "I can tend to my own needs this evening."

"Of course, you must be exhausted," she said, though I could hear the slight disappointment in her voice. "Shall I run you a bath? Bring some wine?"

"No, no, I'll take care of myself," I said. "Thank you."

I dismissed her as I stepped into my quarters. I needed time to myself. I stepped into our fine ensuite bathroom.

Maybe I needed to talk to Elias. As I peeled myself out of my dress and changed into a light nightgown, I turned the possibility over in my mind. I knew it was a strange thing King Draunar had done, but I was still unsure if it was worth it to bring it up to Elias. I couldn't get a grasp on how he might react. What if his possessiveness interfered with the negotiations? Or worse—what if he decided to keep me hidden away for the entirety of the trip?

I could handle King Draunar on my own. But I wasn't sure if I wanted to.

I sighed and ran the brush through my hair, then washed my face, rinsing the evening from my skin. When I stepped out of the ensuite, Elias was in the room as well, unbuttoning his silk shirt with a grimace on his face.

"Oh!" I said. "I didn't hear you come in."

"Are you as exhausted as I am?" he asked, throwing me a weary smile. "That event dragged on a little too long."

"It was quite a party," I murmured. I paused in the doorway of the ensuite and pressed my lips together, still unsure.

He glanced over at me again and his happier expression was replaced by a look of careful concern. "Are you okay?" he asked.

I blinked. "Oh, yes," I said. "Fine. Just tired."

"Something's on your mind." He sat down on the foot of the bed. "Did something happen?"

"No," I said, then rubbed the back of my neck, where my wolf was making my nape itch. She was alert again, pleased to see her mate, and begging me to move closer to him. I hadn't realized how stressed and exhausted I was until I had the possibility of relief in his arms right in front of me. Well, relief for *her*. Maybe not for me. "I mean, nothing *happened*. It's just... It's nothing."

"Reyna," he said softly. "What happened?"

He could be like a dog with a bone—or a wolf with one, I supposed. He wasn't going to let this go.

And I realized I did want to tell him. This would be easier to navigate if he knew what was going on—easier for both of us.

I wanted his support. I wanted *him*.

"King Draunar asked for me in his private study today," I said.

Elias' eyes flashed gold. "He *what?*"

My wolf thrilled at the show of possessiveness. "I know," I said. "I had the same reaction. I almost turned him down but I was worried what that might do to the negotiations."

"The negotiations—Reyna, *fuck* the negotiations. He *asked* for you alone?" A low growl sounded from his chest. "I should gut that bastard tonight."

"That's really not necessary," I said, fighting back a smile. "I would've done it myself if he tried anything. Plus, I brought Fina and Adora with me, just in case."

That seemed to ease his anger a little. "I don't doubt you would have," he said.

"He said he wanted to give me a wedding present," I said. "Come look at this."

On the small table, I unfurled the map King Draunar had given me. Elias leaned over the table to look at it, his hand at the small of my lower back.

"Wow," he said. "This is older than anything we have in Frasia. Where did he get this? And why would he give it to you?"

"That's the thing," I said. "He wouldn't tell me."

"He gave it to you but refused to give you any context?"

"No, he said if I want to know more about the map, I need to have a private lunch with him tomorrow." I sighed and rolled the paper up.

Elias straightened up. "What did you say?"

"I said I'd let him know in the morning. I wasn't sure what I should do—what would be a worse outcome? Saying yes, or saying no?" I pushed a hand through my hair. "I don't want to cause problems with the peace talks."

Elias set his hand at my waist, then slid it again to my lower back as he pulled me closer. His eyes burned golden as they looked over my face, and my wolf squirmed with delight at the closeness.

"Smart wolf," he growled. "Did he say what he wants?"

"I don't know," I said. I wound my arms around his neck, resting them on his shoulders as we spoke. The closeness felt so good—so grounding. "He said it was just lunch, and that he and I should get to know each other as leaders."

Elias exhaled through his nose. "I doubt that's his true intention."

"I doubt it, too," I admitted.

"What makes you say that?"

"You know why," I said.

"I suspect," Elias said. "I want to hear what *you* think."

I sighed as I toyed with the fine hair at his nape. "You saw how he greeted me when we first arrived. In his study, it was more of the same. Getting too close. A not-quite-polite kiss on the knuckles. Nothing overtly inappropriate, just…"

"That bastard," Elias growled. He pressed his fingertips into my lower back. "I should call off the negotiations altogether. The gall of that man—he invites us into his home and then treats you like you're his to take. Sickening."

"I can handle it," I said gently. I could feel his rage escalating, threatening to boil over.

"You shouldn't have to," he growled. "You're his *guest*. The *queen*. And you're *my wife*." He bared his teeth in anger, and they were slightly elongated as his wolf threatened to push to the surface.

"Hey," I murmured. I leaned forward close enough that I almost breathed the words into his mouth. "Relax."

"How can I?" he asked. "You're not safe here."

"I'm safe," I said. "I'll be safe as long as you swear not to fuck up the talks because the king's a creep."

He growled again.

This time, I laughed, and kissed him gently on the mouth. I couldn't resist—his attention was intoxicating, and the possessiveness thrilled my wolf.

"I suspect there might be a lot of creeps in this world, Your Majesty," I said. "You'll have to trust me to handle it. This visit isn't about us—it's about Frasia."

"I know that," he said. "But I can't let this behavior stand."

"Let's get through the negotiations first," I said, "and then decide what to do."

Elias bared his teeth again, frustrated, but they weren't so animalistic now. He'd calmed down some. My wolf warmed with the knowledge that I'd been the one to do it.

"You're right, though," I said.

"What part?"

"I'm the queen. And I'm your wife." I punctuated it with another gentle kiss. "You don't need to worry about Draunar."

Something in Elias seemed to snap. He pulled me impossibly closer with one arm around my waist, and the other tangled in my hair as he embraced me in a deep, passionate kiss. I gasped and melted against him. It was dizzying in its intensity, all lips and teeth and tongue and growls of pleasure rumbling in his chest. All my worries suddenly melted away—all my thoughts, too, caught up as I was in the sensation, the pleasure, the desire. Heat burned low in the cradle of my hips. As soon as he started kissing me, I wanted more. He just had that effect —like one touch could never be enough.

"Reyna," he growled as his hands roamed over my back. He slid one hand lower, over the curve of my ass, and squeezed gently.

I giggled at the contact and hitched my leg up—more for him to grab. He slid his hand down to my thigh and hiked it up around his hip. His touch burned on the bare skin where my nightgown rode up.

"C'mere." He gripped my other thigh, too, and hauled me up into his arms.

I squeaked in surprise, clinging to his neck as he held my weight easily in his arms. He walked us both over to the big, soft bed, and tossed me into the center of the mattress. I couldn't help but laugh as I bounced.

He stood at the foot of the bed, shirtless and flushed, his dark hair loose around his face as he gazed down at me.

"Reyna," he murmured again, so soft my name sounded like a prayer. He set one hand at my ankle and smoothed it up to my calf. The touch sent waves of sensation up my spine. "You're so beautiful."

I blushed at the compliment—not at the words, but at the sheer open earnestness in his voice. Our gazes met and his eyes were warm chocolate brown again, but still full of wolfish hunger.

"Come here," I said, and reached for him.

The kiss had made desire burn through me, and I needed more. I needed intimacy, needed to feel his body against mine. I swallowed, my mouth watering at the easy shift of the toned muscles of his bare chest and arms as he crawled onto the bed. He moved over me, so his knees were straddling my thighs, his arms bracketing my head. I was surrounded by him, lost in his warm eyes and the familiar scent of his sweat.

He leaned down and kissed the curve of my jaw, then moved down to my neck, leaving kisses as he went. He inhaled deeply right at the join of my neck and shoulder, then dragged his tongue there, like he couldn't get close enough. I dug my fingertips into the muscle of his lats, then dragged my nails gently down his back, making him bare his teeth against my skin. I felt his growl vibrate through my palms as I touched him.

"Gorgeous." He pulled back, then slid his hand over my breast, my belly, then my hip. At my thigh, he dipped his fingertips under the hem of my nightgown and began to pull it up. As he lifted it, he glanced up at me with his brows raised in question.

"Yes," I managed to gasp. "Oh, yes, please."

I lifted my hips enough for him to slowly slide the nightgown up. As he did, gold flashed in his eyes, and his lips parted. His touch was soft but so steady as he pulled it up, revealing my pale skin and small breasts. A flush built in my cheeks—he was looking at me like he wanted to *devour* me.

And I loved it.

I pulled the nightgown over my head and tossed it aside, then flopped back onto the bed, trying to will any shy feelings away as he looked at me. He ran one hand from my thigh, over my hip and my waist, to the curve of my breast, then squeezed gently and smoothed his thumb over my nipple. It hardened under his touch, and I gasped as an unexpected bolt of sensation coursed through me; I arched up toward his touch.

"So sensitive," he growled, pleased, then leaned down and sucked that same nipple into his mouth.

"Ah!" I gasped, instinctively burying my hand in his hair.

"Hm?" he dragged his mouth over the soft skin of my breast, to my ribs, and sucked a kiss there. "Okay?"

"Feels good," I murmured. "Really good."

He grinned, then sucked my other nipple into his mouth, this time adding a hint of teeth. The sensation was dizzying, and my back arched again as I desperately sought out more. Then he sat up and maneuvered on the bed until he was kneeling between my spread legs, with his hands curled around my waist in a sweet, possessive gesture. His face was flushed, lips already slightly reddened from the kissing; sweat beaded on his temples.

I reached out instinctively for his bare chest, tripping my fingers over the warm flat plane of his abs. My tongue brushed the lower lip as I dipped my fingertips into the waistband of his pants and tugged. I wasn't sure what I wanted—just that I wanted to see him. All of him.

He grinned. "Not yet, little wolf," he promised, then leaned down and kissed my hip.

I gasped at the sensation. Everything felt heightened. He gripped my thighs and guided them over his shoulders.

Only then did I realize how wet I was. Every touch had made desire burn warmer and warmer inside me, low within my hips, and now it was like all my attention narrowed to the space between my legs—how wet I was, and how much I wanted him to touch me.

He dragged his mouth over my hip, the fine hair at my mons, then to my other hip. He kissed my thighs, both of them, then nipped at my inner calves, making me squeeze my legs around his head.

"Please," I gasped.

"Please what?" he teased. His breath rushed warm and promising over my center, the hottest, wettest part of me, and I shivered at the sensation. At the promise of it.

"Don't tease." I was close to begging.

"Never would," he growled.

He kissed my thighs again, then parted my legs wider. He was giving himself better access. Access for more kisses, a breath away from where I wanted him most—close enough that I raked my nails over his scalp and tugged gently.

He chuckled, pleased by my show of desperation.

Then, finally, he dragged the flat of his tongues through my wet folds.

I couldn't hold back the moan, low and long as I gripped his hair with both hands. The pressure of his tongue on me felt incredible—even better than I remembered from the one and only time we'd fallen into bed together. He worked his tongue over me like I was the best thing he'd ever tasted, long, slow licks with hard pressure that ended right on the sensitive nub of my clit. Every touch made me shiver as pleasure raced over me, dancing along my nerves, chasing any remaining thoughts from my mind.

He kept going, working his tongue a little faster as he gripped my thighs hard. Something low in my gut began to coil tighter and tighter, warm and promising, as he licked me. My thighs quivered on either side of his head, my muscles flexing involuntarily as he brought me closer to the edge.

"Elias," I gasped as I tugged on his hair. "Gods, please."

He pressed the flat of his tongue to my clit, moving it harder and faster, and I arched up harder, toward his mouth like I needed more, more, and I was right on the edge of it, the tightness in my gut pulling tight, tight, tight, almost enough to snap, and then—

He stopped.

He dragged his tongue up the crease of my thigh and to my hip and kissed me again.

"Ah." I couldn't make words, I could only grip his hair tighter and tug again, wordlessly begging for him to lick me again.

He grinned and slid up my body. His mouth was shiny with my slick, and that made my wolf rear up with sudden animalistic desire as I tugged him down for a wet, dirty kiss. He growled as I plunged my tongue into his mouth, tasting myself on his lips. It was dizzying. I was still so wet, so desperate I was throbbing between my legs. It only worsened when Elias placed two fingers over my folds, over my entrance but not dipping inside. Never in my life had I felt so *empty*. I needed him. Needed him closer, needed him inside me.

Elias rocked his hips down and I felt the hard line of his dick pressing against my hip.

"Please," I said. I wormed a hand between us and, ignoring my small spike of nerves, wrapped my small hand around his thick cock. "Let me see."

He groaned at the contact. I squeezed gently and watched in awe as his mouth dropped open in pleasure.

Just from that? Just that touch, even through the fabric of his pants?

He maneuvered off me just enough to wrestle out of his pants and toss them aside. Again he crawled on top of me, except this time heat radiated from his bare body. His dick was thick, hard, dark with desire; he kissed me deeply and I slid my hand between us. I slid my palm over his chest, abs, then down to his erect cock. It was so hard in my hand, and so hot, but the skin was velvety-soft, and he groaned gorgeously when I gave it one firm stroke from root to tip.

He broke the kiss to rest his forehead against my temple and groan, "Fuck, Reyna."

"Please," I said again. It felt like the only word I knew. "I want you."

He mouthed a sloppy kiss to my cheek. "Yes?" he asked. "You want me inside you?"

I nodded desperately. I *did* want that—I was a little nervous, but I wasn't scared. He always made me feel good. Somehow I already knew this would be even better.

"Really?" he asked.

I stroked him again, firmly this time.

He panted. "You're sure?"

"You want me to beg?" I asked, then squeezed his dick gently in punctuation.

"Maybe a little," he teased, then caught me in another burning hot kiss.

He settled between my legs, then gripped my thigh again and hiked one leg up around his hip. I dropped my hands to the bed above my head and gripped the sheets to ground myself, gasping in anticipation as I waited for him to slide inside.

But of course he had to torment me a little. He gripped the base of his cock and guided it to my center, then dragged the head over my wet folds, slipping over me like his tongue had—like a promise. I moaned and arched toward him. He gripped my hip hard, staring down in awe at me as he slid his cock over my pussy just like he had with his fingers.

"Come on," I gasped. "Fill me up."

"Gods above," he growled. "Who taught you to talk like that?"

I was too far gone to even blush. "I need it—I need *you.*"

Elias moved forward, pressing on his elbow on one side of my head, then leaned down and caught my slack mouth in another deep kiss. Finally, *finally,* he guided the head of his cock to my entrance.

He exhaled hard into the kiss. I nodded minutely and wound my arms around him.

Slowly, excruciatingly slowly, he slid inside.

I gasped, clinging hard to him as he groaned into the kiss. "Gods, Reyna," he murmured. "Tight."

Any coherent words I had were driven from my mind. It felt unlike anything I'd felt before. I'd pleasured myself before, sure, with hands and sometimes even toys, but it wasn't anything like this. His cock was burning hot inside of me, so deep I thought I could feel it in the back of my throat; there was a delicious stretch and a deep, intense pressure. He slid slowly inside until his hips were flush against mine, and I whined low and long into the kiss.

"You okay?" he murmured.

I glided my hands down his back and gripped his ass hard. "Move," I managed to plead.

His lips curved into a smile against mine as he slowly withdrew his hips, then pressed forward again.

"Oh, gods," I gasped.

Time melted into nothing but sensation. We traded messy, gasping kisses, and I clung desperately to him, legs hooked around his waist. He drove into me, slow and rhythmic, grunting with each thrust, driving in deep. The pleasure was sweet and slow and overwhelming, rich like chocolate, animalistic like running under the moonlight. He kept a steady rhythm, and again pleasure began to pull tight inside me, but this time it was deeper. When he used his mouth, it crashed over me like a wave breaking on the shore. This time it felt like a tsunami, a rumble in the distance, something big and powerful rushing toward me.

"That's right," he growled into my mouth. "Want you to come. Come with me inside you."

I clung so tightly he was pressed flush against me. His thrusts were shorter, but still deliciously deep, and the movements were so easy with how wet and desiring I was. The pleasure built and built and built. My quads flexed around him, my whole body tensing as my release approached. He didn't let up at all this time, his rhythm deep and steady as he dragged his tongue over my neck.

I tipped my head back. "Elias," I gasped.

Then, the tight coil of pleasure inside me snapped.

I came hard—harder than I ever had in my life. My eyes screwed tight as I arched as much as I could with Elias' weight pinning me to the bed. Pleasure rolled over me, from the crown of my head to my fingertips, so all I could feel was the delicious tingle of it over my skin, all I could hear was the rush of blood in my ears. My body clenched around him as I somehow became even *wetter*, and he growled low and possessive into my mouth.

"So fucking beautiful," Elias growled.

I slumped back against the bed. Elias pulled out slowly, and I whined at the loss, despite how sensitive I already was. He stayed as close as he could as he stroked his cock hard and fast. It was barely a dozen strokes before he groaned, long and low, then muffled the sound by biting down on my shoulder as he came across my belly.

The dual sensations of dull pain in my shoulder and his release wet and hot against my skin made desire curl through me again. He shivered through the aftershocks of his release, and then slumped down against me, panting and sweating into the crook of my neck. His body was deliciously heavy, half-pinning me to the bed and indifferent to the mess he'd made on my skin.

I wrapped an arm around his shoulders and exhaled into the crown of his head. I felt like I'd just spent hours running through the woods with him. I was sweaty, exhausted, sated—and *happy*. Almost deliriously so.

"Mm," he murmured against my neck. "Made a mess."

"Whose fault is that?" I teased.

He kissed my skin again, then rolled to the side, but only so he could shimmy down my body again.

"Wait." I petted over his sweaty hair and he looked up at me, warm brown eyes curious. He was *so* handsome it nearly took my breath away. Well—if I had any breath left after all that exertion. "I—I'm sensitive right now."

He grinned that familiar wolfish grin at me again. "Not going there again," he said.

Then, to my shock, he dragged his tongue over my belly and the white stripes of his release staining my skin.

I gasped, stunned to stillness as he licked my skin. He was cleaning me up—cleaning me up and claiming me at the same time. It was so nasty it made me flush, now that my head was cleared by my post-orgasmic state. It was nasty, but it was also *sexy*. The force of my own desire shocked me, and my pussy throbbed at the sight of it, even though I was far too exhausted to go another round.

Elias finished cleaning me up, and punctuated it with a kiss under my navel. I hummed with pleasure, wiggling a little under his ministrations, then tugged at his shoulder to encourage him to rest next to me. He grinned and did so, plopping down next to me, and tugged me close. I kissed him again, licking the taste of my sweat and his release from his mouth—it should've been gross, but in my sex-stupid, post-orgasm state, it was an intoxicating combination. He growled low and pleased as he returned the kiss. Then he rolled onto his side, propped up on one elbow, and brushed my sweaty hair off my forehead.

"How was that?" he asked.

I giggled. "You couldn't tell?"

"It was amazing for me," he said. "*You're* amazing. More than I ever dreamed."

"You dreamed about this?" I'd had my fair share of fantasies about him, but something about knowing he'd thought about me sent a swoop of warm, affectionate desire through me.

"Of course," he said. "Every night." He traced his fingertips over the bruise forming on my shoulder in the shape of his mouth. "Was I too rough? I know I…struggle with controlling myself, sometimes."

"I like it when you get like that," I admitted in a whisper. "I like knowing that I do that to you."

He grinned and kissed the bruise on my shoulder. "You're the only one who does. You're sure you're okay?"

I hummed as he ran his hand tenderly over the curve of my shoulder, then the dip of my waist. I was a little sore, sweaty, and exhausted—but good. Really good.

"Will you draw me a bath before bed?" I asked.

"Of course," he said. "Wait here."

He stepped into a pair of soft cotton slacks, then padded into the ensuite to start the bath. I sighed and sat up in bed, but only so I wouldn't pass out before I cleaned up. I pushed the hair off of my forehead and stretched my arms.

When I'd imagined my first time before, I'd always imagined it with Griffin—nice and romantic, but maybe a little perfunctory. With Elias, it'd been different. Intense, but somehow right. It felt like part of a connection, like an extension of what we already had. Like it was what we were meant to be doing. It felt safe.

I stood up and walked a little clumsily to the ensuite. My legs felt like I'd been walking for miles, quivering from the exertion.

"I was about to come get you," Elias said, half-teasing. "Thought you might need to be carried."

"I'm a little shaky," I admitted as I climbed into the immense copper tub. The water was deliciously warm on my skin and fragrant with lavender essential oils. My tiredness increased as soon as I stepped in. I reached for a washcloth, but Elias snatched it from my hand.

"Relax," he murmured. "Let me take care of you."

I sank deeper into the bath and leaned my neck over the edge. Elias took care of me as he promised, gently washing my body and working his fingers through my hair. I melted into his touch, my attention drifting somewhere between waking and sleeping.

I'd never felt such tenderness from him. Or—never felt such tenderness when he hadn't already shifted. I felt like we were wolves again, curled up against each other in the safety of the woods, away from all the complications of Nightfall life. I never thought I'd feel this way with him in our human forms.

And yet here I was, pliant under his touch.

I didn't want it to end.

Chapter 8

The next morning, Elias rose at dawn. "Send word to Draunar that you will attend lunch," he murmured, as I was still half-asleep. "If you still want to. I'll go with you."

"Oh, I will. He'll love that." I hummed a laugh into the kiss. Elias' lips curved into a smile against mine, and then he hurried out of our quarters to start his morning meetings.

I didn't see him again until just before the scheduled lunch. I was in the bedroom changing into a finer gown, after spending the morning with Fina and Adora exploring the main grounds. I couldn't bring myself to tell them what happened between Elias and me the night before. It still felt sweet and private, something I wanted to hold close to my heart. They'd known *something* had happened between us, though—Adora had made a comment about how I seemed like I was walking through a dream.

In a way, it did feel like last night was a dream, but it was the best kind. I felt connected to Elias in a way I hadn't before now. Not just from the sex, but from the way he'd taken care of me, both during and afterward. I wasn't sure what it would mean for our relationship, yet, but it had settled something in my wolf. And maybe something in my heart, too.

Elias stormed into the bedroom in a huff when I was in the midst of braiding my hair.

"Oh, hello," I said. "Should I ask how negotiations are going?"

Frustration radiated off him in waves. He stormed over to the small bar cart in the corner and poured himself a finger of brandy even though it was barely noon.

"We're going in circles," he groused. "One minute, Draunar is demanding more land, and the next his advisors are suggesting they not look power-hungry, lest they make Askon suspicious. Then, the tax advisor wants adjustments to the proposed trade policy, then the general wants more land, and then Draunar is the one questioning if that will make Shianga look power-hungry, and around and around they go." He shook his head. "It's exhausting. I almost wonder if they're doing it on purpose to stall the talks."

My dreamy mood was suddenly doused in cold water. My anxiety spiked a little. "What do you mean? Why would he try to stall the talks?"

"I don't know," Elias said. He sighed and leaned heavily against the wall, then stared into his brandy glass. "I'm probably just being paranoid. He might just be peacocking. Trying to make me feel like he has the upper hand."

"Does he?" I asked.

Elias looked up. "Certainly not. He doesn't have the Queen of Frasia on his side." He padded over and put his lips to my temple as I finished my braid. "How are you feeling?"

"Good," I said. "A little nervous about this lunch. He's not going to be happy to see you."

"Probably not," Elias said. "But it's better than you going to see him alone. I have a feeling he'd try something shady if you did."

"You don't want me to murder the King of Shianga in an act of self-defense?" I teased. I turned and caught his lips in a brief kiss.

"I wouldn't be totally against it," he said, "but that wouldn't be great for the negotiations."

"Let's get it over with," I said. "The girls want to go into town afterward."

"Well," he said, straightening up, "we certainly can't leave them waiting."

King Draunar had invited me to lunch in the conservatory, located in the courtyard behind the throne room. It was a beautiful building, covered in pebbled glass and filled with well-tended bright flowers and a few small gurgling fountains. In the center of the conservatory, King Draunar had set up a polished wooden table, small enough to be intimate but grand enough for a king. It was a gorgeous setting, and though there were four chairs at the table, it was clear Draunar had only been expecting to see me.

He stood as I entered, and tugged at the embroidered sleeves of his fine, pale linen robes. "King Elias, welcome." He narrowed his eyes at Elias he entered. "My manservant will fetch another place setting for our unexpected guest."

"My apologies, Your Highness," I said as I took my seat at the table. "Was I not supposed to invite my husband to this fine meal?"

"I'd hoped to speak with you privately," King Draunar said, "as I'm sure your husband is quite sick of hearing my voice already."

"Nonsense," Elias said as he dropped into the seat across from me. The servant the king had called swooped in and set his place with impressive speed. "I greatly enjoy your presence, Your Highness. Though" —he flashed King Draunar a charmer's smile— "I can't let you swoop in to court my wife."

"I'd do no such thing," King Draunar shot back, matching Elias' teeth. "I simply wished to enjoy the queen's company. Is she not allowed to go out alone?"

Elias' eyes flashed. "She's *allowed*—"

"My lord," I interrupted. "Please. Let's not bicker. We're here to develop peace between our nations, are we not?"

Elias and Draunar stared at each other for a long moment. Elias' eyes were shot through gold, and Draunar's burned bright green. The air seemed to crackle with tension, and my wolf raised her hackles—both Draunar's dragon and Elias' wolf were just under the surface, ready to burst forth and handle the conflict physically.

But then Draunar leaned back in his chair and flashed us both a beatific grin. "You're right, of course, Queen Reyna. We're all friends here, aren't we?"

"Of course," I said. "Shall we take a breather from the negotiations and enjoy lunch?"

Elias smiled back, but it looked more pained than anything else. Lunch was tense, and more than a little awkward. Every time I tried to bring up the map, King Draunar deftly sidestepped the question and brought the conversation back to safe, dull topics, like the design of the gardens and the history of the gilded paintings in the throne room. His conversation was as skillful as his flying, and there was no way he was going to tell me anything about the map. From the look in his eyes, it was clear I hadn't held up my end of the deal, so he wasn't going to hold up his, either.

After lunch, King Draunar excused himself for a meeting with his generals. As soon as the door to the conservatory clicked closed, Elias slumped down into his seat, pressing the heels of his hands to his eyes.

"Gods above," he said. "That man is exhausting."

I had a bit of headache myself from playing verbal volleyball with him for the entirety of lunch. "I see why negotiations are so frustrating."

"Do you still plan to go into town with Fina and Adora?" he asked, with his eyes still covered.

"I'd like to."

"Might I join you?" he asked. "I need to get out of this palace. The second I make it back to our quarters, I promise you there will be an attendant knocking at the door, asking me to come review some tax forms I've already looked at a hundred times."

I bit back a smile. "Sure. Some fresh air will do us good."

I hadn't seen any of the town at large, not since we'd rolled through the palace gates and into the courtyard. The four of us took a carriage to the center. Fina and Adora were nearly vibrating with excitement, and Elias looked pleased just to be out from under King Draunar's thumb.

The town outside Shianga was beautiful. It was quieter than Efra, with low buildings made of stone and clay, cobbled streets, and shop doors painted in bright colors like jewels. Fina hopped out of the coach first and adjusted her wide-brimmed straw hat against the afternoon sun.

"Wow!" she said, and spun on her heel, taking in the town square with a wide smile. "This place is amazing! Come on, Adora!"

Adora hurried out of the carriage, looking a little more hesitant than Fina did. She tugged at the collar of her linen dress. "Where did the attendants say the tailor was?"

I stepped out of the carriage. "The tailor?"

"Yes!" Fina said. "Did you see the golden robes the king wore? Apparently, that's a fabric you can just *buy* here. Not in great quantities, of course, but I simply must have a gown that uses it. It's so gorgeous. I've never seen anything like it, it will stun in the Nightfall Court."

Elias stepped out of the carriage and stretched his arms. The four of us stood near the center of the town square, by an immense, gurgling fountain in the shape (of course) of a dragon spewing water from its long snout. The townsfolk gave us a few sidelong glances as whispered to each other. Apparently, word of the Nightfall envoy had gotten around.

Even in his plain clothes, Elias still had an unmistakably regal air around him. I wondered if I was developing something similar.

"Shall we?" Adora asked. "I've heard the dragon tailors are fantastic. She's expecting us."

I hadn't exactly been thrilled to step into yet another tailor shop—I was beginning to think if I'd been in one, I'd been in them all. And there were so many other things to see in Shianga, and I still had so many questions about the map King Draunar had given me. "Ah, well—perhaps I'll meet you there in a bit?"

Elias chuckled low, and slid his hand around my waist to my hip. "I have an idea of where you might want to go."

"Of course," Fina said. "You enjoy the smallest, strangest, most tightly packed bookstore you can find, and we'll see you at the tailor's."

I laughed and leaned closer to Elias. "Am I that predictable?"

"Yes," Fina and Adora said in unison. Laughing, they strolled arm in arm toward the tailor.

"You don't think I'm predictable, do you?" I asked as Elias guided me the other way. The heels of his fine boots clicked on the cobblestone.

"Only in this regard," he said. "If you have a free afternoon in town, you will *always* find the bookstore. Other than that, I can barely keep up."

I laughed. "Good answer."

Elias led the way out of the town square and down a narrow alley. Pale canopies of fabric were stretched between the buildings, shading us from the sun, and the noise of the town melted away as we went deeper into the alley. He opened up a slender, deep blue door; a bell jingled softly as we stepped inside.

"One of Draunar's policymakers recommended this shop," Elias said. "Said it had the best selection of historical materials."

"You asked for a recommendation?" I asked.

He glanced over his shoulder at me. "Of course," he said. "I knew you'd want to find one eventually."

Affection flared in my chest. Even though he'd been so busy with the details of the negotiations, Elias still managed to find time to ask something for me. Something I hadn't even asked him to do. It seemed like a small thing, but the knowledge that I was on his mind even when he was caught up in the mess of negotiations made my heart beat a little harder.

"Good afternoon," the shopkeeper said. He was a tall, rail-thin man with thick glasses and a bird-like nose. "Welcome in, is there anything—oh!" His eyes widened. "Oh, oh, gods above, the Bl— Your Highness, oh, my, no one informed me—"

"What did you call me?" Elias rumbled in a low growl.

The shopkeeper took a step back, stumbling. "Nothing, um, I mean, Your Highness, that is—if I can be of service—" His face paled. He looked like he expected Elias to shift on the spot and maul him. Elias was not helping with that reputation, either, with the way he was glowering.

"Relax," I said, and placed a hand on Elias' forearm. Then I turned my attention to the shopkeeper and smiled warmly. "This is a beautiful space. Are you the owner?"

"Um." He visibly shook himself, then straightened up and cleared his throat. "Yes, yes, I'm Gulde, the owner here. I don't have any employees, you see, it's just me who runs this place."

"Well, you seem to be doing a good job," I said. I meant it, too—I wasn't just trying to ease his nerves, though that was part of my goal. The shop *was* beautiful. It was bursting at the seams with books, bound in leather and fabric of many colors, the shelves running all the way to the exposed beams in the ceiling. Books were all over the tables, too, stacked over the hearth on the far wall, and even open haphazardly all over what I assumed was Gulde's desk in the back. The dim space was cool, and smelled strongly of ink and paper. I already knew I could spend plenty of hours in this small space. "I'm Reyna, of—"

"Of Frasia, yes, the King and Queen of Frasia are in my bookstore. Yes." Gulde was clearly trying to convince himself this was actually happening. He took a steadying breath, then clapped his hands together. "Well, what can I help you find?"

"I'm looking to learn more about the history of Shianga and Frasia," I said.

Gulde glanced nervously at Elias. Something in Elias' expression made him grimace and turn back to me. "You've certainly come to the right place," he said. "Right this way."

"Take your time," Elias said. He dropped into a rickety chair by the hearth with a relieved sigh. The sight made me bite back a smile—he was clearly savoring this brief moment of peace away from the palace.

I followed Gulde to the back of the shop. He waved me behind the desk, and then guided me through a tiny doorway I never would've even noticed if he hadn't directed me to it.

"This is where I keep the rare books," he said. He tapped the wall and sconces, mounted high on the interiors, glowed warmly. The walls were lined with glass cabinets, sparsely filled, but they were clearly well-tended. Gulde unlocked one of them and peered inside. "What exactly are you looking to learn more about?"

Curiosity gnawed at me. Some of the books in here looked nearly as old as the map the king had given to me. Were they even in a language I could understand? If I had my way, I'd spend hours in this room alone. Gods knew what kinds of secrets books of this age held.

"I'm specifically interested in knowing more about the Fae," I said, "before their disappearance."

"The Fae?" Gulde asked, glancing over at me, unsure. "Why so?"

I didn't answer. It wasn't often that I wielded my queenly reputation, but it sure was handy in situations like this. I raised an eyebrow.

"Right." Gulde turned back to the cabinet. "Yes. Queen of Frasia. Here, this one might be helpful for your, um, research."

He pulled a heavy tome out of the cabinet and turned to hand it to me gingerly, like it was made of crystal.

I opened the plain leather cover. "History of Fae," I murmured. "I have something similar." I peered at the authorship of the book. "Blaylock," I said. "Yes. I believe I've already gone through this book, Gulde, is there anything else?"

"Pardon my forwardness, Your Highness, but I doubt you have," he said with a small smirk. "You may have encountered 'History of Fae in Frasia' by Hae Blaylock?"

"Yes," I said, surprised. "Is this not the same?"

"Certainly not," Gulde said. "This work was written by one of Blaylock's forefathers, Orohil. History runs in the family. Much of his scholarship has been lost, but I've been able to get my hands on a few of his works. This one in particular focuses on the Fae prior to the establishment of the borders as we know them today. It's as much an anthropological document as it is a history."

"I'll take it," I said immediately.

Gulde balked. "Well, Your Highness, this book isn't exactly for sale. You see, we're in my private collection."

I pressed my lips together. "Well—there must be a reason you brought me in here, then? If not to sell me some of these books?"

He sighed. "It's not often I meet another who is as interested in history as I am," he said. "I'd be honored for my collection to aid you in your research, it's just…"

"You want to make sure you'll get it back," I said with a grin.

Gulde grinned as well and said nothing. It wasn't like he could ask the Queen of Frasia for collateral. But I knew he wanted it, and if this was a way for me to build trust with a connection like this, I was happy to do it.

"Here." I pulled the fine silver brooch from my cloak and offered it to Gulde. "Take this. I'll bring the book back before we leave Shianga."

He nodded. "Your understanding is much appreciated, Your Highness."

I left the bookstore with the heavy tome wrapped in canvas and tucked under my arm. Elias glanced at it with his eyebrows raised. "Find something interesting?" he asked as we strolled out of the alley.

"I must recuse myself from negotiations for the foreseeable future," I said primly. "I have to bury myself in this book. The shopkeeper wants it back."

Elias laughed and wrapped an arm around my shoulders. "Absolutely not," he said. "I won't make it through another boring meeting without you."

When we made our way back to the carriage, Fina and Adora were already waiting for us, seated at the edge of the fountain and chatting with each other. Adora sprang to her feet as we approached, grinning.

"You look excited," I said. "Wasn't I supposed to meet you at the tailor?"

"We finished already," Adora said. "It went marvelously."

"What all did you buy?" I asked.

"It's a secret," Fina said with a smirk.

"Oh, gods," I said, laughing. "What does that even mean?"

"Don't worry about it," Adora said. "Now hurry up, I don't want to be late for dinner. There's this lord in the Shiangan Court I've been talking with…"

In the carriage, I settled into Elias' side with the book in my lap, as Fina and Adora launched into a detailed retelling of their encounter with the evidently skilled dragon tailor. Being here, with my two friends, and in a suddenly improved relationship with Elias… I was beginning to think this whole queen thing might work out.

Chapter 9

"Have you gotten anywhere with that book?" Elias asked. He padded out of the ensuite, toweling his hair dry, then leaned down and pressed a kiss to my bare shoulder.

We'd been in Shianga just over a week. It was mid-morning, and what had started as few lazy kisses exchanged after another breakfast had escalated into slow, unhurried sex—the kind I was really starting to get used to. I was almost ready to admit to myself that I didn't just like it—I *craved* it. Not just me, but my wolf, too.

Ever since we'd been together, she'd been closer to the surface, but less irritable, too. It was a strange sensation. I almost wished we could take a break from all the pageantry of the negotiations so I could ask him to go on a run with me. A moonlight run, a days-long run. I wanted to spend time with him, just the two of us, as our wolves. I'd never felt that desire so strongly before.

It felt like we were on the brink of something, but I wasn't sure what it was.

While he was in the shower, I'd rolled over in bed and grabbed the "History of Fae" from the nightstand to start thumbing through it again in an attempt to distract myself from my circling thoughts. It was so dense, it was almost guaranteed to put me to sleep.

"Not really," I said. "There's so *much* information, and it doesn't even seem to be laid out in any ways that make sense. I keep stumbling across strange little tidbits, though. Did you know the Fae queen influences the movement of all the Fae in the realm?

Like a hive of ants. Their villages and neighborhoods radiate out from her, which is why a lot of early Fae were nomadic."

"Interesting," Elias said in a tone that suggested he was quite sick of hearing these fun facts.

I laughed and set the book aside again. "Sorry," I said. "I know this bores you."

"It's not that." He sighed and sat at the edge of the bed, then pressed his fingers into his temples. "It's these damn talks."

"No progress after dinner yesterday?" I asked.

"He said in the morning he was ready to sign," Elias said, "but then when the documents were on the table, he balked and said he's unsure about the importation tax clause. It's ridiculous. He's demanding more money from Frasia—but I don't think there's anything we could do to make him agree." He carded one hand through his hair. "There's something holding him back. He's stalling for some reason. But I have no idea what the fuck he wants. He's just wasting our time."

King Draunar's green eyes flashed in my memory. He'd looked at me so intensely when he'd called me into his private study, placing his hand on my back, inviting me for lunch.

The talks had dragged on for so long, and for no reason.

Unless the reason was me.

I pressed my lips together. We needed these peace talks to come to fruition to ensure the safety of Frasia in general. If I raised the idea that King Draunar was delaying the treaty because he wanted something from me... Elias wouldn't react well. There was a real chance he'd do something impulsive and even dangerous. Like challenge Draunar. I knew Elias was strong, but there was no way he could take down a dragon in hand-to-hand combat.

"So I asked him if we could take today off," Elias said. "I need a break from all those gods-forsaken meetings."

"That seems like a good idea," I said. "What are you doing instead?"

"Not sure yet," he said. Then with a smile, he leaned down and kissed me again. "I was hoping I'd spend it with you."

How could I say no to that?

We made our way out of the palace to the courtyard behind the throne room. It was a gorgeous day, with a clear sky above and a breeze cutting the temperate weather. The air smelled clean and fresh, and I longed to shift and run. In the past, when I'd wanted to shift, it'd always been out of necessity. I'd kept her locked up for so long that she had to explode forth. But now, it wasn't that she was demanding to come out—I *wanted* to release her. It was a subtle but dramatic difference. My nape itched with the urge to shift. If Elias could feel it radiating off me, he said nothing, but he did throw me a wolfish smile.

"This way," he said. "There's something I want to show you."

At the northernmost end of the courtyard, the gardens gave way to the natural forest. It was a well-tended barrier, save for a narrow path that led into the trees. The trees were different than the ones I was familiar with from Frasia: they were taller, with branches that tangled together, making a dense canopy of rich green through which the sun fell in golden, dappled patches. The ground beneath our feet was spongy with moss and dotted with immense mushrooms.

"It's beautiful out here," I murmured.

"I've been doing some exploring," he admitted. "If I can't sleep. Or if I need a break from the meetings. Come, this way."

A little deeper into the forest there was a small clearing, with a tiny, forgotten gazebo. It was nearly overgrown with ivy, and part of the roof had collapsed, as if the forest was trying to take it back. The mossy ground nearly covered in tiny flowers of white and gold. It was like something from a dream. I inhaled deeply, wishing for my wolf's nose.

Elias pulled my cloak from my shoulders, folded it neatly, then set it in the gazebo. "Reyna," he said with a smile, "shall we run?"

"Oh, please," I said. "Gods, I need it."

"I thought you might," he said. "I love running with you."

My heart barreled into my throat, fluttery with anticipation. Briefly, I couldn't find any words. Elias had said it so casually, like it was the most natural thing in the world. Maybe, a small part of me thought, maybe it was. Maybe this was the closest we could get to a normal relationship, free of all the baggage or our roles as the leaders of Frasia.

Elias pulled his linen shirt up and over his head, then shook out his dark hair. His body was gorgeous in the mid-morning sunlight, glowing and gold. I flushed as I remembered what we'd done just hours prior, and how I'd explored every curve of his chest with my tongue. How was it possible that we'd rolled around in bed together just hours before, and yet I already wanted to get my hands on him again?

Like he could read my mind, he glanced over at me and grinned. I flushed and looked away. I pushed down my feelings of embarrassment and quickly shucked off my lightweight gown, and my underclothes too, leaving them folded with my cloak in the gazebo. I turned around to face him, bare as the day I was born, with my hair falling loose over my shoulders.

Elias' eyes burned gold as his gaze roved over my body. "You'd better shift, little wolf," he growled, "or else I'm going to take you right here."

Desire shot through me. I bit my lower lip. "See if you can keep up and maybe you'll get your way."

Then, with a soft sigh, I shifted.

It was so easy it was nearly effortless, like leaping into cool, welcoming water. My wolf surged forth, and my paws hit the moss with a strong thump. I shook out my white pelt, then tipped my head back and inhaled the cool air. It was better than I had even imagined, layered with the smell of water and mud, mushrooms and fauna, decay and growth. I felt electrically alive. The air crackled with energy as Elias shifted, and the immense, dark paws of his wolf met the ground. He flicked his big ears at me, gold eyes gleaming, and then bared his teeth in a playful challenge.

I yipped once brightly, and then took off into the woods as fast as I could run.

We tore through the woods like pups. I was more agile than he was and leapt easily over roots and fallen trees, darting through the brush following nothing but instinct. But Elias was just as fast as me, and his paws thundered against the dirt as he chased me. Sometimes I let him get close, just so I could take a sharp turn and lose him again. It was thrilling. The world shrank down to the pace of my run, the breath in my lungs, the sense of my mate following just behind me.

In this moment, everything was perfect.

I barreled through the brush and skittered into a clearing beside a gurgling stream. I got my bearings and moved to push off my back paws and leap over the stream. Before I could, Elias exploded out of the brush. He slammed into the side of my body, tackling me to the soft moss. I yipped in delight. The only thing better than being chased by Elias was being caught. I kicked my back legs into his belly, trying to push him off, but my strength was no match for his sheer bulk. He pinned me easily, and then fit his jaws over my neck.

I whined, low and long, as his teeth pressed gently into my throat. I tipped my head back, jaws parted and tongue lolling out, as I submitted to him. My whole body went pliant beneath his, and the sheer release of submission was unlike anything I'd ever felt before. My tail smacked against the earth. Even while under him, I couldn't hide my pleasure.

He growled back, pleased at my display, and released my neck.

Then with a crackle of energy, he shifted back into his human form. He still had me pinned, except now his familiar, handsome face was grinning golden-eyed down at me, as he sifted his fingers through my white pelt.

It was a strange sensation, being in my wolf form while he was human, but something about it was intoxicating, too. I couldn't think of any other time when I'd let a human touch me as a wolf. He slid his hands through my pelt, up and behind my ears, then dragged his nails gently behind them. My whole body shivered in pleasure at the sensation; every touch felt heightened. My tail wagged harder and beat against the dirt.

He laughed, low and quiet. "Such a cute little wolf."

I dragged my tongue over his cheek. He laughed again, bright and unrestrained. Then I shifted back myself, my wolf dissipating to reveal my bare human form, flushed with exertion, beads of sweat immediately forming on my forehead and chest. Even after shifting back, his hands were still tangled in my hair, and his warm, muscular body pinned me to the moss. I wrapped my arms around him.

"Cute, huh?" I murmured, and then caught his lips in a searing kiss.

We melted against each other under the warm midday sun, half-obscured by the thick canopy reaching above the clearing. The forest was quiet and the only sounds I could hear were the rustling of the breeze in the leaves and the gurgle of the stream beside us. It was so easy to imagine that the world extended only to the forest, and the man in my arms.

Our kisses became more heated and desperate as we rolled on the soft moss, hungry for contact, but still thrilled from our run through the woods. This time, when he entered me, it was with my body on top of his, Elias' hands firm on my lower back as he rolled his hips with instinctive, animal ease. He swallowed my moans into a claiming kiss, and it took no time at all for his sweet touch to pull a dizzying orgasm from my body.

I rested my head on Elias' broad chest, lulled into an easy, relaxed half-sleep by the steady beat of his heart. It was early afternoon, but I only knew that because of the placement of the sun in the sky above. It was such a warm, beautiful day, that I wanted to do nothing else but lie in his arms.

His thumb traced circles on my shoulder where his arm wrapped around me. "So," he murmured, "once we've finished up negotiations in Shianga, where would you like to go next?"

"Next?" I asked. "Aren't we going back to Frasia?"

"Well, yes," he said. "But for our next trip. Hopefully, just a vacation. Where have you dreamed of going?"

I wriggled closer. There were so many places I'd imagined visiting: the sandy beaches of Osna, the dense lush forests of Askon, even the far deserts of northwestern Shianga. But before I could say anything, a great shadow fell over us, blocking the golden sunlight.

My hackles rose. Elias' did, too, and his grip tightened on me. He squinted up at the sky. The great shape above circled a few times, swooping dramatically, causing the shadow to cover and uncover us like a blanket. The dragon then arced down, cutting through the canopy with expert ease and landing with a thump in the clearing.

The rich green scales shot through with gold were unmistakable. The dragon folded his immense wings to his back and stood on his back legs, surveying us, eyes flickering as he bared his golden fangs.

Elias sat halfway up, concealing me from view. "Draunar," he said, low like growl, the lack of title akin to an insult.

Chapter 10

King Draunar bared all his teeth in a draconic smile. He took a step closer. His long, lizard-like tail swept the moss behind him. Then, the air sang with energy, and King Draunar shifted back into his human form. It was unlike the ceremonial change he'd done to welcome us to his palace when we'd first arrived. He wasn't draped in gold fabric or dripping in jewelry—he was as nude as we were, his tan skin seeming to glow under the dappled sunlight and his green eyes blazing. I felt my face heat, both from embarrassment and from a not-insignificant amount of fear.

I didn't want King Draunar to see me like this, not in this vulnerable moment that was meant only for my husband. I shifted back into my wolf form. I felt safer, with my jaws to defend me, and my bare body hidden from King Draunar's bright desiring eyes.

Seeing me shift, King Draunar only looked more interested. He grinned as he approached. Elias climbed to his feet, and I stayed low to the ground behind him, my ears flattened back against my head and my tail low.

"What a gorgeous wolf," King Draunar said. "I've never seen a pelt so pure white."

My hackles raised, and I had to fight my instincts in order to not bare my teeth.

"What do you want?" Elias said. "Why have you sought us out? We had no obligations today."

Draunar chuckled quietly. He clasped both hands behind his back, once more indifferent to his naked state. Something about that only made me more afraid. Inside the palace, when we were surrounded by other court members and dressed up in our fine silk and leather, Draunar and Elias had to play their royal roles. Out here, stripped of all finery like animals, glaring at each other, those roles were dissipating. They faced each other, both in wide, defensive stances—anger radiated off Elias. I nudged my nose against the back of his thigh, trying to remind him silently to keep his temper under control.

"I've come to a decision," King Draunar said, grinning coolly, "regarding our stalled treaty negotiations."

"It couldn't wait until tomorrow?" Elias asked.

"I thought you might want to hear it sooner rather than later," Draunar said. "I know you're eager to see these negotiations come to a close."

"So what is it?" Elias snapped. "What was so important you had to interrupt us?"

"I require one more amendment to the treaty in order to sign it," Draunar said. "A show of good faith from Frasia, to ensure that our kingdoms live in peace for generations to come."

Elias said nothing. He tensed from his shoulders down to his feet. I pressed closer to his legs, steadying myself against his body.

"The queen," he said.

"What?" Elias said. "What about her?"

"I want Reyna," Draunar said. "You must give me your queen as a tribute to prove your good faith. Only then will I sign the treaty."

My blood ran cold. I bit back a whine, then bared my teeth at Draunar. How dare he make such a crazy request?

Right? It was crazy, wasn't it?

Elias laughed, sharp and angry in the quiet of the forest. "You must be a fucking fool," he said. "You think my wife is something to be traded, like a pawn in a chess game? That was never on the table. You offend me by even requesting such nonsense."

The cool smile didn't budge from Draunar's face. "Those are my terms." His green eyes flashed. "Either you give the woman to me, or the treaty falls apart."

"That's ridiculous," Elias snarled. "You would cast aside all the work we've done for our nations on a foolish whim?"

"It's no whim," Draunar growled. "These are my requirements."

"Selfish bastard."

"Selfish?" Draunar asked with a laugh. "Tell me, Elias, does the wolf know how you took the throne? Would she be so keen to hide behind you if she did?"

"Do not speak of what you do not understand," Elias growled. "Have you no consideration for your country?"

What did Draunar mean, how Elias took the throne? He had succeeded his father, fairly young, but it had been nothing remarkable. I nudged my nose against Elias' thigh again. I wanted him to defend me—but I didn't want him to prod at Draunar's temper. Not while we were still technically guests in his home.

"I only have consideration for my country," Draunar said. He took another step closer, so he was looming over Elias, staring down the bridge of his nose at him. "Should you refuse this request, and thus let the treaty fall apart, it will not only be a single treaty that falls apart. I will bring Shianga to your doorstep. We will not be tenuously neutral as we are now, King. We will be at war."

Elias bared his teeth. "You're crazy."

Draunar flashed his golden incisors back. "It'd be easier for you to understand if I were, wouldn't it?" His gaze drifted to me, blazing with desire. "But I'm not crazy at all. I simply know the truth—the truth that Shianga is much stronger and much more stable than Frasia is. My dragons have trained under my family for centuries. We have no coups here, no messy lineages decided by foolish competitions for seats at the royal table. The Shiangan army could crush the wolves of Frasia like bugs. And I will, Elias, if you refuse to give me what I desire."

Elias said nothing. Hatred and rage rolled off him in tangible waves. I could feel his wolf surging closer to the surface, and I knew he was moments from shifting and ripping Draunar's throat out with his teeth. If there was one way to ensure we were at war, instead of just listening to royal threats, that was how to do it.

"Consider what I've said," Draunar said. He took a step back. "I'll give you until the ball at the end of the week to make your decision." He smiled at me again. "I look forward to it, Reyna."

I growled in response, but that only made Draunar laugh. "Feisty thing." Then, he shifted back into his dragon, extended his immense wings, and took to the skies. The impact from his flight sent gusts of wind through my pelt, and made me shiver like it was an unwanted touch.

Once the dragon had disappeared from view, Elias growled low, then shifted back into his wolf without saying a word. He trotted to the stream and dunked his face into the cold water, then waded in. Some of the tenseness in his muscles faded as he shook in the icy water.

I lay down on the soft moss, nose closer to the dirt as I soothed my own nerves with the sweet, earthy smell. I watched him paw around in the stream. My heart was sinking slowly the longer I watched him.

War.

Not just war—an *invasion*.

The threat seemed to linger in the air like a bad stench. Was it real? Or was it just Draunar peacocking? Elias would have a better sense of that, but from how rapidly he'd shifted, it was clear he didn't want to talk about the details right now.

He loved me. He'd made that clear.

And yet I knew he loved Frasia more.

The side comment Draunar had made itched at me again. How Elias had taken the throne. Was there more to the story of Nightfall's grab for power? That was the pit in my stomach. That was the truth I couldn't ignore. If it was a real threat, and there was a chance that Draunar would turn this entire treaty process against us to have an excuse to invade Frasia, was Elias the type of king who would use me as a tribute? Had he done something similar to obtain the Nightfall throne? Was I being naive again?

He would have to. He couldn't sacrifice the safety of our country for something as minor as our marriage. We hadn't been together long at all, and it'd be just as easy for him to marry Adora and get on with leading Frasia.

He'd said I wasn't a pawn, but that wasn't really true, was it? I'd been a pawn in my father's schemes, a pawn to Griffin in his bid for power, a pawn in the Choice and now I was just a pawn that would move from Frasia to Shianga to ensure the safety of both nations. What was the alternative? Would I let war descend on the two nations because Elias loved me?

Because I loved him?

I'd never admitted it to myself, but it was true. I did love him. I loved his seriousness, his wisdom, his loyalty; I loved his laugh, his teases, the secret looks he could give me from across the room. I loved his touch, his kiss; I loved running with his wolf; I loved leading by his side.

But love wasn't enough to save a nation.

I exhaled hard. I wished I could sink into the soft earth and disappear. I'd let myself get too caught up in the fantasy here in Shianga. I was so naive—how could I let myself think that it would be this easy? That it would be as simple as that—a partnership, leading, vacations, ease?

It would never be so easy. Our relationship would never come first. Not when Elias had a country to lead. Not when *I* had a country to lead beside him.

He climbed out of the stream and shook out his dark pelt. He trotted over to me, ears back and tail low, and nudged his nose against my neck. *Let's go,* his voice murmured in my head.

I wasn't going to get any answers from him tonight. I knew him well enough to know that. We made our way back to the gazebo, where we shifted back into our human forms and pulled our clothes back on. Elias' expression was dark and distant. He turned to lead the way back toward the palace, and I caught his wrist in mine.

"Hey," I said. "Are you…"

"It's fine," Elias said. He tugged me close to him and kissed me briefly, but something about it felt perfunctory. When he pulled away, his gaze met mine, and there was something in his eyes I couldn't quite read. "I'm going to fix this, all right?"

"I know," I said. "I know you will."

I just wished I knew what fixing it meant.

We made our way in silence back through the garden to the palace. It was mid-afternoon—we'd been in the forest most of the day. At the doors, Elias sighed and pushed one hand through his hair, still damp from the romp in the stream. "I've got to go find Kodan," he said. "Straighten this all out."

"Right," I said. "What's the plan?"

He shook his head. "Don't worry about it."

I swallowed and tried to push down the frustration building in my chest. "Well, considering he wants *me*—"

"Please, Reyna," he said. He pressed his forefingers to his temples. "Go have lunch. I'll handle this."

"Right," I said quietly, but Elias didn't seem to hear me as he hurried inside.

When I made my way inside, he was nowhere to be seen. I realized I had no idea where Kodan was staying, or where they were having strategy meetings. So much for me being involved in the decision-making. I made my way back to the guest quarters, where luckily Fina and Adora had just called in afternoon tea from the kitchens. When I stepped into their room, the table was spread with fine meats and cheeses, and hot spiced tea that I accepted eagerly.

"Are you all right?" Fina asked, peering from over the rim of her own teacup with concern. "Wasn't today a day off? You should be resting."

"It was certainly supposed to be a restful day," I said. "I went on a run with Elias."

"That seems lovely," Adora said. "Especially with the weather here. Perfect day for it."

"You'd think so," I said. "And it was, until King Draunar butted in."

"He crashed your date?" Fina gaped at me.

"I know," I said.

"I hate to say this," Adora said, with her voice lowered, "as he's been such a lovely host, but he's been giving me a strange feeling most of this trip. Like he's hiding something."

"You can just say he's creepy," Fina said. "He *is* a bit creepy."

Adora hid a laugh behind her hand. "I wasn't going to say it!" Then she shook her head. "But it does seem to be mostly directed at you, Reyna. I've noticed the way he seems to watch you."

I sighed. "So I'm not imagining things?"

"Definitely not," Fina said. "What did he do?"

"He said he was ready to sign the peace treaty, but with one additional requirement," I said.

Fina and Adora glanced at each other, like they knew where this was going.

"He wants me," I said. "He wants Elias to give *me* to him as tribute."

"Well, that's ridiculous," Adora said. "The king would never do such a thing."

"Exactly," Fina agreed. "He's smitten with you. I mean, he chose you—and if I learned anything about him during the Choice, it's that the man is seriously possessive. There's no way he'd ever go along with such a disrespectful request."

"I know," I said as I stared into my tea.

"Don't let King Draunar get to you," Adora said. "This is just two men having a dick-measuring contest."

Fina squawk a surprised laugh. "I can't believe you just said that!"

"What?" Adora asked, even as her cheeks reddened. "It's true!"

"It's absolutely true," Fina said, "but I can't believe you just said 'dick-measuring'! Say it again!"

"Oh, gods," Adora said, blushing even harder, "you're ridiculous."

Fina broke down into giggles. I offered them both a smile, too, but their familiar teasing didn't make me feel any better. I knew they were both right—Elias was possessive, and certainly didn't want to give me up—but they hadn't heard the second half of Draunar's threat.

What Elias wanted and what Frasia needed were two disparate things. And in this case, I wasn't sure if they could be reconciled at all.

Chapter 11

"It's here!" Adora squealed, nearly leaping out of her seat. We were having mid-morning tea in the conservatory, enjoying the fine plants under overcast skies. The servant who had brought the news to Adora reeled back, visibly surprised by her reaction. "Oh, we have to go back to our quarters. Come on, I'll have someone bring the tea in."

"What is it?" I asked. "What's so important?"

"You are going to love this," Fina said. She grabbed my upper arm and tugged me through the gardens and back toward the palace. "Remember how the staff told you your gown for the ball tonight was already taken care of?"

I nodded, even though I didn't really remember. It'd been a week since Draunar had made his demands in the quiet of the clearing, and Elias had refused to discuss it since. He'd been tied up in negotiations each day, and we only saw each other for a few moments in the morning and the evening. We barely had time to speak, and when I tried, he pushed me away.

Things had been improving between us—I'd really thought this trip to Shianga might be what we needed to build a real marriage. And yet now things were back to where they were before this journey. Perhaps even worse. Worse because *he* was the one stonewalling *me*. There wasn't any cruelty in it, he was just…distracted. Absent. Like he was too busy to make time for me.

Or like he was trying to put distance between us.

If he was going to use me as a tribute, that would make sense, wouldn't it? He would be trying to make the loss hurt less.

"You thought the Shiangan Court had something put together for you, didn't you?" Adora asked.

"I suppose I did." I hadn't thought about the ball at all.

Fina and Adora glanced between each other like they knew that. Fina just sighed gently and led me back into the guest wing and back to my bedroom.

"Come on," Adora chided. "This is the farewell ball. It should be quite extravagant. Aren't you even a little excited?"

"At least excited to go home?" Fina asked. "I know I'm looking forward to it. If not the journey."

"I'm sorry," I said. "I just—I'm worried about the treaty. I know nothing's been signed yet."

"King Draunar is all about pomp and circumstance," Adora said. "I'm sure he's just waiting to sign it in front of everyone at the ball so he can force everyone to cheer and applaud."

"Elias said he had it all worked out, didn't he?" Fina said. "Once this ball is over, we'll be able to go back to our normal lives."

I pressed my lips together. If only it were that simple. If Elias had worked everything out, he would've told me. His continued distance made it clear the two kingdoms had not come to an agreement.

The girls didn't know that without one, we would be doomed to war. Was that going to be my first real action as Queen of Frasia? Drawing our nation into a conflict we couldn't win?

"You've got that look on your face again," Fina said.

"What look?" I asked guiltily. I tried to focus on my two friends. There wasn't anything they could do about this situation—the least I could do was give them my full attention when they were trying to make me feel better.

"That bored-sad look you get when you're trying to solve some unsolvable problem in your mind without telling us about it," Adora said.

My face heated. "It's not—"

Fina waved her hand. "Don't worry," she said. "I know there's a lot of royal stuff you have to deal with that we don't. I don't expect you to tell us everything." She sighed. "It's just... I wish there was something we could do to help."

A surge of gratitude finally put an end to my spiraling thoughts. "I'm sorry," I said. "You're doing more than you know just by being here."

Adora smiled. "Good," she said. "Now look at this gown we had ordered at the tailor."

I blinked. "You had something ordered for me?"

"Of course," Adora said with a laugh. "We had it made that day you were all wrapped up in the bookstore. It came out gorgeous. Amity, is it ready?"

"Sure is," Amity said. She hurried out of the ensuite with a dress box in her arms. She set it on the bed, then slowly removed the gown. Fina and Adora giggled in excitement as my jaw dropped.

"This is gorgeous," I said. "You had this made for me?"

"Do you like it?" Adora said.

"I love it," I said, and I meant it. The dress was black organza, but embroidered with silver that shimmered like the golden fabric the royal dragons wore. It looked as if the tailor had reached up to the night sky and cut the fabric from the stars. It was gorgeous, and it perfectly represented Nightfall.

"It has pockets, too," Fina said. "You know. Just in case."

I smiled at her. "You really thought of everything."

"I do try."

Fina guided me behind the dressing screen. "This really is a remarkable gown," she said as she helped me into it. "The tailors here are truly remarkable."

"Shianga is an amazing place," I murmured.

I hoped I wouldn't have to get used to it here.

Fina tied the ribbon on the back. It was mostly a wrap dress, comfortable and soft against my skin, and as promised, it did have pockets perfect for a small knife.

As Fina was smoothing out the skirt, the door to the bedroom opened.

"Oh, Your Highness!" Adora chirped. "Pardon us, we were just helping Reyna try on the gown for the ball. I'll get out of your hair—I'll meet you in our quarters, Fina—see you tonight, Reyna!"

The door closed.

"I didn't mean to run her off," Elias said softly. Then he sighed. "I was just coming to get ready for the ball myself."

I was still behind the dressing screen and couldn't see him, but the gentleness in his voice made my heart leap into my throat.

Fina stepped out from behind the screen first, and murmured a brief greeting to Elias before she left us alone in the room, scurrying out just as quickly as Adora had. I lingered for a moment, still concealed from Elias, taking a few steadying breaths. I felt dangerously close to tears, but why, I wasn't sure.

I just had a feeling something was going to change at this ball. I didn't know what—but my wolf's instinct knew. Nothing was going to be the same.

I stepped out from behind the dressing screen. Elias was at the dresser, fastening cufflinks into the sleeves of his shirt. He looked exhausted, especially with his shoulders curled forward and his hair tied back. Even his fine ball clothes, made of dark silk, couldn't mask the distant look in his eyes and the furrow in his brow.

He glanced up, lips parted like he was about to say something, but then his eyes widened. "Reyna," he murmured. "You look gorgeous."

I swept my hair over one shoulder and smiled gently, directing my face closer to his feet than his eyes, as I wasn't sure I could meet his gaze and maintain my composure.

"I had nothing to do with it," I said. "Fina and Adora had it made for me."

"Well, they did well," he said. He crossed the space between us, then stood in front of me, all square shoulders and serious expression. "Reyna."

I kept my eyes down. Or I tried to, but then his forefinger was beneath my chin, gently tilting my face up to meet his. Those brown eyes were warm, but concerned. "Is everything okay?"

I didn't even have the energy to be mad. "Okay?" I asked incredulously. "What do you think?"

"I know I haven't been around much this week—"

I laughed, but there was no humor in it. I placed both hands on his chest, feeling the warm familiar muscle under my palms, the steady beat of his heart. "That's an understatement."

"I'm sorry," he said.

"I just wish you would talk to me," I said. "You haven't told me anything about the negotiations in days. About what Draunar demanded."

His expression darkened. "There's nothing to say."

I took a step back. "That's what I mean," I said. "You're keeping me out of this."

"I'm trying to keep you safe."

"I know." I was so fucking tired. "But you're pushing me away."

Elias closed the distance between us again, and this time he wrapped his arm around my waist and pulled me flush to his body. Despite my frustration and exhaustion, I sighed in relief, leaning against that familiar warmth. The worst part of this week was that I'd *missed* him.

"I'm sorry," he murmured, and then leaned in to softly capture my lips.

I wound my arms around his neck instinctively. The kiss felt good—it settled my nerves just a little. His touch still had that power.

"Don't lock me out," I whispered against his lips. "I want to do this *with* you."

"I know," he said. "I'm just—I'm worried about what this will mean for the kingdom. I just need to make sure tonight goes well. Please don't worry."

Somehow that only made me worry more.

"What would 'going well' look like?" I asked, with my arms still around his neck. "What do you mean?"

"I've taken care of everything," he said. "It's under control."

I sighed and pulled away. He wasn't going to tell me anything. As much as I longed to be close to him, I wasn't going to let myself do that, not now, not when I was just another pawn on the royal chessboard.

Even when I asked him directly to tell me what was going on, still he kept silent. That was almost worse than the distance.

"All right," I said. "If that's what you want."

He sighed and looked away.

I stepped into the ensuite to brush out my hair before the ball—and to get some space from Elias. In the mirror, I squared my shoulders and set my jaw.

I was the Queen of Frasia. Elias said he chose me not to be a trophy, but to be a leader. I wasn't going to let him treat me like a trophy when I was supposed to *be* a leader. And I wasn't going to let Elias' devotion to me draw our nations into war.

Whatever tonight brought, there would not be war in Frasia. Not while I was queen.

I stepped back into our quarters. "Shall we get this over with?"

Whatever he saw in my face made his expression harden with determination. "I suppose we shall."

Arm in arm, we made our way back out of the guest wing and toward the throne room.

As we approached the fine door to the room, two guards bowed to us, and then pushed the doors open with a dramatic sweep of their hands. Elias barely suppressed an eye roll.

"Your Highness," the guard called, "may I present the King and Queen of Frasia."

We'd had a few dinners with the royal court at this point, and I was beginning to feel irritated by the incessant announcements, the pomp and circumstance. At that point, I had to suppress an eye roll myself. We strode into the throne room, which had been set up for a massive feast for the royal family, court members, and some of the city residents as well. The immense skylights overhead were thrown open to let in the cool evening air, and the floor space was crowded with dragons all dressed in Shiangan finery.

And what finery it was. The women were dressed not in gowns but what looked like slips of golden and silver fabric, each of them wound delicately around their waists and hips. Legs, shoulders, and waists were all exposed—so much skin surrounded me that I felt my face begin to heat. It was so unlike the balls I was used to in Frasia, especially in Daybreak, where everyone was buttoned up and barely touching when they danced. Here the dragons seemed to be one drink away from turning the dinner and ball into an orgy, with the way hands were finding hips and shoulders and thighs.

I stood out like a sore thumb in my organza gown. But the looks I received from the guests as we moved through the crowd were not judgmental—they were almost desiring, from men and women alike. Elias wrapped his arm around my waist and tugged me closer, a barely audible possessive growl rumbling out of him like instinct. My wolf led me to lean closer, pleased by the minor display of possession and protection.

We made our way onto the low dais, where a long table was set up for the king, his attendants and generals, and the Nightfall Court members. The Shiangan generals were already seated at one end, and Kodan, Adora, and Fina were at the other. Fina was watching the crowd with unfettered delight, and Adora was a little more focused on her wine, ears red and eyes downcast. To her left, Kodan, dressed in a fine white silk shirt with leather bracers, was lounging in a chair, with her arm propped on the back of Adora's chair. She threw a wink at Elias as we ascended onto the dais.

Standing at the center of things was King Draunar. He was dressed in fine gold cloth again, but this time it was only a pair of high-waisted slacks. He had on so much golden jewelry it almost looked like a shirt itself, pendants and gems and chains hanging over his muscular chest so densely it looked like chainmail.

"Good evening," he said with a wide grin. He spoke loudly to be heard over the jaunty music and the rumble of conversation. "Please, sit. Have some wine. Dinner will be out shortly."

It was clear from the way the table had been set that King Draunar wanted me at his side, with Elias next to Draunar's generals. Elias scowled at the setup. It only took a glance at Kodan for her to sigh with understanding. She leaned closer and whispered something in Adora's ear, then stood up, glass of wine in hand, and ambled over to the Shiangan general.

"Boys!" she called. "Listen, I've been watching some of your training sessions down at the barracks, and I've got to pick your brains about some of the sword styles I've been seeing…" She dropped into the seat by the generals and turned toward them, unperturbed by their sour expressions.

Elias guided me to the seat Kodan had vacated, while he took the one next to it, positioning himself between King Draunar and me. This made Draunar stare at him with thunderous rage, which Elias met with a demure smile.

I sat down. A servant immediately swept in and poured me a glass of wine, which I accepted gratefully, taking a sip to ease my frustration and my immediate irritation at the level of noise.

Here I was again, a pawn in the two kings' game, relegated to the sidelines as they postured and butted heads.

"That's nice," Adora murmured, "him making sure you don't have to sit right next to him."

"I could've handled it," I murmured back. "Your ears are *so* red, is everything okay?"

Adora squeaked and reached up to touch her ear like she could will the flush away, but that only made her cheeks change color as well. "What?"

"Is it the outfits?" I asked, glancing out toward the crowd where the dragons were dancing—or, more accurately, writhing—to the music. "It's a lot different than Frasia, that's for sure."

"No, it's not—I'm not a prude, Reyna," she huffed. "It's nothing." She swallowed and looked up. From the other side of the table, Kodan caught her eye, and she grinned. Adora bit her lower lip and turned her attention to her wine again.

Before I could start to ask any nosy questions, the music increased in volume as servants streamed from the side doors into the throne room. They were dressed in plain dark outfits, carrying trays and trays of food: steaks, ribs, stews, flatbreads, lush greens, bright roasted root vegetables, fruits and more carafes of rich wine.

King Draunar took his seat at the center of the table and gestured dramatically to the food as the servants set the plates down. "Please," he said with a grin, "eat, eat!"

He started first. We didn't get plates of our own—apparently the custom for a feast like this was to eat directly from the shared plates, knocking hands and spilling onto the table. Fina dove right in, delighted, and Kodan kept her pace with the generals. Elias sat back, waiting, and I stuck mostly to the fruit.

King Draunar set his gold canines into a seared, bleeding steak, ripping the tender meat with ease. His green eyes burned into me the whole time. I took a sip of my wine and looked out into the crowd instead, ignoring the shivery feeling that crawled up my spine under his gaze. The servants carried platters of food into the dancing crowd, and guests snatched meat and bread from them, eating as they danced and drank. There was something hypnotic about it, about the ease with which they moved and ate and laughed. There was something almost animalistic too. I half-expected them to shift on the dance floor.

We ate in relative peace—or as peaceful as the space could be, with the wild dancing and the loud music and meat spilling off the platters and onto the tables.

Then, the air crackled with power. King Draunar stood from the table and shifted—his dragon burst forth like a wave, wings extended and green scales dotted with gold gleaming in the dim light. He parted his immense jaws, golden teeth shining, and released a low, guttural roar. The sound vibrated through the air and into my bones like an earthquake. It carried easily over the music and brought the dancing to a sudden stop.

The guests turned their attention to the king, then began to stomp their feet in anticipation of whatever he was going to say. The music ceased but the stomping continued, intense enough that it rattled the dishes on the table. I snatched my wine glass from the table before it could spill as my eyes widened at the display.

Then the king shifted back into his human form with just as much ease, still dripping in gold fabric and jewelry. The roar earlier seemed to linger in the air like smoke. He spread his arms wide and the stomping ceased.

"Dragons of Shianga," King Draunar boomed. "We are here this evening with this fine meal and fine music to wish our new friends, the King and Queen of Frasia, a good future and a safe journey, and to celebrate a new bond between the two nations."

His green eyes fell to me again. This time, I held his gaze steadily.

As far as I knew there was no new bond, and from Elias' stiff posture, he was thinking the same. The treaty hadn't been signed. There had been no resolution to Draunar's demands. This was just a simple way to placate the crowd—and a way to push Elias into agreeing.

"Now, my friends," Draunar said grandly, "please enjoy the wine!"

Then he swept into a dramatic bow, smiled at us, and left out the side door of the throne room.

"What's that about?" I asked Elias. On the dance floor, the party got somehow even more energetic, as if the chaperone had just left the event. "Where'd he go?"

"I'm not sure," Elias murmured back. "I don't have a good feeling about it, though."

I didn't either. I sat back in my chair, wine in hand, and racked my brain for why King Draunar would just leave the room after such a big speech. A dragon stepped onto the dais, briefly grabbing my attention, but he simply asked Fina for a dance. She grinned and nearly leaped to her feet in her eagerness to join him on the dance floor. Then another dragon came to invite Adora; she glanced at me for confirmation and all I could do was nod. She looked a lot more hesitant as she stepped of the dais.

Elias threw a look at Kodan, who tore her gaze away from Adora to nod, then stepped off the dais to prowl the dance floor and keep an eye on the girls.

I was about to ask Elias if we were expected to dance, as well, when a young servant dressed in black hurried up to us, her brown eyes flashing. "Pardon the interruption, Your Highness," she said, "but His Majesty has requested your presences."

"And where is that?" Elias asked.

"In his study, Your Highness."

Elias sighed and pushed a hand through his hair. From the dance floor, Kodan looked up inquisitively, but Elias just shook his head.

I stood up first. "Lead the way," I said.

I half-expected Elias to put up a fight, but he seemed to know as well as I that there was no getting out of dealing with Draunar. Better to do it in private, anyway. The servant led us out of the throne room and through the same side door Draunar had left through himself, and into the same small study in which he'd first tried to entice me with the map. He murmured a thanks and closed the door behind us, leaving us three alone in the study. The noise of the party was muffled through the thick stone walls, and the sudden quiet made my ears ring.

King Draunar leaned against his desk, one ankle crossed over the other, a picture of relaxation and ease even as tension rolled off Elias in waves. I set my hand on Elias' forearm, trying to calm his temper down. The muscle was tense beneath my hand.

"So," King Draunar drawled, "have you made a decision regarding our little treaty?"

"There's no decision to be made," Elias said. "My wife is not a thing to be traded as part of our negotiations. You can't have thought that was a serious request to make."

He stood with his shoulders square and his feet wide, in a defensive stance like he thought Draunar might launch himself at me and forcibly take me away.

Draunar stood up, mirroring Elias' stance. "Do you think these negotiations are a game?" he growled. "Do you think I ask for this tribute as a joke? Do you think war with Shianga is an empty threat? You will give me the girl, or else Frasia will fall to the dragons. Those are your two choices."

"You're crazy," Elias growled right back. "You would put the lives of both our nations at risk for this? For your ego?"

"The girl is mine," Draunar said. "This is your last chance."

"There will be no tribute," Elias roared, "and no war! You will cease this madness and sign the treaty as we agreed! Frasia has done nothing but defer to your wishes, but this has gone too far!"

"You dare speak to me in my own palace like that?" Draunar growled.

"Please," I said, glancing between them desperately. "Stop this."

"I should strike you down where you stand," Elias said.

Draunar laughed, high and cruel. "My generals would have your pelt as a rug. And I still will, once I take Frasia from your grimy paws."

Elias bared his teeth and growled, and Draunar matched it, his gold canines flashing. The air crackled; Elias was moments from shifting, and I knew Draunar was, too. Internally, my wolf whined. If they actually fought, here in the study, all the work Elias had done developing this treaty would be for nothing. If he hurt the King of Shianga while we were *guests* here, all of Frasia would pay the price.

Elias would never agree to the terms.

But if there was a wolf in the Shiangan Court, a wolf who could bend Draunar's ear and support the growth and development of Frasia, one who could guide Shiangan policy delicately from behind the scenes... Maybe it would be worth it. Maybe we could salvage this diplomatic visit yet, even if it was in a way almost too painful to bear.

"Stop it!" I shouted. I shoved myself between them and braced my hands on either of their chests, forcibly separating them like dogs. "Stop it, both of you!"

To my surprise, they both did. Elias' face softened, and Draunar watched me with interest.

"That's enough," I said.

"Reyna," Elias said. His brow furrowed. "What are you...?"

"This is the only way, Elias," I said. "I am Queen of Frasia, and I won't let war descend upon our nation."

"What?" Elias asked. "What are you saying? What do you mean?"

I stepped back, and turned to Draunar. "I accept the terms," I said. "If my hand is what is required to ensure lasting peace between Frasia and Shianga, that's a price I'm willing to pay."

"Reyna," Elias growled. "I am *not* willing to pay it."

"It's not only your choice," I said. "It's mine."

A grin spread across Draunar's face. "You see, King Elias?" Draunar said. "She's a wise wolf. She knows my threats aren't empty—at least one of you knows how to prioritize the well-being of the nation."

"No!" Elias roared. He whirled to face me, then stalked forward. Instinctively, I moved backward, until my back was pressed to the cool brick wall of the study, and Elias was caging me in, looming over me. "No," he said again. His eyes burned gold. "I will not allow this. There will be no war in Frasia. He's bluffing. You will not leave my side to remain with this beast."

"And what if he's not?" I said quietly. "What if you refuse and all of Frasia pays for your shortsightedness?"

"I don't care," he growled.

"*I* care," I said. "I won't let innocent wolves die. Isn't that why you became king? To prevent things like that? To keep your pack, and all our packs, safe?"

"I won't be bullied like this," Elias snarled. "Not by a dragon."

I pressed my lips together then set my hands on his chest, smoothing over the fine silk of his shirt and the familiar curve of muscle. His rage was palpable, rage and frustration, but now it didn't scare me like it used to. I knew he wouldn't hurt me, even as his anger glowed golden behind his eyes. On the contrary, I knew I had to be the one to hurt him.

Behind him, Draunar was leaning against his desk again, a smug look on his face.

"This is my choice," I said low. "Listen to me, Elias."

He stepped closer, tipping his head down so his brow was nearly pressed to mine. "You can't be serious."

"I am," I said. "I'm not going to risk wolves dying because you wanted to keep me as your own."

His face crumpled. "*Keep* you? Reyna, that's not—"

"It is, and you know it is," I said. "Our marriage was never *ours*. It was always your decision. I was just a plaything in the contest."

"Reyna," he said again, his voice cracking with desperation.

I steeled myself. I wasn't going to back down now—even as my wolf howled out her despair in my chest. She wanted me to wrap my arms around his neck and pull Elias into a kiss, soothe the pain so obvious on his face, but that wouldn't solve anything. He'd always put Frasia first. He'd killed Griffin for that very reason. And yet now here he was, turning his back on his nation to preserve his ego.

"This was never a marriage based on love," I said coolly. "It was always a practical arrangement. And this is the practical decision. Take Adora as queen in my stead; she'd be thrilled."

"Reyna," Elias said. "You can't do this. I love you—*you're* my queen. My *mate*. I can't just—"

"You can, and you will," I said. I pushed him away.

He stumbled back, eyes wide and disbelieving.

"This isn't your choice," I said. "It's mine, and I made it. I will stay here in Shianga, as proof of Frasia's continued good will toward Shianga. And this way we will ensure peace between the nations."

"Excellent," Draunar said. "I'm glad to know one of you has any sense."

"Please," Elias said, quiet and soft as a dusting of snow.

My heart cracked. My wolf howled. But I was more than a pawn in their game. If we returned to Frasia together only to find the city razed by dragons, I could never forgive myself, or him. It wasn't a risk I was willing to take—even as tears prickled hot behind my eyes.

I'd been foolish to think we could be together. Could be happy. Our marriage was one of politics and convenience—not of love. Regardless of what he said now, and whatever bond had grown between us, it was still first and foremost a political agreement. As much as it hurt him, and myself, I owed it to the nation of Frasia to do this. I'd been raised for this role, primed for it—of course it would come to fruition this way.

Draunar swept forward and took me by the wrist, then tugged me close to his side, arm wrapped around my waist. His body was strangely cool to the touch, but his grip was strong where his fingers dug into my hips. I shoved down the instinct to squirm away. My wolf whined and wailed internally.

"How wonderful," Draunar drawled. "I'm so grateful we could come to an agreement for this treaty. The bond between our nations will last for generations."

Elias bared his teeth and growled, head tipped down and shoulders forward. I could feel his wolf just under the surface, but Draunar didn't look concerned at all. If anything, he looked amused, grinning with amusement at Elias, while his thumb moved in circles on my hip.

"Don't," I whispered to Elias. "Don't, it's not worth it."

The air crackled again, but this time, it was Elias who shifted.

Chapter 12

Elias' wolf surged forth with a growl. His immense dark paws hit the polished hardwood floor of the study with a whump, and he bared his immense teeth. His eyes burned gold and his hackles lifted. A ceaseless growl rolled from his chest.

"Silly dog," Draunar said. "She made her choice, and she chose me. You think this little show will change that?"

Elias lunged forward, mandibles parted to clamp down around Draunar's neck. Draunar stepped to the side, pushing me out of Elias' range, and lifted his arm. Elias' immense jaws closed over his forearm, and I gasped, hands flying to cover my mouth. I expected a torrent of blood, a howl of pain, an enraged escalation of the fight—but Draunar only laughed.

How was that possible?

Then, Draunar shook his arm with ferocity, dislodging Elias. Where Elias had grasped him, his skin was covered in rich green scales like armor. He slapped Elias hard across the muzzle with a disrespectful backhand, the scales now over his knuckles, causing Elias to yelp and stagger to the side from the force of the blow.

Draunar scoffed. "Pathetic."

He threw his head back, barked another cold laugh, then shifted himself. His wings exploded from his back first, then scales raced from his nape down his arms. He grew taller, his tail burst forth, and then he was in his full dragon shape, those draconic jaws parted into a reptilian grin.

Elias reared back to lunge again. Draunar stepped in front of me, shielding me behind his immense wings. Before I could fight to get out from behind him, desperate to see what was happening, his body surged with sudden heat and then the room did, too.

Heat and light.

Fire. He was *breathing fire*.

I gasped again and stumbled to the side. "Elias!" I shouted, the name escaping me as a cry.

Elias cowered away from the flame, his ears low and haunches pressed to the back wall as a narrow wall of flame separated us from him. The flames didn't do any more than singe the desk, but they lingered as if enchanted, keeping a barrier between us. Draunar tipped his head up toward the skylight above and roared; the glass slid open under his command revealing the starry sky above.

Draunar beat his wings. It whipped up a wind in the study like a tornado, sending the loose papers on his desk swirling toward the flame, and even knocked down books from the shelves along the walls. Elias yelped and barked desperately as Draunar took to the air. I stumbled backward, stunned and dizzied. Before I could even realize what was happening, Draunar's immense back feet, clawed and flexible, gripped my shoulders and curled around helpless arms.

"No!" I cried, scrabbling uselessly at his ankles as my feet lifted from the floor.

Elias barked again, then leaped through the wall of flame, suddenly indifferent to the sparks dancing over his pelt as he lunged for me again. He jumped up, as high as he could, and closed his jaws gently over my foot—but it was too late.

He couldn't hang on. I slipped from his grasp, my shoe sliding off of my bare foot. Elias was left with only the silk in his jaws. Draunar rumbled something that sounded like a laugh as we flew up toward the open skylight.

Elias leaped up again, desperately snapping his jaws. The fire in the study faded away. Below us, Elias paced in a circle, then sat back on his haunches and howled a long, low cry. The sound was so powerful it seemed to reverberate through my bones, breaking my heart all over again with how painful it sounded. I clung to Draunar's ankles as he took us higher and higher, until I couldn't see Elias at all and I could only hear his mournful wolf's song. My heart crawled into my throat and finally I stopped holding back the tears that had been threatening to spill over.

I was cold, terrified, and alone, as the wind rolled over my skin, feeling like ice on bare flesh. It roared in my ears as Draunar's wings beat. His grip was tight, claws pricking into my skin, yet I still clung to his ankles in desperate terror.

I'd thought I'd be brought back into the throne room and announced. I thought this would be political—a show.

I hadn't expected him to fly off with me like some kind of beast.

I didn't regret it, though—I couldn't. I couldn't let myself begin to feel regret, otherwise it would overwhelm me. I'd done this for my country. For the wolves of Frasia. What happened to me was secondary as long as peace was maintained. As long as these foolish kings didn't risk innocent lives over me, it would be worth it.

And yet Elias' mournful song echoed in my mind, and in my heart.

We'd been so close to something real.

I closed my eyes against the wind. Behind my eyelids, all I could see was his face, his smile warm and lazy with sleep, his brown eyes attentive and flecked through with gold.

Everything I'd said to him had been true. Our marriage *was* a political marriage of convenience. I *hadn't* had any agency in deciding what I wanted out of the Choice. I *was* being used like a pawn in the negotiations between him and Draunar. I didn't miss the Bloody King of Frasia. I missed *Elias*. I missed his hands on me, his laugh, his gentle kiss, the sweet roughness of our runs through the woods. In a different life, maybe we could've had that. Simplicity, and partnership.

But not this life. Not when so much hung in the balance.

Draunar carried me west, high enough in the air that my fingers and toes went numb from the cold. The pain in my heart was doubled by the terror rolling through my veins as we flew higher and higher. The ocean was visible on the horizon to the north, but Draunar was carrying me toward a mountain range near the coast. I tried not to look down, but I couldn't help it—his grip was firm on my arms, but how could I trust him? It'd be simple enough for him to decide he'd gotten what he needed by simply taking me away from Elias. He could drop me.

I tried not to think about that—about the rush of wind around me as I'd plummet to my death.

Powerless.

The mountain range loomed as we raced toward it. Draunar only beat his wings faster and harder, picking up speed. The rock face filled my vision as I saw textured gray stone dotted with ice and snow, racing closer and closer—and closer—and there was nowhere for Draunar to land—no caves, no ledges, just sheer rock—and yet his wings beat faster and faster.

I clung hard to his ankles and, closing my eyes, turned my face away, choking out a desperate shriek as we careened toward the mountain.

Then, the cold dropped away, replaced by a stuffy humidity and warmth. I blinked my eyes open, still half-terrified, but there was no longer any mountain visible. The rock face was behind us, shimmering like a mirage, a mask over the entrance to the cavern. It was dark, a darkness so thick it was almost tangible. Draunar beat his wings and slowly lowered me to the ground. My knees quivered as my feet hit the cave floor. I wrapped my arms around myself, dazed from the journey. The dust in the cavern made my nose itch.

Draunar landed next to me, then folded his wings into his body. Then, he shifted back into human form. He stretched his arms overhead. "I trust you enjoyed the flight?" he asked with a wide smile.

I swallowed and said nothing.

He murmured something in an unfamiliar language—draconic, I assumed—and waved a hand toward the cavern.

Along the cavern walls, torches flickered to life. Each one seemed to light the next a few paces away, until warm light filled the cavern.

"Welcome," he said grandly. He spread his arms wide and stepped backward, inviting me into the cavern.

The cavern was full. Full of *gold*.

I'd thought his jewelry was excessive, but this was beyond my wildest imagination. The cavern was piled in gold, gems, and treasure: trunks of coins, golden statues, furniture, weaponry, and armor. Everywhere I turned, something gleaming caught my attention. Here a fine crown, there a full-size statute of a dragon with its wings spread, and nearby were unfamiliar-looking heavy coins, piled so high they nearly touched the stalactites hanging from the roof of the cavern. Some of it looked brand new, other piles looked ancient, covered in cobwebs and dust.

He was a dragon, and this was his hoard.

"Beautiful, isn't it?" he asked. "And it all belongs to me."

"Why am I here?" I asked. "Aren't I to be your wife?"

"Come," he said. "This way."

I didn't move. I felt pinned to the spot, frozen, and unsure my legs would carry me if I tried to walk. But there was nowhere I could go. There was only the cavern, and the empty air outside its mouth.

Draunar rolled his eyes, then padded back over. He wrapped his arm around my waist the same way it had been in the study, steadying me as he guided me into the cavern.

"You see," he said, "I understand that in Frasia, the queen leads alongside the king. Or at least, that is how your Bloody King prefers to do things."

Don't call him that, I thought viciously.

"But, my rule in Shianga is a bit different," he said. "Other Kings of Shianga have had their preferences, but I don't find it necessary to have a queen at my side to lead."

"What?" I balked. "I thought—with the treaty, I thought this was to be symbolic—"

"Symbolic of what?" Draunar asked. "Frasia's ability to roll over?" He laughed heartily, and the sound echoed through the cavern.

My blood ran cold. I thought I'd be living in the Shiangan palace, alongside Draunar, making my place in his court. I hadn't exactly been looking forward to that, but it would've been a life. An acceptable life. But from what he was suggesting...

"You see," Draunar said, "you were given to me as a tribute. Not as a leader."

He paused, then turned and trailed two fingers down my cheek. My skin still felt tight from the wind outside, and tear-stained, too.

"Worry not, wise wolf," he said with a cruel smile. "You've made the right decision. You've saved your country. And in time you'll know nothing but me—and it will be more pleasurable than any life you've ever known."

I swallowed hard and tried to pull my face away from his touch, but he only gripped my waist harder.

I thought I was a pawn before, but this was—this was something else entirely. I wasn't a woman at all to him. I was just another pile of gold for him to stash away.

"This way." He released my waist and strode further into the cavern. It seemed endless, winding deeper and deeper into the mountain.

I paused, swaying unsteadily on my feet. I was overwhelmed by the sheer amount of gold in this cave, gleaming and sparkling in the dim light. How had he even gotten it all in here? Was it all him, or was this hoarded by the dragons that had come before? What was the purpose of it all? Did he use it for anything, or just keep it here in this secret cave?

I stepped closer to an immense, detailed statue of a ship, one made entirely of gold. It was taller than me, with elegant, delicate masts and thin sails frozen in pursuit of an unknown wind. I traced my forefinger over the edge of the ship's railing, and when I withdrew it, the pad of my finger was coated in dust and dirt. Most of the treasure hadn't been touched in what seemed like years.

The further Draunar walked, the more alone I felt in the hoard. Even with the singular path that led from the cavern straight back into the depths of the mountain, I felt like it would not be hard to get lost moving through it. There were weapons scattered around throughout the piles of gold as well. That spoke to Draunar's confidence—or his lack of confidence in me. He clearly didn't consider me a threat at all, if he was fine with leaving all these weapons around within reach. I knelt down and quickly picked up a small knife. It was a flat silver blade with a golden hilt encrusted with rubies. I tucked it into the pocket of my gown, then strode after Draunar.

Finally, after a walk that felt like a mile, the cave widened.

Behind the piles of treasure was a vast space with a smoothed floor, and columns carved directly from the mountain itself. An immense rough-hewn table dominated the area, and at the far end Draunar was seated in an ornate wooden chair with massive dishes of food in front of him. There was wine, cured meats, cheeses, breads, fruits, and chocolates. Where had they come from? I glanced around looking for servants or other dragons, but the room was empty of other occupants. Just Draunar, alone, smacking his lips as tore a piece of jerky with his gleaming canines.

"Sit," he said. "Eat."

I sat at the other end of the table, so the entire length of the table was between us. There were plenty of dishes on my side as well, and a carafe of dark wine. I poured the wine, but the food made my stomach turn. I'd eaten a little at the ball, but the dim stuffy silence of the cavern was doing nothing for my appetite.

I folded my hands in my lap and watched him methodically work through the platters of food, putting away more meat than I'd thought a man of his size ever could. I supposed he had the diet of a full-sized dragon, even in a human body. He was in no hurry, though, taking his time as he surveyed the meal judgmentally. It wasn't until he'd eaten his fill that his gaze finally flickered up to me. "You're not eating."

"I ate at the ball," I said crisply.

My organza gown was beginning to itch at my skin, sweat building under my arms in the stuffy warmth. The knife my pocket felt as heavy as a brick.

His green eyes narrowed. "Eat."

This time it wasn't a request. It was a threat.

I swallowed and reached for the pile of rustic rolls stacked near me. I tore one in half then took a small bite of the dry, stale bread. I halfway expected something to happen, some sort of entrapment like the rumors I'd heard about Fae food, but nothing happened. It was just stale bread in a stuffy room, with an asshole sitting across from me.

He grinned, pleased. "Good wolf."

Internally, my wolf bared her fangs. The only thing worse than being Draunar's wife was being his pet.

"Why did you bring me here?" I asked.

"You're smarter than that," he said. "I think you can figure it out."

"Just be forthright with me," I said. "What do you want?"

He laughed, low and pleased, like I was a child who'd asked a particularly endearing question. "Come on, now, Reyna," he said. "Isn't it obvious?"

"It's not," I said. "You said you wanted me as your wife."

"I never said anything of the sort," he said with a demure smile. "I believe things worked out just fine. You've served your nation well, and now you don't need to worry your pretty head about the details."

I resisted the urge to bare my teeth in my human form, too. He reminded me of my father—keeping me in the dark about what was happening. Expecting me to remain quiet and pretty, a decoration of the court instead of an active member. I'd tried to develop in my role as queen—and I'd done a good job—and here I was again, relegated to powerlessness.

But I'd chosen this. I'd done it myself.

It was worth it to ensure that Frasia was safe.

But now, I wouldn't even know if that was the case. I wasn't a part of the Shiangan Court at all.

"When will we be returning to the palace?" I asked.

Draunar didn't answer. He continued working his way through the dishes.

"King Draunar," I said, a little louder, "when will we be returning to the castle?"

He took a massive gulp of wine, then heaved himself to his feet. "This way, wolf," he said. "I'll show you to your quarters."

"My quarters?"

"This way!" he shouted. It was almost a roar. His eyes gleamed rich emerald, and scales danced down his shoulders, appearing on his skin like armor.

I clambered to my feet. I didn't want to make him angry, not yet—not until I had a plan for what I was going to do to next. I swallowed my anger down and followed him away from the table, through a stone door, then impossibly deeper into the mountain. The walkway opened to the right, but the blackness was so dense in the empty space that my skin crawled. We continued past the dark opening, deeper into the narrow hallway, where two doors were set into the same side of the rough stone walls. Draunar passed the first, then opened the second, and ushered me across the threshold.

"Rest well," he said. "I must attend to some business, but I will return soon."

The door clicked closed behind him, and then the lock turned too.

"Wait!" I called. "King Draunar, wait!"

There was no response. He was already gone.

The stillness of the room was suffocating. I turned to the door and went to try the handle—but there was none on this side. I was well and truly locked in. I smoothed my hand down the obsidian door, looking for any gaps or secret latches, but there was nothing. Just smooth, polished stone, so shiny my own devastated expression was reflected right back at me.

I sighed and turned my face away from the door, leaning against it heavily. At least I was alone, without Draunar's creepy presence looming over me.

Small blessings.

I surveyed the room. It wasn't nearly as fine as the guest quarters in the Shiangan palace. This was more like a den. The stone floors were covered in sheepskins, and the bed was a low platform with a straw-filled mattress covered in furs. There was no fireplace, but dim sconces lit the room. A small restroom was built into an alcove.

There was nothing else in the room. No books, no clothes, no food—nothing.

Terror rushed into my throat like bile. I had no idea when Draunar would be back. No idea when I would be released from this room—from this *cell.*

At least I could get out of this dress. I shucked off the fine organza gown the girls had ordered for me, folded it as best I could, and placed it in a corner on one of the sheepskins. In just my silk underclothes, I stretched my arms overhead and tried to release some of the tension from my tight muscles.

Would I ever see Fina and Adora again?

I pushed the thought from my mind. Of course I would. This was just temporary. Draunar would return and we'd go back to the palace.

And if we didn't, I'd figure something out. I always did. That was why Elias had chosen me to be the Queen of Frasia—I could hold my own. I figured things out. And though I was frightened and alone in this stuffy cave, without a single other soul, and without anyone in Shianga knowing where I was—I'd made this choice. I'd done it for the wolves. And I was going to fix this.

Fix it or bear it.

I crawled onto the mattress and sprawled out on the soft furs. Sleep first. I had no idea what time it was. No idea if it was the depths of night or if the sun had broken over the horizon. My wolf whined internally. I wondered if I would ever see the full moon rise ever again.

Chapter 13

Sleeping fitfully in the stuffy cave, I had a dream.

I was hovering high above the throne room, looking down into the open skylight. It was the same view I'd had when King Draunar had taken me in his claws and flown upward, but now there was no dragon holding my body in mid-air. I was just there—floating. Witnessing.

The throne room was empty, save for Draunar in his emerald dragon form. Elias and Kodan stood in their human forms, weapons raised; then Elias roared and shifted into his wolf. He lunged forward, teeth bared. Kodan tried to grab the king and drag him backward, but she was no match for his bulk as a human, and he knocked her aside easily. Elias growled and slashed at Draunar's body until his jaws were covered in blood. He fit his teeth around Draunar's throat and bit down hard. Draunar thrashed under him, roaring and shrieking as he clawed at Elias, but eventually fell still. Elias staggered off of his corpse. He tilted his head up toward the sky and howled, long and mournful. Kodan stood, staring at the scene listlessly. Then, the wind shifted, and I began to plummet toward the throne room.

I woke up mid-fall, spasming awake with a gasp.

I swallowed hard and unclenched my fingers where they were grasped tight around the furs. I was covered in a thin sheen of sweat, and my heart was racing from the imaginary fall. I rubbed my forehead. How long had I been asleep? What time was it? I had no way of knowing.

My wolf perked into alertness, and I looked toward the door. My instincts prickled, and I pulled the fur higher up on my body as I propped myself up on one elbow.

Draunar burst through the obsidian door, his eyes blazing, rage radiating off him like a stench. "Did you plan this?" he roared.

I reeled back. "What?" I asked. "Plan what?"

"This little coup of yours," he hissed. "Did you think this would work?"

"I don't know what you're talking about," I said. "What coup? What plan?"

Draunar exhaled hard, and the air shimmered with heat where he breathed. My eyes widened. Could he breathe fire in his human form too?

"Your idiotic *king*," he said, spitting the word like a curse, "has broken the peace treaty we worked so tirelessly to craft. He broke it almost immediately. Was this your plan? Did you know he would do this?"

"Broke it?" I asked. Confusion and terror soured my stomach. What had Elias done? I'd made this decision to prevent war— and he'd immediately gone against that and launched an attack? Had he acted so impulsively? He didn't understand that I'd done this *for Frasia,* and now he was making my sacrifice for naught.

Even though I felt betrayed, a small, wolfish part of me was relieved. He hadn't waited for Shianga to attack Frasia. He'd brought the fight to Shianga instead. He'd gone to war for me. And at least if there was to be a battle, it was Shiangan buildings that would burn.

Guilt immediately raced through me at the thought. I hadn't wanted any fighting at all. Or, more accurately, my human side hadn't. My instincts did. My instincts wanted Draunar to pay for what he had done.

"While I was here with you," he said, "your king and his generals launched an attack on my palace. As if the king had his forces here and were waiting for a chance to attack. You wouldn't know anything about that, would you?"

I said nothing. I hadn't known about that—not even a word. But it made sense. Perhaps when the king first suggested he wanted me as part of the negotiations, Elias or Kodan had called for reinforcements. Yet he hadn't told me. *Why hadn't he told me*?

"Why would I be here with you if I had known that?" I asked. "If I had wanted a battle, why wouldn't I have just pushed for it by refusing your terms?"

Draunar sneered, then cut his gaze to the side. He knew I was right, even if this infuriated him. I never would've agreed to his terms if I had known Elias was truly ready to start a war. Would he have done it if I hadn't agreed?

I'd never know. All I knew was I was trapped deep inside the mountain, while a battle raged on the polished grounds of the Shiangan palace.

"He is a fool," Draunar growled. "Soon his pelt will adorn my throne, and Frasia will be mine." He grinned cruelly, showing his golden canines. "Perhaps your king has done me a favor. Soon I will have not only the wolf queen as my trophy, but all of Frasia, too. Your silly little army is no match for the royal guard. You will stay here, safeguarded, while I deal with this nonsense. Then I will decide if you deserve to be punished for the King of Frasia's mistakes." He nodded, satisfied with this decision.

I said nothing.

Draunar turned back to me. His gaze skittered over my neck and shoulders, over the curve of my breast covered in the silk of my underclothes. I hiked the fur a little higher.

"You will be a lovely reward," he said. "Something special for me to look forward to, once Shianga has claimed Efra." Then he sighed dramatically and smoothed one hand over his hair. "First, though, I may be absent from your quarters as I deal with this situation. In my stead, Corrine will be managing your needs."

"Who?"

Draunar waved a hand toward the door.

A woman stepped through the doorway. She was tall, with a narrow face and shimmering white hair that fell pin-straight nearly to her elbows. She was dressed in slacks and a long, loose robe, and moved with an almost otherworldly grace. She was so pale she looked almost translucent. I wondered how long it had been since she'd seen the sun.

"Corrine," Draunar said, "show Reyna the space. I'll return once I've dealt with the mess at the palace."

Then, without another word, Draunar swept out of the room. I felt the air crackle over my skin as he shifted in the hallway and beat his dragon wings, stirring up the stuffy room of the cavern.

Corinne paused, her head tilted for any sounds. Then, once she was sure Draunar had left, her posture slumped and she sighed heavily. Her left hand moved to her right wrist, and she worked a forefinger under a tight emerald band there, like it was irritating her skin. "He's gone."

"You can tell?" I asked. I climbed off the mattress, with a fur wrapped around me like a robe. My underclothes weren't immodest, but I'd just met the woman. "I thought I was alone in here."

"I'm the only other one, as far as I know," she said. "Though Draunar may have other hoards unattached to this one."

"How long have you been here?" I asked.

She smiled faintly. "Come," she said. "I'll show you the rest of the quarters. And get you a change of clothes."

"Thank the gods," I said. "I only have a formal gown."

"There's not much finery here," she said, "but there are things that are clean."

I blinked as Corinne opened the door. "We can just leave?"

"He locked you in for the first night, I assume?"

"Yes, it was a little disorienting."

She hummed a low, humorless laugh. "There's a door to the dining room he keeps secured when he's gone. The rest of the cavern is available for our perusal."

"How big is this place?" I asked.

"Not big enough," she said with a sigh. "I'm terribly sorry you've been brought here, but I must admit, it's nice to speak to someone who isn't Draunar or Sini."

"Sini?" I followed her out of my quarters and back into the hallway.

She led us to the dark open mouth of the rest of the cavern. She lifted her left hand, then murmured a word in that same unfamiliar language Draunar had used. Throughout the space, dim sconces lit. Corinne grimaced, like activating the light hurt her. I placed a hand on her shoulder to steady her. "Are you all right?"

"Fine," she exhaled. "Just fine."

The sconces illuminated the rest of the cavern. I gasped at the sight. The roof of the cavern dripped with stalactites, dripping single drops of water into still pools. The floor was smooth, but the walls were rough-hewn, with steam rising from the water. It was gorgeous—if I wasn't trapped in here against my will, I'd liken it to a fancy mountain spa resort. Across the space, the cavern continued in both directions.

"This place is huge," I breathed.

"You think that now," Corinne said with a sigh. "Oh, here. Sini's come to say hi."

"Who—oh!" I stumbled backward. A large silvery salamander, shot through with blue, crept out of the neckline of Corinne's shirt and wound down her arm to her wrist. Its body was nearly the length of her forearm, gripping her with its legs and its long tail now wrapped around the bicep. It tipped its head toward me, nostrils flaring, and only then did I realize its eyes were almost completely white.

"He's a cave salamander," Corinne explained. "He doesn't need sight. It's handy having him around to help me navigate when I don't want to use the sconces."

Did using them hurt her that much that she'd resorted to using a guide animal? What kind of magic was this? What kind of magic user was *she*? There was a strange sort of familiarity to her too, like I'd met her before, but I couldn't quite remember how.

"Over here," she said. In an alcove beyond the smallest pool, there were shelves built into the walls. They were lined with anything I might need: soaps, towels, fragrances, combs, anything for a luxurious bath. Next to the shelves stood an armoire, which Corinne opened with ease. She pulled out a pair of slacks and a robe for me, similar to the one she wore. She kept her attention on Sini as I changed briskly, relieved to find the clothes were soft and lightweight, like elegant linen. At least I wasn't stuck with just my silk and organza.

"There's not much else to see," Corinne said once I was changed. She led me across the bathing area to where the cavern continued. To our right, the hallway was sealed with another great obsidian door. "Those are Draunar's private chambers."

"Have you been inside?" I asked.

She shook her head. "Thankfully, no. I spend my time either in my chambers, or here." Across the hallway, there was another alcove, with a lower ceiling. The alcove was dotted with stacks of books, furs, and immense cushions big enough to cradle my entire body if I sat on one.

"Oh, thank the gods," I sighed. "At least there's something to read."

"I've read them all, if you need recommendations," Corinne said.

She must've been here a long time. I watched as she traced her finger over the stacks of books tenderly, like she was stroking the spine of a beloved pet. Then she sighed and turned to face me with a sad smile.

"And that's it," she said. "That's all there is."

I nodded as a chilly fear crept up my spine. That was really all there was?

A few books, a few heated pools, and a bedroom? Sleep, eat, read, bathe?

And never see the sun again?

Suddenly cold in the stillness of the cave, I wrapped my arms around myself and shivered. There was no way I could discover a way out of here alone.

But something about the graceful way Corinne moved continued to pique my curiosity. There was something about her I couldn't place—but if I could get her to open up to me, we could figure out a way out of here together.

Chapter 14

The days passed in relative quiet. Or at least, I thought they did. I couldn't be sure of the movement of 'days' at all. There were no clocks in the caverns, and no access to the outside world, with the inner door to the caverns locked. I followed Corinne's schedule. The sounds of her movements would wake me, and then we'd share a simple meal at the long dining table where I'd watched Draunar scarf down cured meats. The food was always waiting for us when we stepped into the room, though how it appeared I had no idea.

Then, we'd take our time bathing in the warm baths, change into clean slacks and robes, then make our way into the reading alcove and spend some time picking through the books. Whenever I tried to ask Corinne details of how long she'd been here, or about her life outside of the caverns, she'd deflect and change the subject. As much as I wanted to lash out and demand answers, I needed her to trust me if we were going to work together. So I let it slide.

By day four, I was getting antsy. My wolf was beginning to knock against my ribs, demanding attention, and I was dreaming of moonlight runs with Elias nipping at my heels behind me. At night, in the privacy of my chambers, I'd taken to shifting into my wolf form and pacing in circles, just to release some of the pent-up energy to try to sleep.

On day five, or what I *thought* was day five, I woke up after another night of fitful sleep. I'd had the same nightmare I'd had the first night. The blood. The fight. The falling. But this time, there were more wolves in Draunar's palace, and more dragons clawing them to pieces.

My own wolf whined internally. I couldn't take it anymore—the uncertainty was driving me mad. Draunar had yet to reappear in the cavern. Corinne was unfazed by his absence. Had she even heard what he'd said when he left?

I climbed off the mattress and made my way into the dining room. Seated at the end of the long table, Corinne was sipping coffee as she sliced an apple into impossibly thin pieces. Anything to kill a little time.

"Good morning," she said. "You're up early."

I dropped into the wooden seat next to her and poured myself a coffee from the waiting carafe, mysteriously refilled and refreshed as it was every morning.

"How can you tell?" I asked. "How do you even know what time it is?"

"Mm," she hummed. "Internal sense, I suppose."

It was one of those evasive answers again. I sighed and wrapped both hands around the warm mug. "Listen, Corinne," I said. "When do you think Draunar will be back?"

"I have no way of knowing," she said mildly. "He must attend to his business."

"You heard him say what that business was, though, didn't you?" I said. "Shianga has been attacked."

"Mm," she said again. "Kingdoms rise and fall."

"It's more than that," I said. "It's *my* husband who he's fighting right now. The King of Frasia. He's fighting to get me out of here—to ensure Frasia is safe from Draunar's overreach."

"How romantic," she said.

It was like talking to the stone walls. Corinne was numb to the world, because her world no longer extended past the exterior of this cavern. Did she even have anyone outside of the cavern anymore? The thought made my heart go cold.

"He could be dead," I said with an edge of desperation. "He could need my help. And there's nothing I can do here—there's no way I can know what's happening."

"You'll know eventually," she said. "When Draunar returns." She held a small piece of apple between her pinched fingers. Sini appeared out of nowhere, it seemed, darting up the table leg and onto the surface to take the fruit from her grasp.

"What if he doesn't?" I asked. "What if Frasia is the victor, and there's no one to come rescue us? Does anyone know about this cavern other than Draunar?"

Her mild expression briefly flickered into something more anxious, before it melted back into its neutral flatness. "That won't happen," she said. "Draunar will return."

"Do you want him to?" I asked.

She sighed. Sini curled around her forearm, then Corinne stood up. "I need to bathe," she said, striding purposefully out of the dining room and toward the vast bathing chamber.

I snatched up the finely cut apple and followed her. "You don't know that, though," I said. "Elias is a strong fighter. But if Draunar won't tell him where I am, there's no way for us to escape. We can't count on Draunar returning. It's been days—

isn't he possessive? Don't you think he would've come back for us by now?"

Corinne closed her eyes briefly. She shed her clothes and stepped into the warm bath.

I stepped to the side of the pool and sat down at the edge, cross-legged, and watched her as she sank deep into the water until only her head was visible. Her silvery hair floated on the surface like spider-silk. But there was a small furrow in her usually smooth brow. I was getting to her.

"Don't you want to get out of here?" I asked.

Then Corinne opened her pale eyes slowly. Her expression was briefly thunderous, so enraged I rocked backward where I sat—but then that expression passed too, like a thunderbolt.

"You think I like it here?" she asked.

"I don't know," I said. "I can barely get you to talk to me at all. I thought you were glad to have someone else around."

"Having company has just proven Draunar's threats are real," Corinne said. "Having you here brings me no solace. We won't be getting out."

"We haven't even tried," I pressed. "And what threats? He didn't threaten me with anything other than being trapped here. Is there more?"

Corinne sighed. She pulled herself out of the bath. Sini crept out of the water too and clung to her calf as she toweled dry and pulled her robe back on. "I can show you," she said.

"Show me what?"

"Here. Draunar doesn't know I know about this, and we should keep it that way."

"What?" I asked. "What do you mean?"

Corinne already looked exhausted as we padded down the hall toward our quarters. The hallway dead-ended just past the door to my quarters. I stood behind Corinne, blinking in confusion as she faced the wall. Then she lifted her hand, squared her shoulders, and murmured in low draconic. Her whole body shuddered with the effort of it, and briefly her knees buckled, but she regained her balance, keeping her hand up as she faced the wall. The cave began to shudder beneath me, vibrating under my feet. Then, the wall groaned and shimmered.

"A mirage," I said, eyes wide. It was just like the one Draunar had flown through when he'd first brought me to this place.

It dissipated in front of us, revealing a long, winding hallway.

"We don't have much time," she said. "I can only hold it open for a few minutes. But come, look." She led me into the hall.

Inside, there were more obsidian doors that looked exactly like ours. Every time Corinne pressed her palm to one as we passed, it swung open, revealing a small chamber just like the one I stayed in. Some were furnished with furs, some with ponds, some with hearths, some with shelves built in as if for climbing.

"What are these?" I asked. "There's no one here at all."

"There will be," she said. "You're just the beginning."

"What do you mean?" I asked.

"He wants more women," she said. "More royalty. More queens."

"They're cells," I said as a dawning, horrific understanding set in. "How many of these are there?"

"A lot," she said. "I haven't made it to the end. I can't hold the hallway open long enough."

Before I could make my way further into the tunnel, she grabbed me by the shoulder and led me back, over the threshold and into the hallway leading to our two quarters. She sighed, slumped against the door to my quarters, and then the mirage shimmered back into place. Sweat beaded on her sallow skin, right at her hairline. Sini crept up to her shoulder and curled around her neck, nuzzling close.

"Are you okay?" I asked anxiously. If she was totally drained, I was shit out of luck.

"Fine," she murmured. "It's just tiring." She held her arm up where the emerald green bracelet was tight around her skin. "He tries to keep my powers harnessed, but there's only so much a shifter's magic can do. Even a draconic shifter."

"Your powers?" I asked. I knew there was something about her, but I thought she was just a magic user—not a creature of magic herself. But it would make sense. "Are you a shifter, too?"

"I'm no shifter," she said. She walked out of the hallway and back toward the bathing chamber, then to our shared alcove full of books. She folded her long limbs onto one of the big cushions and sank down into it, half-reclined. Sini crawled onto her chest and curled up like a cat. "I'm a queen, like you."

"Oh," I said, sinking down onto the cushion next to her.

"I haven't seen my kingdom for a long time." She closed her eyes.

"What kingdom is that?" I asked quietly, half-afraid to shatter the delicate silence between us.

She set her hand on Sini's back, then breathed out slowly. For a moment I thought she might fall asleep like that, exhausted from breaking Draunar's mirage. But then she sighed out, "Faerie."

I nearly fell backward. "Faerie?"

She nodded.

"Faerie. You're the Queen of the Fae?"

Again she nodded, eyes still closed.

I stared at her slack-jawed. I had so many questions I didn't even know where to start. And she seemed so exhausted I knew I wouldn't be able to grill her the way I wanted to.

"I try not to think about it," Corinne admitted. "I've been gone for so long… I can't bear to think about the damage it may have wreaked on my people."

The text I'd read in Blaylock's book rocketed to the forefront of my mind. "They need your presence," I said. "The Fae need you in order to maintain a presence in Frasia."

That made her look up and open her eyes. "How do you know that?"

I shrugged, then pulled my knees into my chest. "I'm interested in the Fae," I said. "There… Well… There used to be more Fae in Frasia, and I was trying to figure out what happened."

Sorrow carved its way into her brow. "Now you know," she said quietly. "I had hoped—foolishly—that maybe the Fae had found a way to thrive without me. But there's only so much we can do."

"Well," I said, "there have been more, recently, in Frasia."

She blinked. "The Fae are returning?"

"In small amounts," I said. "A different pack took over the kingdom—my husband—and since then, the Fae have been slowly returning."

"No longer under the rule of Daybreak, then," she said. "Well, that's a small silver lining. What pack has taken control?"

My stomach turned. Daybreak had done more harm to Frasia than I had ever known. I was filled with a renewed desire to get out of here and return to Elias' side. To fix all the damage my father had done.

"Nightfall," I said.

"Nightfall," she echoed. "Interesting. They never seemed like a strong pack. They must have a good leader."

"They do," I said. "Or—they have one good leader. Looks like I may have fucked everything up."

"Perhaps in the short-term," she said with a small smile. "Interesting that the Nightfall king has aided in the resurgence of the Fae in Frasia… And now I find myself here with the queen."

"That only matters if we can get out of here," I said. "Some of the reading I did said that high-ranking Fae can open and use portals to travel. Stepping into Faerie from one place, and then stepping back out into this realm in another."

"Hm," she said. I could see her interest fading even as I spoke.

"Can we do that?" I asked. "Can't you open a portal to get us out of here?"

"Don't you think I would've done that were it so simple?" she asked. Then she raised her hand again. "Draunar keeps my powers limited. I can't access them. And even if I could, opening a portal is not innate to Fae—it requires elemental materials."

"Like what?" I asked.

She sighed. "I need two scales from a dragon," she said. "One to remove this ward, and another to use in the spell. The draconic scale helps me channel the power of fire. Then I need something to help me channel the earth."

"We're in a cavern," I said. "Is that not earthy enough?"

She narrowed her eyes at me. "The cavern lacks life," she said. "It has to be something that lives, or once did."

"Like an animal," I said.

"Mm. And no animals come into this cavern. It's just me and Sini."

"You can't—"

"Sini is a being of water," she said.

"Then..." I pressed my lips together.

Finally Corinne looked up. She looked mildly interested, but defeated at the same time. She looked like she'd felt defeated for a long, long time.

"What about me?" I asked.

"What about you?"

"Would I work?"

She raised her eyebrows. "As the channel?"

"Not like this, of course," I said. "Not in this form."

Corinne sat up. "You mean as a wolf."

"Would it work?"

"I don't know," Corinne said. "I've never tried to create a spell using a shifter. I don't know if your power would work."

"Can you check?"

Corinne tilted her head.

In response, I stood up, pulled off my robe, then let my wolf surge forward easily. I shifted gracefully, then shook out my white pelt and peered at Corinne. In this form, I thought I could smell the magic still buzzing, trapped, under her skin.

She stood up from her relaxed position sunken into the cushion, then stepped closer. She held out a hand. "Can I touch you?" she asked. "To better understand if this would work?"

I nodded, then lowered my head, baring the back of my neck to her touch.

Delicately, she set one hand at my neck, working her nimble fingers into my thick fur. Her touch was firm and strong, despite how weakened she was. Then, magic sparked over my skin, and something deep inside me surged awake and rushed to meet it. It was a strange, disorienting experience—it was similar to the way I felt during a full-moon run, powerful and animalistic, but drawn out of me by force instead of by the light of the moon. It made me dizzy, and I yelped quietly and shook off her hand.

She nodded, eyes wide. "Yes," she said. "This will work. If we can get the scales—this will work."

Chapter 15

Four more days passed. I was about to try to break down the door to the hoard and thus the cavern entrance myself when finally, *finally*, I felt the air crackle with Draunar's presence.

Corinne felt it, too. "He's here," she murmured. She climbed out of the bath and dressed in a hurry, then disappeared into her quarters without even a second glance back at me.

I waited in the dining room with my pulse pounding. I heard him rumbling around his hoard, and the weight of his steps and the prickle of magic on my skin suggested he was still in dragon form. My throat felt dry with anticipation. Would he be thrilled? Upset? He was still alive, which was good—and bad. Did the palace still stand?

Was Elias alive?

Draunar stormed into the dining room, eyes blazing as hot air spewed from flared nostrils. He folded his wings against his body as his gaze landed on me. He shifted back into his human form in a crackle of energy. It'd only been just over a week, but it looked like he'd been at war for months. His face was sallow, and his skin tanned from the sun. Even though he was in his human form, his shoulders were dotted with scales, and his eyes glowed bright still. His dragon was close to the surface.

He bared his teeth in a cruel grin and said nothing.

"What's going on?" I asked. "The king—"

"I am the king," he growled. "I am the only king. And soon I will be the King of Frasia, too."

Soon, I thought. That meant Elias was still alive.

My heart swooped in relief, but I didn't let it show on my face.

He sneered, then dropped down into his ornate seat at the table and ripped into a crust of bread. "That fucking mutt," he growled, more to himself than anything else. Then he set his gaze on me. "All you wolves will pay for the trouble he's caused me. Irritating bastard."

Again I said nothing, but bit back a smile. Draunar had not expected how tenacious Elias and his wolves could be. As much as I'd hated the thought of war—I loved the thought of the wolves causing the dragons a lot of trouble.

"I need rest," Draunar snapped. "Do not interrupt me."

I nodded and stepped out of the doorway. Draunar brushed by me, clearly still enraged, and stormed through the bathing hall toward his quarters. He turned the corner toward the door, and though I couldn't see him, I recognized the rumble of the cavern floor under my feet. He was dispelling a mirage, or a ward, the same as Corinne had. Then the movement stopped.

I crept back toward our quarters and pushed open Corinne's door. "What do we do now?" I whispered.

I closed the door behind me. Her quarters were exactly the same as mine, but with sheepskins worn thinner from her footsteps over gods-knew-how-long. Corinne was curled on her own mattress, thumbing disinterestedly through a book. She looked up. "We get the scales."

"How?" I asked.

"Depends," she said. "Did he have any on him?"

I nodded. "A lot, it looked like. All over his shoulders."

"That's good." She sat up, looking a little more alert. "That's why he's back."

"What do you mean?"

"He has to shed those scales," she said, "but they're too valuable to shed in the palace right now, where a wolf could potentially get their hands on them. He's come back to do it here."

"So we can get them," I said. "How? Where does he leave them?"

"They're a part of his hoard," she said. "You'll have to get them before he hides them."

"Me?"

"I can't get close enough to his quarters." She gestured demonstrably to the band around her wrist again. "Even when he's here and so the ward is dispelled. But you can." She paused. "Is he in there now?"

"He said he was going to rest," I said. "He looks pretty beat up from whatever is happening at the palace."

She nodded. "Give it a few hours," she said. "Tonight. You can sneak in to his quarters and retrieve the scales."

"Where will they be?" I asked.

A small, cold smile curled her lips. "On his body."

I balked. "What? I have to pry them off?"

She nodded. "They'll come off easily. But yes, you'll have to pull them from his body before they come off themselves."

"While he's asleep?"

"Ideally."

"That won't wake him up?"

"Shouldn't."

"And if it does?"

Corinne raised one pale eyebrow. "Make an excuse. Don't get caught. But once we get them, we can get out of here. That's what you want, right?"

I nodded, then chewed on my thumbnail, mildly anxious. My wolf whined internally. She wanted to pace. Something about this plan felt off. Reckless. But I didn't have another option. If we needed the Draunar's scales to get out of here—I could get them. I *had* to.

Down in the palace, Elias was still fighting. I needed to be by his side. He needed to know about Draunar's plans, his current captive, and his future ones too.

Corinne and I passed a few quiet hours in the alcove across from Draunar's quarters. I had a book open in my lap, but I kept reading the same passage over and over, unable to process any of the words. My nerves chewed at me, and the small knife I'd pulled from his hoard when I'd first arrived felt like it weighed as much as a brick in my pocket. Corinne was not interested in talking or telling me more about the process of building this spell.

Every time I tried to ask a question, barely whispered, she only shushed me and returned to her book.

So I was left alone with my circling thoughts.

Even though I knew it was risky to try to pull this off, I didn't see any other option. Even if Draunar caught me, what could he do that was worse than the fate I was doomed to now? It was better to have a tiny chance of getting back to Elias than no chance at all. No one knew where this cavern was. No one could get me out. Corinne and her Fae magic were my only chance.

Finally, she closed the book and nodded. "He should be asleep now," she whispered. "He is a deep sleeper, but still, move carefully."

I nodded, then set my book aside and climbed to my feet. I threw Corinne a playful salute in an attempt to cut the tension hovering in the still air, but she only narrowed her eyes and nodded toward the door on the other side of cavern.

I swallowed, then checked for the hundredth time that the knife was still in my pocket. Then I approached the carved obsidian door with trepidation.

The door was immense, larger than any other in the cavern. It was one great block of obsidian, nearly twice my height, and decorated in a detailed carving of two dragons facing each other with their fangs bared and their wings wide. In the center, between their clasped claws, was a recession in the shape of a handprint. It was bigger than my own hand, made for the King of Shianga to push open. I paused, as my open hand hovering over it, then closed my eyes.

I brought my wolf closer to the surface. I didn't shift, but I leaned into her senses. I let her attention overtake my nerves, and let her examine the door. My nape prickled with her awareness, and still air felt a little denser in my nostrils, a little more layered with the scents of stone and sweat and water. Even with my hand this close to the entrance, there was no magic I could sense. Not from Corinne, and not from the door. I could feel the sconces, distantly, like the way my wolf could sense an oncoming storm. There was magic here, in the cavern, but not on the door.

I opened my eyes and let my wolf burrow deeper. Then, gently, I placed my hand in the divot. I half-expected it to push me away with some advanced draconic magic I hadn't been able to sense, but there was nothing. It was just a door.

It wasn't even locked. The door moved silently over the cavern floor. It was heavy, but opened fluidly.

I glanced over my shoulder. Corinne nodded at me. With her encouragement, I steeled myself, and slipped into Draunar's quarters.

Inside, the cavern was dark, dimly lit by what appeared to be a fire, glowing in a hearth carved into the side of the long, narrow chamber. But there was no ventilation in the chamber, and no smoke either. As I stepped into the room, I saw it wasn't fire in the hearth, but a glimmering, glowing light, dancing behind a foggy glass screen. The light moved over the stone walls, which were inlaid with gems and gold in a tiled mosaic pattern that went all the way into the ceiling. The sheer amount of color was dizzying. The floors of the cavern were covered in elegant, plush, colorful rugs—none of the ratty sheepskins like the ones in my room. These were thick, hand-woven, and layered in stacks of three, as if Draunar had so many he couldn't choose one.

I crept slowly through the narrow cavern, careful not to disturb the hoard stacked up against the walls. It was unlike the treasure hoard in the rest of the cavern, which was mostly gold and other valuables—this one held *things*. Empty birdcages, piles of shoes, kites hanging from the ceiling, dartboards, bookshelves stuffed with tiny carvings of animals, a massive aquarium full of gently waving green plants, bronze kettles, seashells, sewing machines. There was no rhyme or reason or organization to any of it, it just spilled everywhere. I moved extremely slowly in order to avoid knocking down any of the delicately stacked goods.

In the back was a massive four-poster bed, with thick velvet curtains pushed open. The bed was covered in blankets and pillows, stacked so high it looked more like a nest, with Draunar asleep on his side in the center of it. He looked almost childlike amid all his stuff, curled up and breathing steadily in his sleep.

All I had to do was pry two scales off his shoulders and get out. Piece of cake.

I reached into my pocket to grasp the hilt of my knife. I was too focused on Draunar's sleeping form, though, and my elbow tapped against a precariously balanced stack of bottles piled against the walls. I bit my lip to keep from gasping as I whirled to face the stack, both hands open, as the bottle sitting on the pile that I'd knocked clicked against the others, and then toppled.

I caught it on my hand right before it hit the ground, but it was full of what appeared to be marbles, clattering moodily against each other as they resettled in the sealed bottle. The pile still swayed, and I stared at it completely motionlessly with the rogue bottle in my hand. *Don't fall. Don't fall. Don't fall.*

The bottles stopped moving. The pile stayed intact.

I remained bent awkwardly over with the bottle in my hand as I slowly turned to look at the bed.

In the center of the mattress, Draunar shifted, but his breathing remained steady.

I exhaled slowly and placed the bottle at the foot of the pile. Then, keeping my elbows close to me, I pulled the knife from my pocket. I crept closer, until I was just a pace away from the edge of the bed.

There wasn't a damn book in his entire library about draconic shifters. Corinne had said he was due to shed the scales that gleamed on his shoulders, but I had no idea what that process entailed. I blinked in the dim light, then leaned closer to get a better look at the scales on his shoulders.

Draunar was on his side, bare-chested, with the heavy comforter pulled up around his waist. The scales started at his nape and ran over the width of his shoulders to his deltoid muscle, then appeared more sparsely down nearly to the elbows.

I stepped closer so my thighs were almost pressed to the edge of the mattress. It was so silent and still in the room that every exhalation of my breath seemed loud enough to potentially wake him. Yet he didn't stir.

The scales were about as big as the palm of my hand and were layered over each other. But they weren't lying as flat as they did when he was in his dragon form—or even as they were when he had summoned them to the surface to block Elias' attacking jaws. They were craned upward, like they were about to peel off the skin one at a time. I took the knife in hand and peered at the scales as close as I could, holding my breath so he wouldn't feel my exhalations on his skin.

There were two right at the top of his nape. That must be where the shedding started. One green and one gold, and both looked like they were moments away from falling off on their own; they were peeling up off the skin much more than the ones on his arm. I reached out and touched the sharp tip of one of the scales.

Draunar didn't move.

I gently pushed the scale upward, away from his skin.

Still he lay there in sleep.

I slid the edge of the knife under the scale, careful not to touch his skin or his other plates. The flat of the blade was now along the scale, until the tip barely pressed the place it was still connected. I pushed the knife in a little closer. The barest amount of pressure.

I pushed up, then the scale released itself like dead bark from a tree. I gripped it tight between my forefinger and thumb in complete stillness, like I'd been catching the bottle again.

Draunar shifted and sighed in his sleep but didn't wake. I gazed for a moment at the gleaming emerald scale in my hand, then tucked it into my pocket.

Then I repeated the process on the other scale. Lift it up carefully. Slide the blade beneath. Pop it off. It came off just as easily as the emerald one had, and I tucked it into my pocket like a prize. I smiled to myself, inordinately pleased with my success, as I gazed at the pale pink lines on his nape where the scales had set.

The knife briefly felt heavy in my hand.

With the scales in my pocket, I had a sudden thought:

It'd be easy, so easy, to take this small knife, and slide the blade into the side of his throat. It'd only take a moment for me to draw it across his flesh and stain the mattress with his blood.

Or I could push it into his temple. Or roll him over onto his back and slam it into his heart before he awoke.

I gripped the hilt tighter.

Could I do that?

I'd killed before. I'd killed Rona with a knife barely larger than this, driven into her flank when she'd attacked me. But I hadn't *meant* to—I'd just wanted to injure her and keep myself alive. I hadn't known about the poison. I'd never killed intentionally. I'd hardly even fought someone in a setting that wasn't an arena.

If it were Elias standing here, he'd kill him without question. He wouldn't stand here with sweat beading onto his palms, wondering if he could do it. He wouldn't even need a knife. I'd seen him dispose of a traitor with a quick snap of his neck. He knew when it was necessary to take a life.

And this was necessary. Draunar had kidnapped me, and now Elias was fighting for my freedom below in the palace.

I had the scales. Corinne could craft the spell now. We had a way out—as far as I knew. The battle would be even easier if I removed Draunar from the equation. That'd be one way to prove myself as a worthy queen. Not just a pawn, not just a prize, not just a treasure packed away for Draunar to covet—I could be a warrior.

I was a wolf of Nightfall.

I could be the Bloody Queen.

I gripped the hilt and leaned forward. One quick motion. One slice across his throat and this would be over.

"Mmf," Draunar murmured. He stirred, then raised one hand and rubbed the back of his neck where I'd pulled the scales off. I stumbled backward and stuffed the knife into my other pocket. My footsteps were muffled by the carpets, but were still audible, and I barely avoided crashing into another precarious pile of trinkets and tchotchkes.

Draunar rolled onto his back, then his green eyes flickered open. "Reyna," he murmured.

"Your—Your Highness," I stammered. "I didn't mean to wake you, I apologize."

Draunar propped himself up on one elbow, blinking awake more as he peered at me. "How did you find yourself in my quarters?" he asked, half-suspicious. His gaze flickered around him, like he was accounting for all his things. Did he think I was interested in his hoard? Did he even have a mental record of all he had in here?

"My apologies," I said again. "I—um, I was outside the door when I heard you—you were talking in your sleep." I pressed my lips together. "I wanted to make sure you were okay."

"Is that so?" Draunar asked. "The little wolf is worried about me?" He smirked and did not look convinced at all.

"I missed you," I lied. I dropped my voice low, and my gaze, too, trying my best to look demure and shy. "It's been lonely here. I wanted—I just wanted to spend some time with you."

I looked up at him through my lashes. The suspicious expression had been replaced by something closer to hunger. "Corinne didn't take care of you?" he teased.

"Of course she did," I whispered. "But it's not the same."

"The same as what?" he encouraged.

"As the protection of a king," I said.

He liked that. His eyes glowed a deeper green, and his smile showed his golden canines. "I knew you'd come around," he said. "Being a woman of Shianga is not a bad fate, is it?"

"It's nice here," I said. "Peaceful."

"Come," he said. "Lie down with me."

I bit my lower lip in between my teeth. I hadn't thought this far ahead—of course my role as part of his hoard was more than just my presence. Eventually, he'd want me. All of me.

I sat down gingerly on the side of the bed, grateful for the depth of my pockets but still hyperaware of the scales and the knife. If he found either of those, that'd be it for me.

"I'm glad you came to your senses, little wolf," Draunar said.

If only I'd come to my senses earlier. If only I hadn't been too cowardly to draw the knife when I had the chance. Regret was sour in the back of my throat as I smiled at him.

Draunar trailed his fingers gently up my back, from the base of my spine, all the way up to my nape. They felt cold, even through the thin linen of my shirt. I suppressed a shiver as he wrapped a hand around my sensitive nape, nails digging into the sides of my neck in an obviously claiming grip. Internally, my wolf growled and bared her teeth, but I didn't let it show on my face. I kept a demure smile on my face as he tugged me down, and I let myself be bent at the waist.

He kissed me. His lips were cold against mine, and I tried to keep my lips mostly closed while he fit his lips around my lower lip. He tightened his grip on my nape, clearly wanting more—a deeper kiss—but I resisted delicately.

"Your Highness," I whispered against his lips, "you need your rest."

"I need you more," he growled.

"I know," I sighed. I reached out and stroked my fingertips gently over his arm, avoiding his scales as I traced patterns on the skin. "And we have plenty of time."

"Do we?"

"Yes," I said. "I know you'll succeed in battle and I—I'm not ready."

"Hm," Draunar said. He narrowed his eyes again, then released my nape and set his hand at my waist instead. From the sharpness in his expression, it was clear he was deciding if he wanted to respect my wishes or not. My wolf was huddled in my chest, hackles up, ready to explode forth to defend us if necessary.

But then he dropped his hand and nodded. "You're right," he said. "Your presence will be my reward when I save Shianga and Frasia from the terror of the Bloody King."

"Exactly," I said with a soft smile. "I'm sorry for waking you. Get some rest."

I stood back up, then stroked Draunar's brow in a measured act of tenderness. Then I hurried out of the room, careful not to disturb any of his treasures, waiting for him to change his mind and call me back into bed.

But he didn't. I pushed the obsidian door open and slipped out, leaving it closed behind me. This time, a lock in the door clicked closed.

Corinne stood in the alcove, wide-eyed.

I nodded, then gestured for her to follow me. We hurried back through the bathing chambers toward our quarters, into my room. I closed the door behind us and slumped against it with an exhausted sigh. The adrenaline bled from my limbs, and my wolf settled, relieved.

"Did you get it?" Corinne hissed. "Both of them?"

"I got them." I slipped my hand into my pocket and retrieved both scales. They sat stacked in my palm, one gold and one emerald, gleaming in the dim light of my quarters. Corinne's mouth dropped open as she gazed at them, then extended one finger delicately to trace over the shape of the scale.

"Incredible," she said. "You really got them."

"He woke up," I said. "But he didn't seem to notice."

"You're sure?" she asked, her expression suddenly sharpening. "He doesn't know we have them?"

"I played it pretty well," I said. "He doesn't suspect anything."

Her lips flattened into a line, but then she nodded curtly. "Good. If things go as I expect, he'll shed the remainder of his scales when he wakes, and then he'll go back to the palace. Once he's gone, we'll be able to craft the spell." Her gaze lingered on the golden scale. "How I wish I could cut this band off right now. But we'll have to wait until he's gone."

I nodded. What would she be like with her power unleashed? The thought made a small curl of anxiety tighten in my gut. Corinne was my only way out of here, but I hardly knew her at all.

"Good work, Reyna," she said. "Hide the scales. Try to get some sleep."

Corinne slipped out of the room, leaving me alone. I tucked the scales under my pillow and settled down on the mattress. We had to get out of here. When Draunar came back next, if I hadn't already escaped, I'd have to handle his advances one way or another.

I turned the knife over in my hand, tracing its fine blade with my forefinger.

I'd come so close to killing him. If he hadn't awoken, would I have? Would I have been able to slide the blade through his flesh while he slept?

If I had, I knew it would've changed me. I'd be a different woman now, if I had his blood on my hands. Whether she would be better or worse, I didn't know.

A strange part of me felt like it wasn't quite time.

Maybe there would be a day when I was called to be a warrior. But maybe it wasn't today. Not like this, in the silent depths of this cavern, in secret.

I tucked the knife under my pillow as well to try to snatch a few moments of sleep. Tomorrow, if all of this worked, I'd be out of this cavern for good.

Chapter 16

I awoke the next morning -or what I assumed was the morning, considering I hadn't seen the sun since my arrival) - to the rumbling sounds of Draunar moving around the cavern.

I leaped to my feet and smoothed out my plain linen pants and shirt, then hurried out of my room. The last thing I needed was Draunar trying to come inside and potentially uncovering the scales. From the hallway outside our quarters, I could see into the dining area, where Corinne was lounging at the table with a coffee. Draunar was half-sunken into one of the bathing pools with his back to me. His flesh was shiny and pink across his shoulders, like new skin beneath a burn, and all the scales were gone. Before he noticed me, I scurried into the dining room. Corinne had a glass waiting for me.

"No scales," I whispered.

She nodded, then gestured for me to sit next to her. "Don't make a show of it," she whispered. "You shouldn't know the power the scales hold."

I sipped my coffee and tried to act relaxed and casual.

After a moment, Draunar stepped into the dining room. He was dressed in plain dark slacks, with leather bracers on his forearms and a plain short sword sheathed on his hip. He still looked exhausted, but better than he had coming in. He grabbed a hunk of cured meat from the table and ate most of it in one enormous bite, his green eyes burning as he surveyed the table.

"I will return in three days," he said. "By then the wolves will be no more. Then our lives can truly begin. Reyna." He gestured for me to stand, and I did so, stepping to his side with some trepidation.

"Remember what I said," he growled. He wrapped his arm around my waist and pulled me close. "When I return, you will be mine."

I swallowed, then placed my hands on his shoulders. It was as close to a gesture of intimacy that I could manage. "Of course," I said.

Draunar grinned, then kissed me harder than he had last night. This time it was deeper, his lips still cool, and the flavor of the cured meat still on his tongue. I suppressed my shudder as I allowed it.

Then he released me, nodded, and made his way to the doors that blocked off the dining room from the rest of the hoard. He smiled at us both once more before he closed the door behind him. Even separated, the air still crackled with energy as he shifted into his dragon form, and I heard his great wings beat as he took to the sky, soaring out of the cavern and presumably back to the palace.

"Eat," Corinne said.

"Shouldn't we get started?" I asked.

"He said three days," Corinne said. "And you will need your strength. Eat."

She fixed me a plate from the breakfast spread, as vast as it always was: hard-boiled eggs, bread, cheese, and fruit. Thankfully, she bypassed the meat. I dispelled the taste from my mouth with a sip of too-hot coffee.

"Where are the scales?" she asked.

"My bedroom," I said. "Under my pillow."

She stood up, then strode down the hall into my quarters. She returned with both in hand, then dropped back into her seat. Corinne stared at the scales in her palm like she couldn't quite believe we had them.

"Finally," she whispered. "After all this time."

Before I could ask how long that was, exactly, Corinne slid the pointed tip of the golden scale under the band on her wrist. She gripped it tight, then flicked it upward.

The band stretched.

Suddenly all the air seemed to be sucked out of the room. My lungs flattened in my chest, and I struggled to hold my mug in hand. The air all seemed to be drawn toward Corinne; she tipped her head back and her silvery hair fell like a waterfall. Then, she exhaled, and the air rocketed back, filling the cavern and bringing my breathing back to normal. But now, the air crackled with power, power stronger than Draunar's but lighter, too, like stardust dancing all over my skin. I blinked, dazed, unsteady on my chair.

Corinne was glowing. It was faint, barely noticeable, but there it was. A pale white glow emanating from her skin, her eyes, her hair. She looked lighter in her body, like gravity couldn't quite touch her.

"Ah," she sighed, in her voice newly bright and musical. "Oh, it's been so long."

She was the Fae queen. It was easy to forget that truth when we were scheming and plotting like jailbreakers. But now her power was laid out in front of me. It was undeniable.

It was frightening.

"Eat," she said again.

I turned back to my breakfast but found I'd lost my appetite.

"Once you are energized and dressed, we'll begin the spell preparations," she said. "We have everything we need now." She took the emerald scale in hand and smoothed her thumb over the surface. "I feel good. With your assistance, we should be able to open a portal without any trouble."

"We'll be able to get to Frasia then, right?" I asked. "We'll both be safe there. We can regroup there and make our plan of action."

"Of course," she said. "I would be honored to be a guest in the Court of Nightfall."

I drained my coffee, then stood up and nodded.

"You're ready?" she asked.

"I think so," I said. "I can't say I'm exactly sure what this entails."

"You'll see," she said. "Come."

I followed her into the bathing chamber. In the center of the space, she spread her arms wide, tipped her head back, and sighed deeply. Her silvery hair seemed to move differently now that she had her powers back, gently shifting as if she was underwater, instead of weighed down flat. I watched her from a slight distance. She gazed around the bathing chamber, then nodded as if making a decision.

Corinne extended one dainty bare foot, placed her toe in the dirt, and then spun on her other foot in an elegant spin, using her balletic momentum to trace a perfect circle in the dust. Then she turned to face me, standing in the center of the shape with a gentle smile on her face.

"Step closer," she said. "Just don't break the circle."

I stood right at the edge of the circle, my toes close to the marking in the dust. "Give me your hand," Corinne said.

From her pocket, she withdrew the small knife—the knife I'd had under my pillow. The same knife I'd almost used to kill Draunar. I balked and folded my hands together in front of my body.

"Why?" I asked.

"It's like I told you," Corinne said. "I need your help to open the portal."

"Why the knife?" I narrowed my eyes at the blade. "I thought you only needed my presence, like when you had me shift to see if this would work."

That small smile didn't leave Corinne's face. "That was just a way to see if you were connected to the earth-magic I need to access," Corinne said. "Actually accessing it is different. Don't worry, I only need a small amount of your blood."

"*Blood*?" I asked. "What? Why?"

Corinne's eyes narrowed with irritation briefly before she schooled her face back into a neutral expression.

"Blood is life force," she explained as if she were speaking to a small child. "Your blood will allow me to easily tap into the earth-magic. I need to access all four major elements that make up this world in order to open the portal. Your blood is earth, the scale is fire, then water, and air." She gestured to herself demonstratively. "Only by controlling the four elements can I manipulate them in order to open the portal. Think of it like weaving. I will pull strands from the tapestry you see around you, the world in which we live and speak now, and weave them into something different. The portal."

"And the blood will help you do that?" I asked.

"Portal magic is a muscle," she said. "One I haven't exercised in many, many years. I need a little assistance to use it again. Now please." She extended her hand.

I swallowed down my trepidation and placed my hand in hers. She tightened her grip around me, then raised the knife and slowly, carefully, pulled the blade across the flesh of my palm. I hissed at the sudden sting of pain, and tensed, but didn't withdraw.

"Good," she murmured. She squeezed my hand and turned it sideways, so blood dripped from the shallow gash on my palm onto the dust. Then she led me to walk in a circle, around the edge of the dust line, dripping blood onto it as I went.

"Earth," she said when the circle was completed. "Step back."

I did as she said, and pressed the linen of my loose robe to the wound to staunch the bleeding. Corrine's eyes gleamed. She took the emerald scale in hand, smoothed her thumb over it, then snapped it in two. The sound was a shockingly loud crack, like a porcelain plate shattering. My eyes widened as blood oozed from the scale—not a lot, but a small amount, dark and rich, coagulating. It was more like an aloe plant dripping its dense innards than a wound, but the coppery-sharp smell was unmistakable. Corinne walked it in a circle as well, dripping the blood onto the circle.

"Fire," she said.

The tension in the air seemed to shimmer like heat waves. I didn't know if it was her power or my nerves causing it.

Corinne knelt in the center of the circle. She clicked her tongue, and Sini, her cave salamander, peeked its head out from the hem of her trousers. She held out her hand and Sini crawled into her palm, comfortably winding onto her wrist. She stood up, then gripped the salamander's body and flipped it over, revealing the creature's vulnerable belly.

I clapped my clean hand over my mouth, eyes widening. Part of me wanted to leap over the circle and stop this. I'd assumed the water in the equation would be just that: water, pulled from the bathing pools around us. But she'd said blood, and she meant it, blood from a water-dwelling creature that had built its life in the cave. She slit the salamander's throat deftly; it thrashed once in her hold then fell still. She dripped its blood over the circle, then placed the lifeless body outside of it, directly across from me. There was still tenderness in her motions, in the gentleness she held the salamander's body, but there hadn't been a moment of hesitation.

Again I wondered. Would I have been able to do something like that? Take a pet's life in hand like that and end it, if that was the only way I had to survive?

"Water," she said. She tilted her gaze up to the roof of the cavern again and breathed in slowly. The air hummed with power.

Then she drew the knife's blade across her own palm and spun in a circle again, just as balletic as the first turn, and her own blood dripped onto the circle.

"Air," she said.

She knelt in the center of the circle and placed both palms flat on the floor of the cavern. The air crackled even more, like it was carrying lightning with it, and prickled over my skin. My wolf roused into alertness, both curious and anxious. Corinne's clothes shifted in an unfelt breeze, and her hair floated around her again like she was underwater. Her eyes shone, and the faint glow under her skin became brighter and brighter. She channeled the energy down into her hands, then it was glowing under her palms, like she had trapped light under her hands against the earth.

From the place she touched the ground, a portal began to spiral open. It spread out like a stain, a shimmering silvery light—more of the same light that had been under her skin. It flowed until it was contained by the bloody circle like a new bathing pool in the cavern.

She stood up. Her eyes glowed the same silver as the portal beneath her. I stared at the portal, hypnotized by the unfamiliar shine, and how it seemed to shift under her feet like water. I'd imagined it differently, like she'd wave her hand and open a gash in the world to step immediately through into somewhere else. The opaqueness of the portal frightened me. Internally, my wolf laid her ears back, unsure.

"Come," Corinne said. "We did it. Now we can escape."

Again she held out her hand, just like she had when she was creating the portal.

This time my anxiety writhed in my throat like it was alive. "To Frasia, right?" I asked.

She nodded. "To the Court of Nightfall."

I'd come this far. All I could do now was trust her. We both wanted the same thing—freedom. Fae magic was the only thing that could give it to us.

Internally my wolf whined. She wanted to pull away from that mysterious portal and rush back to our private quarters, tail between our legs. But if I stayed here, I'd have to face Draunar again. Face him... Or worse, be *his*.

The shudder that raced through me at the thought was enough to drown out my wolf's plaintive whines. I took Corinne's hand again and stepped across the circle onto the portal. I held my breath as I did so, feeling like I was stepping onto a very thin layer of ice. The portal was soft under my feet, plush like moss. It was unnerving walking on it, and I stared at my feet, unsure of its solidity. Corinne took my other hand in hers. The gash on my palm had slowed to an ooze, but hers still dripped blood, bright red that sank into the portal and disappeared.

"Ready?" she asked.

I met her glowing eyes. "Yes," I said. "Let's go home."

Corinne squeezed my hands reassuringly. Her power sparked over both of them, not painful but strange, and then the portal shimmered beneath us.

We fell.

I tried to scream but there was no air in my lungs. I didn't know what I was expecting—Drifting? Floating?—but *falling* wasn't it at all. The darkness was abyssal, dizzyingly deep, and I closed my eyes tightly rather than strain to see Corinne through the thick inky blackness. I focused on her grip as we fell, and fell, and fell.

Then, through my tightly closed eyes, light flooded in, red through my eyelids. I gasped and my lungs filled with crisp, cold air; the inhale was almost intoxicating after weeks of stale cave air. My back hit the soft ground with a whump, gentle as if I'd tumbled off a hammock instead of falling for what felt like ages through the darkness.

I dropped my hands to the ground beside me and slowly opened my eyes.

I was in a bed of soft grass. Overhead, plush clouds drifted in the cool breeze, and the sky was so blue it didn't exactly look right. It was almost *too* blue. Had I forgotten how bright the sky could be in Frasia after only a few weeks locked away?

Internally, my wolf whined. I'd thought she'd settle in Frasia, but my nerves only worsened.

Slowly, I sat up, then groaned as a headache roared to the front of my skull. I pressed my fingers to my temples and closed my eyes again.

Corinne patted my back gently. "Portal travel can be overwhelming if you're not used to it," she said gently. "Now come, we have much to attend to."

I took a few deep breaths. The air was so crisp—did it always feel like this in Frasia? Almost sharp in my lungs?

"Up, wolf," Corinne said. Her voice was colder now, and laced with impatience.

"I'm coming, I'm coming," I said with a groan.

I staggered to my feet.

Then, on the horizon, I saw it.

A palace.

But it wasn't the manor in Frasia.

It was a white stone palace, with silvery roofs and windows inlaid with pale pink glass that shone in the sunlight. It wasn't nearly the size of the Shiangan palace, not even the manor, but it shone like a gem tucked into the lush, hilly landscape. It was built right at the edge of a vast lake sitting between the building and the mountain range across from it. We were in a valley, dotted with tall trees which burst with lush green leaves and pale pink flowers. As Corinne stood near one, it leaned toward her, its branches swaying against the breeze of their own accord. She flattened her palm on the trunk of the tree and smiled like greeting an old friend.

We weren't in Frasia at all.

We weren't even in Frasia's *realm*.

The sky was too bright. The air was too crisp. The trees spoke. The queen was glowing.

I was in Faerie.

"We need to go to Frasia," I said desperately. "The court has to know where I am. Surely this is a mistake."

"I'm sorry, Reyna," the queen said in a gentle, musical voice. "But the wolves cannot be expected to defeat the dragons of Shianga. And after what Draunar has done to my people, by keeping me locked away for so long, I must make him pay for what he's done. I will raise my armies here and return to Shianga to see it through."

"I understand that," I said. Desperation was rising in my throat. "I do. But we must go to Frasia first, Corinne, we *must*. I can't be here. I need to find my husband—I need to make sure he's okay."

"Your husband doesn't matter," Corinne said sweetly. "Do you know how many Fae lives have suffered in your realm? Not just because of what Draunar has done—but because of what Constantine of Daybreak did as well." Her silvery gaze hardened. "You should be grateful I haven't asked you to atone for those cruelties."

"I have done nothing but help you," I said. "Please. Please, just send me back."

"I can't do that," Corinne said. "If I send you back, surely you'll tell your wolves of my plan, and of what Draunar did."

"If you want me to maintain silence, I will," I said immediately.

She sighed. "I wish I could trust you, but I can't take the risk. I need Draunar surprised." Her gaze turned distant and cruel. "I want him to suffer."

"I do too," I said. "Isn't that obvious? He captured us both. I wouldn't put that at risk."

"You would," she said. "I know you'd tell that husband of yours, the one you miss so much. Now come, I need to alert the court of my return."

"I won't," I said, more desperate now. Desperate because I knew she was right. More than anything, I wanted to be back in my realm, on my way back to Shianga with an army of wolves, prepared to fight at Elias' side. "You lied to me. You didn't have to *lie*. You should've just told me this was the plan all along."

"You never would've helped me if I did," she said. She placed both hands on the trunk of the tree and sighed with pleasure as she pulled power from the Fae lands. "We both know that. Please, stop whining."

Embarrassingly, my frustration and rage and betrayal coalesced into the hot prickle of tears behind my eyes. I had felt something was off about Corinne and her plan, but I'd ignored it. I'd just wanted so badly to get out of the cavern—to fix the stupid mistake I'd made by agreeing to go with Draunar in the first place.

Now I was even further away. Still trapped. Still just a pawn in the game.

"No," I said. "I'm not going with you. I'm getting back to Frasia. I won't be treated like this."

Corinne sighed. "Don't be childish."

"I'm not being childish," I shot back. "I'm a queen, just like you. We should be working *together*. I won't be dragged around, gone from being his prize to yours."

She looked at me for a long moment, and something in her expression softened.

"You're right," she said. "You've been through a lot recently. I know this is an unexpected development in our path back to Shianga, but I promise you, you will see your husband very soon."

She stepped forward and caught my hand in hers before I could back away. She gripped it so tightly that pain throbbed through the gash still raw on my palm.

"Hey!" I tried to pull away, but her grip only tightened.

Her power coursed over my skin. It wasn't like it'd been in the cavern, where I could feel her power nearby. This time, it was directed at me, crawling over my skin like tendrils, and then going deeper.

I gasped as her power reached inside me, into my chest, and woke my wolf. My wolf howled in rage, teeth bared internally as we both thrashed, trying to break her hold. But it was no use. She'd gained power being in Faerie, more magical power than I'd ever felt in one place. I couldn't form a coherent thought, I couldn't fight, all I could feel was the cold glow of her power wrapped around my wolf like a vise. She laughed once, high and cold, and then drew my wolf forward.

My paws hit the soft grass of the meadow. The differences between Faerie and my realm were even starker now with my sharpened animal senses. I could smell the magic in the air, bright and layered, like the air itself was sweetened. Everything about the Faerie was slightly different than what I was used to in Frasia, and even Shianga, from the hints of animal musk and humanoid sweat, even the dirt, even the wind. Everything was just different. I shook out my pelt and bared my teeth at Corinne, hackles up. I had half a mind to leap forward and tear her throat out myself. My inhibitions were not nearly as strong in my wolf form.

Corinne laughed, bright and musical, and then waved her hand idly in the air. She conjured a delicate silver muzzle out of the air, and it fit itself over my snout and snapped close. I snarled behind it and shook my head rapidly, trying to shake it off, but it was locked in place, fastened to a delicate silver collar that had made its way around my neck.

I snarled at her, drool dripping from my teeth through the silver muzzle onto the grass.

"Now, wolf," she said with that cold smile, "I have much to attend to in the palace. You'll be a fine companion. Come."

She began to walk through the meadow at a leisurely pace, and I began to trot after her. I could still feel a small tendril of magic that attached me to her, like a leash.

She was controlling me.

Behind the muzzle I growled and snarled, but I couldn't stop walking.

How was I going to make my way back to Elias now?

Chapter 17

There was a small bustling village outside the Fae palace, not unlike the town close to the Shiangan castle. As we approached, Corinne waved her hand through the air again, conjuring a long, plain brown cloak that settled over her shoulders. She lifted the hood, concealing her hair and face, and pulled me closer so I was trotting right at her side.

We made our way through the narrow quiet streets, up to the entrance of the small palace. There were no doors to push open, just an immense white stone archway which led into a grand entrance hall that apparently doubled at the throne room. The floors were polished white stone, with gorgeous, intricately carved columns leading up to the high arched ceiling. The vast windows were inlaid with pink stones, overlooking the still lake outside.

At the far end of the hall, a white stone stood on top of a tall dais. The chair was empty, and looked like it had been for many years. Instead, the room was occupied by a handful of tall, beautiful, white-haired Fae dressed in clothes of fine pale colors, and a few in armor stationed by the dais.

"Pardon me." A Fae man with silver hair tied back in an intricate braid approached. He was dressed in pale blue, and holding a quarterstaff in hand that was clearly not ceremonial. Despite the lack of armor, from the way he carried himself, I knew he would be a formidable foe. "We're not hearing grievances today, the best time to return to the throne room would be early next week."

Corinne lifted her head and pulled the hood down off her shoulders.

The man dropped his quarterstaff. "Your Highness," he gasped.

"Adrian, my right hand," she said with a smile. "I trust you've been taking care of the kingdom in my absence?"

"Milady," he said, still clearly stunned. He fell to his knees in a bow. "You've finally returned."

Recognition rippled through the throne room like a wave. Gasps and murmurs followed, the clatter of more things dropped, as the royal Fae fell to their knees to welcome back their queen.

No one paid any attention to me. I supposed in Faerie it was no surprise to see wolves—or perhaps the shock of having the queen back overpowered any curiosity about me. I was grateful for the lack of attention. I stuck close to Corinne's side as she made her way through the throne room, greeting her court members delicately.

After what felt like a century of tearful greetings and handshakes and bows, finally Corinne turned back to Adrian and led him back behind the dais. They walked side by side through the spectacular courtyard behind the throne room, and then to a spiral staircase built into the side of the castle itself. I followed them up the winding white stairs to the second level, which opened up into a grand banquet hallway. I couldn't hear what they were saying as they spoke in low voices, heads tipped toward each other. Corinne kept me at a short distance behind them, likely for this exact reason.

Finally, we reached the end of the banquet hall, where a white stone door stood carved with an ornate decoration of an immense tree, similar to the one Corinne had leaned on in the meadow. It was one of the first entryways I'd seen in the entire palace. Corinne embraced Adrian, and then he briskly turned and strode back through the banquet hall, only giving me a sideways glance as he left.

Behind the door was what I assumed were Corinne's quarters. They were vast, elegant, and more than a little dusty. The furniture was covered in sheets, which Corinne methodically pulled off, revealing a dresser, an immense mirror, a stone hearth, and a few pieces of art. When she was done, she finally went to the grand four-poster bed and smoothed down the white linens.

"I never thought I'd see this place again," she murmured, half to me and half to herself. "I thought I'd be sleeping on those ratty sheepskins forever."

I sniffed and made my way to the rug by the hearth, and plopped down in front of it.

Corinne glanced over at me. Then she waved her hand and the hearth roared to life, bursting into cozy flame. I started a little, but then the warmth washed over me and I settled back down. That was nice of her at least.

"I've instructed Adrian to let us rest for a day or so," she said. "I'll regain my strength, and then we'll begin the preparations to return to Shianga."

I flicked an ear in acknowledgment. I was still angry, and wanted her to see that in my expression, but I did want to know the details. If I was stuck with her in this form—I could at least get those.

I slept fitfully by the fire, and before dawn, when Corinne unceremoniously jerked me to my feet with a pulse of her power. I shook into wakefulness and padded after her, through the quiet white stone hallways of the palace, to a meeting room at the far end. This was much smaller than the other grand rooms we'd walked through, with nothing more than a low table and a vast window overlooking the still lake. When Corinne stepped inside, the three Fae seated at the table stood and bowed deeply in greeting.

"Your Highness," Adrian said. "Welcome."

"Adrian," Corinne said warmly. "And my council members. General Eodwin. Lady Fretha."

The other two members smiled in return. All four of them had the same shining silvery hair, but only Fretha wore hers long and loose, flowing nearly to the waist of her elegant pale blue gown. They took their seats and a servant swept in and poured a light, fragrant tea from an ornate silver teapot.

"And who is this?" Fretha asked, nodding at me.

"A wolf of Frasia," Corinne said without hesitation. "She was also kept as a part of Draunar's hoard. It was with her assistance I was able to escape. You'll have to excuse the muzzle—she can be a bit, how should I say, spirited."

Titters of laughter rang out around the table. Anger raced through me and made itself known as my upper lip peeled back from my teeth.

"Oh, my!" Fretha said with another bell-like laugh. "The wolf appears ferocious."

"Pay her no mind," Corinne said. "I couldn't risk her exposing my plan to the wolves on Shianga before our strategy was settled. But first, let us discuss the kingdom's developments in my absence..."

The council meeting was long, and excruciatingly detailed, and I tried to absorb the details I thought would be important. But there was so much detail—Adrian laid out dozens and dozens of grievances they'd sorted out with Fae villagers, Eodwin narrated the changes in the barracks and who had been promoted and who had not, and Fretha explained how she had managed the day-to-day upkeep of the manor. In this conversation, the long lives of the Fae were clear. They had systems to keep their community running even in the queen's absence—it was like they had all known, despite the damage, that eventually she would return.

Once they had caught Corinne up on everything, she nodded thoughtfully and sipped her tea in the comfortable silence. "You've all done well," she said.

"My only regret is we could not locate you, Your Majesty," Eodwin said. "In your absence we struggled to maintain a presence in the other realms."

"I don't believe even Draunar knew what he had done to the Fae when he locked me away," she said with a sigh. "His only interest was keeping a queen as a toy. He is a simple, stupid man, and his subjects will be better served under our leadership."

"He will pay for what he did," Adrian said mildly. Despite the quiet tone, there was an edge of clarity to his words that sent a shiver down my spine. Corinne was right about one thing—Draunar had no idea what he was getting into when he kidnapped the Fae queen.

"Eodwin," Corinne said. "Keep an eye on the battlefield in Shianga. Do not engage or let them know you are there. Fretha, you and I will gather our finest soldiers and prepare them for battle. When the time is right, Eodwin, we will surprise Draunar in Shianga and take their palace from his claws."

"I will leave immediately," Eodwin said briskly. "I look forward to returning with news."

Corinne hummed her dismissal and Eodwin left. When the tea was finished, another Fae in tiny glasses and a frazzled expression burst in with a large leatherbound tome in hand. "Your Highness!" he squeaked. "We simply must balance the ledger, it's been a mess the past several years!"

Corinne sighed and gestured for the accountant to sit down. I settled down for another long, boring meeting.

As the days passed, Corinne held more catch-up meetings as she retook the throne. There were breakfasts, banquets, small meetings, large ones, tours of the grounds, rooftop cocktails, and so on and so on. For all of them, I was latched to her side like a plaything or a spoiled pet, muzzled and kept close so she could show me off. I never caused any problems. I sat quietly at her feet, lingered at her side, kept my ears and tail low, and even bit back my growls when the occasional Fae deigned to pet me like a dog. It was humiliating. But my demure behavior paid off.

On the fifth day, I lingered by the fire in her chambers, dozing as usual as Corinne went through her extensive dressing and bathing rituals. I had almost drifted back into sleep when she approached and placed her hand on the fine collar around my neck.

"You've done well this week, wolf," she said.

I glanced up, ears twitching with suspicion. Then, her power briefly flowed through me, sharp and uncomfortable.

"There," she said. "I've adjusted the hold some. You will be relegated to stay within the palace walls, and in this shape, but feel free to enjoy the courtyards. Some sunshine will do you good."

I blinked. Within the palace walls?

Then, Corinne left the room.

Without me.

I was alone in her quarters for the first time in what felt like an age. I stood up, shook out my pelt, and then glanced around.

When I was sure I was alone, I closed my eyes, then tried to find my human form under my wolf's wild nature. She was there still, pacing irritably—but I couldn't shift back. Corinne's magic still had a hold on my abilities, and I was locked in this form until she loosened her hold. In Daybreak, my tutors had always instilled in me that one was not to spend too much time in her wolf form, lest the wolf take control and the human couldn't re-emerge. I'd thought after five days shifted, I'd feel less like myself, and more like an animal. Perhaps that's what all the recent runs had done, though—made it easier to *be* myself while in my wolf shape.

My paws itched at the thought of a run. Gods, that was what I needed now. A long, moonlit run, moving quickly through the trees with Elias on my heels, just waiting for the right moment to tackle me, to land in the soft moss and shift back, wrap my arms around him, bury my face in the familiar curve of his neck—

I stopped the thought in its tracks, and shook my head as if dispelling it. If I thought too hard about Elias, I'd get sucked down into the cavernous despair threatening to open up inside me. I couldn't risk getting lost in my emotions. I had to focus on my newfound freedom.

Corinne had seen how bored I was in the meetings, dozing off sometimes against my will as she went over more tiny inconsistencies in the accountant's ledgers. But why would she release me now?

She'd suggested I go to the courtyard. I paced around the room, unsure. My hackles were up, attention newly sharpened. My instincts were telling me there was a reason she'd put some distance between us. She'd had me at every meeting she'd been to thus far—why now?

Something was different. There was something to which she didn't want me privy. I slipped out of her quarters then padded through the empty banquet hall, ears forward and nostrils tuned attentively to the scents of Fae in the air.

I'd spent so much time with Corinne, it was easy to follow the faint ozone-scent of her power in the air. I padded through the banquet hall, then the main courtyard, and up the stairs to the top level of the palace. This part was sparse, without the fine ornate décor of the lower floors. Simpler. I'd only cut through here on our way to have rooftop drinks. I'd never attended a meeting in one of these cold rooms.

I padded slowly down the hall, careful to keep my nails from clicking on the stone floor. I approached a closed wooden door, and behind it, with my head pressed to the wood, I could make out the voices behind it.

"And you're sure this will work?" Corinne asked.

"I'm sure," an unfamiliar voice said. "We've had all the royal sorcerers working night and day on this spell. With your power, it will execute flawlessly in Shianga."

"Hm." A pause in the conversation. Then Corinne said, "Will it force a shift?"

"It will not," the voice—a sorcerer, I assumed—said. "But it will be able to entrap King Draunar in either dragon or human form. Once activated, it will draw power from here in Faerie and forcibly cage him. You will be able to manipulate Draunar as easily as you manipulate the she-wolf."

"Good," Corinne said, pleased. "And will it affect the other dragons?"

"No," the sorcerer said. "We have only focused on the king, to ensure the spell is as strong as possible. He is strong, Your Highness, and he may have some resistance to Fae magic, due to his proximity to you for so long."

"That's less than ideal," she said, "but I understand."

"The other dragons will be easily dispatched once they see their king trapped," Eodwin's voice said. "They are nothing without him."

"I hope you're right," Corinne said coolly. "Ideally, I'd like as little bloodshed as possible in Shianga."

"After what they did to you?" Eodwin said. Rage tinged his voice. "We should slaughter them all."

"We could," Corinne said, "but we won't. We'll do better to convert as many dragons as we can to our side, and then execute those who resist. But remember our plan, Eodwin. We need time to build our strength in Shianga. It is not just their kingdom we will be taking."

"Of course," Eodwin said.

"If this appears to be a simple act of revenge, we will not inspire retribution from Shianga's neighbors," she said. "Better to build our strength in peacetimes, and take the remaining kingdoms when their defenses are down."

"Wise as always," the sorcerer said.

"It was not only the dragons who did this to our people," Corinne said. Her voice sounded in a low, cruel hiss. "Every leader of that realm who drove us from their lands will pay for what they have done."

A door at the far end of the hallway swung open. I leaped back, still quiet on the stone. A servant Fae girl walked unsteadily down the hall with her arms piled with folded, clean laundry, so high it appeared she couldn't even see around them. I scurried back toward the staircase and slipped out before she saw me.

I made my way back down to the main courtyard, ears back, my hackles trying to rise as I kept forcing them down. It was a gorgeous day, as every day was in Faerie. There was a strange hypnosis to my settings. The weather never seemed to change, the sun never seemed to move much in the sky. The breeze carried the clean scent of the lakes and the sweet scent of the pink flowers bursting into bloom on the branches of the pale tree in the center of the courtyard. I lay down in the shade under it and exhaled heavily.

Corrine's plan weighed heavily on my mind. It wasn't just Shianga she wanted. Surely, she'd come for Frasia next, what with the way the Fae lands had dissipated in our nation. She'd already spoken ill of Daybreak. And then after that, surely she'd use her power to take Osna, Cruora, and Askon, too.

From spending time at her side, I knew how conniving and convincing she could be. I knew she would try to build a diplomatic relationship with those nations while she built up her army in our realm. She'd try to woo us all into a sense of safety, and then she would strike.

But now I knew. Now, Frasia would be ready.

Now, I could bring the fight to her.

For the next two days, the queen continued to give me freedom to roam the palace during the day, but she did insist that I remain at her side during the dramatic banquets that happened every night without fail. It was part of the ongoing celebration for the queen's return, but I was well sick of it. The first Fae banquet I'd been dragged to had been remarkable: piles and piles of unfamiliar fruits and suckling pigs, enchanted to dance and squeal before they flopped onto the tables, fast-paced and thrilling music playing from bands perched in the rafters, complicated dance routines, ever-flowing wine, and Fae kissing and laughing and disappearing into side rooms for privacy.

From her table on the dais, Corinne overlooked it all. She sat at the table with Adrian at her side, lounging in her carved white throne and dressed in white robes embroidered in silver. She swirled her wine in its glass as she overlooked the revelry with an impassive gaze.

None of the activity in the banquet hall interested me. I lay down on the dais, ears low as the party went on. Being stuck at a banquet in wolf form was even more boring than the ones back when I was a Lady of Daybreak. I longed to be return to Corinne's quarters, just so I could pass out in front of the roaring fire, but for events like this she used me like an accessory, an example of her power and influence.

I was moments from drifting into an uneasy doze despite the raucous noise when a horn sounded abruptly. The music cut. General Eodwin, dressed in fine silver armor stained with dirt and blood, marched into the entryway, his gaze stern and commanding. The crowd parted around him, and he waved one gloved hand dismissively. The band began to play again, and the dancing and partying resumed, as if Eodwin wasn't there at all.

Eodwin climbed the stairs to the dais and took at Corinne's left side. I inched a little closer, still on my belly under the table, ears pricked to better hear the conversation.

"General," Corinne said as she poured him a flagon of wine. "I trust you come with an update from Shianga?" She glanced at his breastplate. "It seems you're straight from Shianga?"

"I thought you'd want to know as soon as possible," Eodwin said. He took a long drink from the wine. "My spies and I have kept a close eye on the fighting the past few days. Both the wolves and the dragons are engaged in a war of attrition at this point. The wolves' ranks have been thinned, and the defenses at the palace are weak. If you wish to strike, I suggest you move soon, before Frasia calls for reinforcements from Efra, and while the palace is still reeling from their latest hit. This is a narrow window."

She nodded, and a cold smile turned the corners of her lips upwards. "And what of the wolves?"

Eodwin popped a grape into his mouth and crushed it between his front teeth as he grinned. "They struggle," he said.

My ears flicked as I suppressed a low whine.

"Their morale is dropping steadily, but they fight on." Eodwin said. He rolled his eyes. "They frustrate Draunar."

The whine broke through my clenched jaw. Corinne glanced down at me and her expression hardened with irritation. I scooted further away before she could kick me in retribution. Why was their morale dropping? What of Elias? Was he alive? Was he battling alongside his wolves? Desperation rushed through me, renewed, like the dry leaves of my sorrow had been set alight. I had to get back to Shianga. I had to see him again.

Corinne only sighed. "Tomorrow," she said. "Under cover of darkness, we will strike. Ready the warriors."

"Yes, Your Majesty." Eodwin stood up and hurried back through the raucous dance floor.

"Rest well tonight, wolf," Corinne murmured. "Tomorrow will be interesting."

Another whine slipped out. I could only hope that when I was dragged into Shianga as the queen's pet, Elias would still be alive. If he wasn't... If my leaving with Draunar had led to his death, I'd never be able to forgive myself.

Chapter 18

I snarled at the Fae blacksmith as he approached me with silver plate mail in hand.

"I see why you keep the beast muzzled," he said with a low laugh as he knelt down in front of me.

I was in the armory with Corinne and Eodwin, and the cavernous room beneath the palace bustled with activity. Fae soldiers strapped into lightweight silver armor and sharpened their weaponry, throwing sparks off the grinding wheel. They spoke in low voices, and the sounds that filled the underground armory were mostly the clanking of metal on metal as they readied for battle.

Battle... or war.

The blacksmith strapped the plating onto me. It was a silver breastplate fastened with leather, and layered plates over my front legs. It was so lightweight it hardly hindered my movement at all. Behind the ever-present muzzle, I bared my teeth and tossed my head in frustration. If I was going to go onto a battlefield, I'd be a lot more useful with a sword in hand rather than with my main weapon restrained.

Corinne smiled faintly as if she could read my thoughts. "I know, wolf," she said. "You'll have your human form back soon enough. You know I can't risk you running off while we're in Shianga, though. If the wolf king is still alive, I might need a little bargaining tool."

She fastened the clasps of her own armor, the same fine silver as mine, though hers was ornately engraved with a carving of a many-branched tree. She looked so different than the woman I'd spent those weeks with in the cavern—now she was a warrior queen. She removed the muzzle. I gnashed my teeth and shook my head, relieved to have it off. The blacksmith glanced at her, clearly nervous, but I wasn't about to ruin my chances of making it back to the realm by launching a foolish attack now.

She didn't know if Elias was alive or not. My heart beat into my throat. I was terrified to face what awaited me in Shianga—terrified to be turned into a war-beast at the queen's side—but the thought of seeing Elias propelled my spirit forward. I'd gone from being a pawn in Draunar's game to Corinne's. But once I was in Shianga—once I was in my own realm, I'd break free. I'd find Elias.

I'd make this right, whatever it took.

Corinne led the way out of the open back entrance. The castle opened directly to a sturdy stone bridge that led into the lake, and then terminated into nothingness. It was a bridge to nowhere in the center of the lake.

I walked at her side, nerves burning through me as we approached the end of the bridge. Behind us, the Fae soldiers marched in step, their boots pounding heavily. Corinne held up her hand, and the soldiers stopped. A heavy silence descended, and all I could hear was the gentle lap of the lake water against the columns of the bridge.

"Now," Corinne said, low, "onward to take what is mine."

She held out her hand. The lake below began to churn, building into a swirling whirlpool. I stepped back nervously. The wind picked up, dancing through my fur and making me shiver. Corinne's silver hair whipped around her face. The water in the whirlpool rushed and sped up, and then with a shimmer of power, a portal rose from the shape like a shadow. It raised up, appearing as a round, churning doorway at the end of the bridge. I couldn't see anything through it. It appeared just like the whirlpool, except instead of water churning, it was bright Fae magic.

Corinne whistled once, a long, low sound like a birdsong, and behind her the soldiers shouted in unison and thumped their fists against their breastplates.

Her power over me tightened as we stepped through the portal.

This time, there was no sensation of falling, no endless travel. The darkness swept over me, and three steps later, there was moonlight shining on my face. Turned out portal travel was easier for her when she had access to all the power of Faerie. My eyes adjusted to the darkness.

I couldn't hold back the low whine that sounded from my throat. My ears lay back flat against my head. I couldn't stand the sight in front of me, but even with my tail low between my legs, all I could do was move forward.

The portal had opened directly into the front gardens of the Shiangan palace. The moon shone full and high overhead, but no wolves howled at its presence. The gardens were quiet. Few plants still stood, the beds had been burned or destroyed. The palace stood in front of us, but it was dirtied and damaged, with turrets fallen and immense holes blasted into its sides. What was once well-tended grass in the gardens was now wet mud sucking at my paws. Mud—and worse.

There were wolves in Shianga, but none of them were howling, because they were left in motionless heaps on the ground. Bodies were stacked in low piles, both wolf and man, adorned in the dark colors of Nightfall. Left on the grounds like corpses at a slaughterhouse. I couldn't bear to look at them, at the way the moonlight danced over their motionless flanks, nor could I escape the rancid smell of rotting blood.

My heart shattered. Pain roared through me, making my blood pound in my ears. All I wanted was to throw my head back and sound out my despair, my hate, to let any remaining wolves know they were not alone. I wanted to break loose of Corinne's hold and leave all of this behind, flee, find Elias where ever he was. Our kingdom needed him now more than ever.

I needed him.

Corinne's hold was still too strong though. I couldn't shake her magic.

"Draunar!" Corinne roared. Her voice echoed through the still night, ringing off the dilapidated sides of the palace. "Draunar, come out and face me!"

The immense doors to the palace swung open.

Draunar stepped out into the gardens, flanked by exhausted-looking soldiers in battered leather. Draunar himself was dressed in gold armor, bloodstained and slightly askance, like he'd just pulled it on in a hurry. His expression darkened as he bared his teeth.

"Corinne," he said, low and poisonous. "You've returned."

"For you," she snarled. "I've come to take what is mine."

"I'd like to see you try," he hissed back. "You'll be back where you belong momentarily. You and the stupid she-wolf."

He leveled his green eyes at me and then spit off to the side, a gesture so disrespectful I snarled at him.

Draunar laughed, and then shifted. His dragon burst forth, snarling, wings spread and claws out. The soldiers at his side followed his lead, changing into their own draconic shapes. He launched forward, roaring, and Corinne sidestepped him easily. The soldiers behind us spread out, circling the other dragons, while Corinne withdrew a long, thin sword strapped to her back and brandished it at Draunar.

"When I'm finished with you," Corinne shrieked, "I will take your head and hang it above my throne in this very palace!"

Her hold on me slipped as she focused on Draunar. I backed up, crouching low to the ground as I deftly dodged the soldiers and the other dragons. I glanced around looking for any wolves in the tree line, but I could barely see at all with the chaos of battle escalating around me.

Draunar roared again, then beat his powerful wings, lifting his immense body into the sky. He inhaled, then exhaled a column of flame directly at Corinne. I cowered back from the sudden brightness as the heat rippled through the air.

Corinne lifted the sword over her head. The blade blocked the column of flame as if it were a shield. The flame spilled over the edges, but none of it touched Corinne. Her eyes glowed pale, and then her hair moved like it was underwater as she channeled her power. The blade of the sword began to glow.

I realized it then. The spell she had been discussing with the sorcerer—it was tied to the blade itself.

She roared, sounding like a dragon herself as she pushed the spell through the blade. Glowing white light traveled up the column of flame, wrapping around it like ropes and extinguishing it just as easily. Draunar's eyes widened in shock and fear as he realized it. He beat his wings harder to put distance between himself and the spell.

"You fool," she called, her voice cruel and layered as if she was speaking from a different realm. "You thought you could trap the Fae queen with no consequence? You doubted my power?"

Draunar moved to blow another column of fire, but the spell traveled to his jaws before he could expel it. He roared as the queen's air of magic coiled around his head and neck. He shook his head wildly as if trying to knock it off. His claws dragged through the light to no avail. Then, he fell from the sky like a goose struck by an arrow. His body hit the ground with a loud thump. The other dragons turned their attention to the king in sudden confusion; a Fae soldier took advantage of their momentary distraction and drove his sword into the dragon's belly. He roared, then gurgled and fell sideways, writhing in pain as his death approached.

Corinne approached him, sword still drawn and glowing. The spell worked its way around Draunar's body like a net, pinning his wings to his body. He thrashed against it, roaring, but he could blow no fire, nor could he break her hold. Corinne's power crackled through the air like a thunderstorm. She walked, but her feet hovered an inch off the ground. The power spilled from her like light trapped from within. I'd never seen her this powerful. I'd never seen Draunar so cowed.

If she had taken Draunar down so easily, the other nations didn't stand a chance.

She laughed, high and cruel, and then drove her sword into Draunar's clawed foot. He shrieked in pain, writhing on the ground in agony but unable to shake the sword from his flesh.

"Kill the guards," Corinne roared. "Take this disgrace to the dungeons."

The two dragon soldiers were dispatched easily by the Fae soldiers, and their bodies were left in a heap on the grounds. Adrian stepped forward and took the sword from Corinne's hand. He controlled the spell now, apparently, and dragged Draunar roaring and hissing behind him like he was a sack of potatoes.

Corinne's hold tightened on me again. I was forced toward the palace itself, trailing behind the marching Fae soldiers as they thumped their fists against their breastplates and shouted a low rhythmic war cry in warning.

"Come out, dragons!" Corinne shouted over the din. "Your king is dispatched, pledge to your queen or face your death where you stand!"

The war cries continued as soldiers filtered through the palace, dragging the sparse number of servants and dragon fighters from their chambers and into the throne room. Corinne took her seat on Draunar's throne while Adrian dragged Draunar, still roaring uselessly, down the west staircase into the underground level I hadn't yet seen.

I stood in the center of the room, under the dais, while the chaos escalated around me all under Corinne's watchful, glowing gaze. Beneath my feet, Draunar's rage rumbled helplessly. He was trapped in his own palace—just as trapped as I'd been in the cavern. But gazing up at Corinne, I knew I had only traded one imprisonment for another.

Chapter 19

It took less than a day for Corinne to solidify her takeover of the Shiangan palace. Some of the lower-ranking dragons had pledged their allegiance without question, especially once those who refused had their bodies dragged through the streets of the town as proof of Corinne's strength. King Draunar was under lock and key in the dungeons, and more Fae had crossed into Shianga from Faerie.

The throne room was an explosion of celebratory activity. Corinne lounged in Draunar's ornate throne, with a flagon of wine dangling from her fingers, her pale cheeks flushed red and eyes glassy with drink. Dragon and Fae servants both worked in a flurry, bringing in endless plates of food from the kitchens, and the wine poured like waterfalls. Music played loud and raucous, and Fae danced and sang loudly to honor the queen and her victory under the open skylights of the throne room.

I made myself small, pushing close to the furthest wall of the room. I was free of my muzzle, finally—the queen trusted me enough to keep me unrestrained now that she'd had her victory. But I could still feel her power squeezing gently around my chest. It was a similar hold that she'd had in Faerie: strong enough to give me boundaries, but not tying me directly to her side.

I was trying to make myself forgotten. As the party raged on, I stayed still, and tucked myself half-behind a statue of a dragon by the entrance.

Her hold was loosening.

I could feel it. It wasn't intentional—she was just drunk and distracted. Susceptible to the same mistakes that we all made, it seemed.

Adrian, a little unsteady on his feet, approached the dais and offered Corrine his hand with a dramatic, playful bow.

Corinne laughed, though I couldn't hear it over the din of music and noise, but I could imagine the sound when she threw her head back. She accepted his hand, then drained the rest of her wine and followed him down to the dance floor. He swept her in close, and then I lost sight of them as they disappeared into the raucous crowd.

The music picked up even louder, faster, and cheers erupted as the Fae realized their queen and general were dancing with them.

Then I felt it.

She slipped.

The control dissipated to barely a touch. I turned on my heels and bolted out of the open front doors, as fast as I could, moving quickly and silently over the grounds before anyone could notice I was gone. I didn't even a risk a glance back at the damaged castle, still brightly lit with Fae power.

The grounds were soft and muddy under my paws as I raced through and toward the tree line. I kept my eyes fixed on the forest, ignoring the piles of bodies rotting in the mutilated garden, and the smell of decay poisoning the crisp night air. It wasn't until I was under the cover of the trees that I slowed down.

I paused at a clearing in the forest and lifted my nose to the sky. I swiveled my ears, carefully listening for any sign of being followed.

There was nothing. I was alone in the forest. Even the usual rustling of animals in the underbrush was muted, as if the battle had driven all the wildlife from their homes.

I closed my eyes, took a slow breath, and then shifted.

It was a slower process than usual—I struggled to bring forth my human form after so long in my wolf shape, but after a few breaths, I was standing on two bare feet, naked in the middle of the forest. I shook out my hands and stretched my arms overhead, then took a few steps, testing my balance.

"Okay," I said gently to myself. My voice was scratchy with disuse. "Okay. I'm okay."

There were no wolves in the palace, other than those left for dead on the grounds. I had to believe that Elias had retreated back to Frasia—the alternative was impossible to imagine.

He had to be in Frasia. He had to be preparing the wolves to return and strike again.

Right?

I took a deep breath of cold night air. I couldn't think too far ahead. All that mattered right now was that I make it back there alive.

I shifted back into my wolf shape and took off at a run, heading toward town. If I was going to make it to Frasia, I needed supplies. I wasn't sure if there was anywhere safe I could go—

but there was one place I was willing to try.

I made my way through the silent streets of the town outside Shianga. What was once a bustling place had been reduced to a shell of its former self. The streets were empty, and some doors of the taverns and shops stood open, like the residents had left in a desperate hurry. The silence was not the silence of the night, but of absence. It was eerie. I crept through the streets with my ears low. Guilt chewed at me—this was my fault. This trip was supposed to avoid an outcome like this. I'd thought Elias and I were going to make our mark as diplomats, building a new relationship between Frasia and Shianga. I'd accepted Draunar's terms to avoid a battle like this.

All this suffering. All this death.

Corinne had to pay. I would be sure of that.

I made my way down the familiar narrow alley just off the town square. The blue door of the bookstore still stood, and behind the dusty, dirty window, a light glowed faintly.

I shifted back into my human form. It was easier this time—like now that I needed to be human, it was easier to draw that shape forth. It was almost instinctive, like regaining my balance when I stumbled. Uncaring of my nudity and the dirt on my hands and feet, I knocked rapidly on the door to the shop.

"Gulde!" I called in a low voice. "Gulde, are you in there?"

The door opened a crack. Gulde's birdlike nose appeared in the visible space, and his small eyes narrowed behind his thick glasses.

"We're closed," he hissed, then blinked, eyes widening as he realized who I was. "You—it can't be. Your Highness?"

"Please," I said. "I've just escaped the Fae, please, I need help."

Gulde pressed his lips together in a thin line.

"I understand your hesitation," I said.

"Hesitation?" Gulde snapped. "Your wolves have been slaughtering dragons for weeks."

"Only after Draunar took me as part of his hoard," I said. "The Fae queen, too. She's taken her revenge."

"I'm aware of that," Gulde said, then, "You were in his hoard? That's why the wolves arrived?"

"Please," I said again. "The queen will realize I'm gone soon. I've been her captive. I need to get back to Frasia and fix this."

Gulde sighed and stepped away from the door, ushering me in. From behind the counter, he pulled a heavy cloak and tossed it to me. Gratefully, I wrapped it around my shoulders and sat in one of the small chairs by his roaring fire.

"Draunar has never been a wise king," Gulde said. He stepped into the back room, and then re-emerged with a bowl of lukewarm soup. I took it gratefully and slurped it down, savoring the meaty broth and tender vegetables. He sat across from me and gazed into the fire. "And you understand your husband does not have the finest diplomatic reputation either. I had assumed these peace negotiations would fall apart due to someone's ego." He sighed. "But not to this scale. I never imagined anything of this scale."

"It's only going to get worse," I said. "The Fae queen... She's been trapped in Draunar's hoard for a long time. She carries a lot of wrath."

Gulde hummed thoughtfully, then stood up. "You're probably right," he said. "When you say fix this, what do you mean?"

"I mean I'm going to deal with the queen," I said. "Whatever it takes."

"Good," Gulde said. His voice was low and chilly with anger. "That gives me adequate time to leave this wretched city. I wasn't going to leave without my materials." He looked around his shop with a definitive nod. "But now I will. Far, far away."

I swallowed, gazing into the fire as guilt turned my stomach.

"Let me get you something," Gulde said. He went into his back room again, and then returned with a small, faded piece of parchment. He handed it to me and I unfolded it gingerly in my lap.

"This is the safest place to cross," he said. The parchment was a map of the southeastern border of Shianga, where it connected with Frasia. A red dash marked part of the boundary leading into Cruora. "Cross into Cruora first, slightly north, and then circle back down toward the old Nightfall pack lands. This is an old smuggling route. I expect the Fae will be keeping a closer eye on the border with Frasia itself. The route opens into a no man's land. You won't have any trouble."

Then he handed me a small pack. "Here's this, too. Some food for the journey. It shouldn't take more than a week on foot." Then he clicked his tongue. "And keep the cloak. You can't just be showing up to shops bare as the day you were born. You're a queen."

"Thank you, Gulde," I said. I tucked the map into the pack and slung it over my shoulder. "Once Corinne is dealt with, you'll be rewarded handsomely."

"Honestly, Your Highness, I hope by that time I'll be long gone." He ushered me toward the door.

Chapter 20

What would've taken me a week on my human feet only took a few days in my wolf shape. I traveled only during night, moving through the woods under the moonlight swiftly and quietly, and spending the days curled under the brush of the forest, sleeping in snatches and keeping my attention attuned to any Fae patrols. But as it turned out, Gulde was right. I only saw patrols on my first day of travel. The closer I got to the border with Cruora, the further I was from them. During the night, I carried the pack in my mouth, which was cumbersome at first, but better than wearing a muzzle day and night.

On the third night of travel, I crossed the border into Cruora—or what I assumed was the border. As Gulde had promised, there was no activity in this scrubby part of the country. No Fae, no eagles, no wolves. I made my way east, through the scrubby grass, only stopping to sleep in a small, abandoned den built into a hill when the sun rose. I ate the last of my hard tack in human form, then settled down for sleep as my wolf.

Shifting between the two forms was as easy as breathing now. I barely felt any separation between us at all. It was strange to think of the girl I was before I'd ever met Elias, riding in the carriage from Daybreak to Efra, dreaming of one day seeing the world. I'd never imagined I'd see it like this. I never thought I'd be capable of doing anything like this—traveling on my own, living as my wolf, escaping from the Fae queen's grasp to find my husband on my own.

I was scared, I was anxious—but more than that, I was determined. I was still the Queen of Frasia, and I was going to prove I could still lead. I was going to fix this. I knew once I found Elias, once I explained everything that happened, we'd be able to figure out what to do. I wasn't going to let Corrine take Frasia. Not ever.

As soon as the sun set, I kept loping southeast, crossing the border out of Cruora and into Frasia. I paused in a small patch of trees to review the map. Gulde had suggested I move through the old Nightfall pack lands. It was more than a possible route that drew me there, though. My instincts were drawing me there, like my wolf knew where her pack was.

I could only hope she was right. I put the map away, shifted back into my wolf, and continued toward the old pack lands. Throughout the night, I moved through the brush, swiftly and quietly, my nose and ears attuned for any sounds of activity, friendly or otherwise. But the night was quiet. It wasn't until the sky was turning pink with oncoming dawn that I saw a small, rustic village in the distance, nestled amid the rolling hills.

I approached quietly, loping with head dipped and my tail low, as if to make myself smaller. There wasn't much to this village. It was surrounded by a dilapidated fence, easy enough to slip through. Only a few buildings were standing, plain wood and stone with thatched roofs, but the dirt roads were still hard-packed and well-trodden. So there had to be people here. In the privacy of a narrow alley between the fence and a building, I shifted back into my human form and quickly pulled the heavy cloak around me.

There had to be someone here who could help me. I could only hope that the people I found here were still wolves, and not dragons scouting their way into Frasia. I crept around the edge of the building, looking for a window or doorway I could peer inside, to see if there was light, or even better, food—

When suddenly a knife pressed against the center of my back.

"No sudden moves," a low voice said.

The spike of fear was suddenly doused in the cool water of relief. "Oh, thank the gods," I breathed. "Kodan."

Behind me, Kodan inhaled sharply and dropped the blade. I whirled around, and she stared at me slack-jawed. "Your Highness?" She gripped my shoulders and squeezed, as if checking to see if I was real. "By the moon and stars. How— Gods above, are you all right?" Then she hauled me into her broad arms and squeezed so tightly it knocked all the breath from my lungs in a whoosh.

"I think so," I managed. "You're crushing me."

She released me and then shook her head, amazed. "You look like you've been traveling for days."

"I have been," I said.

"Come on." She wrapped her arm around my shoulders and guided me toward the house. "I'll need to hear everything, of course, but let's get you some warm food first."

My stomach rumbled at the suggestion, and Kodan laughed. She pushed me over the threshold.

"Where's everyone else?" I asked as I looked around. The inside of the house had been turned into what looked like a makeshift war camp: a few cots pushed against the wall, a fire burning in the hearth, and a table spread with maps and candles. But there was only one cot that looked like it'd been used—Kodan's, I assumed—and the rest of the town was quiet.

"I have a few scouts here with me," she said, "but most of the others have gone out for reinforcement. Fina and Adora took small convoys to their packs, following the messengers. Hopefully with the letters I've sent with them, and their connections to the pack, we'll get some reinforcements to Siena."

"Siena?" I asked. "Is that where we're drawing everyone to?"

Kodan nodded. "It's closer to the border with Shianga, and less likely to be targeted by the remaining dragons."

So word had not yet reached of Corinne's attack on the palace. There was so much I had to explain. Where to even begin? Exhaustion sat heavy on my shoulders. Kodan must've seen it on my face, because she pushed me to sit down on one of the plain wooden chairs by the fire.

"Here," she said. "There's coffee, too."

She poured coffee from the carafe on the table into a small tin cup and handed it to me. I wrapped my hands around it and sighed with pleasure as the fragrance wound around me like an embrace.

"You're leading things here?" I asked.

Kodan nodded. She braced both hands on the table and gaze down at the maps, her lips pressed into a hard line.

"Where's Elias?" I asked quietly. I almost didn't want to ask at all, too afraid of whatever answer I would get. "Is he... Is he okay?"

"He's alive, if that's what you're asking," she said.

I slumped down in the chair slightly as relief coursed over me once again. He was alive. Despite everything, he was still alive. "Where is he?" I asked. "Is he in Efra?"

Kodan sighed heavily. "I wish I had better news, Your Highness."

"Reyna, please. And—what do you mean? Where is he? Is he hurt?"

"I don't know where he is," she said.

"What?" I stared at her. "What do you mean you don't know?"

"Those last few days at the palace..." She closed her eyes and shook her head slightly. "It wasn't easy. We took a lot of casualties. Lost good soldiers. Even more got hurt. The dragons beat us back over the border, and we retreated back here to this outpost with our tails between our legs. I didn't know how we were going to recover, but I was sure Elias would have an idea. Some sort of rousing speech or new plan of attack, something creative and cunning and wise—he excelled as a strategist." She sighed. "But as soon as we got back here, something in him just snapped."

I took a sip of my coffee, but I didn't taste it at all. My heart pounded hard in my chest.

"I think he couldn't bear the reality of what had happened," she said. "The attack on the palace had gone disastrously. We didn't have the Nightfall forces to launch an immediate counter. Which meant, I think, that he had no way of getting you back."

The unspoken truth hung in the air between us. I was the one who had left. I was the one who had chosen to go with Draunar. It'd seemed like the only way to save my pack from exactly this outcome—this kind of devastation. I stared into the fire, numb with exhaustion and pain.

"So what did he do?" I asked.

"He left," she said.

I stared at her. "He wouldn't do that."

"Well, he did," she said. "Grief makes you do crazy things."

I pulled my feet up onto the chair and wrapped my arms around my knees, tugging them close to my chest. Guilt writhed like a living thing in my gut. "Where did he go? I—I'll go to him. I'll talk some sense into him."

"I don't know," Kodan said. "He shifted and left. I didn't have time to chase him down—I had to manage the casualties here in Siena. I'd assumed he'd come back, but he hasn't. I had to send word to Efra." She pinched the bridge of her nose. "And that, of course, was a mess."

"Surely the court is fine, right?" I asked.

"Your father heard about what happened."

I balked. "My father was in Efra?"

"He came at the duchess' request, as soon Efra got word of the fighting in Shianga. He raised some... concerns."

"Is a king no longer allowed to expression emotion?" I asked sharply. "He'd just lost members of his pack, and I—I wasn't there--" I swallowed around the sudden knot in my throat. "He'll be fine once I find him. I'll find him."

"You might think that, but Duke Rodthar doesn't," Kodan said. "He likened it to what happened to Elias' father. The duchess didn't like hearing that, of course, and the court doesn't like being reminded of it, but—"

"What happened?" I asked. "What would that have to do with Elias?"

Kodan's face paled. "You don't know," she said, like she was just figuring something out. "Forget I said anything. The point is, the court installed the duchess and your father as the queen and king."

"*What* happened?" I asked. I couldn't even wrap my head around what Kodan had said—my father, installed as King of Frasia? "Why would they do that? What don't I know?"

"Here," Kodan said. She turned to her cot and began to rifle through her things. "I'll get you something clean and dry to wear, that cloak smells like wet wolf."

"Kodan." I stood up and set my coffee on the table. I grabbed her shoulder, and she stiffened under my touch. "Just tell me. I'm so sick of being the last to know things. Please, if this will help me understand what's happening, how to make this right, just tell me."

Kodan sighed, then straightened up and turned around. She handed me a thick quilted shirt and a pair of trousers. "Fine," she said, like it pained her to agree. "If you'll put these on."

I did so, shucking off the cloak and replacing it with the thick pants and shirt. I was grateful for the cleanliness and the warmth, and I sat back down by the fire, resting my heels on the hearth. The warmth melted away some of the pain from the hours and hours of travel. Kodan sat across from me and poured herself a cup of coffee.

"I shouldn't be the one to tell you this," Kodan said.

"There are a lot of things that haven't gone the way they should recently," I said.

She smiled weakly. "Well, that much is true."

She stared into the fire, then took a sip of her coffee. The silence that hung between us was tense—heavy with the promise that whatever Kodan had to tell me might change everything.

"There's something strange that runs in Elias' family's blood," she said. "Some people in the old days says it was a curse. I don't know what it is. They're… Close to the moon." She sucked her teeth. "Elias' father, Drogo, was a strong leader. A vicious leader. He took Efra from Constantine of Daybreak by brute force alone, leading in his wolf shape. And what a wolf he was. Pelt as dark as night, eyes like lava, nearly the size of a horse."

She took another sip of her coffee.

"He was always more comfortable in his wolf shape. As things settled down in Efra, and his kingly duties became the day-to-day duties of the court, he grew frustrated. Bored. He cast the leadership duties off to his wife, our duchess, more and more. He spent all of his time on the grounds, in the woods, running and hunting and conditioning the soldiers. All in his wolf form." She pushed her hands through her hair. "And one day, he couldn't change back."

"The sickness," I said.

Kodan nodded.

"I didn't think it was real," I said quietly. "My tutors used to tell me stories about it to scare me, back in Daybreak. They said if I shifted too often, or for too long, one day I'd be stuck a wolf forever."

"It's exceedingly rare," Kodan said. "Part of me wonders if Drogo wanted to go crazy. He'd done what he needed to do—he'd secured a good, safe place to for his pack to live and thrive. But he was always a warrior. He was never cut out for a life inside, running the daily affairs of a city. Maybe he just liked things as an animal more." Again she sighed and stared into the fire. "But I'll never know. I only know how it ended."

I said nothing. I only waited.

"He went crazy," she said. "Simple as that. He entered the manor in the dead of night, under the full moon. Broke into rooms. Murdered court members. He was making his way to the duchess' chambers when Elias intercepted him. Killed him where he stood."

Simple as that. Killed him where he stood. My hands trembled around my mug.

"He did it as a man, too," Kodan said. "Not as a wolf. A knife in his hand outside his mother's bedroom door."

I closed my eyes.

Draunar's cruel voice echoed in my memory. *Does the wolf know how you took the throne?*

"Quite a way to start your time on the throne," she said. "And he was young. Barely seventeen summers."

"So when my father heard that he had shifted and run off…"

"He compared it to Drogo," Kodan said, confirming my suspicions. "That the stress of the battle, the loss, and your…" She trailed off, grimacing as she searched for the right word.

"My betrayal," I said dully. "You can say it."

"Your *decision*," Kodan said. "He suggested those things might trigger the wolf craziness. That it runs in his family's blood."

"That's nonsense," I said.

I was gripped by the urge to take off into the woods myself. To shift into my wolf, put my nose to the ground, catch his scent and find him. He needed me, now more than ever. I'd sent him to this brink, and now I had to bring him back. This story about wolf craziness was nonsense—unless it wasn't.

"I'll go." I stood up. "I'll find him. This is all my fault—my father cannot be on the throne. This is what he wanted all along. I won't let him slip through the cracks like the snake he is."

Kodan raised her eyebrows at me. "I can see your hands shaking from here," she said. "Sit back down. Eat. Clean up. Then we'll go."

I sat back down heavily. "We?"

"Of course," Kodan said. "I'm a good tracker. Between the two of us, we should be able to find him. If I went alone, he'd only run from me. But you—he can't resist you."

"He might be able to now," I said, low. "After what I did."

"I'm sure he'll be angry," Kodan said, "considering he has the temperament of a teenage girl sometimes. But I said *resist*. When he picks up your scent again, he'll come to you."

I rubbed my hand over my forehead. "I hope you're right."

"Now," Kodan said, "as much as I want to hear everything about where in the gods' names you were, you look like you're about to fall over. Sleep a few hours while I make breakfast. We'll leave tomorrow, before dawn."

"It can wait," I said. "But I promise. I'll tell you everything."

"We'll have some time on the road," she said. She gestured for me to take one of the spare cots. I was asleep before my head even hit the pillow.

Chapter 21

After a few meals of hot food and a full night of rest, I felt much more like myself. I dressed in the heavy, comfortable clothes Kodan had given me, and tied my hair back in a neat plait, keeping it well out of my way. When I stepped out of the small house into the dim light of morning, the village was still quiet, though a few scouts had begun their days tending to the horses in the nearby stable.

Kodan was finishing packing up sturdy backpack. "We'll be on foot," she said. "Don't want to risk the horses drawing any attention."

"Where are we going?" I asked.

"I was going to ask you the same thing," Kodan said with a grin. Despite the early hour, she was wide awake and looked almost excited, with leather armor strapped on and her red hair pinned back in a plait like mine. "Your wolf led you here. She should be able to lead us to Elias, too."

"How?" I asked. "I can't track his scent—he's been gone too long."

"Not using scent," Kodan said. "Just trust your instincts. If he were hurting, where would he run to? What kind of environment would he seek out?"

I sighed and closed my eyes, then took a deep inhalation of the brisk morning air.

I let my wolf creep closer to the surface, letting our senses blend together. With the right focus, I could trace the smell of everything a little more clearly, and feel the ground firm under my feet as clearly as if I had paws.

Where would he run?

Efra was to the east. To the north, the bay separating Frasia and Cruora.

The bay. If I inhaled deeply enough I thought I could smell the salt on the air. He'd want to be close to Efra, but far from the borders. He'd want open space to run. And maybe... Maybe the ocean would remind him of me.

"Northeast," I said.

"Northeast," Kodan agreed. She didn't ask why, or offer any other alternative. She just hiked the pack onto her back, and we headed out of the village and into the balds of Frasia.

It was chilly, but there was no wind, just a delicate breeze as we started off. The hilly landscape stretched out to what looked like eternity in every direction, broken only by the occasional toughened tree and jutting boulders. As we walked, the sun rose higher in the sky, and despite the guilt and anxiety that still chewed at me, the landscape had an inexorable effect on me. Being outside, with a friend, with a mission—I felt better.

I was going to fix this. I had to.

After about a few hours of walking, Kodan pulled hard tack from her pack and broke off a piece for me. "So," she said.

I accepted it gratefully. "So."

"What happened?" she asked. "All I know is that you agreed to Draunar's terms, then were hauled off in to the sky, and then you showed up in my war camp bedraggled and wrapped up in a terrible cloak."

"Did I really look bedraggled?" I asked.

"Absolutely," she said. "Where did he take you, when he flew off with you?"

"To his hoard," I said. "I thought he wanted me as a queen—that I would rule Shianga with him. I didn't realize how naive that was. I thought it was the only way to prevent war between the nations. I thought a good queen would be willing to make such a sacrifice."

Kodan said nothing. For that I was grateful.

"His hoard is deep in the northern mountains of Shianga," I continued. "Plenty of gold, as expected, but there was a hall that led deep into the mountain. Full of small rooms—like cells."

"Cells?" Kodan asked. "Were they occupied?"

I shook my head. "I was just the beginning. He wanted to keep queens as part of his hoard."

She snorted a stunned laughed. "How very masculine."

"There was one other woman already there," I said. "She'd been there a while, it seemed, though I'm not sure how long. Corinne. The Fae queen."

Kodan stopped dead in her tracks. "Draunar captured the Fae queen? How in the gods' names did he do that?"

"I don't know." I kept walking, following my feet toward the mountain range looming in the distance, which separated the lowlands from the coastline. "But we developed a friendship while we were in there, and then she was able to use some of my wolf-magic to open a portal so we could escape."

"A portal," Kodan said. "To Faerie?"

I nodded.

"You were in Faerie," she said, slow and disbelieving.

"She was not pleased at having been held hostage," I said. "While I was in Faerie, I was privy to some of her plans. Shianga is only the beginning. Once she's settled in her control of that nation, she's going to begin expanding her reach. I don't know when, or where she'll start, but she's not going to be satisfied with only taking control of one kingdom."

"When will that happen?" Kodan asked. "When will she attack Shianga?"

I gazed toward the mountains. "She already has."

The silence between us seemed to last for days.

"You were there, weren't you?" Kodan said.

I nodded.

"She must've had scouts in the area," Kodan said. I could almost hear the gears working in her mind. "She was waiting for the dragons to be weakened and off guard. She waited until they fought us back, while the dragons were injured and busy licking their wounds."

Again I nodded.

"Did she win?" Kodan asked. "Does Draunar live?"

"I don't know," I said. "She captured him. When I escaped, he was in the dungeons."

"Gods above," Kodan said. "The Fae queen in Shianga. I never thought I'd hear anything like it in my lifetime."

"There were moments when I thought I'd never escape her," I admitted. "She's stronger than Draunar. And she craves power—real power, not just wealth and treasure. She shouldn't be taken lightly."

"Reyna," Kodan said. "I'm sorry."

I blinked, glancing over at her. "What? Why? Because I was the one who chose to go along with Draunar's terms?"

"It never should've gotten to that point," Kodan said. "We should've pulled out of the negotiations when Draunar dared to suggest such a ridiculous thing. Elias can be so bullheaded."

"So can I," I said. "This was our first negotiation as king and queen. We both wanted it to work."

We walked in silence after that, stopping for a few short breaks for food and coffee. After spending so much traveling in my wolf form, it was nice to be on foot again, even if it wasn't quite as efficient. It helped me settle back into humanity again—into this new version of me, who wore mostly pants and boots and functional leather armor. How long had it been since I'd worn a gown? The young woman in Daybreak who had never worn a pair of trousers before would hardly recognize me at all.

After a few hours, the sun was beginning to set low in the sky as we approached the mountain pass. The air had grown colder, and snow still lingered, crunching under my boots as I walked. Kodan cast her gaze around the base of the elevation.

"We should camp here for the night." She dropped her pack onto the ground. "Better not to travel through under threat of darkness. We can continue in the morning."

"Wait," I said.

Kodan paused, hands stilling on the pack where she was about to unfasten the bedrolls.

I gazed toward the mountain pass. I focused my senses on the brisk air, the rustle of the breeze in the sparse trees. My wolf was now awake and alert.

"You sense something?" Kodan asked.

"I should shift," I said. "I could find him."

My wolf howled with delight at the suggestion, up and bounding around inside of me. The desire to shift prickled over my skin. With my canine nose, it'd be easy to find him, surely. I'd just take off, leave Kodan behind, and Elias and I could be together again.

I was a breath away from shifting and taking off into the pass when Kodan gripped my nape roughly and shook it, like one might do a misbehaving puppy.

"Do not," she hissed. "Do not shift."

"What?" I wrenched out of her grasp. "Why not?"

"Because," she said, "then you two will run off together into the wilderness, and all of Frasia will be fucked."

"I wouldn't do that," I said. But even as I said it, I knew she had a point. My wolf longed to find his, to nuzzle close, and take off away from all of this. To build a life together as wolves, free and wild in the snowy mountains of the north.

"We need to find him," Kodan said, "and get him to come back as a man, not a wolf. If you approach him as a wolf, he won't want to shift at all. He's already been living as one for too long."

I nodded. Kodan was right. In either form, I was his mate, but I wanted to meet him as a woman, and for him to meet me as a man.

"Which way?" Kodan asked.

I nodded toward the notch. Kodan left the pack in the snow and gestured for me to follow.

We clambered up the snowy slope, and my wolf longed to escape—we both knew her claws would function on this icy landscape better than my boots slipping and sliding. I crested the hill and gazed down at the narrow pass, with the quartzite mountain jutting out on either side.

In the snow along the path, I saw a pawprint.

A single one. It looked like it'd been there for a while. But it was big, bigger than an average wolf, with deep points in the dirt from the claws. I knelt down and swept my hand over it.

"He was here," I murmured. "I know it was him."

"You found a print?" Kodan dropped next to me. She looked closely at the print, then glanced around. "Here," she said. "This way."

Kodan was clearly an experienced tracker, and she led me in a hurry down the notch, where it turned and split in two. She knelt down again, then glanced up toward the pass to the right and looked over her shoulder at me for confirmation.

"Yes," I said. My wolf whined. We were close. I could sense him, his presence prickling over my senses like an oncoming storm.

Then I saw it. Carved into the side of the mountain by years of erosion was a small, shallow cave, the entrance half-hidden by a dying tree.

"There," I said. "He's there."

From the darkness, golden eyes glowed.

"Elias," I whispered.

The wolf drew back its upper lip and growled.

Internally, my wolf whined, desperate to burst forth and press close to him, to soothe the rage radiating off of him.

"Careful," Kodan said. She held out her arm in front of me, as if to hold me back. I shoved her away and took a step closer to the cave.

"Elias," I said again. I crouched down, so I was at his eye level, and my heart pounded desperately as I gazed into his familiar golden gaze. "It's me. It's Reyna."

He snarled again. I'd never seen him behave like this; even when he was in wolf form, he always moved with an easy regality, a self-assuredness. I'd never seen this cold, feral look.

"Please," I said. Was Kodan right?

Had he gone crazy?

"Please, Elias. Don't you know me?" I begged.

He lunged forward.

He moved so quickly I had no time to react. Kodan shouted but Elias easily knocked her aside with the bulk of his body as he slammed me into the ground, barely avoiding slamming my skull into a nearby boulder.

"Kodan, no!" I shouted.

Kodan kept her hand on the hilt of her sword, but stayed still, leaning heavily against the mountain.

Above me, all I could see was Elias. His familiar wolf, his pelt dark as night, his golden eyes, his teeth bared as he stared down at me. I was on my back beneath him, supine and vulnerable, but I didn't try to throw him off.

He was still Elias. He was still my husband. I didn't just believe it, I *knew* it—my wolf knew it. But I wasn't going to shift. Not until I knew he still could.

"It's okay," I whispered. I moved my fingers through the thick, coarse fur at the ruff of his neck. He was so warm to the touch. "It's okay. I'm here."

Elias' ears dropped back and he lowered his head. He snuffled at my neck and shoulder. His breath was warm, and his teeth were so close to my skin, but I didn't feel afraid. I closed my eyes and kept my arms wrapped around his neck, fingers wound tight inside his coat.

He whined, low in his chest, and the sound made my heart shatter. I clung harder to him and swallowed around the lump in my throat.

He reared back, shaking off my grasp. He snarled at me again, and then the air crackled with power as he shifted. It wasn't an easy one, done in a breath like I was used to seeing—it was slower, and looked a little painful as his human form fought its way to the surface.

"You left me," he said in a rough, cracked voice.

I was pinned by the weight of my emotions, propped up on one elbow as I drank in the sight of him. His eyes still burned gold. His hair was long, and a rough beard had grown on his defined jaw. He'd lost weight, and his muscles were starkly defined. Dirt covered his tan skin. "Elias," I said. I wanted to get closer, wanted to wrap my arms around him, kiss him, remind him who he was. Who *we* were.

"You *left* me," he snarled again.

"I had to," I said as I clambered to my feet. "But I'm back now, Elias, please—the kingdom needs you. They need *us*."

He bared his teeth. "Go."

"I need you," I said softly. I took a step closer. "Come back to me. Please."

"Go!" he roared. "You left me once. Now do it again. There's nothing for you here."

"Elias," I begged. "Just listen to me."

"Go back to the dragon."

His words were like a blade through my heart. I took a staggering step back. Something that looked almost like sadness—or regret—briefly flashed over his features, but then his expression hardened again. He shifted back into his wolf, and bounded down the pass and out of sight.

"Elias!" I called after him. I started to move after him, ready to shift and make chase, but Kodan caught my upper arm before I could.

"Don't," she said. "Let him go."

"Let him?" I asked incredulously. "How can I just let him leave me behind?"

"He'll come around," she said. "You got him to shift back. That's more than I thought he'd be able to do." She sighed and gazed in the direction in which he'd ran. "Come on. We've got to let him come back on his own terms."

She wrapped her arm around my shoulders and led me back toward the way we'd came. Guilt weighed heavily on me, and I leaned against Kodan's sturdy body.

"What if he doesn't?" I asked. I felt like a petulant child even as I said it.

"He will," Kodan said. "I saw the way he looked at you. He'll come back."

Chapter 22

We camped under the stars just outside the mountain pass. The bedroll was thin, and the frigid earth seemed to suck the heat from my bones. I longed to shift into my wolf form—at least I'd be warmer—but Kodan had cautioned against it. She still didn't trust that I wouldn't just run off with him, were we both wolves the next time we saw each other. Instead, we huddled on the same bedroll, backs pressed against each other in an effort to conserve body heat.

I slept fitfully, my wolf whining with the desire to seek out our mate, and my human self shivering from the cold. It was only the sheer exhaustion, from the journey and the emotional turmoil, that allowed me to rest at all.

At some point during the night, I slept deeply. At least for a few hours. It was a warm presence near me that allowed me to do so, familiar fur, slow breaths. I wasn't sure if I dreamed it, since it was gone before I awoke.

At dawn I roused and stoked the fire, then heated water to make coffee. As I waited for the water to boil, I huddled closer to the fire and pulled my cloak around my shoulders. My skin prickled with the memory of that heat.

Was Elias nearby? Had he not run off at all, but was just lurking in the pass, keeping an eye on me?

The thought made my lips twitch up in a small smile. I could only hope Kodan was right, that he would come back around and return to himself.

We didn't do much that day. I went back into the pass, looking for Elias, while Kodan stayed at the campsite and sharpened our weapons, mostly for something to do. We hunted—in human form—and caught enough rabbit for a stew.

That night I slept fitfully again. At least until sometime in the depth of night, when I'd finally fallen into something resembling a deeper sleep, a familiar warmth settled next to me and drew me in deeper. But the feeling was gone once more before morning could break.

Again, nothing in the pass. Again, a day spent poring over Gulde's map, just for something to do. Again, rabbit stew.

We ate sitting across from each other at the campfire. The mountains stood high and imposing, with the balds wide and seemingly endless all around us. The sun sat low in the sky, and the wind whistled, making me pull my cloak tight around my shoulders as I held my bowl of soup in shivering hands.

"We'll give it two more days," Kodan said. "Then we'll head back and regroup."

"He'll show up," I said. "I know he will."

Kodan looked less convinced, but she didn't argue.

We ate in silence.

Then, something caught my attention. What it could be I wasn't sure. A breath? A cracked twig?

Or just the mere feeling of Elias, close by?

I looked up. At the top of the mountain pass, the same hill I'd scrambled up in my boots, Elias stood in his immense wolf form.

The low light of the sunset touched his fur, bringing out the rich browns in his dark coat.

Kodan followed my gaze. "Shit," she murmured. "Guess you were right."

Elias padded down the hill and approached the camp slowly, ears back and tail low. His hackles were up, but he was moving defensively, like he expected us to lash out at him. It was all I could do not to leap to my feet and rush toward him with my arms open.

His nostrils flared as his eyes flickered to the pot on the fire. I pressed my lips together, hiding a smile. I should've known the stew would be the thing to lure him out of the mountains.

At the edge of our campsite, he glanced between us, and then shifted back into his human form.

"Ugh," Kodan said. She reached into her pack and grabbed a cloak, then tossed it at him. "It's cold. Make yourself decent."

Elias said nothing, but did wrap the heavy cloak around his body.

"There's stew," I said, gesturing toward the pot. "Plenty of it." My voice was quiet. I felt like I was talking to a spooked animal, like if I said the wrong thing, he'd run off again.

Still silent, he took a seat by our campfire, and accepted the heaping bowl I handed to him.

I tried to touch his knee. He pulled away.

Each rejection made pain and guilt flare in my chest. But I knew what I felt was nothing compared to the pain he'd felt when I'd left with Draunar. I tried to tamp down my emotions. My guilt wasn't what was important here. I had to fix what was between us—so we could keep our kingdom safe.

Ours. Together.

"I had help escaping from the dragon's hoard," I said.

Elias' gaze flickered to me, then returned to his food.

"I wasn't the only queen the dragon was interested in. He had another locked away. The Fae queen."

Elias didn't look up, but his fingers flexed around the bowl.

"She's taken control of Shianga, now," I continued. "She overpowered Draunar after he had been weakened by the wolves. She'll come for Frasia next."

A low growl sounded from his throat, an uncontrolled noise. At least I was getting through to him.

"If I had known what Draunar meant, Elias, I never would've—"

"Stop," he growled, low. "I don't want to hear it. Not now."

I wanted to keep pressing, to force him to listen to me, but we were equal in our stubbornness and I knew I wouldn't get anywhere. But he'd said not *now*. Which meant maybe he'd be willing to listen to me soon. I clung to that shred of hope as we ate our stew in silence.

Once he was finished, he shifted back into his wolf form and settled down by the fire. His golden gaze lingered on me as I settled onto my own bedroll onto the freezing ground. I wasn't going to get any sleep tonight, that much I knew—not with Elias so close, yet so far away. Under the starlit sky, I pulled my blanket up around my chin and tried to keep my teeth from chattering.

It wasn't long before I heard Elias stand up. He padded around the fire to me, and settled down at my side, his immense furry back pressed to mine through the blanket. The heat from his huge, muscular body flooded through me as I wiggled closer, pressing on him as much as I could. It staved off the worst of the cold.

He'd been doing this every night. Keeping me warm. Watching over me.

I wanted to roll over and bury my face in his fur, slide my hands over his familiar body and breathe in the soothing animal scent—but I also knew I couldn't press my luck. I didn't want to ask for too much. Right now, this was enough. Proof that he still cared about me, despite his fury. I matched my breathing to his and eventually fell into sleep.

When the dawn's sunlight woke me, Elias was no longer lying at my side. He had stoked the fire, and was dressed in clothes I'd assumed were pilfered from Kodan's pack: plain slacks and a quilted shirt similar to the one I was wearing, with his cloak folded and set aside. I sat up, shocked to see him still here. He raised one eyebrow at me, and the expression was so playful and familiar my heart clenched to see it. I'd missed him. I'd missed him so much it was like an aching wound, and being so close, but still having so much distance between us, was worse than being apart.

Kodan woke up with a groan as the sunlight fell over her face. She pushed the heels of her hands into her eyes and sat up, then looked just as surprised as me to see Elias. "You stuck around?" she asked.

"Is what Reyna said about the Fae queen true?" Elias asked.

I put coffee on the campfire as Kodan began to pack up the campsite. "I haven't independently confirmed anything," she said. "I only know what Reyna told me. I've been a bit busy with the happenings in Efra."

Elias' expression hardened. "What happenings?"

Kodan sighed. "What exactly did you think would occur when you ran off like that?"

"What?" Elias asked. He stoked the fire. "Something wrong?"

"You weren't thinking at all," Kodan said. "You went too deep into your wolf."

"Kodan," I said quietly, as I interrupted their conversation by handing her a cup of coffee.

She glanced at me, then closed her eyes briefly and sighed. We both knew this wasn't the time to start to prod at Elias' motivations, regardless of how irritated she was with his behavior. She'd have time to chew him out later.

"The court wasn't exactly comfortable with your taking off like that," she said. "Comparisons were made."

"Comparisons?"

"To your father."

His hands stilled, and his pupils narrowed as they stared into the flame. I said nothing, though my wolf whined with the desire to leap to his side. He didn't know I knew. Seeing him push down the memory, without being able to do anything to support him, made my heart ache more.

"Who was making those comparisons?" he asked. "The duchess?"

"Of course," Kodan said.

Elias grimaced.

"It wasn't just conversation, though," she said. "She called on Rodthar of Daybreak."

"She summoned that mutt?" Elias snarled. "After everything he did?"

"The court agreed to install them as king and queen," Kodan said. "I only got word from a soldier in Efra still loyal to you. I would've stopped it otherwise. Tensions are high in the city, it seems. I don't believe most of the citizens support the current leadership, the soldiers certainly don't, but there's no one to step in."

"There is now," Elias said, low. "Daybreak will not lead Frasia. Not under that man." Finally his eyes met mine. "And you," he said. "You will remain loyal, as a wolf of Nightfall?"

"Of course," I said in a small voice. It felt like a blow that he even had to ask. Yet I understood why. I could only hope that when we had a chance to be together, to be alone, I could make him understand why I'd gone with Draunar, too. It was a mistake, but one I'd made trying to protect Frasia. We put our nation first. We both did. Surely he would understand that.

I had to hope he would.

"We'll go to Siena," he said gruffly. "Summon the wolves that are still loyal to Nightfall. We'll have to move swiftly, before Daybreak gets too settled in Efra. We'll have to strike soon and remove Rodthar from the throne by force. Let the wolves of Frasia know that the king does not let treason go unpunished."

Again his gaze slid to me. A shudder ran through me—treason? Surely he didn't consider my agreement to Draunar's terms *treason*. "Elias, please, can we just—"

"No," he said sharply. Then he softened minutely, the tiniest amount of tension leaving his expression. "No. We have to focus. Siena isn't far, if we move briskly we'll be there before sundown."

As if proving his point, he doused the fire.

"Sir," Kodan said in agreement. She threw the rest of her coffee back and we quickly took the rest of the campsite down. By the time we'd packed the site up, Elias was already heading east across the balds.

Kodan hiked the pack high onto her shoulders. "Of course he didn't even offer to carry anything," she grumbled.

"Why Siena?" I asked. "Why not back to the outpost you were at?"

"Siena's a little bigger," Kodan said. "We're likely to be able to gather some reinforcements there."

"We'll be expected?"

"No," Kodan said, "but Elias and I grew up there. If there were any wolves that would back us now, it's those in Siena."

"Your hometown," I said.

"From there we'll send messengers," Kodan said, "have everyone meet in Siena. I can only assume Elias is already developing a plan."

I nodded. I just wished he'd let me be a part of it. All I could do was watch the familiar breadth of his shoulders as he led us across, not even sparing a look back.

Chapter 23

Just as Elias had said, the rough-hewn wooden buildings of Siena appeared on the horizon before the sun had fallen. It was larger than the outpost in which I'd found Kodan, but it was less a town and more of a village. The perimeter was surrounded by a rough wooden fence, made of tree trunks cut free of their branches and sharpened at the top. Under the thatched roof of the lookout tower, a woman leaned out curiously.

"State your purpose," she called.

Elias stood in front of the gates and grinned up at the lookout. Kodan and I stood behind him. My feet ached from the hike, and I was tired down to my bones. It was like the consistent ache in my heart, like a fresh bruise, was making my exhaustion more impossible to ignore than ever.

"Elias of Nightfall," he said. "I've come to speak to your pack leader. And hopefully break bread."

The lookout gasped and clapped her hand over her mouth. She ducked down in the tower, and then the wooden gates slowly began to crank open. They only opened just enough for us to slip through, and then closed immediately behind us.

"Thank you," Elias said, clapping the lookout on the shoulder.

She stared at him wide-eyed. She looked no older than fifteen. "Your Highness," she said. "We—I—I'll announce your presence."

"Relax," Elias said with a warm smile. It was a kinder expression than I'd seen since I'd coaxed him out of the cave. "I grew up in this town. No need for any theatrics."

The lookout was still stammering as she led us through the narrow streets of the village. As we walked, people peeked out of the taverns and houses and shops, murmuring to each other with expressions of awe and delight. Siena was small but charming, made up of functional wooden buildings with the same thatched roofs as the lookout tower, a few with stone facades and carvings of wolves. It looked old—old and sturdy, like it had been here for many years, and would be here long after its current inhabitants were gone. Kodan sighed as she looked around.

"It hasn't changed at all since we were kids," she murmured. We passed by a tavern, and Kodan nodded at it. "That's where I got drunk for the first time. I was nine."

The main street terminated at a stone building with a low, arched doorway. It was quieter than the rest of the town, and inside, it was dim and warm despite the cold weather. A fire roared in the hearth, and in front of it, an older man in plain but well-tailored canvas clothes was in deep discussion with a man in worn leather armor.

"Thaddeus," the lookout said. "I apologize for interrupting, but—"

"There's the old man," Elias said. His booming voice echoed around the stone room.

The older man stood up, eyes widening as he strode across the floor. The heels of his boots cracked on the stone. "Gods strike me where I stand," he said with a shake of his head. "King Elias." He smiled at the lookout. "Thank you, Hela," he said. "Take the news of Elias' arrival to the house. See what kind of dinner we can pull together on short notice."

The girl nodded and hurried back out under the arched doorway.

"That's not necessary," Elias said.

"Certainly it is," Thaddeus said with a grin. Then he turned his warm gaze to me. "This must be Queen Reyna," he said. He took my hand in his own strong, callused hand and squeezed. "Word of the Choice traveled far. It does appear the king has chosen well."

"Honored to make your acquaintance," I said with a nod.

"And my finest general, Kodan of Nightfall," Elias said. He pointedly did not confirm nor deny Thaddeus' comment on the Choice, but it was just pleasantries.

"One of my own is with me here," Thaddeus said. "General Artin. We were discussing the happenings in Efra. I assume that's what brings you here to Siena."

"Will you retake the throne?" Artin said, low, from his seat by the fire.

"I will," Elias growled. "I did not win the throne from Daybreak only to have the duchess return it."

"Good," Artin said. "The Nightfall wolves of Siena will stand behind you. But you know our numbers are small."

"We've sent word to Starcrest and Duskmoon," Kodan said. "If you can assist me with messengers, we can have the reinforcements come here, to prepare an assault on Efra without Daybreak's knowledge."

"Ah, and that's why you've come here as well, is it?" Thaddeus said.

"It's convenient," Kodan said with a smile. "Your falconers are things of legend."

"Legend seems a bit strong," Thaddeus said. "My servants will take you to the falconer's hold."

She turned to Elias. "And after that, Your Highness?"

"Go to Efra," he said. "Remain hidden. Gather what information you can safely. Don't stay long—I need you to help prepare."

"Sir," she said.

She hurried out of the room, guided by Thaddeus' servant.

"Come," Thaddeus said. "I'll show you to the guest quarters. You can rest and clean up while we're preparing dinner. Discussions of strategy will be a bit easier once we've all had some wine, don't you agree?"

Artin nodded demurely. Thaddeus led us up a narrow staircase to the second level of the building. The ceilings were so low, Elias had to duck his head to keep from knocking against the rafters. At the end of the hall, Thaddeus pushed a heavy wooden door open and gestured for us to step inside. There was already a hastily built fire burning in the hearth, and the covers of the simple bed had been turned down. Obviously the servants had worked in a hurry. The bed called to me—after so many nights on the ground, or in a cot, or a freezing bedroll, a straw-stuffed mattress with a thick cotton comforter appealed to me more than any royal silk sheets.

"I'll send word up for dinner," Thaddeus said. "There's some whiskey tucked in the built-ins, should you need to lift your spirits before."

"Thank you, Thaddeus," Elias said. "Your kindness is deeply appreciated."

"Of course," he said. "No less for the true King of Frasia."

Thaddeus closed the door behind him.

Finally, in the tiny guest bedroom with its low ceiling and crackling fire and cool stone floors, we were alone.

Elias stood in front of the fire, shoulders square and his gaze fixed on the flickering flame.

I wrapped my arms around myself. Even with him so close to me, I'd never felt so alone. "Elias," I said. "Please talk to me."

"What is there to talk about?" he snapped. His voice was cold and stiff with restrained anger. "You left me. You chose Draunar. And I had been foolish enough to think that what was between us was real." He shook his head, laughing softly.

"I had to," I said. My voice rose in desperation. I had to make him understand. "I had to, Elias, with his terms—"

"I believe you called our marriage a 'practical arrangement?'" he said. "Isn't that right?"

I snapped my mouth shut. After all that had happened, I'd almost forgotten what I'd said in order to force Elias to let me go. I *had* said our marriage was just a forced agreement—a practical decision. Not rooted in love.

That had been true, at the start. But things had changed.

"I didn't mean it," I said meekly.

"Then why would you say it?" He whirled to face it, golden eyes blazing. "You chose him so easily. Hardly any hesitation. How am I supposed to trust you? How am I supposed to call you my queen when you are willing to abandon me at the smallest obstacle?"

"In what realm was that a small obstacle?" I shot back. Frustration was beginning to clash with the guilt in my chest. "He was threatening to bring dragons to Frasia. To kill our subjects. And we were just supposed to let that happen? For our own comfort?"

"You are naive," he said. "It was never that simple."

"What other option did we have?" I asked. "I couldn't let war come to Frasia."

"And yet it did," he said coldly.

Shame, guilt, anger, all blended together, icy and nauseating. "You did that," I said. "Not me."

"Because you are my queen!" he roared. "You expected me to stand by while that beast hauled you into the sky like a common cow picked up for prey? You imagined there was any way I would accept that? That I would live happily in Frasia with some other wolf, with the image of your body in Draunar's claws burned behind my eyelids?" Pain leaked into his voice. He scowled and looked back toward the fire, as he rubbed one hand roughly over his face.

"I just wanted to do what was right for our kingdom," I said. "What other option did we have?"

"There are always other options," Elias said. "*That* is why you are naive. It is never so black and white. He was threatening us, certainly, and complicating negotiations, but there are always other avenues. Negotiations are not choosing a dress from a handful of options—it's weaving a tapestry. It's complicated. And you threw out all the work we'd done when you accepted his ridiculous terms."

I bit my lower lip. I had felt so righteous when I had made that decision. I'd felt like a strong, serious queen. A queen willing to sacrifice for her people. A queen who would do whatever it took to do the right thing. But through Elias' eyes, it was shortsighted. Foolish. Again, we weren't working as partners—we were working separately, but side by side.

"How was I supposed to know all of that?" I demanded. "You didn't include me in the negotiations at all. If I had known what your method was, what *our* method was, I wouldn't have felt so cornered when Draunar proposed the terms."

"Diplomacy is not an immediate privilege," he said. "It takes time to learn."

"You should've told me that, too."

"I should've done a lot of things. But even so, how can I trust you after this?" he asked. "How can I know you won't leap at the chance to leave me again?" The rage had finally melted from his gaze. Now, there was only hurt in his expression, as if now in the relative safety of Siena, he had allowed himself to feel his betrayal.

I stepped closer. When he didn't move away, I carefully set my hand at his upper arm and slid my hand to his shoulder. He shivered slightly under my touch, and his eyes fluttered closed.

"You're right," I said softly. "I never should've agreed to his terms."

He exhaled hard out of his nose.

"I didn't see another way," I said. "I was afraid—afraid it would escalate to war if I refused. I didn't think there would be fighting *because* I agreed. I thought—I thought we would both put Frasia first, and accept the conditions."

"Putting Frasia first does not mean sacrificing ourselves," Elias said. "It never has."

"You make it sound so easy," I said.

"What?"

"Being the leader." I set my hand at the joint of his neck and shoulder. My wolf was purring at being this close—at finally connecting with him. Even if I couldn't soothe his pain just yet, at least we were starting to understand each other again. "I was doing what I thought was right. I realized how wrong I was when I ended up in his hoard."

"I thought I'd lost you," Elias admitted. He said the words with his jaw clenched, like it hurt to even admit the fear. "I thought you were gone forever. I didn't see a way to lead without you at my side. I couldn't see past my own pain. I just ran." He shook his head slightly. "If I had known the duchess would call on Rodthar—"

"And if I had known Draunar wanted me for his hoard, not as a diplomat," I said, "we both would've made different choices." I sighed softly. "Elias, I'm sorry."

His brown eyes, flecked with gold, met mine. My heart beat hard in my chest.

"I'm sorry," I said again. "I never wanted to leave you. I fought my way out of Draunar's cave because of it. I fought my way back to you."

Elias' brows pulled together. He closed his eyes again and then bared his teeth briefly, an uncontrolled response, like being this close hurt.

I wrapped my hand around his nape and pulled him down for a kiss. Even if he couldn't forgive me, or even fully understand me, I knew from the pain in his eyes that he still cared about me. Loved me. And I loved him, too, even though I'd left him alone in Shianga.

His lips met mine. Softly at first. Just the barest touch of my lips against his, and for a moment the stiffness made me think he might pull back and shove me away.

But then it was as if something inside him snapped. He growled low and possessive in his chest, then wrapped his arm around my waist and hauled me flush against him. His other hand raked through my hair; he kissed me so hard I bent back with the force of it. I wrapped my arms tightly around his neck and moaned into the kiss, a sound of desire and relief both. My wolf was just as pleased as I was, close to the surface, heightening the sensations. It felt like it'd been years since I'd kissed him. Now I couldn't get enough, chasing his lips, deepening the kiss, even nipping at his lower lip.

He growled again when my teeth set into him, and this time we were pressed so close I could feel the vibrations rolling through me. Desire settled low in my hips. It'd been so long since I'd felt this way. It licked over my skin like delicious flame. I whined at the sensation, a wolfish sound, and that only made Elias dig his fingertips harder into the muscle of my waist. He wanted this just as badly as I did.

Our wolves were right at the surface, reaching for each other, heightening the sensations. My whine then morphed into a bright laugh as he hauled me toward the bed and tossed me onto it. I felt my back hit the straw-filled mattress with a whump, but all my exhaustion melted away under the heat of his gaze. I met it steadily, my lips slightly parted as his stare traveled hungrily over my body. I felt vulnerable, and exposed, but desired, too—and I wanted him just as badly as he wanted me.

"Come here," I said, reaching for him. "I missed you."

He exhaled hard, then crawled onto the bed on top of me, his knees straddling my thighs, his forearms bracketing my head.

"I missed you too," he said, so quietly I almost thought I imagined it. "I'd thought I'd lost you forever, Reyna. I thought when he took off with you, I'd never see you again."

"I'm here," I said through the tightness in my throat. I wound my arms around his neck.

"You chose him," he said again, half in despair and half in disbelief. "You chose him, and I was never going to see you again."

"Elias," I said again desperately, then pulled him into another burning kiss.

I didn't know how to explain any further what I'd done. Even if Elias understood logically why I'd gone along with Draunar's terms—that didn't mean his heart could accept it. I could feel the hurt radiating off him, and my wolf whined internally at the sensation. Words wouldn't fix it now. He met my kiss with equal intensity, kissing me like he'd never get a chance to kiss me again.

Maybe part of him still felt that was true. His wolf still felt betrayed, abandoned. I'd told him I wanted him—told him I'd made a mistake. I had to show him, too. Had to make his wolf believe me when I said I wasn't leaving again.

I slid my hands under the hem of his shirt and over the skin of his back. I pulled it up and over his head, revealing the sinewy, tan plane of his chest, dusted in dark hair. I slid my hands over the curve of his shoulders, drawing my nails gently over the skin. He dragged his mouth hungrily over my jawline, then my neck, then down to my shoulder where he could reach over the hem of my shirt. The scrape of his beard was a delicious contrast to the softness of his mouth, an unfamiliar sensation, but it heightened the pleasure all the same. His breath rushed hot over my skin, and each kiss made the need spike inside me as I pressed my fingertips into his muscles.

Desire coursed through me like magma, burning hot, melting my coherent thoughts away. All that was left was desire, want, need, *Elias.*

He set his teeth against my neck and bit down, not hard enough to break the skin but hard enough that the sudden sharp pressure made me gasp and arch my back, pressing my breasts to his bare chest. He exhaled hard against my skin, then shoved his hands under my quilted shirt and wrestled it off, freeing my breasts too. Elias began sliding his hand up my torso, up to cup my breast. He squeezed gently, smoothed his thumb over the hardening nub of my nipple, and I moaned into the kiss and the delicious sensation.

I needed more. I couldn't get close enough. I gripped his hips, then the hard curve of his erection in his slacks. Just the feeling of it, thick and hard in my palm, made me gasp into our messy kiss. I squeezed; his length twitched. He groaned, then nipped at my jaw, neck, and shoulder, in animal desperation.

"Please," I said. "Need you, Elias."

Elias reared back, just enough to gaze down at me with his eyes burning gold. His lips were slightly darker from kissing, swollen, framed by his rough beard. There was a high flush on his cheeks, and his black hair stuck to his temples with sweat. He looked wild. I felt like prey beneath him, and it felt good. I wanted to submit to him—to show him I meant it when I said I wouldn't leave him again.

He wrestled me out of my slacks, so I was nude beneath him, my center already throbbing with desire. I squeezed my thighs together, still a little shy so exposed under his heated gaze. That made him hum a laugh low in his chest, and my ears burned hot. I turned my head against the mattress, eyes fluttering closed.

"Don't hide," he growled. "Look at me."

I bit my lower lip, then turned back to meet his gaze.

"Good," he said. He slid his hand over my belly, delicious pressure that made me squirm, and then gripped my thigh and tugged my legs apart. I gasped, gripping his upper arm hard. He exhaled hard, eyes landing between my legs, where I was already wet and ready for him.

"Gorgeous." He traced his fingertips gently up my inner thigh, then slid two fingers against my pussy, not pressing inside but just sliding over my wet folds. I gasped, moving my hips down toward his hand as pleasure licked up my spine. It was overwhelming, but still not enough, just slow steady pressure that had me rocking my hips to match it.

"Please," I begged. "I need you."

Elias swallowed my repeated pleas in another kiss, wet and messy, tongue and teeth clashing. He shoved his pants down just enough to free his length, and as much as I wanted to get my hands on him, my *mouth* on him, I didn't want to stop kissing him. I hooked one leg around his waist and sighed more needy pleas into his mouth. He slid the wet head of his cock over my folds, teasing me until I was dizzy with pleasure and anticipation.

Then, after what felt like an eternity but was in reality only the space of a few breaths, he pressed inside me. The slow push of his hardness into my body had me breaking the kiss to throw my head back, moaning around an exhale. He dragged his lips over my neck, licking and biting as he slowly slid inside until his hips were pressed flushed against me. The sweet pressure of being filled was so good—I hadn't realized how much I missed it. How much I needed it.

"Please," I said. "Please, move."

Elias hummed. He gripped my hips as he withdrew his length slowly, then moved back inside. The slide was so good. So slow. So not enough.

"More," I said as I clung to him. I wrapped my arms around his neck, keeping him pinned close to me. His breath washed over my neck as he began to move—really move. He pulled out and thrust back in deep and steady, building a fast, animal rhythm that made the bedframe shake with the force of the moment. Each deep thrust pulled a small sound from inside me, rhythmic *ah ah ah*s I couldn't seem to stifle even with my face pressed into the crook of his neck. He held tight to my hips, keeping them tilted up so his pelvis pressed right against my sensitive clit with each deep thrust. I lost myself in the sensation, caught on the wave of pleasure.

"Elias," I gasped against his neck. "Yes—like that—"

He growled, only holding me tighter and fucking me faster. Pleasure built and built inside me, molten-hot, and my whole body tensed and pulled, as taut as a bowstring. Elias rolled his hips just right, and I cried out as my orgasm rolled over me like a wave. The feeling ran from the cradle of my hips all the way to the crown of my head and my toes, wiping out all other thoughts as I clung to him.

As the intensity subsided, I slumped against the mattress, held up only by Elias' strong hands on my hips. He thrust into me a few more desperate times, faster and shallower as he chased his own pleasure. He stifled his groan into my skin as he thrust deep inside me, then pulled out and came, spilling hot stripes of his seed across my hip.

Then he slumped down on top of me, his body warm and heavy. It felt good to be covered by him. Safe. I scratched my nails through his hair gently as we caught our breaths. I tipped my head against his, my eyes fluttering closed as we held each other quietly. We stayed like that for a few long moments, then to my dismay Elias exhaled hard and sat up.

"No," I whined. "Don't go."

He smiled, then swept the sweaty hair off my forehead and kissed me again. Soft and sweet this time. "We'll get stuck together."

"That wouldn't be so bad," I teased.

He stood and walked to the basin in the corner of the room, then returned with a dampened washcloth. He cleaned me up, his touch gentle and tender—so tender it made me want to burst into tears. I just wanted everything between us to be fixed.

If only it were so easy.

He put the washcloth away, and then sat at the edge of the bed, feet flat on the floor. Some of the tension had returned to his shoulders. I petted at his lower back. "What is it?" I asked quietly.

"Draunar took you to his hoard," Elias said.

"Yes," I said. "It was only me and the Fae queen."

"Tell me." He looked over his shoulder at me, his deep brown eyes concerned, with a furrow in his brown. "Did he force himself on you? Ravish you? Or..." His nostrils flared. "Did you sleep with him willingly?"

"No!" I said. I sat up, staring at him wide-eyed. "Of course not. He made it clear that's what he wanted, but I refused him. I would never. *Never.*"

Except for the kiss.

I could keep it a secret. I could take it with me to my grave. There was no way Elias would ever find out, with Draunar locked up in the dungeon under Corinne's hold and likely not long for this world.

But I didn't want to. I didn't want to build our relationships on secrets. I'd already hurt Elias so badly. I had to prove I still trusted him. I had to be honest, even when it terrified me.

"What?" Elias asked. "What are you thinking about?"

"When Corinne was preparing the spell to escape the cave," I said, "I had to sneak into Draunar's room while he was asleep, to get two of his scales."

I scooted back on the mattress, my back against the headboard, knees pulled to my chest. Elias still sat on the edge with his gazed fixed on me as I spoke, those great hands gripping his legs.

"When I was leaving, he woke up. I couldn't let him see the scales, so I told him I was just…checking on him. That I wanted to see him."

Elias nodded.

"He invited me into his bed. I told him to wait until he was better rested, since he was so injured and exhausted. Hoping to the gods that the spell worked so I wouldn't have to see that promise through." I propped my chin on my knees. "He demanded a kiss, and I gave it."

"You kissed him," Elias growled.

I nodded. I couldn't meet his eyes.

"That foul beast," he said. Rage radiated off him in waves. "I can only hope the Fae queen keeps him alive so I can slaughter him myself for what he did."

"Can I ask you something?" I asked.

The anger was still palpable in the air, but he nodded.

"When I was in his room, I had a knife on me," I said. "To pry the scales he was shedding off. And when I was done and I had them, there was a moment when I had the knife in my hand and I realized I could slit his throat. Right there. I was trying to decide if I could do it, but then he woke up."

Elias said nothing.

"What should I have done?" I asked. "What's worse? Would it be easier for you if I had slit his throat in his sleep? Or kissed him to escape?"

Still he was silent, his eyes fixed on me.

"Had I killed him, Corinne and I would've escaped immediately," I said. As I calculated what would have happened next, the implication dawned on me. "The wolves would've still been in Frasia."

They would've been there, still battling to take the castle, worn out and nearly pushed back—and Corinne would've emerged and stomped on them like ants.

"Why did you hesitate?" he asked. There was no anger in his voice, just curiosity.

"I'm not an assassin," I said. "I'm a fighter, but I'm not an assassin. I don't know, I just—I wasn't ready. I didn't consider it until I was standing there with the knife in hand. If he hadn't woken up, I think… I think I would've. So answer me." I pressed my lips together. "Would you have preferred that? For me to have murdered the dragon king in his sleep?"

Elias took my wrist, peeling my arms away from where it was wrapped around my knees. He tugged me forward, maneuvering me until I was straddling his lap, my thighs astride him. I kept my hands at his shoulders as he held my waist, gazing up into my face with grave, gold-flecked eyes.

"I would've," he said.

Something in my heart shattered. I wasn't sure what I wanted—did I expect him to tell me I'd made the right decision? I wanted to defend myself, to say it would've been wrong to kill the king like that: dishonorable, cowardly. But perhaps it was more cowardly to let him live. More dishonorable to kiss those lips.

I expected Elias to grow frustrated again, but he just leaned close and put his lips on my neck.

"Killing with purpose is not something to be done lightly," he said. "It changes you."

"I was afraid," I whispered to him. His lips felt so soft on my neck, so possessive. He pressed his teeth there too, gently, like a shadow of a bite.

"I am a warrior," he said. "My queen should be a warrior, too. But that takes time."

I closed my eyes, face still tipped to the ceiling. Worse than his jealousy was the sense that I'd disappointed him. That he would've been thrilled to know I'd slit the king's throat.

I wanted to be that queen. I wanted to be strong, and diplomatic, and independent, and fearless when need be.

"I will be," I murmured. "I promise, Elias, I will be."

His grip tightened on my waist. I wasn't sure if he believed me, but some of the tension had left his body. He kissed me, a soft kiss on my sternum, close to my heart.

"Come," he said. "We should get ready for dinner."

The meal that evening was boisterous: full of laughter and beer and simple, filling food, braised lamb and dark bread and potatoes roasted to perfection. It was dim and loud in the room, with wolves seated and laughing along the wooden benches, with me tucked by Elias' side. Even though the town was unfamiliar, it felt like home here. I knew things weren't completely settled between us, but the foundation was there. It was good to see Elias smile and laugh, and let me wipe the beer froth from his upper lip. The warmth in the room, and in his eyes, was enough to make me believe that we'd make it through this.

Somehow.

Chapter 24

The next morning we rose early, with the sun, and made our way down the stairs to the main room of Thaddeus' home. The table was still laid out from dinner before, but now only Thaddeus, his general, and the servants were there. It was strange to see attendants eating at the same table as their leader, but things were different in Siena.

Elias and I had just taken our place at the quiet table to partake in coffee and warm oatmeal sweetened with honey, when a youngster pushed open the door, flooding the room with early morning light.

"Sorry, milord," the boy said, "there's word from Efra."

He stepped out of the way, and Kodan loped through the door in her immense wolf form. Her coat was dirtied, and her paws were coated in mud, leaving tracks as she walked with her head held low. Her eyes were bloodshot. She looked exhausted.

"General," Elias said. "Is everything all right?"

Kodan padded to the table, then exhaled hard. She shifted with some effort back into her human form. Her leather armor was dirtied, and her hair was pulled back into a tight, functional plait. She all but collapsed into a seat at the table with us.

"Did you run all night?" I asked.

One of the servants stood and fixed her a bowl of oatmeal and a mug of coffee, which she accepted with an exhausted, grateful sigh.

"I did," she said. "It's worse than we expected."

"What do you mean?" Elias asked.

"Rodthar has not just taken the throne," she said. "He's made the manor into a fortress. It's as if he's brought all of Daybreak with him. There are guards swarming the place."

"I see," Elias said coolly. "He's expecting retribution."

Kodan nodded. "There's no way we can get into the castle. Not without a lot of help, and not without killing a lot of wolves."

"The reinforcements are coming," Elias said, "but a man like Rodthar won't hesitate to throw his guards on their swords if he must."

"I must admit," Kodan said, "If what Reyna said about Corinne is true, I don't think we should risk our forces fighting the Daybreak guards."

"Nor do I," Thaddeus said. "The wolves of Siena are strong, but few in number. I won't lead them into a slaughterhouse."

"No one is going into a slaughterhouse," Elias snapped. His eyes flashed gold as frustration radiated off of him. I set my hand at his knee under the table and squeezed reassuringly.

"There's another way in," I said.

Kodan raised her eyebrows. "Into Efra?"

"No," I said. "Into the manor."

Elias relaxed minutely, and nodded. "We don't need to fight through all the guards," Elias said. "I only need to get to Rodthar. Just as my father did."

"The tunnel?" Kodan asked. "I thought that was a myth."

Elias shook his head. "It was safer to spin it as a myth," he said, "rather than let others know about the access."

"You snake," Kodan said with a slow grin. "I can't believe you never told me. You told Reyna?"

"No," I said, smiling, "I found it."

"Ah, so you're a snake too," Kodan teased. "A match made by the gods."

"You mean there's a way inside?" Thaddeus asked. "Without alerting the guards?"

"It might still be guarded," Elias said. "Rodthar might know of its existence. But even if it is—it won't be defended nearly as well as the rest of the city. I will not hesitate to strike down a few wolves to regain my rightful throne."

"How do we get in?" Kodan asked. "Is it just a way to move around the manor?"

Elias looked at me expectantly.

I looked at the table in front of me, and then closed my eyes. With a steadying breath, I tried to recall the map I'd studied when I was planning on breaking Griffin out of the dungeon. The tunnels that wound through the map of the manor like veins, and then one that went from the dungeons to the north wing and straight out. I could see it there, the illustration of the exit of the tunnel deep in the forest.

"Do you not know?" Kodan asked.

Elias said nothing.

Was this a trial perhaps? My lips quirked into a small smile as I focused my memory on the image of the map. At least this was one test I knew I could pass.

"The entrance is in the forests northwest of Efra," I said. "On the east side of the Lake Argoen, below the mountain range between Efra and the old pack lands. There's an outcropping of rocks on the west side." I remembered the illustration on the map, three immense boulders pushed together. "The entrance is below them."

"Lake Argoen?" Kodan asked. "That's barely two days' journey."

"I'll take a small convoy to the tunnel," Elias said. "We'll get into the manor that way. The rest of the soldiers, those of Siena, Duskmoon, and Starcrest, will wait outside Efra, camping in the woods and hidden from view. I'll take care of Rodthar myself. Once he's dead, I'll call for the reinforcements to come into Efra and clear out the remainder of the Daybreak guards. I expect they won't have much reason to fight back once their king is dead."

"Simple as that," Kodan said.

I swallowed. Nothing was ever that simple with my father. "I'll come with you," I said.

"No, you won't," Elias said. "I need you here. I need you safe."

"I won't stay here and wring my hands while you go to Efra," I said. "I need to be at your side."

"Come," Elias said. "Let's discuss this privately."

"Your Highness—" Kodan started.

"It'll be just a moment," Elias said coolly. "Get some rest, General. We have a long few days ahead of us."

He stood up, and nodded for me to follow. I brought my mug of coffee with me, following behind him, trying to walk with the easy confidence of a queen and not show any of the imbalance I felt.

Outside, he led me to the side of the building. I thought he was taking me to a private room, or something like that, but instead we just ducked into the narrow alley, kicking up dust on the rarely trodden path. He leaned heavily against one of the barrels stacked against the stone wall, half-sitting on it, and then pressed his fingers into his temples.

He looked exhausted. I realized then why he wanted to step away—he didn't want Thaddeus or Kodan to see him like this. Not before we were planning to strike at the heart of Daybreak.

I rubbed my free hand over his shoulder. He sighed, then looked up at me with a small furrow in his brow. "Reyna," he said, "must you make this so difficult?"

I risked a small smile. "What do you mean?"

"Coming with the convoy through the tunnels," he said. "You should ride with Adora and other reinforcements. As soon the deed is done, you can come into Efra. Once it's safe."

"You know I won't do that," I said gently. "It's my father—stepfather—who has taken the crown. I won't sit back and let him try to take the kingdom again. He'll stop at nothing."

"I know that," Elias said. "I don't want you there when I do what I must."

"Which is what?" I asked. "Kill him for treason?"

Elias nodded. "Regardless of how you feel about him now, no woman should have to see the man who raised her slaughtered."

"He didn't raise me," I said, my voice hard.

Elias looked up, curious.

"He barely spoke to me," I said. "I was never good enough for him—never ladylike enough, too opinionated, too cold. Barion is the one who raised me. The duke always seemed like he didn't want anything to do with me." I chuckled, but there was no humor in it. "I guess that much was true."

"You'd see him pay for his crimes?" Elias asked.

"I'd do it myself," I said. "If given the opportunity."

Now it was Elias' turn to chuckle. He set his hand at my hip and tugged me in between the open spread of his legs. Then he took the mug of coffee from my hand and took a sip. I huffed in faux indignation.

"Would you actually?" he asked.

I knew he was thinking of the cave, of my hand wrapped around the knife, hesitating as I looked down at Draunar.

"I would," I said. "With you at my side. Knowing it wasn't just for my revenge—but for us. For Frasia. I would. Without hesitation."

"Spoken like a warrior," he said. He set the mug of coffee aside and pulled me down again to kiss me gently. "I still want you to stay here."

"I still won't."

He sighed. "Somehow I knew this is how this would go."

"Do I need to remind you how our sparring went during the Choice?" I teased.

He hummed. "It's a fond memory of mine."

"I will be an asset," I said. "I know those tunnels the best of all of us."

"I should order you to stay behind," Elias said with a small smile, "but I have a feeling you'd find a way around that."

I bit back a smile. "Would you rather me come with you, or sneak into the tunnels on my own?"

"You're impossible," he said with a fond shake of his head.

The bright clang of a heavy bell rang through the quiet morning. We broke apart and hurried back to the front of the building. "Reinforcements!" a lookout called from atop the tower by the gate. "Reinforcements have arrived!"

The gate swung open, slow and heavy. Two white horses trotted through first, in shining steel armor with pale blue detailing. Even from this distance, I'd know that white-blonde hair anywhere. Adora led a battalion of Starcrest wolves, marching in step behind her.

Thaddeus hurried out of the arched doorway. "Starcrest," he said. "Duskmoon won't be far behind."

The horses approached, then nickered as they came to a stop in front of the building. Adora leaped off her white mare.

"Adora," I said, "it's so—"

"Reyna," she cried, and threw her arms around my neck. The force of her hug nearly knocked the wind from me, and I grinned as I returned her affection. She pulled away and touched my face, looking dangerously close to tears. "I wasn't sure if I'd ever see you again. I was so grateful when the hawks sent word."

The man astride the second white horse stepped off, landing heavily on the dusty earth. He was tall, taller even than Elias, broad-shouldered and dressed in steel armor inlaid with moonstone. A broadsword hung on his hip, with a cloak trimmed in furs of the same color hung on his shoulders. His face was lined with age, crow's feet and laugh lines, but his expression was stern. He had short dark hair and the same blue eyes as Adora.

The same blue eyes as me.

The same nose. The same wide shoulders. The same high cheekbones.

"This is my father," Adora said. "Lord Ealric of Starcrest."

"Your Highness," he said. "It's an honor to finally meet you."

I was stunned to silence. He looked so much like me—was it possible? I looked to Adora, but she only pressed her lips together curiously.

"Ealric!" Thaddeus said gregariously. "Come inside, please, you've had a long journey. I'll have Artin take your men to the barracks. This way, this way. You as well, Elias, we have much to discuss."

Elias nodded to Adora and me, and then followed Thaddeus and Ealric.

"Adora," I said quietly, "do you think—"

"Lady Adora?" Kodan stepped out of the building, still looking exhausted, but a little better than when she'd arrived, after a meal and some coffee. She smiled broadly at Adora. "How was your journey?"

Adora flushed slightly. "No trouble whatsoever. We were grateful to receive word from the hawk at the right moment."

"Good," Kodan said. Her gaze lingered on Adora. "It's rare I see you without your finery," she said. "It suits you."

Adora flushed harder and smoothed out the heavy canvas of her riding gear. "Please, it's just for functionality—"

The bell sounded again, and Adora whipped around, clearly grateful for the distraction. "Duskmoon was close behind us," she said.

Whatever curiosities I had about Adora and her father would have to wait.

The gate opened again, and Duskmoon marched in on foot. Fina led them, with a general at her side. The Duskmoon battalion was dressed in leather armor and thumped their fists against their chests rhythmically in greeting. Fina bounded up the road, and her general rolled his eyes, as if used to this, before jogging after her.

"Reyna!" she shouted. "Adora!" She flung her arms around both of our necks, pulling us in close. "I'm so glad to see you both. I was so worried." Then she pulled away and nodded to her general. "This is my aunt, General Sida."

Again Thaddeus stepped out and welcomed Duskmoon, then sent the battalion to the barracks and welcomed Sida into the main room. With some reluctance, Kodan stepped back inside as well.

"Come," I said, "we'll get breakfast. There's much I need to catch you up on."

We ended up in the kitchens, seated at a small wooden table in the corner while the servants fried more bacon and cracked more eggs into the cast iron on the immense fire. They didn't seem to mind us, and I was happy to let Elias catch the generals of Duskmoon and Starcrest up on our plan to take back Efra. I caught them up on everything—my time in Draunar's hoard, Corinne's takeover of Shianga, and now Daybreak's opportunistic coup in Efra.

"Do you really think this will work?" Fina asked. "Going through the tunnels?"

"It's the best option we have," I said. "We've been hurt enough by battling Shianga. I don't want us to lose any more wolves trying to fight through the soldiers of Daybreak to get to the duke. If we can take out the duke first, Daybreak will fall back." I nodded to myself. "I know they will."

"How do you know?" Adora asked.

"The duke has lost sight of the pack," I said. "First he sent me to Efra, where I promptly dropped all affiliation with the Daybreak pack—surely that wasn't good for them."

"I got word of some surprise in the court when that happened," Adora confirmed.

"Then he lost another wolf to a failed challenge, and now he's trying to take Efra through a connection with the Duchess of Nightfall. The wolves of Daybreak must know Elias will return."

"It's well-fortified," Fina said, "according to the Duskmoon scouts. But yes, there's a sense of... Anticipation. Nervousness."

"The duke has proven himself rash and impulsive," I said. "Daybreak would be better served by a different leader."

"Like who?" Adora asked.

I sighed. "That I don't know." I thought immediately of Barion. He was a loyal man—foolishly loyal to my father, but a good man at heart. I wondered what he might do if my father were removed from power. If he might be willing to lead the pack.

I pushed the question aside. That could be resolved later. What was important now was removing the duke from this farcical takeover. Elias was still the true King of Nightfall—and I was still his queen. Somehow. Against all odds.

In the tunnels under the manor, I'd prove it.

Chapter 25

Two days later, I stood on the west side of Lake Argoen, as the sun dipped low in the horizon. We'd set up camp on the banks of the lake—just those of us who would be going into the tunnels for the initial push. Elias would lead us, with Kodan at his side, then a handful of the finest wolves of Siena, Duskmoon, and Starcrest. There would be a few wolves between Elias and me. It was a compromise I was willing to make to be a part of the initial convoy.

"You ready for this?" Fina asked as she sharpened the edge of her short sword.

I'd been surprised when Fina had insisted on coming, but I hadn't tried to talk her out of it. She was just as stubborn as I was. Adora was with Sida and Thaddeus, leading the rest of the battalion to the woods outside Efra to lie in wait until the king called for their presence.

"More than." I had my own steel armor from Siena's barracks, a sword on my hip, and determination in my heart. I was ready.

At the edge of the lake, Elias fastened his bracers over his forearms. He was in leather armor, for ease of movement, with a sword on his back and a small knife at his hip for use in close-quarters fighting. He'd shaved his face and tied his dark hair back. He was deep in conversation with Ealric of Starcrest, who had traded his polished ceremonial armor for studded leather as well. His jaw was set, gaze hard as he talked with Elias.

I'd never seen him like this—war-ready, with his wolf close to the surface, but still in possession of that regal air about him. It was different than when he moved around the manor in Efra, on his own turf. It was different than when he was alone and wild in the mountains. It was almost like I was seeing his true self for the first time—all of the roles he played coming together to make up the man.

He finished his conversation with Ealric, then looked over like he could feel my eyes on him. Heat shot through me; I held his gaze a little unsteadily. Things still felt delicate between us, like we were on opposite sides of a frozen lake, trying to make our way over cracking ice back to each other.

He strode over. Fina glanced up, then muttered an excuse about getting a few more knives as she shoved her sword back in its scabbard. I was grateful for the imagined privacy as the rest of the soldiers readied themselves around the campsite.

"Reyna," he said. "You're certain about this?"

I smiled gently. "Of course I am," I said.

He nodded. I knew he'd prefer that I stay with Adora and the rest of the soldiers in the forests outside Efra, but we both knew that wasn't going to happen. "Remember," he said, "I'll be at the front—"

"And then Ealric and Kodan behind you, and then the soldiers of Siena, and then Fina and me," I interrupted. I set my hand at his shoulder and tugged him closer. "I know."

He sighed, then set his hands at my waist and pulled me almost flush against him. "Be careful," he said. "Stay safe."

I kissed him briefly, like a promise for later. "I will if you will."

Elias laughed, low and private between us, then flashed me that familiar wolfish grin. My heart did a somersault. He squeezed my hip fondly, and then stepped away.

"Wolves of Nightfall," he said. "Today you are all wolves of Nightfall."

The soldiers looked up from their tasks and hooted in agreement.

"Prepare to move out," he said. "We'll traverse the tunnels under cover of darkness. The traitor will be dead before dawn."

More hoots and howls of agreement and thrill. It wasn't much of a speech—but these wolves didn't need much encouragement. These were the finest wolves Frasia had to offer.

The outcropping of boulders by the lake concealed a pit, which contained a simple wooden ladder descending into the depths. Elias went down first, carrying a single torch. Then Ealric and Kodan, a few more wolves, and then finally Fina and myself.

As I descended, nerves began to crawl up my spine. The tunnel was strangely familiar, deeply dark and rough-hewn, with only the flicker of Elias' torch ahead to illuminate the path. The light cast the soldiers ahead of me in shadow. I crept quietly behind them, feet soft on the dirt.

The tunnel stretched for what felt like miles. I had no idea how long I walked for, quiet and tense with nerves. It must've been hours. Finally, we stopped walking where the tunnel suddenly narrowed.

"We're close," Elias growled, low, to the wolves behind them. "I can feel wolves' presence. Where does this lead?"

I stepped closer. "The dungeons," I said quietly. "There's a secret door in one of the storerooms."

Elias nodded gratefully over his shoulder at me, then he told Ealric, "Stay close."

At the dead end of the tunnel was a rough-hewn, dusty door. It didn't take much work for Elias to pop the lock with a small knife and slowly, slowly, he pushed it open.

I held my breath, but there was no reaction. As it had said on the map, the room behind the entrance was dark and quiet. But with the door in the tunnel opened, sound from the dungeons filtered in: the drunken idle laughter of the guards, the crackle of a fire, the rattle of chains.

Energy and anticipation rustled over the soldiers. Ahead of me, the wolves widened their stances and drew their weapons. At my side, Fina exhaled slowly and withdrew her own sword, too.

I drew mine. The weight of the short sword was a small assurance. But there was no turning back now.

Elias shouldered the storeroom open with a roar.

Ealric was right behind him, and then the other wolves rushed out of the storeroom. For a long moment I was pinned by my nerves, my feet feeling as if they were nailed to the dirt path, as the remaining soldiers rushed around me, gnashing their teeth with their weapons drawn. The laughter in the dungeon was replaced by shouts and growls as the clanging of steel on steel filtered in.

At my side, Fina looked as terrified as I felt, her short sword shaking in her hand.

"For Frasia," I whispered to Fina, but also to myself. "And for Nightfall."

I rushed into the dungeon.

Inside was chaos. Battles raged around me, drunken soldiers swinging their axes sloppily at the wolves as they dodged easily; one struck a soldier in the temple right in front of me and the man collapsed into a heap. In the cells, Nightfall wolves yipped and howled, slamming their great wolf shapes against the bars like they could break free. The room smelled of vomit and blood, and the heat made sweat break out across my forehead.

In the center of the room, Elias dragged the sharp edge of his knife across a soldier's neck. He spun to the side and the man collapsed into a heap. He bared his teeth, growling, his eyes savage with anger as he whirled onto the next guard that dare approach him.

"Fall back," he snapped at me, eyes blazing. He drove his foot into a guard's chest, sending him clattering back toward the cells. "Wait by the door. It isn't safe here."

He planted his foot on him and sneered down, knife in hand as he put enough pressure on the guard's chest to make him wheeze and scrabble uselessly at Elias' ankle.

Behind him, a short, stocky guard buried his blade in the chest of one of the Sienan soldiers. The wolf crumpled to the dungeon floor, and the guard, invigorated, dragged his blade from the body and then whirled toward Elias. His eyes blazed with rage as he lifted the bloody blade again, shoulder height, ready to drive it into Elias' back where he stood over his fallen enemy.

I didn't think at all. It was pure animal instinct that guided me as I charged forward, sword drawn, and clanged my blade against his before he could strike. The guard bared his teeth at me and shoved forward, trying to set me off balance, but I easily shifted my weight, then ducked to the side. I pulled my sword with me, swinging it at an angle to knock the guard's weapon out of his hand. Then, still moving with muscle memory and pure instinct, I drove my blade into his ribs.

It was a sequence I'd learned from Barion ages ago—parry, rebalance, redirect, strike. It worked beautifully. The guard groaned and staggered back, hand on his gushing wound, and fell to the ground.

There was no guilt that ran through me, no question, no lack of certainty. I gripped my sword and took a step closer to Elias, blade up, prepared for the next attacker.

Maybe in Draunar's cave, I learned I wasn't an assassin. But I *was* a warrior.

"I won't fall back," I said.

Elias huffed a small, surprised laugh, but said nothing else.

Soon enough, we'd dispatched with most of the guards. Ealric rounded up the ones that weren't dead and shoved them into the cells after the Nightfall prisoners were released. One of the prisoners was a young soldier, no more than eighteen; his eyes blazed yellow when he shifted back into his human form.

"What was your crime?" I asked.

The young man pulled the clothes and armor off one of the guards and put them on with no hesitation.

"Loyalty to the true King and Queen of Frasia," he said. "I'm honored to fight alongside you."

"Are there others?" I asked quietly. "Are the wolves still loyal?"

"Of course," the young man said, looking at me with his brow furrowed, like he couldn't believe I'd asked at all. "Rodthar only cares about his own power. Not about anyone in Efra. We've been waiting for the king to return."

I nodded. The young man's gratitude sent a rush of adrenaline through me. We'd made it into the manor—now we just had to make it to the man who was once my father.

"Which way?" Elias asked as we approached the other side of the dungeon. "How do we get into the throne room?"

"I can get us back to the quarters I stayed in when I was part of the Choice," I said. "That's the only part of the system I know."

Elias nodded. "That's enough. That's close enough. Wolves—this way."

I led us out of the dungeon to the secret door I'd found when I'd first snuck down here with the intention of freeing Griffin. This time, I was just behind Elias and Ealric as we moved up the long, gradual incline of the tunnel. Fina and Kodan followed at the back of our small battalion.

Finally, we reached the heavy door. The familiarity was strange, almost unnerving, standing here in the tunnel with a bloodstained sword in my hand and Elias at my side. The last time I stood at this door, all I wanted was to leave Efra behind. I'd thought I'd be starting a life anew, traveling with Griffin, leaving all the demands of court life behind. And now here I was, the Queen of Frasia, breaking *in* instead of out.

This was where I was meant to be. At Elias' side. Defending our kingdom from the man who had tried—and was still trying—to take everything from me.

No more.

Carefully, Elias pushed the door open. It swung slowly open, thankfully silent, and Elias crept into the hall first. I stepped out after him.

In the hallway, a servant girl stood with a stack of sheets folded, her eyes wide as dinner plates. Elias stood still, one hand raised in a show of peace. We both looked a state—sweaty, dirty, covered in blood, with gore on our blades as well. Not exactly the king and queen this servant was used to seeing.

I half-expected her to drop the laundry and run screaming, alerting the guards of our presence. But she just curtsied as best she could with the sheets in hand.

"Your Highness," she said. "Welcome back."

Elias nodded. "Thank you," he said delicately, like he was still unsure how this girl would react.

She cleared her throat. "The Duke of Daybreak enjoys an evening nightcap about this time in the throne room," she said. "With the duchess. He won't be expecting you." Her lips curled up in a tiny smile. "I'll be in the kitchens if you need anything. As will the rest of the servants."

"Thank you," Elias said. "Do stay there until you hear summons, please."

She nodded, then hurried out of the hall.

"Ah," Elias said with a wolfish grin. "It's good to be home."

The rest of our battalion crept into the hallway.

"Kodan," Elias said, "take Fina and half the wolves through the west corridor to servant quarters behind the throne room and lie in wait. I will go with Ealric and the others through the main hall and meet Rodthar of Daybreak."

"I'm coming with you," I said.

To my surprise, Elias nodded in agreement. "Good," he said. "You should show him the woman you are now."

We crept through the halls with just a few wolves behind us. No guards roamed inside—I supposed most of them were outside, flanking the entrances to the manor and the city alike, expecting Elias' dramatic, enraged return. The inner chambers had been left undefended as well. A few servants still moved through the halls, finishing up their evening tasks, but none sounded an alarm. Those who saw us only bowed their heads in greeting, looking shocked but almost delighted.

We approached the throne room from the side. Ealric peered around the corner. "Two guards," he whispered. "One bored, one almost asleep."

"Dispatch them quietly," Elias said to two of the wolves. "Don't let them sound any alarms."

The two soldiers nodded, then glanced at each other and shifted into their lean, dark animal forms. With teeth bared, they leapt around the corner and onto the guards. It was remarkably quiet—a clunk and a clatter as bodies hit the floor, and then a cut-off sound of pain as the wolves' jaws closed around their throats.

"Now," Elias hissed.

He shoved his shoulder into the immense ornate doors of the throne room and stormed inside, teeth bared and eyes blazing gold. He had two knives, one in each hand, blood staining his armor and his wolf's power crackling on his skin. I followed behind him, my own wolf gnashing her teeth close to the surface, ready to explode forth if necessary. His rage fed my own anger—it tamped down my fear and made my blood run hot and hungry.

The throne atop the dais was empty, but an immense, ornate table had been brought into the room. Rodthar and Duchess Alana of Nightfall sat side by side near the center of it, the duchess with a glass of deep red wine and Rodthar with a whiskey. Alana looked just as stern and horrible as she had during the Choice, and the duke looked as pleased as a cat after a successful mouse hunt. He looked surprised for only a moment, before he stood up, drained his whiskey, and strode around the table.

"Elias," he said, voice dripping with faux warmth. He was dressed more casually than I'd ever seen him, in a plain linen shirt and slacks due to the late hour, a light robe hanging off his shoulders. "You've returned, I see. I was so certain we'd lost you to the woods forever."

Then his gaze cut to me. He didn't mask his openly disdainful sneer in the slightest. "I expect *this* has something to do with it." He spat the word out like it tasted bad in his mouth.

"What?" I shot back. "I am the rightful Queen of Frasia."

Daybreak guards emerged from the side doors, stumbling like they'd just been woken from a nap. Rodthar cast them an irritated look, then held a hand up to hold them back. Behind us, our battalion of wolves bared their teeth at the guards, ready to strike if necessary.

"You were supposed to be a little treat for the King of Shianga," he hissed. "How in the gods' name did you end up back here?"

"What?" I asked. My rage was shot through with confusion. "How do you know about that?"

Duchess Alana sighed and took a sip of her wine. "Did you really think we were uninformed of the negotiations in Shianga?" she asked. "Of course we had to keep an eye on things ourselves, too."

"In what way, *Duchess*?" Elias hissed. He spoke the title with such vitriol—I couldn't imagine how it might sound if he had called her 'mother.'

"Frasia belongs to Daybreak," Rodthar said with cold venom in his voice. "Your father took the throne from us dishonorably, and went crazy for his trouble. I've known since the first day I laid eyes on you that the craziness ran in your blood too. Frasia needs stable rule. Not the violent, impulsive leadership you've shown."

"You've aligned yourself with this fool?" Elias roared as his mother. "You've turned your back on your pack?"

"There was a test," Rodthar said, "one you failed."

"What fucking tests?" he snarled. "What did you do?"

Duchess Alana sighed again, then leaned forward, elbows on the table like this was a casual dinner conversation, and not an argument between two wolves about to tear out each other's throats.

"I'd hoped it wouldn't turn out like this," she said, in a tone that suggested she had hoped for just that. "But Rodthar was right, when he said you wouldn't be able to take it."

"You planned it," I said. The pieces began to come together in my mind. "The same as you planned the coup with Griffin. You nudged Draunar."

"Just slightly," Rodthar said with a grin. "He's a man who likes pretty things. It wasn't a grand plan. It was just a small message, sent to him during the negotiations. A suggestion that if he were to add the queen to his hoard, then the new King and Queen of Frasia would be more than happy to allot some territory to him at the border as a show of good faith. No treaty required." He sucked his teeth. "But it appears I overestimated Draunar. He'd assured me it was impossible to escape the hoard."

"Rodthar suggested the loss of your pet would drive you to craziness," Alana said. "And a wolf prone to craziness is not fit to lead. Simple as that. I thought it was a ridiculous claim, but he was correct. How quickly you lost control of your senses and fled your responsibility. You are an embarrassment to Nightfall."

"I will not be dressed down by traitors in my own kingdom," Elias growled with his teeth bared.

Rodthar sighed. "This really is such a disappointment. I'd hoped for a two-birds-one-stone situation, where I'd be rid of my waste of a daughter. Since you were too weak to do your duty to Daybreak, it'd be best to just be rid of you."

I was shredded. Nausea roiled my stomach. It wasn't just Draunar who'd wanted me—the man who had raised me also hated me so much he wanted me kidnapped. What kind of man could feel that way about a child he'd reared? How could the duchess have agreed? How could so much hatred drive those two? So much hunger for power? My hand shook where I gripped my sword.

"If you think yourself worthy to lead Frasia," Elias growled, "prove it. I challenge you for the throne."

Chapter 26

"A challenge?" Rodthar asked, eyebrows raised. "You would challenge me?"

"I slaughtered the last wolf you sent to challenge me," Elias said. "And I'll do it again."

"Griffin was a weakling," Rodthar said with a roll of his eyes. "I was a fool to think he would be able to handle such a request."

"Then accept," Elias growled. "I challenge you. Right now. Right here."

"I accept," Rodthar said. "On one condition."

Elias said nothing.

"We fight as wolves," Rodthar said. "As is traditional."

I balked. No one else seemed as surprised as I did. Elias seemed pleased, and Ealric beside me was nodding with agreement. Even Fina looked relieved. They all knew Elias was strongest when he'd shifted.

Why would Rodthar of Daybreak suggest a battle in wolf form? Growing up, I'd always been taught that shifting was uncouth. It was something that must be done, but should be kept in check when it wasn't necessary. It was savage. It was feral.

Maybe, I realized, it was something I wasn't supposed to have.

Power.

The wolf form was power.

Was Rodthar totally comfortable as his wolf? Had he gone running whenever he wanted? Was he connected with his animal in a way I was just developing now?

Had he done this intentionally? Cut me off from her? Kept me weak and unsure, ignoring her?

I was too stunned to even feel any anger. I was frozen in disbelief. All this time, he had led me to believe that a good citizen of Daybreak kept things on a tight leash. Internally, my wolf whined in frustration, and my hackles lifted.

Elias grinned. "I accept."

Rodthar waved his hand instructively, and the few Daybreak guards in the chamber moved to the edges of the room. Elias stepped toward the center of the throne room, feet silent on the polished floor. The rest of the Nightfall wolves moved as well, creating a wide ring around Rodthar and Elias as they faced each other. I stayed where I was, near the door, and Duchess Alana crossed the room and stood at my side.

She said nothing, but I realized this was part of the ritual. Only one of us would be queen, as only one of the men in the center of the room would be king.

Ealric locked the front doors and took his place at Alana's other side, and stood with his hands clasped behind his back. The Daybreak guards locked the doors on either side. If Kodan wanted to get in, she'd have to break the entry down herself, which I didn't doubt she was capable of doing. But still, the click of the lock made nerves shiver up my spine.

A tense silence fell over the room. The hair on my forearms stood up as power crackled through the two men. They bared their teeth at each other, then paced in a slow circle, sizing each other up in human form.

Rodthar shifted first. His wolf burst forth, and as it did, smoothly and effortlessly, I realized I hadn't seen him like this since I was a little girl. He was a huge wolf, bigger even than Elias. His pelt was a deep, chocolate brown, and his eyes burned bright like copper. He shook out his hulking body, then laid his ears back and bared his sharp teeth in warning.

Elias' wolf sprang forth at the same time. His eyes burned golden as he stared at Rodthar, hackles up and head low. He kept his gaze on Rodthar, but didn't bare his teeth—he was assessing. Despite the rage I'd felt radiate off him, when it came to battle, he was always tactical. He wasn't going to do anything impulsive, not until he saw how Rodthar fought in his wolf shape.

They loped in a circle, sizing each other up, and then Rodthar growled and launched forward, jaws open, ready to close around Elias' neck.

Elias ducked low, rushing forward beneath Rodthar, dodging his attack. Rodthar's back legs caught on Elias' body, knocking him off balance, and he landed on the floor of the throne room with an unsteady thump. His immense paws skittered on the slick floor and it took him a moment to regain his balance. It wasn't nearly as ferocious as the battle was in the arena, with the dirt floor easy for wolf paws to dig into—it was almost humorous for a moment, before Rodthar righted himself.

Rodthar snarled, a ferocious, wild sound, and then lunged at Elias again. This time, Elias was ready to meet him. They met in violent clash of muscle and teeth, growling and spitting in range. I steeled myself, resisting the urge to step backward away from the fighting. It was terrifying being so close—seeing every ripple of muscle, hearing every snarl and heavy breath and clack of bone as they snapped their jaws. Equally matched. Equally enormous. I clutched the hilt of my sword in an attempt to stay grounded and steady, watching expressionless, as Duchess Alana did.

They wrestled like that in the center of the room, up on their back legs with the front limbs wrapped around each other. Elias slammed his head against Rodthar's, teeth bared; he tried to get his jaws around Rodthar's ear, neck, snout, wherever he could reach. He couldn't get a hold, though, not with Rodthar blocking each attempted bite with one of his own.

Then, Rodthar heaved himself forward, using his weight advantage to stagger Elias a few feet back. Rodthar managed to get his jaws around Elias' shoulder; Elias yelped and clawed at Rodthar's head, but Rodthar was able to hold his grip. He hurled Elias to the ground with a grunt.

Elias' side slammed against the floor; he rolled onto his back, briefly vulnerable. I held back a small gasp of fear. Rodthar moved to pin him, but Elias was too quick, he rolled over and jumped onto his feet. Enraged, Rodthar lunged forward again, rearing up onto his back paws with a snarl.

Elias was expecting him. He closed his jaws hard around Rodthar's front leg, sinking in deep. Rodthar howled in pain as blood poured from the wound, staining Elias' teeth and snout. Rodthar dislodged him and staggered back, injured paw curled away from the floor, but then he rushed forward and slammed the bulk of his body against Elias'. The injury to his leg hadn't slowed him down at all. If anything, it'd only made him angrier.

Beside me, the Duchess Alana didn't react at all. Her gaze was narrowed, focused intently on Rodthar, as if judging his performance. It was a stark contrast to the way I felt—my wolf howled internally, hungry to leap forward and jump in, to protect my mate from Rodthar's rage.

This time, Elias wasn't quite quick enough to dodge. Rodthar pinned him on his back, but Elias was able to slam his front paws roughly against his face, preventing him from biting him. Then Elias drove his back paws hard into Rodthar's belly, forceful enough to throw him off, giving Elias enough space to scramble back onto his feet.

Again they lunged forward, meeting in the center of the room on their back paws. The air was thick with the dense smell of exertion, of animal, and the ground was wet with blood, dripping from the wound on Elias' shoulder and the punctures in Rodthar's front leg. This made Rodthar's attack unsteady He jerked forward, jaws open to get around Elias' neck, but this time when he shifted his weight, the slickness of blood on the floor made him lose his balance.

Elias knocked him to the side, and then crashed on top of him like a wave. Rodthar tried to shake him off but Elias was too fast. He closed his jaws around Rodthar's shoulders, and then, with a strength I hadn't seen, jerked Rodthar's entire body down hard, slamming his head into the floor. Rodthar howled and thrashed in a wild attempt to throw Elias off, but Elias had him pinned down.

In the arena, when Elias had battled Griffin, this was when he had given him a chance to submit. To escape defeated, but with his life intact.

Elias offered Rodthar no such respite. He tore into Rodthar's throat with feral ferocity, his sharp canines ripping through his flesh and pulling out muscle in a gruesome, visceral display. The wound was deep, vicious, and Rodthar's whines melted into gurgles as blood drained from his body.

Rodthar's body twitched and fell still.

Dead. He was dead.

Elias planted his foot on the unmoving corpse and then tilted his head back, letting out one low, sonorous howl. The sound echoed in the throne room, and around the ring of spectators, the Nightfall wolves beat fists against their leather armor in a show of loyalty.

My heart felt frozen in my chest. I hadn't processed it, still—that Rodthar was dead, that Elias had won, that I was once again the Queen of Frasia. I was still staring at the heap that was once my stepfather, the blood pooling under Rodthar's body, spreading out across the polished floor.

Then, a cold hand wrapped around my wrist and wrenched it behind my body. Duchess Alana caught me in a skilled, tight hold, her chest to my back, and pressed a small, thin blade to my throat.

"Elias!" she screamed, shrill and pained and right in my ear.

Elias' golden eyes widened. He immediately shifted back into his human form, in his bloodstained leather-armor, his eyes still wild. "Reyna!" he called.

I grasped Alana's forearm where she pressed the blade to my neck. The cold metal bit into my throat, a tiny pinprick of pain, and I felt drips of warm blood rolling down my neck.

"No," Alana hissed. "I want him to watch. He took the love of my life, and now I'll take his."

I gasped. I had to do something, slam my foot into hers, something, anything to try to get out of her hold before she could draw the knife across my throat with Elias watching. Her breath was hot and rancid, her grip painfully tight. Every labored gasp of my breath stung now from the sharp edge.

"You failed Nightfall," Alana spat at Elias. "You failed me. At every turn, you failed to choose the right bride in the Choice, you failed in Shianga, and now you have failed to return the crown to the true king. I will not be relegated to the shadows, forced to stand by and watch alone as you drive this kingdom to ruin. This mutt has distracted you from your duties—from what really matters—and now I will—"

Her voice was cut off, interrupted by a screech of pain. Her knife clattered to the floor in front of me, and I wrenched out of her grasp. I stumbled forward, losing my balance; I hit the floor with a gasp, catching myself on my hands. I crawled backward, whipping around to look up and ensure she wasn't about to drive her weapon into my back.

Alana stood with her mouth agape. A small trickle of blood flowed from the corner of her mouth. Her hands twitched by her side.

Behind her, Ealric twisted the knife he'd driven into her back. His eyes blazed with rage and care, teeth bared in a wolfish snarl. He pulled the blade out of her back with a wet sound, then shoved Alana away. Her knees shook as she crumpled to the floor.

"Treasonous bitch," Ealric hissed. "The true king has returned."

Elias surged forward and wrapped his arms around me before pulling me to my feet. I leaned heavily against him, indifferent to the blood staining his leather armor. He then pulled back just enough to peer down at the thin wound on my neck.

"It's nothing," I said.

He smoothed his thumb over the wound. It was so shallow the bleeding had already ceased. It was barely a cut at all. But the truth of what could've happened weighed heavily on me. He kissed me gently at the corner of my jaw, then my lips, then my forehead. I clung to him, suddenly exhausted as the adrenaline began to drain from my system.

"Your Highness," Ealric said.

Elias pulled away, but kept me close with an arm around my waist.

"I apologize," he said, then bowed deeply. "I reacted instinctively, but knowing now—"

"Do not apologize," Elias interrupted. "You did what had to be done to protect the queen. For that I am grateful."

His fingertips pressed hard into my side, and he carefully kept his eyes away from the body of his mother crumpled on the floor. The pain he was feeling must've been similar to my own ache: the knowledge that it had to be done, the hurt of being betrayed, and still the unavoidable grief of losing the one who raised you. Regardless of what Rodthar had done, who he really was, there was still a childlike part of me that mourned him. I wondered if Elias felt the same.

We couldn't talk about that now, though. Not when there was still work to be done.

"Unlock the doors," Elias said. "Nightfall wolves, take the Daybreak guards to the small dining hall. Those who pledge loyalty to Nightfall will be spared. If you choose to maintain loyalty to the traitor Rodthar, you will be dealt with accordingly." He said all this briskly, like it was more irritating than troublesome.

"I see that went well," Kodan said as she hurried in. She wrinkled her nose at the sight of the wolf in a heap on the floor. "Simple enough."

Elias rubbed his hand across his forehead before squaring his shoulders. He turned to me again, his arm still around my waist. "Are you all right?" he asked. His voice was low and private. My world narrowed to just him again, for a moment—just us.

I nodded. I was stunned by everything that had just happened, but physically, I was okay. I was still standing. The reality of what had just happened hadn't hit me yet. It was like it had happened to someone else, in a dream.

"Stay here," he said. "I'll announce my return to the city and dispel the rest of the Daybreak guards. It won't be long."

Again, I nodded. All I could think was: *we did it. It's over.*

For now.

He kissed me again briefly, then with some reluctance stepped away. "Kodan!" he said. "With me."

Side by side, Kodan and Elias each took one of Rodthar's back legs. They hauled his body toward the doors and then out of the throne room, out to the gates of the manor. I intuitively knew what they would do then: they'd drag the body out of the manor and leave it dropped at the front doors, so all the Daybreak wolves would know of Rodthar's death.

"Deal with this," Ealric said to the remaining guards, gesturing at the duchess' body.

Fina rushed to my side. "Are you all right?" she asked. Her eyes were wide and concerned. "Are you hurt?"

"I'm okay," I said, offering her a small smile. "Really."

"Come," she said, "let's go to the kitchens, get you something hot to drink while the king sorts out the details tonight."

"Okay," I said. That sounded nice. A cup of tea, maybe a bite to eat—anything to kill the time and settle my nerves while I waited for Elias.

Fina took my upper arm gently, ready to guide me to the kitchen, when Ealric said, "Wait."

I paused and looked over my shoulder.

"Can I speak with you for a moment, Reyna?" he asked.

Fina raised her eyebrows.

"It's okay," I said to Fina. "You go ahead."

"I'll have something sent to your room." As always, she said it like a promise, and I nodded gratefully. Ealric guided me out of the throne room and through the back doors, to the hallway behind the dais—away from the mess of blood and the soldiers cleaning up the bodies. I followed him to a small balcony overlooking the woods behind the manor. It was nearly dawn, and the sky was turning gray with the approaching sunrise. The air was chilly, and I shivered a little as sweat cooled on my skin. But the crisp air felt good in my lungs, and the familiar tree line grounded me.

Ealric leaned his elbows on the balcony railing and looked over the horizon. "You must understand," he said, "I never knew about you."

"What do you mean?" I asked.

"When your mother was..." He swallowed. "When she left Starcrest, I didn't know she was pregnant. I'm not sure if she did, either." He turned and looked at me, his blue eyes hard with determination. "If I had known, I would've come for you. I want you to know that."

I said nothing. My heart clenched at his words. What would that have been like, I wondered? If someone had swept in and taken me away from Daybreak when I was still just a girl? If I had grown up in Starcrest? Would I be the woman I was today? Would I have been a part of the Choice? Would I have ever met Elias?

It was pointless to imagine the possibilities. Even trying to picture that life was too much for my exhausted mind to grasp.

"I hope we can have some kind of relationship now," he said. "I know you and Adora are close. Almost like sisters."

The word hung in the air between us. *Sisters.* She really was my sister. Before, I'd thought maybe, possibly, we were distantly related. But it was just an idle dream. Half-sisters. It felt unreal.

"So I hope—"

"Lord Ealric," I said, "I— I can't have this conversation right now."

He straightened up. "Of course, your Highness. I don't know what I--"

I held up my hand, cutting him off again. "I— It's not that I *don't* want that. Just. I need some time."

"Certainly," he said.

A sonorous howl rang through the night. It was Elias, sounding his cry to all the wolves still present in Efra, announcing his return and his victory. Kodan's howl joined his, and then more and more wolfsongs rang in beautiful unison. The sound sent goosebumps racing up my arms to my nape, and I longed to shift and join them.

"The king is back," Ealric said with a grin. "Come, I'll escort you to your chambers."

Chapter 27

Ealric left me with a bow at the entrance to my chambers. To my relief, our quarters were miraculously undisturbed—kept just as we'd left them.

Amity and Rue were there, waiting in the room, with a meal covered on the small table. My heart soared when I saw them as I close the door behind me.

"Your Highness," Amity said, moving to sweep into a curtsy.

I rushed forward and wrapped my arms around them both, pulling them both into a hug. Rue squeaked in surprise.

"Thank the gods you're all right," I said.

"We were so worried about you," Amity said. "Word traveled that Elias returned, but we didn't know—it's been so awful here with Daybreak taking control."

"I'm sorry," I said. "I'm so sorry. So much has happened."

"There's nothing to apologize for," Rue said. "We're just glad you're home safe."

I pulled away and smiled softly, but gratefully, at the girls.

"Lady Fina had a meal sent up," Amity said, "and there's a hot bath in the ensuite, and—"

"Thank you," I said. "Please go get some rest."

"But, Your Highness, you've just returned!" Rue said.

"I know," I said. "The king will be here soon, too. I'm sure you heard him."

They both nodded.

"Thank you for taking care of the quarters," I said.

The girls curtsied, and then with some reluctance, left me alone in the big room. I was relieved to see they were okay, and just as relieved to have a moment of privacy.

I managed to eat a few bites of the hot soup the girls had left for me, then padded into the ensuite and cleaned up as best I could, before sinking into the hot bath the girls had left for me. It was strange to be back in my quarters, alone, in the quiet. The bath reminded me uncomfortably of the chambers in Draunar's cave, so I didn't soak for long. I changed into soft linen lounge clothes, and returned to the soup, sipping at the broth as I gazed out the window toward the brightening sky.

I still felt distant from myself, unreal, like the events of the past few weeks had happened to someone else. How was it possible that I was standing safely in this room? How was it possible that the man who raised me had tried to steal the throne? That the duchess' blade had been at my throat just a little while ago? And that just days before that, I'd been a hostage of the Fae queen, and before that, a relic in Draunar's hoard?

I wasn't sure how much time passed as I stood at the window. The sky turned golden with the dawn and the soup cooled to a lukewarm temperature in my bowl. I was about to give up, crawl onto the welcoming mattress and try to sleep, when finally, *finally*, the door opened.

I turned from the window.

Elias stepped over the threshold. The King of Frasia.

My husband.

In the privacy of our quarters, with his exhausted gaze meeting mine, the numbness finally cracked like ice inside me. I dropped the soup and barreled forward, threw my arms around his neck, and pulled him close to me. He hummed a low, surprised sound, then embraced me just as tightly. I didn't care about the dirt, the sweat, or the blood still flecked on his skin. At least he'd lost his armor somewhere along the way. I buried my face in the side of his neck and inhaled deeply. He smelled like home.

"Elias," I choked out. My throat was tight, and tears burned hot behind my eyes. This time, I didn't try to hold them back. I let the sob tear itself from my throat as I slumped against him, trusting him to hold me up.

"I'm here," he murmured. He kissed my temple and just held me, his strong arms wrapped around my body as grief and exhaustion poured out of me. It was a catharsis eased by the rhythmic, smoothing motion of his hands up and down my back.

Eventually, I cried myself out, and then pulled back and rubbed my eyes. "Sorry," I murmured. "You must be exhausted."

"Reyna," he said. "I'll always be here for you. No matter what."

I took his face in my palms and looked at him. Really looked at him. I was trying to commit his face to memory again, the gold-flecked depths of his brown pupils, the crow's feet at the corners of his eyelids, the stubble along his strong jawline.

"I'm sorry," he said. "I'm sorry about your father."

"He's not—he *wasn't*—my father." Still, tears welled up in my eyes again. "You shouldn't be sorry for what you had to do. He deserved it. He deserved worse, for everything he did to me, and for his treason."

Elias said nothing. He just kept holding me close, his hands on my waist. He was patient while I gathered my thoughts.

"But even though he never really loved me… And was never truly my father…"

"He still raised you," Elias said. "You can't change that."

I nodded. "It still hurts. His betrayal, his death—all of it. It just hurts."

"I know," he said.

He didn't have to say anything more than that. I knew he knew. I knew he understood. I closed my eyes and leaned against him again.

"Come on," he said warmly. "I smell terrible. Let me get cleaned up."

"Mmf," I mumbled. I didn't want to let him go, but I didn't put up too much of a fight when he unwrapped my arms and pulled me toward the ensuite bathroom. Inside, he stripped off his sweat-stained clothes, and then stepped into the tub of mostly clean water I'd left behind. It couldn't be more than lukewarm now, but he still sighed in relief as he sank in and began to scrub the grime from his body.

"Here," I said. "Let me."

I pulled up a small stool behind him, guiding Elias to lean his head back against the edge of the tub. To my surprise, he didn't resist. His eyes flickered and closed as he leaned further towards me. I wet his hair, then poured a small amount of shampoo into my palm, working it into a lather before I gently raked my fingers through dark locks. He groaned with pleasure as I did so, seeming to melt even deeper into the bathwater.

For a moment I worked in silence, massaging the shampoo into his scalp. Then I asked, "Are you all right? After everything?"

He sighed heavily.

"After the duchess?" I asked. "Are you okay?"

"It's strange," he said in a low, rumbling voice. "I didn't know she was like that. So power-hungry. She'd always been controlling. Particular. But I never thought... I never thought she'd do anything like this."

"Seems like Rodthar may have had something to do with that," I said.

"Perhaps he encouraged it," Elias said, "but no one could make my mother do anything she didn't want to do."

I gazed down at him, at his closed eyes, and the small furrow in his brow.

"I should've seen it coming," Elias said. "I should've suspected it. How could I have been so blind? How could she have changed so much without me noticing anything?"

"She saw you becoming a leader," I said. "No longer allowing her to lead from the shadows."

"I guess that started from the Choice," Elias said. "The first time I went against her wishes."

"That was the first time?"

He nodded. I began to rinse the shampoo from his hair.

"I wonder sometimes if there was a way to pull my father out of the craziness," Elias said. "We didn't try. Mother said the only way forward was to kill him. That we'd lost him forever. I was so young." The muscles in his jaw twitched. "I trusted her when she told me that was the only way. But when I went into the mountains, I felt crazy too. And yet I was able to emerge from it. You brought me back."

I pressed my palms to his head and leaned down, kissing the crown of his head.

"I wonder if I could've done so for my father," he murmured. "If we had just tried. I wonder now—if Mother wanted him dead. If she wanted me on the throne. I was young. Easy to manipulate."

The thought was so horrifying it rattled down my spine like a physical touch. Had Duchess Alana really been capable of something so awful? Using her son to get rid of her own husband?

"He'd be proud of you now," I said. "That much I know."

He swallowed hard, his eyes closed tight. My heart broke for him—for us both—but there was still a flare of pride there too. It hurt, but we'd done the right thing. For ourselves, and for our kingdom.

"Come on," I said, "let's get some sleep before we have to face your adoring subjects in a few hours."

Elias climbed out of the tub and toweled off, and then we fell into the bed as quickly as we could. We wouldn't have much peace now, not with all the work that needed to be done to heal the city from Rodthar's terrible leadership, and then the specter of Corinne looming in the future. There wasn't a lot of peace to be found, but there was a little here, in this moment. The sun had already crossed the horizon, but with Elias' arms finally around me, sleep came easy.

Chapter 28

Three weeks passed in a rush of activity. There was so much to do to right the city and the kingdom: buildings to repair, grievances to hear, announcements to deliver, plans to be made, meetings to be had. It was an endless, stressful rush, but at the same time, it felt good to be doing it. Elias and I were finally working together as king and queen instead of living our separate lives in the same manor. Our days were spent navigating the endless details of leadership, and during our nights we cherished the moments of privacy we had together.

It was a rhythm. One I was beginning to enjoy, and even thrive in.

It was a beautiful, sunny day in the city when I had scheduled an appointment at Camille's to do the final fitting for the outfit I had made for our upcoming summit. Elias and I had invited delegates from all the courts of Frasia, to discuss what had happened in Shianga, and the threat Corinne posed to all of us. I wanted to show the courts the queen I was now. No longer was I simply the winner of the Choice, a beautiful piece of arm candy for the king to display. I was a leader in my own right.

"Wonderful to see you, your Highness," Aerika said warmly as she welcomed me into the shop. She looked as effortlessly stunning as ever, with her silvery hair pulled up into a bun and her deep brown eyes blinking owlishly. She wore a plain linen suit, with a pincushion shaped like a rose fastened around her wrist. "I hope you haven't been too busy with the preparations for the upcoming summit."

"It's been a bit much," I admitted, "but going well."

"Good, good," Aerika said. "We've just finished up your order. Please, step this way for the fitting."

It was a quiet day in the shop, and I was grateful for the peace. I'd come here alone for a reason, and from the curious gleam in Aerika's eyes, I figured she knew that, too. I stepped up onto the platform in front of the trio of mirrors. Aerika arranged the dressing screen, and then called the tailors out from the back room.

Two tailors emerged, in similar plain clothes to Aerika. One was tall and thin, with silvery hair and pale blue eyes, and the other was a bit shorter, with wispy blonde hair cropped close to her head. They both moved with the same easy grace Aerika did. All three had a similar aura—an aura that was now familiar to me from my time with Corinne.

"Here you are, Your Highness," Aerika said. "Sewed just to your specifications."

Behind the dressing screen, Aerika helped me out of my simple day gown. I'd ordered a pair of fine trousers and matching jacket. Fit for a queen, but unlike anything I'd seen a queen wear before. The pants were dark, silk, and embroidered with silver, with a high waist that tied in the back almost like a corset. Accompanying it was a pale shirt Aerika had made, the same color as the embroidery, and then a long jacket that fell just past my knees, embroidered at the hems. It was elegant, simple, and feminine—but functional.

"It's gorgeous," I said as she pulled away the dressing screen. I turned in front of the mirrors, seeing the jacket from every angle, admiring the detail in the embroidery that ran up the back. "You've outdone yourself."

The Fae tailors smiled then disappeared, returning to the back room.

Aerika smiled, pleased. Then she took the jacket off my shoulders and hung it back on the nearby dressing rack.

"I'm pleased you like it," she said. "Let me just make a few adjustments to the fit of these pieces."

She knelt on the platform and peered thoughtfully at the hem of the pants, then pinched the fabric a bit tighter and pinned it in place. I watched her reflection as she worked. We were alone in the tailor shop, and now there were questions that weighed heavily on me.

"Aerika," I said, "can I ask you something?"

"Certainly," she said, with her eyes still focused on the hem of my pants. "What's on your mind?"

"Do you know what happened?" I asked. "In Shianga?"

Her hands stilled, and her dark eyes glanced up at me. "You'll have to be more specific."

"Draunar has been removed from power," I said. Rumors had been traveling through Frasia, that much I knew, but the details of what had happened in Shianga had yet to be discussed in an official capacity. Not until the summit. "He was removed by Corinne, the Fae queen. He had been holding her captive."

"So it's true," Aerika murmured.

"You've heard word of this?" I asked.

Aerika sighed and turned her attention to the other hem of my pants, making sure the adjustments matched exactly. "I suppose there's no reason to dance around it, is there?" she asked. "You know of my Fae heritage."

"I had my suspicions," I said.

She smiled gently. "Well, I'm grateful to you for keeping them to yourself. Some shifters are not so keen to be reminded of our continued existence."

I nodded, glancing toward the back room.

Aerika caught it. "They have even closer lineage than I do. It's safer for them to stay there. I do the guest-facing work when I can." She finished pinning the hem and moved up to check the fit of the waistband. "There's no word going around. It's more like…a feeling."

"A feeling?"

She nodded. "There was a feeling when the queen was taken captive—though we didn't know that was what happened. I felt like a hole had been struck inside of me, somehow, and my power was beginning to slowly drain out. So slowly I hardly noticed it happening. And then, a few weeks ago, suddenly the hole was plugged. I felt stronger. More awake. More like myself again." She smiled again, softly. "Like I'd been living in a fog, and didn't even realize it until it cleared. I knew something had changed. I had my suspicions, but didn't want to investigate closely."

"Why not?" I asked. I moved carefully, making way for her small adjustments and pins. I'd expected Aerika to be rejoicing at the news that Corinne was back. This slight discomfort was unexpected.

"Just because there is an inherent reaction to the queen's return," Aerika said carefully, "does not mean all Fae are exclusively pleased to see her back."

"What do you mean?" I asked. I was dying to jump down her throat with dozens of questions. I'd thought the Fae in Frasia would be rushing to Shianga to join her when they found out.

"Leadership is complicated," Aerika said, "as I'm sure you know. Corinne's rise to the throne was…" She trailed off and pressed her lips together as she searched for the right word. "Rocky. Not all Fae were pleased with her rule, especially those of us who built our lives in this realm."

"Is her rule the reason you came to this realm?" I asked. "Would you go if she called the Fae back?"

Aerika's expression closed off. I cursed myself internally—my curiosity had gotten the better of me.

"My apologies," I said. "I'm only hoping to understand what this means for Frasia."

"I don't know what it means," Aerika said, "but my life is here. In Efra." She stood up, then peered judiciously at the small adjustments she'd made. "I believe I'm all done here. We'll make the final changes and have it sent to the manor."

Aerika pulled the dressing screen back up, and then helped me out of the pants, careful not to disturb the pins she'd placed.

"Can I ask you one more thing?" I asked.

"I suppose," she said, sounding much less willing than earlier before.

"In the manor," I asked, "there's a small room of Fae artifacts. Have any of the remaining Fae heard of it? Or know about why it might exist?"

"I've heard of it," she said. She fastened the back of my dress deftly. "Again, I wasn't sure if it was real. Just a rumor that had traveled around, mostly after Drogo's death."

"It was Drogo's room?" I asked.

"I don't know," she said. "But as a king, he was curious about what had happened to the Fae around Efra. I think he thought it was an illness at first. But then neighborhoods started just…fading away. Fae, too. Some Fae had particular items, things that helped them move between Faerie and this realm, or to channel some of their power here. If someone disappeared and left their channel behind, sometimes it would end up in the manor for safekeeping. I think some Fae were afraid they'd disappear too, and then these treasured items would be lost forever."

My heart clenched. Those items below the manor—they weren't stolen. They were kept there for safekeeping. I'd thought someone in that manor had been trying to kill the Fae, either Daybreak or Nightfall. But it was Drogo, trying to bring them back.

"Thank you," I said, "for trusting me with this knowledge. It will help at the summit—to figure out what to do next."

Aerika smiled thinly. I stepped off the platform and she walked me to the door. She looked a little pale, nervous, like she wasn't sure if sharing all of this with me had been a good idea. "I trust your judgment, Your Highness," she said. "And your discretion."

I looked at her. "It will remain between us."

That seemed to ease Aerika's nerves, and she nodded briskly as she led me out the door.

Chapter 29

The next evening was the first night of the summit. Elias and I stood outside the throne room, side by side, both in the dark silks of Nightfall.

"Are you sure you're okay with this?" Elias asked. "We can still demand he leave."

"It's fine," I said. "Really. It's strange, I'm almost… I'm almost looking forward to it."

He shook his head in disbelief. "Sometimes I think I'll never really understand what makes you tick."

I smiled, then took his hand in mine and kissed his knuckles. I understood his hesitation. Daybreak had sent word they would be attending the summit, if the King and Queen of Nightfall would allow it. They would attend with just a single convoy.

Barion.

I'd expected a message like that to hurt. It was supposed to hurt, to have to face a figure from my past after so much loss, and yet part of me was excited. I wanted him to see who I had become. I still wanted him to be proud of me. He was more of a father to me than Rodthar ever was.

Elias nodded at the guards, and they opened the ornate doors.

Inside, a round table had been set for dinner. Wolves from each pack were already seated. There was Giles from Dawnguard, a broad-shouldered man dressed in leather armor, with a scar over one eye. From Duskmoon, Isalde, a tall woman who looked remarkably like Fina, wearing an immense necklace of amethyst and onyx. Starcrest had sent an older woman, Marget, whose eyes were clouded with blindness, but not Ealric, and for that I was grateful. It would have been a little much to have to navigate sitting at this table with Ealric and Barion of Daybreak.

We took our seats at the head. I was between Barion and Elias, and anxiety was already crawling in my throat.

"Thank you all for attending," Elias said, "and welcome to Efra. I trust your journeys were not too challenging."

Around the table, murmurs of assent.

"If I may," Barion said. "Before we start, I do believe it'd be best for me to speak on the recent happenings."

He held my gaze as he said it, and he looked…beaten down. Terrible even. So unlike the gregarious man who had trained me all through my youth. His fine clothes were pressed and the bracers on his forearms were clean, but there were dark circles under his eyes, and new wrinkles on his forehead and around his mouth. Whatever had happened in Daybreak had worn him down, too.

Elias glanced at me. I nodded. "Please," I said. "The floor is yours."

"Rodthar's actions do not speak for all of Daybreak," he said.

"He was your alpha," Giles said. "I believe he does speak for your pack."

"He was," Barion agreed. "He is no longer. He was not the man we—not the man I thought he was. The court has stepped in to lead for now but Daybreak, we—" He paused and squared his shoulders. "My pack is weakened now. I've come here as a show of loyalty to Nightfall, in hopes Daybreak can rebuild our friendship."

Elias nodded. "It won't be that simple," he said, "but this is a good beginning. We will need all the wolves of Frasia to work together if we want to keep our nation safe from the Fae queen in Shianga."

"Let's get into that," Isalde said, "I've heard rumors that Draunar was usurped in Shianga. But it wasn't Nightfall that did so? You say it was the Fae?"

Elias moved to speak, but I held up my hand first. "Let me explain," I said.

With all the eyes on me, I explained what had happened in Shianga—all of it. How my father had put the idea in Draunar's head, how Draunar had demanded me as part of the treaty, and how he had kidnapped me and taken me to his hoard. I carefully danced around the fact that I had foolishly agreed to the terms myself. I didn't want to undermine my own authority as queen, especially in such delicate circumstances.

Instead, I focused on the facts. Corinne had defeated Draunar and was rebuilding her strength in Shianga.

"This seems ridiculous," Giles said. "What interest would the Fae queen have in our realm?"

"You may think so," Marget of Starcrest said, "but my scouts have seen strange happenings at the border with Shianga. This explains many of the reports I've been receiving." She folded her hands in her lap, her milky-white eyes fixed on me. "You believe Corinne's desires for territory will expand beyond Shianga?"

"I know they will," I said. "I heard her say it."

"Frasia is not prepared to go to war with the Fae," Giles said. "The soldiers of Dawnguard are well-trained for hand-to-hand battle, but magic users bring too many unknowns. Marching into Shianga could result in our deaths."

"No one is suggesting we march into Shianga now," Elias said.

"Then what are we suggesting?" Giles asked. "Do we wait like sitting ducks until the Fae queen decides to attack us?"

"Calm yourself, Giles," Barion said. "The wolves of Frasia may not have a grasp on Fae magic yet, but we aren't the only shifters in the realm."

"Exactly," I said.

Barion met my eyes and gave me a small nod. We were already on the same page—even without having much time to discuss it.

"You suggest we go to the other shifters," Isalde said. "In preparation?"

"Askon," Barion said. "We all know the stories."

"They aren't just stories," Marget said. "And regardless of whether or not the jaguars of Askon have a history of magic use, it makes sense to ally ourselves with the other nations before Corinne decides to attack."

"Even with an alliance," Giles said, "or a few alliances, it's still crazy to think we could stand against the Fae queen. Gods know how many she has at her beck and call in her realm. We could be doomed before we even begin."

"I know that," Elias said.

The discussion fell silent as the attention fell to Elias. I set my hand at his knee under the table.

"We won't have a choice," Elias said. "She is ruthless. She feels she's been wronged not only by Draunar, but by all the shifters of her realm. She won't be satisfied with just Shianga under her rule. She will come for all of us, sooner or later. If we want to have the smallest chance of survival, we need to work together now. Before it's too late."

Giles pinched the bridge of his nose. "Never in all my years as a general did I think there'd be risk of war with the Fae."

"Someone's got to keep you on your toes, old man," Barion said.

"I'd like for you all to stay here in Efra," Elias said. "I'll send word to Askon inviting the king and queen to open a new round of peace talks."

"I trust they'll go better than the talks in Shianga?" Marget asked.

I was grateful Marget couldn't see the sour expression I knew flashed across my face. Under the table, Elias folded his hand over mine.

"The talks in Shianga were doomed from the start," he said, "courtesy of Rodthar of Daybreak. I hope having you all here, as a show of good faith, will prevent such complications in these talks. Since all of our fates hang in the balance."

The heads of the packs agreed to stay until word was received from Askon. Now all that was left to discuss were the details of the invitation we would send to the jaguars. Elias nodded to the servants posted at the edge of the room, and on his command, they exited and returned with the fine spread of boar and vegetables prepared for dinner.

As the conversation moved away from the more serious topics of politicking to the more casual engagements of wolves catching up, Elias got roped into a conversation with Giles, and at my side, Barion topped off my glass of wine from the carafe in the center of the table.

"Your Highness," he said quietly, "I owe you an apology as well."

I sighed and closed my eyes briefly. "Please," I said. "Not now."

Barion's expression shuttered. "Of course."

"I mean." I took a sip, then turned slightly toward him, keeping my voice low and private. "Frasia has to come first. We have to sort out what we're doing to protect the packs. But…but after all this, Barion, of course there's much for us to discuss."

He nodded in agreement. "You're right. It will come later." He paused and sipped his own glass. "I'm quite glad you're well, Your Highness."

Once dinner was finished, Elias and I excused ourselves, instructing the servants to take our guests to their quarters and ensure everyone was settled.

In the quiet of our bedroom, Elias shucked off his jacket and nearly collapsed into the wooden chair at his writing desk. He sighed, pressed his fingers to his temples, and then reached for a fresh sheet of parchment.

"Tonight?" I asked. I draped my arms over his shoulders and kissed him on the cheek, then knocked my temple against his. "You're going to go ahead and write the invitation?"

"I'd like to get a bird in the sky as soon as possible," he said. "It's not an easy journey to Askon. It'd take too long to send a proper messenger."

"You know the keepers don't like to send a messenger out at night," I said. "It can wait until the morning."

He sighed and smoothed his hand over the parchment. "I'll feel better if it's written and ready to send."

"You'll write better in the morning," I pushed back. "Come on. We both need to sleep."

He turned his head and caught my lips in a brief kiss. "How was tonight?" he asked. "I know having Barion as a convoy is not ideal."

I sighed and let my weight slump onto him in the chair. I turned the question over in my mind, with my nose pressed into the curve of his neck, letting his familiar scent soothe me.

"It was okay," I said, after a long moment of consideration. "It's strange. We have so much history, and I still... I still care for him, but I don't feel like I need him as much."

Elias hummed in understanding.

"I did before," I said. "I relied on him for stability. But now...it's different now. I'm not so reliant on anyone else for my stability, or my safety."

"Not even me?" Elias half-teased.

"That's not what I mean," I said, and kissed his neck. "I mean, I can rely on myself more."

Again he nodded in understanding. "Spoken like a queen."

"Really?" I asked. "Sounded a bit awkward to me. You don't think I sound a bit like a teenager?"

That made him laugh, bright and surprised. He unwound my arms from around me so he could stand up, leaving the parchment untouched on the desk. Instead, he pulled me in and kissed me properly.

"Leave the invitation for tomorrow morning," I murmured against his lips.

Elias tugged the silk shirt from the waistband of my fine trousers, then slid his hand over the bare skin of my back. His touch sent a promising shiver down my spine. "All right," he said with a smile. "You've convinced me."

He deepened the kiss, drawing my lower lip between his teeth before sliding his tongue into my mouth. It was intense, it was claiming. Internally, my wolf preened as I pressed closer and looped my arms around his neck. I scraped my nails through the fine dark hair at the base of his skull, and he hummed with pleasure. Then he drew his mouth over my jawline, the column of my neck. He slid his hands down over my hips and over the fine silk of my trousers.

"I like these," he murmured against my skin.

"What?" I asked. "The trousers?"

"They suit you," he said. "Much better than the gowns."

"You don't like the gowns?" I teased.

He nipped at the skin of my neck. The slight pain made me shiver in delight. "Of course I do," he said. "I like everything you wear. You're gorgeous."

"But you like these best?" I asked.

"Function," he said, "suits you."

I slid my hands under the hem of his shirt and up the broad plane of his back, holding him close. "I like it too," I admitted. "Freedom of movement. Makes me want to run."

He growled in agreement, and his grip tightened on my hips. "I want that, too," he said. "Gods, I want to go running with you."

I guided him back into another deep kiss. We hadn't had nearly enough time to go out running alone with all the work required to get Efra back on its feet. I longed for it now, even with Elias in my arms—I craved the freedom of being in my wolf form, feeling the moss under my paws, inhaling layered scents on the night wind. I wanted to be in the moonlight with him, running full speed, waiting for him to catch me and pin me to the soft ground. I wanted to submit.

There was a part of me that wondered why I still wanted to shift so badly. I'd spent so much time trapped in that shape—shouldn't I be sick of it? Yet I only felt more connected to my wolf. We weren't two separate identities in the same body. We were two sides of the same coin. Connected. One and the same. A run sounded amazing—a break from the responsibilities of leadership—but we had no time for that now.

We could take a break in other ways, though.

I took control of the kiss with a hand on his nape. Elias smiled against my lips, surprised and pleased. I set my hands at his chest and pushed him backward. He took a few steps back until the backs of his legs hit the edge of the bed, and then I pushed him down. He hit the mattress with a smirk, then scooted back, propped up on one elbow. He watched me with one eyebrow raised slightly, curiously, like he was waiting for something.

I felt my face heat slightly. I still wasn't used to being looked at like this—watched so openly, and with so much desire, but I knew with Elias, I didn't need to be shy. Before I could overthink it, I pulled my silk shirt up and over my head, then tugged off my trousers, too, only slowed down a little by the laces on the back. Then I was standing at the foot of the bed, nude and blushing, while Elias sprawled on the bed still in his shirt and slacks.

"Gorgeous," he said. His voice rumbled low in his chest, and his eyes flashed gold with desire. "Get up here."

I grinned and crawled onto the mattress so my knees were straddling his hips. Then I slid my hands back under his shirt, up the solid warm plane of his chest. As I pushed his shirt up, I kissed the revealed skin, licking and biting, claiming him as my own. The brawn of his abs jumped under my touch. He wrestled his shirt off and tossed it aside. I hummed in approval, then resumed my attention to his chest, petting at his shoulders and arms as I drew my mouth over the curve of his pectoral muscles.

Desire settled low in my gut, molten hot, oozing through me as I savored the familiar taste of his skin. His heart raced under my hand. He traced his fingers up my bare back, over the curve of my waist and breasts, then my nape, then raked them through my hair. He was gentle, but touching me constantly. I burned with yearning now, each touch like a flame against my skin.

Finally, I drew my mouth up his neck and back to his lips, kissing him deeply. He gripped my hips hard as he rolled his waist up; the hard line of his arousal pressed against my wet folds. I gasped at the sudden sensation, the proof of his desire. I broke the kiss and planted my hands on his chest, sat up, and shifted my weight back, moving against the hardness still trapped behind his trousers.

"Reyna," he growled. He bared his teeth, eyes burning gold as he watched me.

I threw my head back and savored the feeling of him beneath me. I rolled my hips in a circle, teasing him. Each motion drew small sounds from Elias, huffed exhales and grunts of need. He gripped my thighs hard enough to bruise, shifting beneath me to meet the motion of my hips.

I leaned forward, nearly collapsing onto his chest, and mouthed a sloppy kiss at his jawline. I was almost drunk with hunger for Elias—and with power. I'd never had him under me like this, so open and wanting. It felt like running. Like play, and power, and teasing. I'd never thought sex could feel like this—I'd never known I could feel like this.

"I want you," I said against his jaw. I punctuated it with a teasing bite.

Elias growled in response. Then he wrapped his arms tight around my waist and surged up, rolling us over in a sudden surge of power. He'd been holding back, and this show of strength thrilled me. I laughed as my back hit the mattress. His gaze was warm and hungry as he hovered over me, a smile playing on his features. He kissed me again. "You tease."

"Not teasing," I said. "Never teasing." I petted over his nape and tugged him down for another kiss again. Then I tugged at his waistband with my other hand. "Please."

Elias hummed, then pulled back just enough to shove his trousers down. He caught my lips again, and I hooked one leg around his waist. I was so wet, so open with desire; I gasped into the kiss when he pressed his length teasingly against me.

"Please," I said again into his mouth.

"You're so gorgeous," he murmured. "I'll give you what you need."

He gripped my thigh and slowly pushed into me. I was so sensitive already; the pressure made me break the kiss to throw my head back against the mattress. I dug my fingers into the muscle of his back, hugging him impossibly closer, my leg still hooked around his waist.

Finally, he was flush against me, and my whole body thrummed with the feeling of completion. Wholeness. He pushed his face into the crook of my neck and kissed me sloppily there, then panted his desire against my skin.

"Reyna," he murmured. "Reyna, I love you."

I gasped as he began to move. He thrust slowly and steadily into me, a rhythm that sent deep ripples of pleasure through me. I dragged his mouth back up to mine for a kiss so I could speak the words back into his lips.

"I love you," I echoed. "My king."

Chapter 30

A week later, the convoy from Askon arrived in Efra.

I had never seen such a grand procession of carriages. I had to intentionally keep my jaw shut as they rolled seemingly without end through the gates of the manor. The carriages were pure black, detailed with gold, and pulled by gorgeous horses with sleek black pelts. They carried no markings of the jaguars, but the sheer beauty of the carriages proved they were royal. Two carriages rolled ahead, guided by a few servants hustling on foot—luggage and servants of Askon's own, I assumed. The third carriage in the line came to a stop at the front doors of the palace. The horses tossed their heads, nickering; the driver hopped down and swept into a dramatic bow before he opened the door to the carriage.

I wasn't sure what I was expecting. I had a vision of what jaguar shifters might look like—tall and elegant, catlike and sleek, dressed in gold and jewels, like the dragons of Shianga. But the two that stepped out of the carriage surprised me.

The queen emerged first. She was a short, lean woman, with large brown eyes and hair cropped close to her skull. She had a dramatic birthmark that cut across her face, a dark stain which traveled from her eye across to her neck. Instead of a crown, she wore a shimmering silver veil that fell to her shoulders. Her clothes otherwise were simple: a sleek black gown with a loose skirt for comfort, and a heavy cloak over her shoulders against the Frasian cold.

Her husband, the King of Askon, stepped out behind her. He was much taller, taller than Elias, wearing similar simple black slacks and a shirt with a thick, fur-lined cloak. He had a strong jaw and high cheekbones, dark, narrow eyes, and a silver band around his neck in lieu of a crown.

"Welcome," Elias said. "Thank you for journeying on such short notice."

"We have much to discuss, it seems," the queen said with a curious smile. Then she approached me and took my hand in a warm handshake. "Queen Reyna. I've heard much about you. I'm Queen Enet, of Askon. This is my husband, King Khainan."

"Lovely to meet you," I said. "Please, come inside out of the cold."

"The servants will show you to your quarters," Elias said as we walked through the doors of the manor into the throne room. "I'm sure you'd like to get settled, and then—"

"That won't be necessary," King Khainan said in a rumbling voice. "I'd prefer to hear more about the claims made in the invitation we received. If these issues are as pressing as you've said, I'd like to get right into it."

"Certainly," Elias said, only looking a little surprised. "This way."

In the throne room, the servants hurried to bring out whatever the visiting royals might want: coffee, wine, whiskey, a plate of cured meats and fine cheeses. Seated at the table, Elias laid out the same discussion we'd had at the summit—what had happened in Shianga, and the threat of the Fae building in the west.

After hearing all the details, King Khainan leaned back in his chair and rubbed his short beard thoughtfully.

"We have no history of the Fae in Askon," he said. "How can you know she plans to take over?"

"What do you mean?" I asked. "I heard her say this when I was held captive."

"Draunar of Shianga never caused anything but trouble for Askon," King Khainan said. "His removal from the throne is not necessarily a sign of trouble for Askon. Frasia are the ones who have initiated conflict with the queen—has any diplomatic resolution been attempted?"

"She held my wife hostage in Faerie," Elias said in a low growl. "Would you be keen to initiate diplomacy after such disrespect?"

"If it were to the benefit of my kingdom, I would," Khainan said, meeting Elias' gaze steadily.

"I highly doubt that," Enet said with a teasing roll of her eyes. She patted her husband's thigh, throwing him a fond smile, then turned her attention to me. "If the Fae queen had kept me in my jaguar form for months, he'd be storming the castle by himself for a mere chance at revenge."

Her joke cut the tension building between Elias and Khainan. Both them glanced away, visibly irritated, but Enet caught my eye and threw me a wink.

Some relief cut through my nerves. At least Enet might be on my side—if not fully ready to join an alliance against the Fae.

Elias cleared his throat. "I understand your hesitation, and I'm not opposed to a diplomatic solution. It's only that from my experience with the Fae queen, I can't imagine a situation in which she accepts one. If she wants to take control of the whole realm, we'll be better prepared to meet her if we work together. It's not closing the door on diplomacy."

"What if Askon chooses to reach out to the Fae first?" Khainan asked.

"I can't say I recommend it," Elias said.

"She's wily," I said. "She may lead you into negotiations that seem genuine, but aren't. She's likely to turn on you to get what she wants."

Again Khainan rubbed his beard. "If what you say is true," he said after a long moment, "and the Fae queen is determined to take over the realm fully, where do you believe she'll start?"

"Queen Reyna," Enet said, "do you mind if we have a discussion of our own while the men talk details?"

I wanted to be a part of the strategy, too—but something in Enet's eyes made me nod in agreement. I stood and walked with her toward the balcony just off the throne room. Elias' eyes tracked me as I went. I met his gaze and offered him a small, careful smile, but I could feel the anxiety radiating from him. I knew he didn't want me to leave, not when we were in the middle of tense negotiations. I knew it made him think of Draunar's study, when my foolish decision had led him to haul me into the sky.

He feared I might leave again. I didn't know how long it would be before that fear went away. But I'd wait, however long it took to prove that I wasn't going anywhere. Never again.

I pushed open the door to the balcony and stepped outside, immediately sighing with pleasure in the crisp, cool midday air.

Enet joined me, then braced both hands on the railing and gazed out over the tree line.

"It's beautiful here," she said. "Colder than Askon, but just as lush."

"I've read about Askon," I said. "And pored over the maps and the few sketches we have. Your architecture is incredible."

Enet smiled, looking vaguely impressed. "You're interested in Askonian architecture?"

"It's unique," I said, "building around the trees like that. I hope to include some of that style if Efra continues to grow."

Enet nodded. "What else have you read about Askon?" she asked.

I knew a leading question when I heard one. I stood next to her, gazing out over the tree line.

"There's not much in the library," I said. "Frasia hasn't maintained a close relationship with Askon, obviously. But there's some history."

"History that led you to call on us rather than Osna, or Cruora?"

"We're also both earth shifters," I said. "Our two nations used to be connected by a land bridge once." I thought back to the map I'd found in what felt like a different lifetime in Daybreak. But we both knew that wasn't our real interest in Askon.

She sighed. "It's good for Askon to maintain our historic reputation," she said.

"Reputation?" I asked.

She raised an eyebrow at me. "Don't pretend you don't know what I mean."

No reason to feign ignorance. "If the jaguars of Askon are still magic users—the last real holders of magic in this realm—then that might be a way for us to build up our defenses against the Fae. Our wolves have no magic outside of our shifts."

"It's a fine thought," Enet said, "but the jaguars are the same."

I balked. "What? Everything I read said that the jaguars are holders of ancient magic. I understand the secrecy—if you wish to maintain the secrecy, there's no reason to lie."

"It's no lie," Enet said. She gazed sadly out to the horizon, and I knew then she wasn't trying to hide an existing well of magic. There was too much longing in her eyes for that to be the case. "Generations ago, we did. But the art has been lost. We haven't had shifters with the capacity for it. We have the records, the stories... But no practitioners."

"I see," I said. Disappointment swooped through me.

"Khainan is a good king," Enet said. "I doubted him at first, when he took the throne as a young hothead."

I chuckled. "Sounds familiar."

"I thought it might. He wants to rekindle magic in Askon. It's why he answered your call. A Fae presence in this realm might help us determine what happened to our magic. It's unlikely, but it's possible."

"Does he want to work with the Fae queen?" I asked tentatively.

"No," Enet said. "He's curious. He wants to keep Askon safe. We both do—that's our main priority."

"That much I understand," I said.

"But I'm grateful we answered the call," she said. "Had the Fae approached Askon first, it's possible his curiosity would've overridden his suspicion. Thus opening our doors to potential takeover."

"That's what we're trying to prevent," I said. "The potential for magic access would've just been a nice bonus."

Enet laughed; it was a high, pretty sound. "He's still curious, but he trusts Elias. He will always prioritize Askon's safety. If you're right about the Fae queen's goals, Askon will come to Frasia's aid."

"Thank you," I said. Some of the fluttering nerves in my stomach settled.

"Have you heard word of what is going on in Cruora?" she asked. "My scouts have heard whispers of alchemy across their borders."

I started. "Alchemy?"

"Not natural magic, like Askonians once had," she said, "but rediscovered magic. Created magic. Of course I can't confirm this. It's just whispers."

I nodded as I turned that rumor over and over in my mind. Frasia had never had any alchemists within our borders, as far as I knew. Wolves were physical, tied to the earth, and we fought our battles with tooth and claw. But if the eagles were interested in developing alchemy... There had to be something we could do to stand against the Fae. With the scuffles between rogue wolves and eagles at the border, though, and the mess of what had happened in Shianga, it wasn't going to be easy to get the eagles to hear us out.

"Come," Enet said, "let's leave the boys to their drinking and discussion. I've brought a few artists from Askon, and I'd like to have them perform for you this evening, if that suits you?"

"Artists?" I asked, sounding perhaps a little too overeager. "You don't mean dancers, do you?"

"I do," Enet said, pleased.

"Oh, gods above!" I said. I had to restrain myself from bouncing on the balls of my feet. "Real Askonian dancers? Oh, I've read so much about them—yes, that would be amazing!"

With the promise of an evening of incredible music and dance ahead of us, I was able to push my worries and fears to the side, just for a moment. Things I'd only imagined as a young wolf in Daybreak were now coming to my home. To *my* court.

That evening, Nightfall held a welcome ball for the Court of Askon. The wolves of Efra were beginning to heal from the havoc wreaked by the war in Shianga, and as a result there was a celebratory air in the city, as if we were finally rising out of the ashes. We had thrown open the gates to the manor, welcoming wolves of all social statuses to come in for music, dancing, and a spread of food carried by servants flitting through the crowd.

Elias and I sat at a long table atop the dais, with Enet and Khainan seated at our sides. The band played a riotous, fast-moving song, and the crowd of wolves on the floor engaged in one of Nightfall's many elegant, quick, high-energy jigs. I caught a few glimpses of Fina and Adora in the crowd, exchanging grins as they bounced gleefully between dance partners. Laughter rang through the room as men swung women up into the air, dark skirts flashed like waves, and even a few kisses were snuck on the dance floor.

Looking out over the crowd, with a glass of wine in my hand and Elias' hand on my thigh, I felt settled. I felt like I was at home. Elias gazed over the crowd, too, then caught my eye and gave me a small smile.

We'd been through a lot. In my darkest moments I'd thought I might never see him again.

But here we were. Seated side by side with a convoy from abroad, overlooking our kingdom. I'd survived Draunar and Corinne both. Elias had survived a brush with craziness.

If we'd made it through that, we could make it through anything.

Then the jig came to a stop. On the dance floor, the wolves' attention turned to the band curiously as they awaited the next song. Instead, Lady Glennis stepped forward with a demure smile on her face, and gestured for the band to step aside. In their place, from the side door, a band of jaguar shifters stepped forward, carrying beautiful drums and elegant brass horns.

"The Queen and King of Askon have graced us with their presence," Lady Glennis said warmly, "and brought us from their kingdom a fine show of music and dance. Please, clear some space."

Titters of curiosity rose throughout the crowd as the wolves stepped back, making space on the floor. From the same door the band had walked through came a stream of tall, lithe dancers, dressed in loose, colorful clothes that fluttered off their bodies, with bells strapped to their ankles and wrists.

"You're going to love this," Enet murmured, leaning close to me. "These are the finest in Askon."

The dancers took their places in the center of the room, toes pointed, hands up, backs slightly arched in long, gorgeous curved poses. The drumming began first, heavy and rhythmic, and they began to move slowly, like reeds in the wind, the bells jingling with each movement.

Drums. Horns. The dancing picked up. Now they'd become fast-paced and athletic with turns and leaps, hypnotizing me with their beauty.

And then the doors to the throne room slammed open.

"Your Highness!" Kodan shouldered in, eyes wide, sweat beading on her forehead. "King Elias!"

The band stuttered to a stop. The dancers did too, their motion stilling in a wave as they turned to the doors. "Elias," Kodan said again. She rushed past the dancers to the dais. Her breathing was short and quick from exertion. "Portals," she said. "Portals to the south."

Elias stood up. "Portals?"

"No movement," Kodan said. "No Fae. They just opened. We don't know from where. Don't know where they go. They're just there."

"Yet," I said, low. "No Fae *yet.*"

The Fae queen was testing us. And this was just the beginning.

Made in United States
Troutdale, OR
09/18/2023

13010726R00222